ELITE OF ELMWOOD ACADEMY

DISORDER

USA TODAY BESTSELLING AUTHOR

J.L. WEIL

Published by J. L. Weil
Copyright 2021 by J. L. Weil
www.jlweil.com/
All rights reserved.

Edited by Hot Tree Editing
Cover Design by Wicked by Designs
Photo by Lindee Robinson

ALSO BY J. L. WEIL

ELITE OF ELMWOOD ACADEMY
(New Adult Dark High School Romance)

Turmoil

Disorder

Revenge

DIVISA HUNTRESS
(New Adult Paranormal Romance)

Crown of Darkness

Inferno of Darkness

DRAGON DESCENDANTS SERIES
(Upper Teen Reverse Harem Fantasy)

Stealing Tranquility

Absorbing Poison

Taming Fire

Thawing Frost

THE DIVISA SERIES

(Full series completed – Teen Paranormal Romance)

Losing Emma: A Divisa novella

Saving Angel

Hunting Angel

Breaking Emma: A Divisa novella

Chasing Angel

Loving Angel

Redeeming Angel

LUMINESCENCE TRILOGY

(Full series completed – Teen Paranormal Romance)

Luminescence

Amethyst Tears

Moondust

Darkmist – A Luminescence novella

RAVEN SERIES

(Full series completed – Teen Paranormal Romance)

White Raven

Black Crow

Soul Symmetry

BEAUTY NEVER DIES CHRONICLES

(Teen Dystopian Romance)

Slumber

Entangled

Forsaken

NINE TAILS SERIES

(Teen Paranormal Romance)

First Shift

Storm Shift

Flame Shift

Time Shift

Void Shift

Spirit Shift

Tide Shift

Wind Shift

HAVENWOOD FALLS HIGH

(Teen Paranormal Romance)

Falling Deep

Ascending Darkness

SINGLE NOVELS

Starbound

(Teen Paranormal Romance)

Casting Dreams

(New Adult Paranormal Romance)

Ancient Tides

(New Adult Paranormal Romance)

For an updated list of my books, please visit my website: www.jlweil.com

Join my VIP email list and I'll personally send you an email reminder as soon as my next book is out! Click here to sign up: www.jlweil.com

This book is for my readers! Your kind words and friendship inspires me every day. Thank you for following me through genres and worlds.

CHAPTER ONE

T riplets? Triplets? Triplets!

The phrase echoed in my head like a bad song.

Are they fucking kidding me? How is this possible?

It couldn't be. This had to be a joke. Some kind of mind-fuck. Another Elite game.

They had to be high.

"What the fuck did you say?" I asked, my voice trembling. When the hell had that started? The trembling? The cold suddenly bit into me.

"Grayson is your brother," Brock repeated, more slowly this time as if the words would finally sink past the blockade that refused to believe him. His startling aqua eyes implored me to understand. "You're triplets. Grayson, Kenna, and you."

And in just seconds, my world, everything I thought I knew about myself, about my family, ripped to shreds. I shifted in his lap so we weren't as close, because even faced with disorder, some part of me radiated constant awareness of Brock Taylor.

"No, I don't have a brother or a sister. I think I would know if I had a brother and a sister." Yet, even as the denial left my lips, doubt crept in.

Kenna looked so much like me. Identical almost.

"Would you?" he asked, his expression still hard and tense. It was only because of me that he sat in Grayson's Jeep instead of beating the living shit out of my stepbrother, Carter. Again.

The other back door opened, Micah shoving Grayson inside beside Brock and me before I could demand Brock explain. Seeing Grayson distracted me.

My so-called brother's fists clenched as he hit the back of the seat, releasing a groan of rage. "I want to kill that bastard," he seethed.

Unconvinced any of this was true, I thought perhaps I was living in an alternate universe. No other explanation made sense to me.

Fynn slid into the driver seat as Micah climbed into the passenger front side. As soon as the doors closed, Fynn slammed the running vehicle into gear.

"I'll deal with you later," Brock growled at Grayson. "Fynn, get us out of here before the cops show up," he ordered.

I had a feeling the reason Grayson hadn't hopped into the driver seat of his Jeep was because he would have run Carter down with his car. Rage vibrated off him in waves.

Sneaking a glance out the window despite telling myself not to, I caught a glimpse of Carter as Fynn whipped the car around, tires peeling over the parking lot pavement.

Carter looked... furious.

His blond hair disheveled, blue eyes wild, Carter's little kidnapping plan had been foiled. God knew what he was capable of next. But I got the horrible feeling his target had shifted from Brock to me. My stepbrother wouldn't forget the Elite coming to my rescue.

He despised them.

What I had once thought smacked of envy and jealousy, I now realized burned of bitterness and contempt. It had become a race to see who could take down whom first.

The Elite.

Or Carter.

And somewhere along the way, I got caught in the crosshairs.

FML.

Micah turned in his seat, glancing back at Brock and me, a serious note in his light blue eyes. "She okay?" he asked as if I was incapable of speaking for myself.

I was shaken up, clearly, but not so much that I couldn't talk.

Micah Bradford. The Elite playboy. Flirting came naturally to him, but tonight, he'd been stone-faced and serious, a side I hadn't seen before. I had always considered Micah harmless.

I was wrong.

His firm body wasn't just for show and football.

"He hit her," Brock replied lowly.

"And he will pay for that," Fynn said as he cranked the steering wheel to the right, maneuvering the car onto the main road. The silver piercing on his dark brow reflected off the headlights of cars passing by as he glanced at me from the rearview mirror. "No one hurts what's ours." Over six feet of swoon-worthy male, Fynn Dupree was the shyer member of the Elite. Cool and calm, until you pissed him off.

That seemed to be an Elite theme. They were all okay guys until someone made the mistake of flipping their asshole switch.

"I'm not yours," I said hoarsely.

Brock's hand splayed over the small of my back, keeping me on his lap. "You are, Firefly. The sooner you accept it, the safer you'll be."

The sharp stinging on my cheek said otherwise, but I figured now wasn't the right time to point that out. To be fair, he had come to my rescue after I had gone behind his back with Grayson. I wanted to circle back to the whole triplet bomb. *Later,* I told myself.

I studied Grayson, seeing him for the first time in a different light. So what if we shared the same brown eyes or the same shade of hair? That didn't automatically mean we shared DNA. A picture of Kenna came into my head. When he looked at me, did he see her?

Grayson exhaled, dropping his head back on the seat. "Fuck," he breathed, rubbing his hands over his face.

A weird tingle wove through me as I stared at Grayson, dissecting every feature in his face. The resemblance shone to such an astonishing degree that I wondered how I hadn't seen it before.

Triplets!

Holy! Shit!

How is this possible?

What does it mean? Am I adopted? Or were they adopted?

Question after question tumbled through my head.

How long had Grayson known?

How long had the Elite known?

Why hadn't any of them told me?

Did Kenna know?

What the fuck!

It did explain why there had never been any kind of attraction between Grayson and me, no spark. I'd been certain Grayson hated me.

Now I finally had an inkling why.

He looked at me and saw his sister, which I sort of figured out already. How could he not when I looked so much like her? Did he believe that I knew about them? That I had somehow abandoned them? Because that was the only rational explanation my mind could come up with for this anger he had toward me. My parents had given Grayson and Kenna up for adoption but kept me. If that were true—*if* being the big factor—then I couldn't imagine how he felt, nor could I understand why my parents would do such a thing.

Okay, yes, Angie had me at a young age, but my father stuck around, he married her, provided for us. Had they not believed they could have done so for three babies?

Another gazillion questions ran rampant through my head.

Or... had Grayson's parents given me up? Was I adopted? It might explain why Angie hated me so much, why we never got along. But why wouldn't my parents have told me? Never once had they ever let on that I wasn't theirs. I'd heard my birth story a million times over the years.

One thing was certain: I had to talk to Angie.

I had to uncover the truth. I deserved the truth.

Brock noticed where my attention diverted, reading my range of facial expressions. "Look, I'll explain everything after we get out of here," he whispered near my ear.

My gaze shifted to Brock, and I saw the concern he had for his friend. Grayson was going through some shit, but so was I. I just found out that I might have a sister and brother. Like, holy hell. What was I supposed to do with that information? Keep it to myself?

Other than my parents, Grayson was the one person I wanted to talk to. He had answers I desperately needed, but the closed expression on Brock's face told me not to prod him.

Not now.

Grayson needed to cool off.

And I needed to pinch myself. Or wake up. Nothing that had happened tonight seemed real. How the fuck was this my life?

"I can't go home," I muttered, thinking of Carter. Not tonight. Hell, maybe never. The idea of facing Carter...

I shuddered.

In the dimly lit car, Brock's gaze drifted to my swollen cheek, his eyes darkening. I hated to admit just how much it freaking hurt. "You're not," he said, expression serious.

"Oh." I exhaled as my nails still dug into my palms to stop the shaking, but it appeared to be an ineffective tactic, seeing as I still trembled.

"You're coming home with me. At least for the night," he

added, his breath warm along the side of my neck, doing wonders to thaw the ice in my veins.

"Are you sure that's a good idea?" Micah asked. He forked a hand through his bleached blond hair before resting his elbow on the windowsill of the car door.

Why would my staying at Brock's be a big deal?

I'd spent the night once before, but his parents hadn't been home. Was that the problem? His parents? Did they have a strict no-girl policy? Seemed unlikely Brock had rigid parents, but then I remembered Mads telling me Brock didn't take girls to his house, definitely not to his room.

So once again, the Elite were breaking the rules for me.

Why?

Because I was Grayson's sister?

Considering how much Grayson gave off the impression that he didn't like me all that much, it didn't make sense. I planned to uncover why Grayson hadn't welcomed me with open arms. Or perhaps I already had unearthed the reason why.

He had come to my defense with Carter tonight. That was something... wasn't it?

If Grayson was angry with me, then he had to have his reasons, and until I got some answers, I chose to hold on to the bead of hope that we could be friends, at least while I figured out how I felt about having a brother and a sister.

"I'm not letting her out of my sight," Brock said. "We can think of a better plan tomorrow." Without the radio on, our voices easily carried throughout the car, even over the purring engine. "Drop us off and then you guys go back to Grayson's and kick everyone out. Stay with him," he instructed, falling into his leadership role.

It suited him, giving commands without blinking and expecting them to be carried through, no questions asked.

Ten minutes later, we rolled up past the community gates and onto Brock's driveway. Darkness shrouded the house, only a single porch light casting a soft glow over the entrance. Not a single window was illuminated.

"It's been an... interesting night, new girl," Micah said with a wink, his dimples flashing on either side of his grin.

"Try and stay out of trouble," Fynn added as he glanced over his shoulder, an impossible request considering who I hung out with—the fucking Elite.

Had entangling myself with them been a mistake?

Too late now.

I found myself glancing at Grayson. He leaned forward in the seat, elbows propped on his knees and chin resting on his hands. His left foot tapped agitatedly on the rubber floor mat.

I should say something, right? Like, see you later, bro?

No. Definitely not.

He didn't bother to look up at me, so I took it as a sign.

Brock opened the car door and gave the side of my thigh, close to my ass, a pat. "Come on, Firefly. You and I need to have that *talk*." The way he said the words made it sound like he was about to deliver me a stern lecture.

Like hell would I listen to him scold me over my choice to trap Carter, despite it having completely backfired.

I jumped out of the Jeep and strolled onto the porch, waiting for Brock to key in the code that unlocked the door. He

swung it open and waited for me to walk through. Inside, darkness greeted me, and for a moment, absolute blackness bathed
over me. Panic clawed inside my chest as memories of waking
up blindfolded and with hands bound inside the back of
Carter's SUV came barreling to the forefront of my mind.
Quick pants of breath expelled from my lungs. *Not now. Not
now,* I chanted. I would not lose it.

Brock flipped on a light switch, flooding the room with light.
Fumbling with my rings, I stood in the center of the entryway,
staring at nothing.

"Josie."

The sound of my name snapped me out of that too-fresh
memory. I blinked, allowing my gaze to focus on my surround-
ings. Brock had one of those magazine-quality homes, but I
didn't really see any of it. My brain was so blown by the events
of tonight, it just stopped fucking processing altogether, a
defense mechanism to keep me from having a meltdown.

Who knew how long I'd be able to keep the hysterics at bay?
I suspected at some point, I'd have to let the emotions in and the
floodgates open.

Later.

Right now I had questions.

Millions of them, and yet, I couldn't form the words. I
wrapped my arms around myself, feeling cold again, and wished
to be back in Brock's arms, which was so wrong.

Or right?

I didn't know anymore.

Brock grabbed my hand, tugging me down the hallway.
"Come on, Firefly. You need ice, pills, and a drink."

Blindly, I followed him to the far end of the house. He sat me down in a chair before rummaging around in the kitchen, coming back with a gel ice pack, two white pills, and a glass of water.

"Thanks," I muttered, reaching for the aspirin and glass of water first. The pills went down smoothly. As long as I didn't think about the pain, the throbbing in my cheek was manageable—not that I would recommend everyone to go out and get hit in the face, but there were worse kinds of pain.

And it wasn't the first time I'd been slapped.

"Good," Brock said, pulling out the seat next to mine. "Let me take look at that cheek." Before I had a chance to protest, he slipped a finger under my chin, tilting my face to the side. His eyes flashed, and a sense of danger radiated off him. Not at me, but at the one who had hurt me.

"You don't have to do this. I'm fine," I insisted, captured by the intensity in his gaze. When he didn't say anything and only continued to scowl at my face, I asked. "Is it that bad?"

"You'll have one wicked bruise." He picked up the ice pack and placed it on my cheek, inciting an immediate wince. "I'm still pissed at you. Grayson too. Things could have gone down very differently, and you might have ended up with something a lot worse."

I frowned at him. "You might need to work on your bedside manner."

He shook his head. "You should count yourself lucky. If you didn't look so pitiful, I'd let my temper loose."

"Why hold back?" I grumbled.

He stood and grabbed a bottle off the counter. A shot of

something amber and strong dropped down in front of me. "Now drink this," he ordered.

Was mixing liquor and pills a good idea?

Yes.

I down the shot without a second thought, letting the heat warm my bones. Brock didn't bother with a glass and took a long pull directly from the bottle. "Fuck, I needed that. What a shit night," he grumbled, raking a hand through his dark hair.

It looked like we were finally going to have that talk.

I held out my glass, silently asking for more. Hell, I deserved it. Brock obliged without blinking. "How long have you known that Grayson, Kenna, and I are related?" The question blurted out of me. I blamed the bourbon for loosening my tongue.

Brock set the bottle on the table, keeping a hand secured around the neck. "Since we started looking into your family. It wasn't information I went looking for. And trust me, no one was more shocked by what we read than Grayson. He was a wreck for months. Adding that your mother stole you on top of what happened with Kenna, Grayson reached his breaking point."

Stole!?

Dear God. I couldn't breathe. "I was kidnapped?" This was way worse than being adopted. A part of me, from the moment I found out, had had an inkling Angie was responsible. But kidnapped? Why would she do that? How had she done it? And get away with it for so long? We lived in the same town.

Oh, God. My parents weren't my parents.

I'd never felt more lost in my life as I did right now. This had to be a joke.

The vanilla and oak notes inside the bourbon turned sour

on the back of my tongue. Too damn afraid that my mother had done exactly what Brock implied—stolen me from the Edwardses—I tossed back another shot. Knowing my mother, I was inclined to believe Brock had every right to be disgusted.

A bead of worry and sympathy for Grayson, Kenna, and their parents found its way into my heart. Had the Edwardses hidden their missing child from Grayson and Kenna? Trying to make sense of it all made my head ache more than it already was.

"From what we were able to gather, your mother—Angie," he corrected. "She was also pregnant around the same time as Mrs. Edwards. The details of the switch aren't clear. The three of you were born early like many triplets and spent time in NICU at the same time Angie's baby was there, also born premature. Her little girl had health complications and the baby died. We can only conclude that she somehow switched that baby with you, allowing the Edwards's to believe that one of their little girls didn't make it."

"So they don't even know about me," I whispered.

"No."

I shook my head. "This can't be true."

Brock shoved a hand through his dark hair, exhaling. "I'm sorry to be the one to tell you. And I wish it wasn't like this."

"So your private detective found out what happened."

He nodded. "A total fluke. As I said, it was not something we went searching for. The detective is a personal friend of our families. He was actually Grayson's father, uh, your father's," he added, glancing at me. "...college roommate back in the day. He noticed the date you were born and the hospital on your birth certificate. The same day and location that one of his close friends went through the best and worst days of his life. So for kicks and his own curiosity, Oliver ran a DNA test on you. None of us expected for it to come back as a match with Grayson's."

My finger traced over the rim of my empty shot glass as I stared at the few lingering drops of amber liquid gathered in the bottom. "Can I read the file?" I lifted my eyes, and our gazes crashed.

Brock's brows drew together. "Do you think that is a good idea?"

"I need to know the truth." And I couldn't be sure I would get that from Angie. I could already hear her giving me a sob story about losing her baby, being alone, young, and scared. I'd heard it all before. I had a feeling today was the last day I'd ever consider her my mother or capable of being a decent person. "It's one of those things I have to see for myself."

"Fine," he agreed reluctantly. "Don't move."

As if I had anywhere else to go. I waited until he cleared the kitchen before reaching for the bottle to fill up the small glass and tossing back another shot. He returned a few minutes later holding a familiar manila folder. Setting it down on the table, he pushed it toward me with his middle finger. As Brock took another long drink from the bottle, I opened the file. My fingers shook slightly.

Brock remained silent while I read the details of the hospital records for both Angie and Mrs. Edwards. My eyes hung up on the lab reports where it showed my DNA to be a damn close match to Grayson's and Kenna's. There was no question that we were related. For seventeen years I'd been living a lie. Angie had been living a lie.

Did my dad know?

He wasn't really my father.

And that sudden knowledge stabbed me in the heart.

I had a hard time believing my father would have agreed to steal a baby. He was a decent man—a good man. That definitely would have been a topic thrown around during arguments. They aired all their dirty laundry when things got heated, which they had often. I grew up thinking the arguments I witnessed between my parents were totally normal.

OMG. I have a family.

CHAPTER TWO

According to the birth records, Grayson was born first, and then Kenna. I was born last, twelve minutes after Kenna, making me the baby. "It's true," I whispered, slamming my... I lost count of the number of shots I'd taken, but the bourbon helped with the shock of it all. My heart squeezed in my chest; the pain of being deceived and lied to hurt more than any injury I'd sustained.

What would my life have been like if Angie's baby had lived?

It was a question that would haunt me forever.

"I told you I wouldn't lie to you." Brock's voice drifted across the table to me.

What started as a flutter of anger morphed into something bigger. "No, you just withheld information. You should have told me. I had a right to know."

"This isn't just about you. Grayson's parents think you're dead. We didn't know if we could trust you."

"And when you do shit like this, it makes me wonder if I can trust you," I snapped. My anger wasn't entirely for Brock, but he got the brunt of it, seeing as my mother was not around. She and I would have words. How dare she keep something like this from me for seventeen years!

If she hadn't gotten involved with Steven and the Elite hadn't investigated Angie's past, Grayson and I might never have known the truth.

Fuck that.

The first time I'd learned about the Elite digging into my family, I'd been livid. But now... a part of me was grateful. "Does Kenna know?"

Brock shook his head. "Not yet. And Grayson wants to keep it that way for now. She is finally in a good place. Kenna isn't as strong as you. He doesn't want to risk sending her spiraling again," he explained as my eyes continued to scan the documents, reading the words but not comprehending.

I remembered what Mads had told me about Grayson's sister. She'd suffered from depression long before Carter came into the mix. The way Brock spoke about her made Kenna seem like a fragile doll about to break. But this was my sister too. He couldn't keep me away from her. I realized how much I wanted to meet her. My cheek frozen from the ice pack, I pushed the folder toward the center of the table. I'd read enough. "I don't know what to say. Or how I'm supposed to feel. I need to talk to my mom."

"No," Brock snapped, surprising me. His hand closed over mine where it lay on the table. "Not yet."

"Why? Because of Carter?" I guessed. With all this talk of triplet stuff and the shots I'd taken, the incident with Carter seemed as if it happened months ago instead of just an hour.

Brock screwed the top back onto the bourbon bottle, indicating we were done drinking. "Partially, *but* mostly because of the Edwardses. And you," he added. "This has to be overwhelming for you, and I can't imagine what you're feeling, but we need to be careful with this information. If we expose what Angie did, she will go to jail." He didn't bother to hide the disdain he felt for Angie, or that he thought she belonged behind bars.

My feelings were a fucking mess. On one hand, anger festered inside me, aimed at Angie. She had taken me from my family, pretended to be my mother, and yet, she never really loved me. Not like a mother should. I could see that now, and it finally made sense.

All this time I just thought I was a disappointment to her. I couldn't understand how we could be so different.

This wasn't supposed to be my life.

"You need to be sure you're ready for the consequences," Brock reasoned.

"What am I supposed to do then?"

"Business as usual," he stated, leaning back in his chair and folding his arms over his chest.

I had gone seventeen years without knowing about Kenna and Grayson. How much longer would I have to wait? "What about Grayson? Are things going to be weird with us now?" Did

I want to pursue a relationship with Grayson as my brother? Did he want to? Before tonight, I would have said hell no. Grayson had shown no real interest in me other than annoyance. Had that changed?

Would he continue to look at me and see his sister? Could he get past it? Before tonight, I would have said hell no.

Something flashed in his eyes. Regret? Pain? "I don't know. Give him some time to cool down," he replied. "Grayson is all messed up in the head right now after what happened tonight. He's had it rough the last few years and I think seeing you with Carter snapped part of the grudge he's been holding on to. He has a sister he adores and would do anything to protect. He is all mixed up about you."

"He isn't the only one." Perhaps Grayson and I had more in common than just DNA.

Brock snorted, shaking his head. "The two of you are so much alike."

Wasn't that the definition of triplets? It finally made sense why Kenna and I looked freakily alike. The worse part for me was the chance to grow up with my sister had been stripped away from me.

I dropped my head, refusing to admit how much it hurt having the Elite keep secrets from me, knowing they still didn't trust me, not completely. I'd been willing to put myself on the line to take Carter down, not just for my safety but for the Elite as well. "It's been a long night. I think I'd like to lie down." And be alone with my thoughts. Brock had a way of scrambling my brain; add in the shots, and I might forget that I was just here to sleep.

"Do you need to let anyone know where you are?" he asked.

I shook my head. How pathetic. But then I remembered.

Mads!

Dropping the ice pack, I reached around to my back pocket. I had to text her, let her know I didn't get murdered. I leaned slightly to the side, my fingers sliding into the pocket as I fished for my phone. *Shit! My fucking phone.* Memories I wanted to suppress came flooding to the surface. I had dropped my phone on the floor in the back of Carter's car. "Son of a bitch," I mumbled.

My forehead thumped against my palm as I groaned. I had no hope of ever seeing it again, meaning I had to ask Angie for a new cell phone and come up with a lie for how I lost it. Though, I hadn't yet made up my mind on whether or not I'd try to plead with Angie to take my side for once—to believe me. Most sane people would tell their mother that their stepbrother had kidnapped them, held a knife to their throat, and assaulted them.

I wasn't most people.

And neither was Angie.

She wouldn't believe me, and if she did, she'd be more concerned about her newly acquired status, protecting the Patterson family name, keeping her closet filled with designer clothes, and hiding her own secrets. I was far down on Angie's list of important shit.

I turned my head to the side and found Brock watching me with an odd yet amused expression. He probably assumed I was on the brink of a mental breakdown... and he wouldn't have been that far off.

"My phone is in Carter's SUV," I explained my sudden verbal despair.

"Oh," he said, then shrugged. "Not a big deal. We'll get you a new one," he added as if we were talking about replacing a tube of lip gloss.

"You can't just buy me a new phone, Brock," I argued.

"Why not?"

"Well, for one, they cost money, I might add, and I don't want your money. It's not your problem. I'll handle it."

"I'm not taking no for an answer. We'll go to the store tomorrow. I'll put you on my plan."

That sounded like a horrible idea, but also ridiculously appealing to not rely on Steven to pay for my cell phone bill or have Angie use it as a punishment. On the flip side, there was something too intimate about sharing a phone plan with Brock. That was what couples did.

And Brock Taylor and I were not a couple.

"I'll get it back. Don't worry about it." I brushed off his offer.

"Like hell. You're not going anywhere near Carter's SUV," he said, roughly and firmly.

Anger rose in me. Brock should have known better than to boss me around. I despised being told what to do and like all my emotions tonight, my temper came on swift and strong. "I appreciate the concern, but you don't get to tell me what to do."

His eyes became chips of ice. "I think I earned that right for saving your ass tonight."

A short snort loosed through my nostrils as I dropped the ice pack onto the table. "You're unbelievable. Thanks for the first aid and the shots, but I'm leaving." I stood too fast, but ignored the spinning room and sloppily stormed across the kitchen.

He grabbed my elbow before I made it three steps toward the archway and whirled me around to face him. My palms hit his chest, and my gaze slammed into his chin as I tried to steady myself. "Like hell, Firefly. I said you're not going home."

Lifting my eyes, I jerked my arm out of his hold. Or tried to. He wasn't letting me go far. Releasing my arm, his fingers moved to my waist, keeping me from putting the distance I sought between us. I leaned into him, needing the support as my eyes cleared. "I have friends, you know. Or I'll just go to my dad's," I countered. "Your house is not my only option."

Brock stepped closer, our chests brushing. "Not tonight."

"I'm not sleeping with you, if that's what you think this is." The words flew from my mouth.

His fingers tightened at my hips, a look of annoyance flashing in his eyes. "For fuck sake, Josie. What kind of guy do you take me for? I'm not interested in seducing you tonight. Not when you're still shaken up over what happened. Give me a little credit. I'm not always an asshole."

"Just ninety-nine percent of the time."

His lips grew into a slow grin. "Exactly. Come on. I'm putting you to bed, where you'll stay." His hand slid to the small of my back, guiding me out of the kitchen and into a dimly lit hallway.

And I let him, too fucking tired to put up much of a fight. "What about Mads?" I asked, glancing sidelong at him.

Dark brows drew together in confusion. "What about her?"

My eyes rolled. "I need to let her know I'm okay."

He blinked. "I'll have one of the guys get in touch with her. Satisfied?"

I nodded and asked, "Any chance I could take a shower first?"

He gave me a long stare, one that brimmed with too much heat at the mention of me naked in his shower, which had not been my intention. He blinked, and understanding crossed his features. "Take as long as you need."

I didn't say anything as he led me upstairs to his bedroom, but I wanted to. From what I'd heard about Brock, he didn't let girls sleep in his room, yet he broke that rule with me and looked to do so again. I wanted to know why. Was it because he still had use for me? Because I was a pawn for him to maneuver in this game of chess he was playing with Carter?

Again, too damn tired to dissect his reasons for letting me stay in his room, I just walked inside with him. Leaving me in the center of the room, he opened a drawer and pulled out a plain black shirt. "You can sleep in this."

"Thanks," I replied, grateful. Dying to get out of my clothes, I wanted no reminder of Carter when I went to bed. My favorite pair of jeans was forever ruined now—tainted. Another thing to curse Carter for.

As I took the shirt he offered, our fingers touched for a brief moment, and I lifted my gaze. The startling aqua color of his eyes trapped mine. I should move. I really should. And yet, my feet stood there, doing nothing.

With a grin that made me want to kiss him and hit him at the same time, Brock released the shirt and his tingling touch along with it. I'd be a liar if I said a ribbon of disappointment hadn't woven through me, that I didn't crave his touch. A part of me, a big part of me, wanted to grab him by the arm and pull him into the shower with me just to hold me.

That was my irrational, reckless side that always ended up getting me in trouble.

Turning around, I walked into the bathroom and shut the door, loosing a long breath as I stared at the shirt. "Fuck," I whispered, running a hand over my face, and winced, having momentarily forgotten about my cheek. The pain was a reminder, and alone in the bathroom with just my thoughts, it all came crashing down on me.

Carter.

Grayson.

Kenna.

Panic rose swift inside me, and I reached for the doorknob, Brock's name on my lips.

But as my fingers touched the cool metal handle, I closed my eyes and forced myself to take a steady breath. I could do this. I *would* get through this.

Forcing myself to turn the water on to warm up, I stripped out of my clothes, refusing to look at them as I kicked them into a corner. Poised on a perilous mental edge, it would only take a tiny nudge to send me careening over the edge.

As I stepped into the shower, silent tears flowed with the steady stream of water, the two mixing in such a way that I convinced myself there weren't tears at all.

Twenty minutes later, I stood in front of a foggy mirror, wrapped in a white towel. My hair smelled like Brock, woodsy and with a hint of citrus. Braiding my wet pink hair, I braced myself and glanced into the mirror, half afraid of what I would see. My skin was shades pinker than usual due to the hot shower, but the cheek Carter hit was redder yet. Turning to the side for a closer inspection, I concluded I would have one hell of a bruise in the morning.

"Bastard," I hissed, cursing my stepbrother.

Borrowing a bit of toothpaste from the drawer, I squeezed a glob onto my finger and scrubbed it over my teeth, swirling the paste around in my mouth. Better than nothing. I absolutely could not go to bed without brushing my teeth. It didn't matter how late, tired, or drunk I was.

When I left the bathroom, my gaze immediately went to Brock on the bed. His grin widened at the sight of me in his T-shirt that hit just at the tops of my thighs. "It looks good on you."

And he looked good on the bed... way too good, but I kept that to myself and berated myself for downing those shots. Rolling my eyes, I tugged at the hem, wishing the tee was longer so it didn't look like I was naked underneath.

Did he expect us to sleep together in the bed?

The lush side of me said if I got into the bed with him, all kinds of delicious things would happen.

No, Josie! Sex with the hottest guy you've ever seen is not what you need tonight. What you need is comfort and safety.

And Brock could give me both.

Hell, what I need is a tranquilizer.

I wasn't keen about being alone, but then again, a night in bed with Brock seemed riskier.

"Does that mean I get to keep the shirt?" I asked in a sad attempt to be light and playful when I felt anything but.

He swung his legs over the side of the bed. "Only if you promise I'm the only one who gets to take it off you."

I swallowed. Flirty Brock made my head fuzzy. "I'm too tired to make deals with you."

He patted the bed with his hand. "Get in."

Without argument, I padded over to the bed and peeled back a corner of the blanket, slipping underneath. I kept my legs curled as Brock watched me from the other side, still on top of the covers.

When I was settled, he asked, "Do you want me to stay or go? Your choice. And though I don't think it needs to be said, I promise to keep my hands to myself. For tonight," he added.

I tucked my hand under the pillow, lying on my side—the opposite one of my hurt cheek—and watched Brock. "It's your bed."

"Firefly," he replied firmly, leaning a hand on the other side of my legs.

"Stay," I whispered.

His gaze held mine as he nodded and got up to turn off the lights. The room was suffused in darkness, followed by the rustling sounds of clothes being shed. I clutched the edge of the blanket, forcing my mind to go blank, refusing to let my thoughts go to Brock nearly naked. The bed dipped with his weight on the other side.

He wasn't naked, was he?

I wasn't about to find out.

"Before you harp at me, Fynn called Mads," he said, settling into the bed.

A tiny ache in my chest eased. Tons of pressure still

clamped down on me, but it was one less thing to worry about. "I never harp at you for information."

"Uh-huh." I felt him shift, tucking an arm behind his head on the pillow. "And because I know how your brain works, you can stay with me for as long as you need."

His body brought warmth to the bed. "I don't have any clothes." Gah. Why did I mention clothes? It was as if my brain couldn't stop dwelling on the fact that neither Brock nor I was wearing much. On the plus side, I wasn't thinking about Carter.

His head turned to the side, and I could feel his stare at me through the darkness. "That's what you're worried about? What you're going to wear? It's not a big deal. I'll buy you new clothes."

"Not the point. And I'm not taking your money." No matter how much the Taylors might have. "I'm not a charity case, Brock." First a phone, now clothes.

"Who said you were?" he murmured, his voice closer than it had been a minute ago.

I sighed, exhaustion slamming into me now that I lay in bed. "I'm sorry I didn't tell you what Grayson, Mads, and I planned. It wasn't to cause drama."

"The drama started long before you showed up. As pissed as I am at your choices tonight, Grayson too, this isn't your fault. It's mine."

Yawning, I muttered, "Did I just hear you own up to your shit?" The sheets were cool against my skin, and his scent clung to them. I told myself not to sniff them, that I hated the way he smelled.

Big. Fat. Lies.

I did the unthinkable. I pressed my nose into the pillow and inhaled.

Dear fucking God. Why did he smell so damn good? A ribbon of lust bolted between my legs, and I groaned silently in frustration into the pillow.

His fingers tucked a loose, damp strand of pink hair behind my ear. "I'll deny it. No one will believe you," he replied softly with a touch of seriousness, because honestly, it was the truth. No one would question Brock.

"I'm still mad at you too," I mumbled into the pillow.

Sometime during my incessant babble, I fell asleep. Brock kept the nightmares at bay, banishing the noise, and maybe the bourbon helped a teensy bit. The point was, I made it through the night, but the night was the easy part. It was facing the day that scared the shit out of me. All my problems waited for me when the sun came.

But was I ready for them?

Brock was gone when I woke. A stream of sunlight beamed through the tall windows, blinding me. Groaning, I rolled over, and my hand landed on a piece of paper.

A note lay on Brock's pillow.

I flipped over my hand and lifted it, squinting to read. Two simple words.

I snorted and crumpled the note into a ball. Staring at the ceiling, I chewed on my lip, knowing I should do as the note said: stay here. Not specifically in Brock's bed but in his house.

Except... I had shit to sort out, including clean clothes for school on Monday.

Not to mention my mother—correction, my kidnapper. Until I turned eighteen, I technically was still a minor and had to live by Angie's rules, which meant I stayed in the Pattersons' house, despite it being like living in Hell. I had promised Brock to not say anything, to give Grayson a bit of time, and truthfully, I needed that time as well.

Which meant Angie could still reign over me as my legal guardian.

Not even Brock could go up against the courts.

Could he?

I couldn't take the chance. Angie might not notice my absence for a night or two, but eventually, she'd miss her verbal punching bag. Like her wine, Angie was addicted to unloading her shit onto me. If she had a bad day, I paid the price.

And I needed my phone. Despite Brock offering to buy me a new one, everything I needed was in that phone. I didn't want a new one. I liked my phone.

So I made the quick decision to go home, grab a few things, including my car, and get the hell out, all without seeing Carter. It shouldn't be hard, considering the hour. Carter's late and overindulgent lifestyle meant he slept in on the weekends. No way would he be up before noon, leaving me a few hours to sneak in and out.

Easy peasy.

Brock would be pissed.

But when wasn't he annoyed with me?

I chewed on the inside of my cheek, telling myself I could

do this. That I wasn't scared shitless of going anywhere near that house with Carter in it. But it was all lies. I was scared of my asshole stepbrother and for good reason.

In theory, I shouldn't stop living my life because of Carter. I didn't want to let my stepbrother have that kind of power over me. I didn't want to crawl under a rock or hide behind the Elite.

But talking about being brave and actually being brave were two separate entities.

It was all too soon. And I didn't *want* to go to that house alone, but I also couldn't bring Brock for fear he might actually go postal and kill my stepbrother.

Fuck!

Before I overthought everything, I made a rash decision. Taking advantage of Brock's absence, I quickly tossed on the clothes I'd left on the bathroom floor, the ones I never wanted to wear again, and dialed the main line at Pattersons' from the house phone in Brock's room. One of the maids answered and quickly transferred me to Edmund, who agreed to come get me at once.

Desperate times called for desperate measures, and asking Steven's driver/bodyguard to pick me up was reserved for only extreme circumstances. In light of last night's events, this classified as desperate.

The entire time I waited for Edmund, I thought for sure I'd see Brock's Land Rover speeding up the hill and bust me. He didn't.

Edmund picked me up outside the gated community five minutes later. He didn't ask questions, but at the same time, the thin lips and silent treatment proved disapproving enough.

Edmund would undoubtedly report to Steven my whereabouts and with whom I'd chosen to spend my Friday night. It was no secret what Steven thought of Brock.

I didn't give a flying fuck. Steven could suck it. He was no better than his son, just older and wiser in his games.

Edmund swung the town car into the Pattersons' driveway, smoothly easing to a stop. Steven enjoyed luxury, and the sleek black car with its butter leather seats and blacked-out windows oozed importance and money. Two things my mother always aspired to have.

What a damn match made in heaven the two of them were —the attractive gold digger and the hotshot who wanted a beautiful woman to warm his bed, grace his arm, and keep his secrets. Not difficult when she had some pretty big secrets of her own she'd like to keep buried.

"Thanks, Edmund," I said and opened the door before Edmund could. The sight of Carter's SUV parked outside on the wide driveway caused a whirlwind of anxiety to spin around in my chest. These were emotions I needed to learn to deal with —sooner than later.

Before I lost my gumption, I swung to Edmund. "I left something in Carter's car last night. Can you wait here while I go retrieve it?" I asked, wanting someone to watch over me even if they had no idea they were.

He gave a curt nod. "Of course."

I make quick haste to Carter's Escalade and whipped open the back door. In that single instant, it all came rushing at me. The tight bonds cutting into my wrists. The utter darkness from the blindfold. The smell of Carter's cologne gagging me, burning my nostrils as stark fear dug its claws in me.

I closed my eyes, only making it worse.

Snap out of it.

Deep breath in. Deep breath out. Now again.

A tad steadier, I opened my eyes and glanced over the back seat, over the floor mats, searching for my phone. Nothing. But I knew damn well I had left it in here. With frantic fingers, I peeled back the rubber mats. "God damn it," I muttered, slamming the door shut.

"Did you find what you were looking for?" Edmund asked as I stalked past him.

"Not yet," I replied and strutted to the side of the house, avoiding the main house and taking the stairs the led up to the balcony that connected to my room.

In and out, I reminded. The less attention I drew to my being here, the better.

I slid the glass doors open and stepped inside my tomb. At least it felt that way, as quiet as a grave. The analogy freaked me out.

"Hey, sis."

CHAPTER THREE

otherfucker.

M At the sound of Carter's voice, I lost ten years of my life. Jumping, I backed into the wall, spotting the bastard on the center of my bed. Messy, sandy hair fell over his forehead, and he'd changed into a pair of gray sweats with a white T-shirt.

Had he been here all night? Slept here?

The thought caused a shudder in my veins, and I was certain I could never sleep in that bed again. Another thing in my life Carter ruined.

Staring at my stepbrother, fear paralyzed me, and I regretted stepping foot inside this house. How stupid could I be? Of course Carter was waiting for me. This was Carter. My deranged, desperate, and out-of-his-bloody-mind stepbrother.

Fuckkkk!

Now what, Josie?

My mistake. My problem. I had to deal with this—with Carter—on my own.

Steeling my chin, I dug deep inside myself and pulled out a kernel of strength. "Where's my phone, asshole?"

Carter quirked a brow. "Morning to you too." His voice grated on my nerves.

"What are you doing in my room?" I demanded. My hands fisted at my sides, nails digging into my palms. The pain held me together, kept me centered, kept me from going back to last night. I'd already been down the road once this morning. I refused to go there again. Not in front of Carter.

He made no indication to move from his spot on the bed, hands propped behind his head. "I was worried when you didn't come home last night."

My fists hit the wall behind me. "Bullshit. Cut the crap, Carter. I'm done with your games. I don't want to be part of this." Someone had to be home. The day maids? The cook? Edmund! Surely one of them would hear me if I screamed.

Carter rocked upright on the bed, his long legs stretching so half of them hung over the side. He dwarfed the queen-sized mattress. "It's too late for that. You're the key component."

I scrambled over to my desk, whipping out a pair of scissors from the penholder, and clutched them like a weapon I wasn't afraid to use in front of me. "Get. Out."

He laughed. "Cute. If you get blood in here, Macy is going to have a shit fit." Macy was one of the maids who usually cleaned our rooms.

I kept a firm grip on the scissors. "Like you care about the staff. Or anyone but yourself, for that matter."

He wasn't fazed. "True. But I do care about my future."

"Is this going somewhere?" The longer I was alone with him, the higher my anxiety spiked. He was fucking with my get in and out plan. Truthfully, the entire plan had gone to shit. My eyes flashed to the open sliding door and back to Carter.

His expression darkened, turning into something ominous. "You shouldn't have slept with him."

"Who I sleep with is no concern of yours."

"Did you fuck him last night? I bet you did." His smirk made the act of having sex with Brock dirty when it was anything but.

Well, maybe a little, but not in the creepy-ass way Carter implied.

"And if I did?" I gloated, pointing the tip of the scissors toward Carter's heart, because that was a smart move, baiting the unstable stepbrother.

Scooting to the edge of the bed, his blue eyes never left mine as he said, "You're going to help me."

I blinked. He was delusional. What other explanation was there? "Why the fuck would I do that?"

His lips curved. "I know your little secret."

My heart jerked in my chest. "You don't know shit, dickhead," I replied with a scratchy edge. "Now get out of my room before I scream. And I want my phone."

Standing up, he tossed something onto the middle of my rumbled sheets and stalked toward me. I backed up until I hit a wall. Swearing under my breath, he halted just an inch short of the scissors and said, "You'll change your mind, but I'll give you a few days to think on it."

"What-the-fuck-ever."

His dancing gaze moved to the side of my face before flickering back to my eyes. "Purple suits you."

Rage joined the fear inside me, nearly stifling it. I wanted to carve his eyes out, cut out his tongue, and serve his bloody heart to Angie on a platter. "You'll never hit me again," I vowed, my voice choppy from all the pent-up anger building.

He jerked toward me and then chuckled at my instinctual flinch. "The next time you'll be begging me to save you from them."

"It will be a cold day in Hell before that happens."

His hand reached out as if to touch my cheek but I slapped it away, my self-preservation kicking in. "Don't. Touch. Me," I hissed between clenched teeth.

Chuckling, he walked toward the door, pausing on the threshold. "Welcome home, sis."

Speed walking across the room, I slammed the door shut after him, not caring if I hit his heels with the door, and quickly threw the lock in place.

A good full five minutes passed before the shaking stopped and my heart steadied, yet knowing Carter lingered somewhere in the house kept me on edge.

I went straight for my phone, which Carter had tossed onto the bed. After a quick inspection, consisting of me trying to get the damn screen to turn on, I concluded it was dead. "Asshole,"

I muttered between my teeth. The creep probably spent all night trying to crack the 4-digit passcode. And if he managed to unlock it, you know the asshole went through my phone, reading my texts and jerking off to my photos, all thoughts that made me want to puke my guts out.

Grabbing my charger, I rushed to pack a bag of clothes, a few makeup items, and other bathroom essentials. I stuffed them all into my pink duffel, including my Elmwood Academy uniform. The clothes I wore went straight into the trash as I changed into something clean.

Hauling my duffel and school bag stuffed with my laptop, I snatched the keys off the dresser and went back out the balcony, leaving my bedroom door locked from the inside. I doubted it would keep Carter out, and the idea of him going through my drawers made me queasy.

I took the stairs and went straight to the garage to deposit my crap inside the Lexus, a gift from Steven. I hated the cherry red color. I hated the blacked-out rims. I hated everything this car stood for. But right now, it was the only thing offering me the escape I sought—far, far from Carter Patterson.

My ass slid behind the wheel, and I plugged my phone into the charger as I started the engine. Putting the car into reverse, I backed out of the garage. My foot pressed down on the brake. I stared at Carter's SUV. The urge to ram the SOB rose in me.

My stepbrother loved that stupid car.

Unable to help myself, I shifted the car and revved the engine.

The urge to hurt Carter any way I could whipped like a

wild wind within me. This need for revenge came on strong. Maybe this devilish side of me had been dormant until now— until Carter.

There would come a time when my stepbrother would get what was coming to him. I needed to be patient. I needed to plan—to plot my revenge.

He wouldn't get away with what he did to me.

Cranking the wheel, I gunned the Lexus out of the drive-way, peeling into the street like I was in the Indy 500. Speed and danger curbed the fire for revenge—temporarily. And now that the match had been lit, I didn't think the flame would truly ever extinguish, not until I had my justice.

For the first time, I grasped the Elite's persistent desire for retribution.

My fingers remained firm on the wheel as I glided around the corner. Moments later, my phone chimed a few dozen times from where it charged in the cup holder, messages from last night and this morning finally coming through. I glanced down briefly, a rookie driving mistake, and when my eyes returned to the road, my gaze bulged at the car stopped in the middle of it.

What the f—

I slammed on the brakes, the Lexus fishtailing as it came to a screeching halt in front of a black Range Rover. My heart leaped into my throat, pumping in overtime. The windows were all tinted, and although I couldn't see Brock's burning gaze, I felt the heat of it.

I didn't question how he knew where I'd run off to or that he had been waiting for me. Honestly, I'd been more worried if he hadn't, but was it necessary to scare the shit out of me in the process? "Fuck," I cursed, slamming my palms against the steering wheel.

Leaving his car in the middle of the road, he got out and stalked toward me. I opened my door and stepped out as he said, "What the fuck, Firefly! Do you have a death wish?"

Our front bumpers were practically kissing, but it wasn't like *I* was trying to kill us. He was the one in the fucking road.

Then I realized he was talking about Carter.

Shit.

I hadn't thought this far ahead and assumed I'd have a few minutes in the car to come up with a solid explanation for leaving his bed.

I'd left him.

The protection of his house.

None of that sat right with Brock.

Staring into his face, I could see the damage I'd done, which had not been my intention. His jaw clenched. "I told you to stay put."

Blinking, my eyes swept over the sweatpants that sat low on his hips and the Academy T-shirt stretched over his chest. Even spitting mad and growling at me, I found him utterly attractive.

Someone should send help.

I needed to be saved from myself and my stupid hormones that couldn't seem to behave themselves around this particular guy. I couldn't think straight, and I had a mountain of crap churning inside me.

Stepping around the door, I lifted on my toes and kissed him. As expected, he made me forget.

No more Carter.

No more Angie.

No more anger or sadness.

No more pain.

Only Brock and the red-hot lust his lips enticed.

His lips stayed unmoving for a heartbeat and I thought he would pull away. Then his fingers were at my hips, shoving me up against the car as his tongue pressed against my lips. I parted them for him, my hands moving to frame his face. If I could have managed it, I would have wrapped myself around him like a rubber band.

Hot and hungry, I attacked his lips, searching and falling into that swift punch of lust only he brought on. My fingers trailed down the front of his shirt, fisting into the material as I tried to pull him closer still, and when that wasn't enough, I slipped my fingers underneath the shirt, skimming over his bare skin. The muscles in his lower abs contracted.

"Jesus, Firefly," he hissed against my lips before diving right back in. Our tongues tangled as my fingers dipped into the waistband of his sweatpants, shoving them lower on his hips.

"You're not wearing any boxers," I murmured.

Wickedness glimmered in his eyes. "I didn't bother putting any on this morning."

But that would mean he'd gone to bed naked. Dear God, tell me it wasn't so. I had managed to sleep the entire night next to Brock naked. That had to be a sin of some kind.

"There is no point in stressing about it now," he said, reading my mind too easily.

"Lots of people sleep naked. I'm not stressing," I countered, my breath coming out in quick bursts of breathiness.

"Do you?" he whispered along my neck, pressing his lips right at the spot that I loved.

My neck arched into him, silently begging for him to never stop.

A loud horn blared, followed by a voice yelling, "Get a room!" We broke apart in time to see a car zoom around us, clearly annoyed.

Unable to contain myself, I laughed, dropping my forehead to his chest. "That did not just happen."

Brock tugged at the end of my braid. "Maybe I should get pissed more often. I had no idea being yelled at had such an effect on you. What other weird vices turn you on?"

"Shut up." I flattened my palm on his chest and pushed, creating a small amount of space that allowed me to draw in a breath. Not that it was all that helpful when the air was tinted with his scent. "That was a momentary lapse in good judgment. It won't happen again."

His grin turned wolfish. "Uh-huh."

He didn't buy it.

Neither did I.

Already I was thinking about his mouth. Again.

I clamped down on my lower lip.

"You seemed to have quite a few momentary lapses around me," he said smugly, like a guy who was used to girls fawning over him.

"Get over yourself."

Brock had an ego that skyrocketed to the heavens. "I'm still waiting for you to confirm if you have a death wish?"

Rolling my eyes, I replied, "Rest assured, I don't. I had to grab some things at my house, clothes and homework. You can't buy my math assignment that's due on Monday."

A dark brow rose, contradicting me.

I shook my head. "God, is there anything money won't buy?"

He stepped away from me, the Academy shirt falling to cover his flat-ass stomach. "I haven't found it yet."

"I'll take your word for it. Look, I knew you wouldn't let me go." My shoulders were tight, anticipating a fight.

Scowl lines appeared at the corners of his mouth. "Damn right, Firefly. You need to trust me. I can't keep Carter from hurting you if you constantly run off on your own."

"Like you trust me?" I tossed back. "Besides, you can't always be by my side."

"There are four of us," he reminded me.

As if I needed to be reminded. Brock. Grayson. Fynn. And Micah—the infamous Elite of Elmwood Academy. The four most sought-after guys at school, and somehow I ended up on their radar. Well, I had done my fair share of shit to cross paths with them, thanks to the grand scheme Mads, Ainsley, and I concocted. Little did I know, I'd been on their radar long before my first day at Elmwood Academy. Even before that fateful night I hooked up with Brock at my mother's wedding.

"Fantastic," I mumbled. "I'm not used to having someone look out for me. It's weird."

"Well, get used to it, Firefly."

I groaned as another car swerved around us, laying on the horn. The sound echoed around us, the driver staring with his nose pressed to the glass. My hand flew up in the air with the middle finger extended before I thought about it. "We can't keep arguing in the middle of the road," I complained, concerned some idiot might actually hit us. This wasn't a busy road in general but we'd lingered too long.

"You want to go back to kissing then?" he asked, his gaze flickering to my mouth.

"Brock," I groaned again.

Before he made any indication toward his car, the lightness in his eyes flickered, there one second, gone the next. It was kind of scary how fast he could switch his emotions. "Was he home?"

Carter's name wasn't necessary. I leaned a hand on the Lexus, stabilizing myself from the quick flash of my stepbrother's face. "That's not important."

Something in my voice must have given me away, or perhaps my face lost shades of color. "What did he say to you?" Brock demanded.

The fight I'd been trying to avoid brewed again in his expression, and telling him that my stepbrother was trying to blackmail me to do his dirty work wouldn't help his temper. So I said, "Nothing."

"James," he growled.

"Taylor," I spat back.

His arms folded over his chest, that sexy mouth no longer smirking. "I'm still furious with you."

The rigidness in my shoulders eased. "I know."

"We're not done. Follow me."

"In those sweatpants... anywhere," I said lightly, adding a grin to ease up some of the tension.

He rolled his eyes. "Don't get cheesy on me."

I got back into the driver seat of the Lexus and replied, "Like you don't love it, girls fawning over you. Please, it gets you off."

His lips quipped. "You get me off."

My cheeks betrayed me by going hot. Before I could open my mouth and embarrass myself more, I shut the car door and put the thing into drive. Brock Taylor always had to have the last word, a trait I found so damn irritating... like the man himself.

* * *

"I can't live in your room," I argued as Brock dropped my duffel bag in the middle of his room, after insisting he carry it inside. "There are like a dozen other rooms in this house. Surely one of them is a guest room." I consented to stay the weekend. Come Monday, I would have to figure my shit out.

"We have four. You're still staying in my room," he stated flatly.

"Has anyone told you how insufferable you are?" I huffed, annoyance flaring through me.

Brock peered at me from behind thick lashes, eyes twinkling. "Almost daily."

Brock and I would drive each other mad after a weekend in the same room. "And what will your parents think about you keeping a girl in your room?"

He moved to the window and opened it, letting in the late October breezes. Traces of burning leaves and pine filtered into the room. "My parents are gone for another week."

"Why do rich kids always have parents who are never home?" I mumbled, not expecting a response. I sank onto his unmade bed, sheets still rumpled from our sleep.

Brock shrugged. "Luck of the gene pool. Or cursed. Depends on your viewpoint."

So perhaps he didn't enjoy the freedom as much as he led on? "Wish Angie would become absent now that she's living her dream married to a wealthy asshole."

Brock made a disparaging sound. "You might just get your wish, but then that leaves you with Carter."

A shiver of revulsion went through me. "True." I laid my hands over my knees to keep them from bouncing. "What about the staff? Won't they tell your parents you have a girl staying here?"

He pulled out his phone and glanced at the screen. "That's the thing about being raised by the help; they care about you more than your own parents. They won't say anything," he assured, his fingers tapping on his phone in what I assumed was a text.

I was about to ask who he was messaging when my phone buzzed. Reaching into my back pocket, I stared at the name scrolling across the banner. Angie. Not Mom or Mother. Just Angie, the name she absolutely hated to be called. I declined the call.

A few minutes later, my phone buzzed again, and I scowled at the screen.

"Who keeps calling you? Carter?" Brock's expression said he'd like to go through the phone and rip Carter into his room. Brock would love the chance to get my stepbrother alone. And this time Carter might not make it to the hospital but leave in a body bag.

I stared at the flashing screen. "No, worse. My crazy-ass-kidnapping mother. She is due home tomorrow from Steven's business trip."

Brock walked over and sat beside me. "You need to tell her you won't be home."

I shot him a narrowed glare. "Like ever?"

"Will she go for that?" He was serious.

I shook my head. "Definitely not. But really, what can she do about it? I'll be eighteen soon."

"Stall her for as long as possible. And don't say anything about Grayson." He pinned me with a hard look meant to intimidate, but it just fell short of the mark for me.

"Easier said than done." She had called four times in the last hour. Sighing, I hit the accept button on my phone, knowing I was going to regret this. "Angie," I said dryly after putting the phone on speaker.

"Josephine. Do you know how many times I've called you?" Annoyed, her voice shrilled octaves higher than it needed to be as it blared out of the speaker.

"My phone died."

"It's irresponsible to not keep your phone properly charged. What if something happened to you? What if you were lost in the woods and the police needed to ping your phone?" she ranted.

I didn't even want to know how she knew about such things. "Shit happens."

"I swear, Josephine, you need to be more aware and responsible. Just because we live in a nicer part of town doesn't mean bad things can't happen."

I choked. *No shit. I'm living with a fucking monster.*

"I called the house and was told you didn't come home last night. Where are you?" she demanded, miffed that she'd had to track me down.

How many mimosas had she already had this morning? Three? Five? "I'm staying at a friend's."

"Did you and Carter have another fight?" she asked, and I could picture her pressing a hand to her temples as if a headache brewed.

My gaze met Brock's. "Why would you ask that?" Had Carter already said something to her or his father?

"I know the two of you don't exactly get along, but please, Josephine, don't make trouble." This time her voice turned pleading, bordering desperate. She was preparing her woe-is-me act.

Yet again, I was at fault. It was somehow me that was the reason Carter and I couldn't stand each other. I scoffed. "This is me *not* making trouble."

"Fine," she sighed. "I expect you home for dinner on Sunday."

Brock stiffened beside me and shook his head. "I'm not sure I'll be able to make it," I said.

Her response came through quickly and sharp. "This is not negotiable."

"Kind of like you marrying Steven. Got it." I had no intention of showing up for dinner.

"Josephine, so help me God, I'll see you—"

Brock reached over and hit the end button, cutting off Angie's goodbye. "Wow, your mother is a piece of work."

I stared at the blank phone. "She is one of a fucking kind. And she isn't my mother, not really."

CHAPTER FOUR

T he doorbell rang, echoing through Brock's house in a
chiming pattern. It was about three in the afternoon,
and Brock and I'd just started a movie. He hit the
pause button and checked the security cam on his phone. "I'll
be right back. And there better be popcorn left."

It wasn't bad hanging out at Brock's house. It was nice, and
he somehow managed to keep my mind off all the other stuff.
But when left alone, even for only a minute, my mind went right
there.

Neither of us had forgiven the other, but a silent truce had
been agreed upon, at least for the day. We both needed twenty-
four hours to decompress.

Curious, I leaned over the couch and listened to the voices
coming from down the hallway. They grew louder. Whoever
was at the door, it wasn't a solicitor, not that they could get
through the security gate.

I tossed aside the throw blanket and stood up, setting the bowl of buttered popcorn aside on the end table. I padded quietly down the hall, keeping to the wall. For a second, I had a horrible feeling someone I didn't want to see stood at the door, like my mother.

"I know she's here. Now get out of my way." A pushy female voice echoed from the foyer.

"Mads?" I said, rounding the corner.

And there she was—my best friend from the Academy. Actually, she was the only friend I had at school. I wouldn't exactly call the Elite friends. They were...something else. I hadn't figured it out yet.

White knights?

Fallen angels?

A bit of both, I decided.

Her dark brown hair sat in a ponytail high on her head, wisps of honey highlights framing her cheekbones. Gray eyes shifted over Brock's shoulder to my face. The frown on her lips remained as she crossed the threshold, straight for me.

"Josie," she sighed. "You're alive." Mads wrapped me in a tight hug. She smelled like mint gum, sweet electric perfume, and faint traces of smoke.

"Didn't Grayson tell you what happened?" I shot Brock an accusatory glare.

Maddy Clarke was no dummy. Her eyes darkened upon seeing the bruise that was just beginning to form under the skin on my cheek. "He said you were fine and with Brock. As far as I knew, they were keeping you hostage here."

"He more or less is," I replied, firing him a smirk.

Brock rolled his eyes as he closed the door. "I'm considering handcuffing her to a chair."

Mads ignored him. "When I didn't hear from you..."

"I'm sorry. I lost my phone, and when I finally found it, the damn thing was dead. I planned to call you later tonight," I explained, knowing how lame of an excuse it was. I'd been too shaken last night to deal with anyone.

"Now there's no need," she said, brightening her tone until her eyes skimmed over my cheek again. The bruise was like a beacon that drew the gaze. "I'm glad you're not dead."

Only Mads and Ainsley would be so blunt. I loved her for it. "Same."

Brock's hand went to the doorknob. "Okay, you've seen her. Thanks for stopping by," he said dryly in an attempt to shoo Mads back out the door.

She scrunched her freckled nose at him. "I need a moment with my best friend. Alone," she emphasized and grabbed my hand, leading me to the staircase. She made her way upstairs like someone who knew where she was going. It was still weird to know that Mads was best friends with my sister—the girl who used to pretend date Brock—the girl who was at the center of this entire fucking mess.

Kenna.

Could things get freakier?

Then I realized it could.

Mads was my cousin.

Holy crap.

The temptation to pump Mads for information about Kenna lingered in the forefront of my mind as we climbed the stairs. There was so much I didn't know; so much I wanted to know about her. She left two years ago because of my asshole stepbrother.

Let's set the record straight. She wanted it. If anything, she was using me, trying to get back at Brock for discarding her, just like he does with every girl. You'll be no different.

That had been Carter's warning last night. God, what a sicko. The defense of a rapist, of a guy who got off on hurting someone he considered weaker, on making them feel powerless. The fact that I looked like Kenna probably got Carter hard.

Had it really only been last night?

"Firefly," Brock called after us.

I paused halfway up the stairs and glanced over my shoulder. He gave me a look that conveyed everything on his mind—a crystal-clear warning. *Don't tell Mads anything.*

He seemed to want me to keep secrets from everyone but him.

And despite the warning, the sight of him filled me with security. Carter might know where I was hiding out, but he wouldn't dare come here, not alone. Not unless he wanted his ass beat again, which he might if it meant getting Brock in trouble. Wouldn't that be the perfect setup? And Carter was desperate and crazy enough to put himself intentionally in danger to accomplish removing Brock as an obstacle.

The Elite no longer had to pretend Carter didn't disgust them. It was all out in the open. Battle lines had been drawn.

Mads shut the door to Brock's room, turned, and said, "Okay, now tell me what really happened. I don't want any of the glossed-over crap my cousin fed me."

I had to sit down for this. Waiting until she joined me on Brock's bed, which had been made by one of the staff, I gave Mads a quick rundown. The words came out robotic as I tried to keep myself detached from the events that replayed so clearly in my head. Was it healthy to keep suppressing my emotions? No. But I didn't want to lose control.

Mads didn't seem surprised when I finished. "Oh God, Josie. I can't believe it. Okay, that's not true. Of course, I knew what Carter was capable of, I just never thought... We never should have—"

"I don't regret it," I interrupted before she added any more guilt to the pile I could tell she already felt. "Only that our plan didn't exactly work. What happened isn't our fault." And that was the truth. The blame belonged entirely on Carter.

"I get why they are being so cagey about where you are, but it wasn't hard to figure out," she said, toying with her thumb ring. "All Grayson told me was that you couldn't go home."

I crossed my legs on the bed, surprise fluttering in my chest. "That's all he said?"

"Yeah, is there more?" Her eyes narrowed when I didn't immediately assure her there wasn't. She brought a leg up on the bed, the other dangling over the edge. Her knees peeked out from the rips in her jeans. "Of course, there is. There is always more with them."

"I have to ask you something."

"Anything," she replied with no hesitation.

I chewed on the inside of my lip, thinking over what I was about to do. Brock expected my silence. Grayson too. And I respected that. But did either of them think about what I needed? Grayson wasn't the only one dealing with the choice my mother made seventeen years ago. "Before you say that, I need to ask you to keep this to yourself; that is, if you don't already know," I added, because I still was unsure.

Her soft painted pink lips turned down, sensing we were getting into some serious shit. "Okay, now you have my attention. This secret, who are we keeping it from?"

"Everyone, but most importantly the Elite. Brock would be pissed if he knew I was telling you this. I think." But I had to talk to someone about Kenna. My first choice would have been Ainsley, but she wasn't here. Mads was. Plus, she knew Kenna. It was a connection we shared. And I trusted Mads.

I thought I did.

Perhaps that depended on her reaction to what I was about to tell her.

My eyes shifted to the door, making sure it was closed. Brock probably had his room bugged or was listening in on the security camera. I really hoped not. But just to be safe, I put a finger to my lip. Her brows drew together. I gave a nod and tugged her off the bed, pulling her into the bathroom, where I promptly turned on the sink faucet. Extreme? Most definitely. But I wasn't dealing with normal teenage guys here.

The Elite were extra on so many levels.

Mads jumped up on the counter, and I took a seat on the closed toilet. "Do you know why Kenna and I look so much alike?"

Confusion crossed over her pretty features. "I don't understand. What do you mean? Are you like her doppelganger or something?" she deduced, trying to put together a connection between Kenna and me.

Leave it to Mads to take this to a supernatural level. "Um, not exactly. But I am related to Kenna; Grayson too." And you, I silently added.

"I'm confused." Her reaction seemed genuine, so I was going with Mads had no idea the big secret her cousin was keeping from everyone but the Elite. "Are you saying that Kenna is what, like your cousin?"

I nodded. Taking a deep breath, I whispered, "She's my sister. We're triplets."

Mads blinked. "You're not kidding."

I shook my head. "Definitely not."

"Holy. Shit. You're really not kidding," she said again. "I can't believe this. Ohmygod. This is surreal, but looking at you... ohmygod. How did I not think of that? What are the fucking odds? Zero to none. I hate to sound like a skeptic, but are you sure? Like really sure?"

My sweaty palms pressed into my knees. "Yeah, I saw the papers. My mother kidnapped me; she switched me at the hospital with her baby who had died, to be exact."

She took a moment to process what sounded like a daytime drama. "That's some messed up shit. Explains why Gray has been extra moody lately," she mused, connecting the dots.

"We haven't talked yet."

"You and Grayson?"

"Yeah. This whole thing has me so twisted up inside. I don't know how I should feel about it. You seriously had no idea?"

Her brows drew together. "No, and I'm kind of pissed off he

didn't open up to me. Not that Grayson and I tell each other everything, but I thought we were closer than that. Well, we used to be. Shit hasn't been the same since Kenna left. Oh, my God, Kenna. I'm betting she doesn't know."

Was it a coincidence that both Kenna and I befriended Maddy Clarke? They were cousins, so it would make sense they were friends. Was that also why Mads and I became such fast friends? Some inherent part of us recognized that we shared DNA? "I don't think his parents even know the truth. And you can't say anything."

"My aunt and uncle are going to freak out when they find out, especially after losing Sawyer. It's like the universe is giving them something back. What about your mom? Does she know that you know?"

"No, and I promised Brock I wouldn't say anything until Grayson was ready to deal with it."

"I'm freaking out. How the hell are you coping with all this?" Her eyes were wide, shining with a mixture of excitement and disbelief.

I rubbed at the back of my neck. "Who says I am? A part of me is still in shock... or denial. I'm not sure which anymore."

Her hands gripped the edge of the counter. "Josie, this is life-changing."

"Now you know why I had to tell you. What am I supposed to do? Just go on pretending that I don't have this huge secret, that I don't have a sister? I'm not sure I can do that. I want to see her, to meet her. I don't know how long I can wait."

Mads reached over and turned off the running water.

"Secrets always have a way of coming out, especially when we least want them to."

No longer able to sit, I stood up and leaned against the wall. "To make matters worse, I think Carter might know."

Her gray eyes widened further. "What? Wait, back up a minute. When did you talk to Carter?"

Shit. I forgot. "That's another story," I mumbled, the fairly large bathroom feeling small.

Mads shook her head. "Jesus, you went back home, didn't you? Now the handcuff comment makes sense. I thought Brock was just trying to be kinky. Do know what might have happened?"

"I already got the lecture from his highness." All jokes aside, it could have been bad. Whether I liked it or not, I had to see Carter. Perhaps not at home, because I had no plans to ever go back there, but at school.

"And your mom?"

"Angie," I corrected.

She seemed to understand. "You can't tell her what happened and go to the police?" It was a rational course of action, one most sane people would have already taken.

There was nothing sane about my family.

The back of my head hit the wall. "I wish. I'd be wasting my breath. Angie only cares about how perfect her new family appears. Involving the police or pressing charges against Carter will cause too much unwanted attention. *Elmwood's newest scandal, stepbrother kidnaps and assaults stepsister* isn't the kind of headlines my mother is looking to make. She won't be any help. I'm on my own."

Mads reached out and took my hand, squeezing it. "You're never alone. I'm here. Ainsley too. And you have the Elite."

My lips pouted. "I thought you were supposed to make me feel better."

Mads laughed, jumping off the counter. "What are friends for?" Her fingers reached for the doorknob as she threw me an evil smile. "Holy shit. I just realized we're related, bitch."

I grinned, tossing an arm over her shoulders. "Yes, we are, cuz."

It was a wonder what an hour with my best friend could do for my anxiety. By the time Mads left, the pressure in my chest felt lighter.

I should have known it was too good to last.

At just around midnight, my phone buzzed. The damn thing had been going off most of the night, drunk rambling texts from the mother of the year that ran from threats to sloppy "I love yous."

A jolt of anger rippled through me. *Can't she just leave me alone for five minutes?* Grabbing my phone, I thought about turning the damn thing off. If I weren't worried Mads or Ainsley might text me, I would have. A quick glance at the screen, and my hand froze. Not Angie, but a text from the devil himself.

Was it possible Carter did know my secret? Had he uncovered the truth that I had a brother and sister?

Revealing the information would hurt Angie and his father. It would drag the name his dad prided himself on through the mud. He didn't like Angie, but would he turn her in? I wasn't worried about Angie. I was worried Grayson's parents would find out about it on the front page of the *Elmwood Herald*. I did not want that to happen.

I had to tell Grayson. Brock too... eventually. Grayson first.

It was time my brother and I had a little chat.

CHAPTER FIVE

L ight dappled through the curtains as I tied the laces on my black combat boots.

"Where do you think you're going?" Brock demanded, his shadow falling over me.

I cranked my neck up while I finished securing the laces. "Out," I replied flatly, straightening up. "Unless you're keeping me prisoner here."

Dark brows lifted, a gleam of something wicked flashing in his aqua eyes. "The idea has merit."

"You're unbelievable. Don't turn this into some kind of sex thing." The fact that we'd been under the same roof for almost two days and hadn't ripped each other's clothes off deserved an award. Just looking at him now, I weighed the option of staying here and putting my hands on that damn glorious body or doing this important thing that had been on my mind since Friday.

Self-control. Find your self-control, Josie. Just because you're a hormonal teenager, doesn't mean you have to act on those urges every time you get one.

Right?

This was Brock Taylor.

He was not the type of guy to get mixed up with. Physically? Sure. Emotionally? Hell no.

"Look, I need to see Grayson," I defended my choice to go see my brother, regardless that I shouldn't have to explain it to Brock. What I did was my business.

Brock crossed his arms. "I figured. Do you want me to go with you?"

Was he actually offering moral support? What was happening? "This is something I need to do alone."

His expression didn't change, but his voice softened. "Just don't expect too much too soon."

I nodded. "Noted. I've had years of practice being careful with my emotions."

Pulling a little plastic card from his back pocket, he held it out for me. "Here."

"What's this?" I asked, taking the white card from him.

"It will give you access to get back through the gate."

Why did this feel equivalent to being given a house key? I blinked. "Thanks." Where was the argument I anticipated? The, *James, this is a bad idea?*

Without another word from either of us, I walked out his front door, got into my car, and drove off.

* * *

The bell rang, chiming through the other side of the door. I shifted on my feet and glanced back at my car, second-guessing if this was a good idea or not. The autumn breeze kicked up as I waited, and I slipped my hands into the front pocket of my hoodie.

The door opened, and my gaze met Grayson's, watching as his brown eyes went from mildly annoyed to surprise, which he quickly covered up with a mask of indifference, an Elite specialty. The four bad boys of Elmwood Academy had a way about them. Unapproachable. Respected. Feared. And somehow those traits made them the most attractive guys at school.

And this particular Elite was my brother.

I just stared at him, taking in his face. At least a few inches taller than me, he wore basketball shorts and a T-shirt, despite it being too cool outside for both. Beads of sweat gathered on his brow in a way that looked as if he'd just come back from a run. Perhaps I had caught him in the middle of a workout.

"We need to talk," I stated. No point in beating around the bush.

Regarding me with wary eyes, he said nothing, only pushed the door open wider.

I walked past him into the foyer with vaulted ceilings that made the entryway feel enormous. I'd been in the house before, but this time, it had a different meaning. It wasn't a party house, but the home I should have grown up in. An image of three little kids with the same shade of brown hair running up and down the hallway flashed through my head. I could see it all too clearly, and my heart squeezed for a childhood I'd never have the chance to know.

Grayson shut the door and turned to face me, crossing his arms in a protective stance. Who was he guarding himself against? Me? "I wondered when you'd show up."

"This is weird," I said, hoping we weren't going to have this conversation standing around in his foyer. I needed to sit down or would be pacing the floors.

His shoulders relaxed. "Weird doesn't begin to cover it." Not waiting to see if I followed, Grayson sauntered down the hallway.

I trailed behind into the less formal family room, where a large television sputtered sounds of a football game. Grayson turned down the volume as he sat in one of the rocking recliners. I took the other one, twisting my fingers in my lap. For a moment, just the low hum of the TV filled the room, neither of us saying anything.

Considering Grayson had thrown a rager just two days ago, the Edwardses' house looked halfway decent. No beer bottles in scattered in the yard. No bras swimming in the pool. No bodies lingering around, nursing a two-day hangover.

Color me impressed.

"Your parents still gone?" I asked, scrambling for some sort of normalcy, and wondering if I'd get a chance to see them. I hadn't come to ambush them. I'd come only to talk to Grayson, but now that I was here...

He nodded. "They're visiting my sister—" His hand rubbed awkwardly at the back of his neck.

Right. Kenna. Our sister. Our parents.

I couldn't bring myself to refer to them as such. Not now. Who knew when. None of it seemed real.

The awkwardness between us stretched at the mention of Kenna. An unexpected ribbon of anger went through me. I wasn't sure who I was mad at. "Everyone" seemed like the answer. But mostly, I was upset that I had a sister who was virtually a stranger to me and a brother who confused the hell out of me. I was the odd one out in this scenario, the one who got the short end of the stick. Strong and startling emotions burst within me, one of them being jealousy. I was jealous of Grayson... Kenna too. They had each other. They grew up as a family in this beautiful home, not that I gave a shit about material things. It was more of what this house stood for. Love. Stability. Family. Security.

Feelings of always longing for a sibling reared up inside me. There was a comfort in numbers, and I thought having someone else besides me to deal with my mother would have made my life tolerable. Not that it was always horrible. There was a time when I was younger when things seemed normal, happy.

Then it all went to shit. Angie drank more. My parents fought often. Before I knew it, they were divorcing and I moved in with the Pattersons. What took years seemed to happen in a blink of an eye.

Grayson forked a hand through his dark hair. "I'm sorry, I don't know what to say," he finally said, cutting through the silence.

"How about that you're my brother, for starters?" The statement blurted out of me. "God, you're my brother," I said again, trying to make it all sink in and make sense.

He flinched but otherwise remained unaffected by my tone. "It wasn't my intention for you to find out like that."

It wasn't his intention for me to find out at all. "And how exactly did you plan on telling me? Or should I ask, were you ever going to tell me?" I replied with heavy saltiness. Bottled-up anger leaked out. I didn't know how upset I was with Grayson until I got here.

A part of me was so damn thrilled to have siblings. The other part was spitting mad. I'd been kept in the dark, lied to. I might have gone my entire life not knowing I belonged to another family.

"Honestly, I don't know," he admitted, massaging his temple. "I hadn't made up my mind until I saw that asshole hit you." His eyes blazed as if he too relived that night again and again, a dark memory that never went away.

This morning I'd woken up with one hell of a nasty bruise on my cheek. It was impossible to miss. Concealer helped, but it shone for Grayson to see, deep in color against my ivory skin. "I never did get a chance to thank you for coming to my rescue." Some of the harshness left my voice.

He scoffed, grabbing for an open bottle on the end table between us. "I don't want your thanks. You never should have been alone with him. That's on me."

I eyed the beer. It was a little early to be drowning his problems in booze, but I didn't say anything. Who was I to judge? I had a mother who started each morning with a Bloody Mary instead of a cup of coffee. "It wasn't your fault," I said. I should have known Grayson would blame himself. And we were getting off-topic. Carter wasn't why I was here. I took a breath, regrouping. "Look, I get this is difficult and you're feeling all kinds of crazy shit, because I'm feeling it too. I'm angry at you, at Brock, at Carter, at my mom."

Grayson chuckled, shaking his head, which only fueled my rage.

"This is not fucking funny, Grayson," I snapped.

"No. It is definitely not, but I see what he means," he said after taking a swig from his drink.

"Who?" I asked, though I had a good assumption.

His entire face relaxed. "Brock pointed out once that you and Kenna both have the same temper. It is so strange to have you here, yelling at me. It's what Kenna would have done."

I scowled, my lips pressing together. "I want to meet her." The demand just blurted out of me. I blinked, realizing it was true. I wanted to see her so much, this girl who looked just like me—my sister.

The momentary smile vanished from his lips, the softening of his features going with it. "When the time is right, when it is safe, I will drive you myself."

His response didn't make me feel any better, but I understood how many lives this secret touched. "Fine. But I won't wait forever."

An exhale loosened the tightness in his frame, and he sank a little deeper into the chair. Had he been afraid of what I would do with the information? "Thanks. I mean it. I can't imagine what you're going through. If the roles were reversed, I don't think I'd be this understanding or patient," he admitted. "I'm the hothead in the family."

"Good to know." I flashed him a quick smile, feeling a bit

better after laying into him. "This is difficult for both of us. I need to know where we stand. Do you still hate me?"

He shifted in the chair. "I never hated you, Josie. I was mostly scared."

He used my name, and some unknown emotion spun in my belly. "Of me?"

"Of what you could do. I didn't know if you knew who you were. It was one thing to read about you on a piece of paper. Seeing you... I don't know, I just..."

"Felt wary?" I supplied.

"Yeah, I guess so." His voice grew quiet. "Our history with Carter only added to it."

My gaze shifted to the television, watching the players execute a play, but not really seeing it. "I don't think I'll ever be able to forgive her for taking me. Or for not telling me the truth. But why didn't *you* tell me, Grayson?" I asked, turning my attention back to him. I knew he could see the hurt in my eyes, the raw pain, because I allowed him to see it.

"For the same reason you're here right now. I was angry at first, and admittedly, I still am. Then, suddenly you were here, going to my school. You were this huge secret that could rock my family just after things had settled down. Some of that anger transferred to you regardless of how displaced," he explained gruffly.

"I'm so confused. This whole thing is so fucked-up. What am I supposed to do now?" The question hung in the air between us as we just stared at each other.

He clenched the beer in his hand. "You mean do we keep on pretending nothing has changed?"

Just hearing him suggest it sent a chill through me. "Is that what you want?"

He leaned forward in the chair, pressing his elbows onto his knees. "We can't go back. I know what I'm asking is a lot and difficult, but can you keep this to yourself just for a little bit longer while I figure out how to tell my parents? They've been through so much."

I wanted to press him, to demand he tell them, but that was selfish. I also wanted to know more about the tough times his parents had gone through. I wanted to know everything about them. Kenna too. "I can do that," I said softly. "But eventually I need to confront my mother. I can't let go of what she did. I can't forgive her. I don't know how I'm supposed to keep on living this lie like I don't know what Angie has done."

His face grew grim, and I understood I hit a sore spot. "I don't want you near her. She lost that right the second she took you. Not to mention who her stepson is. You're not safe there."

Understanding, I nodded. It was clear Grayson was fiercely protective of his family, and somehow without my knowing, that umbrella protection now extended to me. "Carter implied that he knows I have a secret."

Grayson's jaw clenched. "And you believe him? Don't let that asshole get under your skin, Lil' J. Even if he does know about us, we'll take care of it." By "we," he meant the Elite. "Got it?"

"I'm staying with Brock for now. And I won't tell anyone... else," I added under my breath.

His brows drew together. "Who did you tell?"

Why hadn't I just lied? "It was too big not to tell someone.

And the Elite doesn't count," I defended, fumbling with one of my stud earrings.

His expression lost some of its seriousness. "Glad to know how we rate."

I rolled my eyes. "Please, don't pretend like everyone at school doesn't worship the four of you. They'd kiss your feet and suck your dick if you let them."

His lips twitched. "I'm not sure how I feel about you talking about my dick."

My cheeks flushed. "This is so weird. I don't know if I'll get used to it."

"So, who was it?" he prompted, refusing to let me dodge answering, ever after trying to distract him.

"I needed to talk to someone who didn't already know."

"Josie," he gritted between his teeth. "Who?"

I gave in, hoping Grayson and I weren't about to have our first fight. "Mads."

He jerked a shoulder up. "Shit. My cousin?"

"She won't say anything," I assured, reaching for his beer and taking long a drink. I needed something to settle the constant churning of emotions within me.

The muscles in his back relaxed through his white shirt. "No, she won't. Mads is loyal to a fault." He made that sound like a bad quality. I could think of a few traits the Elite could adapt.

"Why does that sound like a threat?"

The corner of his lip turned up. "You learn fast. Obviously, you got the brains."

My fingers tapped along the glass bottle. "Mads is my friend. The only friend I have at the academy."

A quick grin came over his face. Grayson didn't smile enough. "Not true. You have us." That might have been the nicest thing Grayson had ever said to me. I just didn't know if it was true.

The fucking Elite.

"Do I?" I responded, a brow arching. "It seems I am only good for your agenda. My only value lies in what I can do to help you take down Carter."

"Ouch." His hand flew to his heart in a mock gesture of pain.

I chewed on the inside of my cheek, unable to believe what I contemplated telling Grayson. "This isn't probably the right time to bring this up, but I'm pretty sure Carter plans to black-mail me. You too."

Other than a slight flinch, he gave no other reaction. "I wouldn't put it past him. He can try. Did he say something to you?" Grayson held out his hand for the beer.

I handed it over. "He might have."

He narrowed his eyes and asked, "When the fuck did you talk to him?"

Oh boy, here we go again. Break out the male testosterone. I had a feeling I would be getting similar lectures from each of the Elite guys once they found out. "Not the point. What's on the thumb drive?"

He shrugged, and I could see in his eyes that what was about to come out of his mouth wouldn't be the entire truth. "Just information about kids at school."

"What kind of information?" I pressed, a knot forming in my belly.

"You're stubborn. And perceptive." A long sigh of resignation left his lips. "The kind of stuff people pay big bucks to bury and hide. Those dark secrets people never want uncovered."

I thought about our own secret and the file on my family. If that was just a slice of what was on the thumb drive, I shuddered to think what else might be on there. "Is this something you guys do for fun? Collect damning evidence?"

"It's insurance. It's what keeps us on top. Being worshiped also means we have enemies. We own that school. If you have a secret, you can assume that we know about it. They think twice about stepping out against us."

"But it just doesn't stop at the kids we go to school with, does it?"

He shook his head. "No. The parents are way worse. Half of them bring their kids into their dirty little side businesses."

"Why don't you turn it over to the police?" I couldn't help ask.

Grayson just looked at me.

"Because there is information on your own families on the drive," I muttered, answering my questions.

"Partially," he verified. "But mostly, it's there for future use. Our intention was never to be vigilantes. It started as a prank for kids at school, but the secrets we found, they were deep shit. So we made a pact. We agreed not to expose the truth unless someone got out of line. We could take down more than half the school. Students. Teachers. Staff. Parents. The list is ridiculous."

I lifted my legs, tucking them underneath me on the recliner. "How does Carter know about the thumb drive?"

Darkness extinguished the light in Grayson's eyes. They were cold and ruthless now. "Micah's dumb ass got drunk, spilled the beans. This was a time when we thought we could trust Carter, before we knew what he did to the girls at our school."

I didn't like where this was going. My pocket buzzed before I could give him my snarky response. It could be Brock or Mads. I pulled out my phone and let a groan. Shit. Sunday dinner. I'd completely forgotten about it. I glanced up at Grayson with apologetic eyes. "Sorry, it's my mom. Angie," I scrambled to correct. "She's probably wondering where I am."

"Answer it," he stated unemotionally. A mask dropped over his features at the mere mention of Angie, but he couldn't hide the underlying anger that resided inside him entirely.

"Hey, Mom," I answered, reminding me I had a role to play.

"Where are you?" she demanded from the other end of the phone.

Her tone caused me to wince, wrinkling my nose. This ought to be fun. "I'm not coming home," I replied, exasperated. This conversation would brew a fight I just didn't have the energy to deal with. It had all been sapped talking with Grayson.

But my mother didn't know anything about that. "Josie, so help me God," she hissed through the phone loud enough that even Grayson's brows lifted. "If you aren't home in the next five minutes, I'll call the police."

I grinned, an evil smirk that matched Grayson's. He rolled

his eyes at me. My sentiments exactly. "Go ahead. I'm sure they'd be very interested in hearing about what happened Friday night."

"Josephine." My name came out in a harsh warning.

I leaned back in the chair, which rocked back and forth in small movements. "Did Carter tell you what he did?"

Silence.

Then a long drawn-out sigh. Someone needed a glass of wine, Angie's cure to a migraine in the works. "Josephine, I'm not in the mood to listen to another of your elaborate schemes to embarrass me and hurt your brother. I've heard enough. My head is throbbing."

Hearing her call Carter my brother when I was sitting across from my actual brother snapped something inside of me. She was lucky we weren't face-to-face, because the urge to hurt her like she had hurt me burst into my chest. "Bye, *Mom*."

"Don't you dare—"

Click.

I closed my eyes for a brief, peaceful moment without her voice making my ears bleed. Grayson chuckled and offered me his beer, which I gladly took. "Got any more?" I asked after draining what little was left.

"You read my mind." Grayson reached under the side table and pulled out another glass bottle, offering me one and grabbing another for himself.

"Think the three of us have triplet mojo?" I asked, pressing the bottle to my mouth.

His lips twitched.

CHAPTER SIX

Monday began with the resumption of the Elite rotation. Once again, I found myself shadowed by one of the guys. And if Brock, Grayson, Fynn, or Micah couldn't follow me, like into the girls' locker room, Mads was there. I was never left alone, which of course didn't go unnoticed.

Murmurs and whispers trailed after me as I walked down with Fynn to Physics, a class I wasn't particularly pleased about taking but it looked good on my school transcripts. How different my life here at Elmwood Academy was than at Elmwood Public. I wasn't sure the reality of it would ever sink in.

I missed my mundane life. And yet, as I walked beside Fynn down the hall, I realized something good had come out of this mess. I'd met Mads, and I'd found out I had a brother and sister.

My relationship with Elite was complicated, and I had yet to decide if it was a good thing or not.

Fynn lightly bumped my shoulder with his. "Ignore them."

I adjusted the strap of my bag higher on my shoulder. "Easy for you to say. You're used to being talked about."

Fynn's boyish smile grew. "True. But their opinions don't matter."

"Let me guess. The only opinion that matters is the Elite's."

Clusters of students forcing their way to class parted as Fynn walked by. "Now you're getting it."

My eyes rolled. "Whatever. See you after class?" We'd come to my Physics room.

Fynn opened the door. "Grayson's up next."

Giving him a half smile, I went inside to take my seat in the back. The classroom was set up with rows of lab tables, two chairs at each. Monica, my lab partner wasn't in her chair yet, so I slid into mine and dug into my bag to pull out my laptop. A body brushed past me, and I assumed it was Monica.

I was wrong.

"Hey, sis."

At the sound of Carter's voice, I nearly dropped my laptop on the ground. I'd already broken one computer. I doubted Angie would be pleased with me if I showed up with another broken one. "What the fuck are you doing here?" I hissed under my breath, placing the laptop on the table in front of me.

Carter stretched his legs out under the table, a lazy smirk on his lips. The tie around his neck hung loosely, his blondish hair curling around the collar of his white shirt. "I did a little rearranging of my schedule."

"Why?" My voice grew louder, not caring who overheard.

Carter chuckled, flipping a pen in between his fingers.

My fingers tightened against the edges of the laptop. "This isn't funny, you shithead. Can you find someone else to torture? I've had enough." I started to scoot my chair back with every intention of skipping this class, but Carter's hand landed on my knee.

The tips of his fingers pressed firmly into my leg, keeping me in the chair. "You didn't show up to family dinner last night."

The legs of a chair squeaked across the floor from the table in front of us as Brad Newman took his seat. "Hmm. I wonder why. Could it be because you were there?" I slid a hand under the table and dug nails into the top of his hand.

"Your mother was inconsolable."

"You mean drunk." I didn't bother to sugarcoat it. I knew exactly who my mother was.

Carter wore a smug grin as he finally released his grip. "You're about to find out the Elite aren't the only ones with pull at this school."

Dread dropped into my stomach like a bomb about to explode. "What are you talking about?"

"You'll see," he said, so cocky, so sure of himself.

I wasn't up for his cryptic bullshit. "Can you try to be fifty percent less of a prick?"

"Probably not... unless you give me what I want."

Professor Dirkton strolled in, dropping a stack of books on the edge of his desk. It was a good thing too, because I was two seconds away from slapping the shit out of my stepbrother. "Once Brock finds out about this, you're dead."

He shrugged in that I'm-untouchable way of his, tapping his pen against the table. "You can't hide behind them forever."

Not forever. Only until I turned eighteen and I could legally get out from Angie's control or she went to jail for kidnapping.

Professor Dirkton glanced up, his eyes landing on Carter. "Mr. Patterson. What are you doing here? This isn't fifth period when you actually have class with me."

"My bad, Professor D. Too much vodka in the coffee this morning." A few of the guys in class chuckled but Professor Dirkton wasn't amused.

"I suggest you get to the proper class."

Gathering his shit, Carter glanced over his shoulder, shooting me a wink.

Bastard.

* * *

Mads and I strolled through the cafeteria on our way to the girls' locker room. I seriously considered skipping out on gym class today. The idea of doing laps around the track made my stomach churn.

Gah. I'd so rather be doing laps in the school's massive pool. Perhaps I'd take a dip into Brock's tonight. That was the only thing I missed about the Pattersons'—the pool.

The rest of the day had been uneventful, which was exactly what worried me. Carter's little threat echoed in my head throughout the entire day, and I kept waiting for the other shoe to drop.

"Have you talked to Grayson since, you know?" I asked, wondering if he had said anything about spilling the beans.

Mads shrugged. "No, not really, other than for him to remind me to keep my mouth shut. I figured you'd know more than I do."

I grimaced. "He hasn't said much to me either. This whole thing takes awkward to a new level. Neither of us knows how to act around the other."

"You'll work it out, cuz." She grinned.

The locker room came into view as we turned the corner, and I groaned. "Think Coach Q will go for the whole cramp excuse?" I asked, still figuring out if I could find a way out of gym.

A hollow laugh came out of her. "Coach Q is a hard ass. He has three daughters. Cramps don't faze him."

"Wonderful," I mumbled, my hand reaching for the door. Something hit me on the shoulder.

Not something. Someone.

Whirling around, I didn't have time to avoid the smoothie as it flew straight at me, splattering over the front of my crisp white academy shirt.

Motherfucker, the shit's cold.

I gasped, my hands flying up in the air.

"What the fuck, Ava!" Mads snarled, throwing her bag down on the ground like she was ready to rumble. She stuck her nose right in Ava's face.

I should've known Ava was responsible. She made her

disdain for me very clear, and apparently we'd moved on to childish pranks like tossing a smoothie on the new girl.

Izzy and Parker giggled beside the redheaded bitch. They were rarely ever seen not glued to Ava's ass. Each wore the signature blue and black Academy plaid skirt, altered of course to show half their thighs, the Elmwood brand embroidered onto the bottom left hem. Izzy twirled her hair, snapping a piece of gum. Parker had her white shirt unbuttoned low, showing the lace on her black bra. Her short hair was angled so it hung lower on one side.

But it was always Ava who demanded attention. She had a blue cashmere sweater tied around her slim waist. "Oops. I didn't see you there," she said, batting her long, fake lashes at me. Her peach glossy lips curved villainously.

The standby whores. Just what I needed.

Mads eyes were hostile. "Like hell, you psycho bitch."

A hush fell over the hallway, drawing unwanted attention straight on us. I glanced down at my white shirt covered in dark blue, probably blueberry and cherry, which meant I wasn't getting the stains out anytime soon. My shirt stuck to my skin in patches.

"Back off, Clarke," Ava retorted, breaking off her stare down with Mads to glare at me. "It really was an accident." The giggles from her posse started again, and I'd had enough.

I lunged forward, shoving Ava with both my hands. She stumbled backward, a look of astonishment crossing her face. Two seconds later, my hands were fisted into her red hair, and I yanked her head back. Through the tangle of nails, fingers, and hair, I slammed Ava up against the locker door, transferring smoothie onto her.

She shrieked a few times, letting loose a string of vile swear words, but I didn't care—I was past caring.

One of Ava's hands attached to my boob and twisted, her other knotting in my pink hair. I sucked in an angry breath. "I'm going to kill you," she seethed, sounding as insane as Mads had called her. Ava fought dirty, but so could I. Had she forgotten where I came from?

I kicked out at the back of her leg, causing the skank to go down, and then I was on top of her. Only vaguely aware of the commotion in the background, my ears buzzed with fury.

No. It wasn't my anger that caused my ears to ring. Someone blew a whistle long and hard.

"Break it up!" a voice full of authority boomed down the hall.

Neither Ava nor I listened as we continued to tussle on the floor. Nails scored down my arm in hot pain, but I gritted my teeth through the sting. Sitting on top of her, I pulled my hand back to slap her across the face, but someone caught my hand midair. A moment later, I was lifted off the cheerleader by strong arms.

"Let me go," I snarled, but the arms that held me remained steadfast. My back pressed firmly against a flat chest, and I bristled, shoving the hair out of my face.

Coach Q fumed in front of the gathered crowd. "Principal's office. Now!" Coach ordered, pointing his finger down the hall from which Mads and I had just come from. His steely eyes bounced between Ava and me.

The hands holding me off my feet relaxed slightly, allowing my boots to touch the ground. "I can't leave you alone for two seconds, can I, Firefly?" Brock's deep voice whispered in my ear.

It would be him.

But I had known, even through the haze of rage, that it was Brock who held me. "I'm not done with her yet," I growled.

His chuckle brushed over my ear, and a different fire stirred low within me. "I can see that. Best to deal with her outside of school." His mild amusement only irritated me.

I attempted to shake his hands off. "I can walk on my own," I grumbled.

"Probably, but we're sending a message here."

My eyes looked up at him in confusion. His lips hinted at a smirk, but his eyes... they were cold. On my other side, I sensed a presence. My head turned to see Micah and Fynn. Micah winked at me. Where had they come from? Then I noticed Grayson beside Brock, his cognac eyes flaming.

I was surrounded by the Elite. He was right. This definitely sent a message. Don't fuck with what's theirs.

I glanced over my shoulder and saw Mads grinning in approval.

By the time I got to the principal's office, my adrenaline had calmed down, and the reality of what I'd done set in.

Shit.

A trip to the principal's office meant a call to Angie.

Ava smirked triumphantly at me as the two of us sat down, waiting to be called in. Had she planned this whole thing to get me into trouble? Anticipating that I would do something reckless? She couldn't have. Could she?

The expression on her face said this bitch wasn't as dumb as she looked.

The Elite stood with their arms crossed over their chests, looming over me. They all wore serious expressions except for Micah, who grinned. His light blue eyes twinkled at me. "Who says Mondays are boring?"

I rolled my eyes. "It wasn't my idea to tie-dye my shirt with a smoothie."

"No talking," the lady behind the desk said sternly. She peered over at us from behind wire-framed glasses.

A dry chuckle left Micah. He made it very difficult to keep a straight face, because now that the escapade was over, all I wanted to do was laugh.

Principal Wallis called Ava and me into her office one at a time. As Ava stood up to go inside first, she met my gaze with a dark look that promised I'd pay for this later. She was up to something.

Oh, goodie, something to look forward to. More bully drama with the cheerleading squad.

Between her and Carter, I needed to be babysat twenty-four seven.

"Whore," Micah said, covering it with a cough as Ava passed by. She shot him a dirty glare, but in those hazel eyes beamed hurt. Ava wasn't used to the Elite treating her like shit. She'd been replaced. She knew it. I knew it. But most importantly, the entire school knew it.

"Mr. Bradshaw," Principal Wallis snapped, inclining her

head toward Micah. She was an average height woman, but in heels and a power suit of navy blue, there was something powerful about Principal Wallis. She didn't seem afraid to take on all these rich kids and their even richer parents. I pegged her to be in her midforties, based on the strands of white hair peeking through her sleek brown waves. "What are you doing here? Don't the four of you have class?" she said to the guys hovering in the lobby with me.

"We're witnesses," Micah retorted with a twisted yet somehow charming grin.

"This isn't a trial, Mr. Bradshaw. Get to class." She didn't wait to see if they complied as she ushered Ava into her office. And that was Principal Wallis's first mistake. The Elite weren't going anywhere.

Micah dropped down in Ava's empty seat, stretching out his long legs in a reclined position.

"You guys are making this worse. You should really go to class," I muttered.

"Not happening," Brock replied like an immovable force. "We've already concluded you can't be left alone."

A cocky smirk came over Micah's lips. "And we're supposed to be the troublemakers."

I rotated my shoulder, the aches and pains of being hit and scratched making themselves known. Like I needed more bruises. "She started it," I mumbled, not giving a fuck if I sounded like a sulking two-year-old.

"And you finished it," Grayson chimed in, his lips twitching as if he was proud of me.

I grinned at him.

Ten minutes later, Principal Wallis's door opened and Ava strolled out. She didn't hide the pure disdain she felt toward me. Pulling her eyes from mine, she turned her attention to Brock. He did and said nothing, but I wanted to jump out of the chair and tackle her again.

My fingers tightened on the wooden chair arms.

Principal Wallis surveyed the lobby, shaking her head. "The four of you just don't give up. I don't know how you manage to have so much influence over the students at this school. I've stopped trying to make sense of it."

Micah shoved his hands into his pockets. "Some people just have that certain je ne sais quoi."

Principal Wallis pressed her lips together and sighed. "Josephine, let's chat." She held the door open and waited.

I nodded and stood up, stepping into her office, half surprised the Elite didn't try to follow me inside.

She walked around the solid oak desk. "Please sit. I want to hear in your own words what happened."

The leather groaned under my weight. "What did Ava say?"

Folding her hands studiously on her desk, she said, "That's not important. We don't take bullying lightly at Elmwood Academy, and I'd like to think my staff is keenly aware of what goes on in this school."

I snuffed a snort. They had no idea what shit went down in and out of school.

"It was nothing. Just a misunderstanding." Tattling on Ava would only bring more misery. Besides, I wasn't a narc. I'd handle Ava my own way... off school grounds.

"I can't help you if you don't open up to me. I'm not the enemy here."

Crossing my legs, I slumped lower in the chair. "As I said, it was an accident."

"Okay, then. Since neither of you will own up to the truth, I have no choice but to give you both Saturday detention. I've already called your mother. She will be here in a few minutes to discuss what happened today."

My jaw clenched. *Son of a bitch.*

What had I been thinking, going after Ava? Now I was stuck facing Angie, who definitely was day drinking and I'd been avoiding. She was the last person I wanted to see.

I didn't know how, but this was Carter's doing, attempting to force me back home so he could impose his blackmail upon me.

Over my dead body would I help him.

My eyes glanced to the door as I contemplated how much trouble I'd be in if I got up and ran.

Principal Wallis must have picked up on my sudden discomfort. "I know it can't be an easy transition for you, starting a new school your senior year, but Josie, you have less than seven months until graduation. I hope that we can get through those months without any more incidents."

"If only we lived in a perfect world."

She cleared your throat. "Is there something going on at home? My door is always open if you need someone to talk to."

My tone went flat. "Is that all?"

"Yes. I hope the next time I have you in my office it will be under more positive circumstances. You can wait in the lobby with Ava for your mother," she instructed, peering at me through her glasses.

Ava scowled when she saw me, obviously blaming me for this crappy situation we were both in. She refused to look at Brock or the guys, who hadn't moved from their spots.

"Let me guess, Josie Jo, you earned yourself a Saturday." Micah sounded as if he was very familiar with the discipline process at the Academy, and I had no doubt he and the others had spent many Saturdays in detention.

Before I could answer, the lobby door swung open, and Angie strolled in full of glitz, false glamour, and... booze. Stumbled into the lobby might have been a more appropriate description. My cheeks flamed with embarrassment. This wasn't the first time she'd come to my school drunk, but for her to do so in front of the Elite, particularly Grayson, and Ava, sent me spiraling in shame.

She already carried the label gold digger. Tomorrow, she'd also be known as the boozy leech. My fight with Ava would be old news by the time Angie and I walked out of the school. Just one more thing to be whispered through the halls.

Her eyes fell upon me. Disapproval gleamed in her expression. Scowling, she went into see Principal Wallis, returning just a few minutes later. The frown still graced her lips. "Josephine, we're going home."

I didn't want to make a scene in school and especially not in front of Ava. My gaze shifted to the hard set of Brock's face. I silently begged him with my eyes. *Not here.*

He blinked.

Poor Grayson looked caught between seeing a ghost and wanting to commit murder.

Only two periods of classes remained in the day, but I didn't even argue that. Standing up, I followed the clicking of Angie's heels, leaving the lobby. The exit doors to the main parking lot were right outside the principal's office. As Angie pushed open the door, she finally realized we weren't alone.

The Elite flanked me on either side, Brock and Fynn on my right and Micah and Grayson on my left.

Her glossy eyes narrowed. "What is this?" she asked as we all stepped out into the afternoon sun. Autumn breezes blew along the building, sending loose strands of Angie's sleek black hair flying.

"Josie isn't going home with you," Brock declared. The cocky expression on his face taunted her to challenge him.

"Josephine, in the car. Now," Angie ordered, sultry red lips puckered in displeasure at being defied by a boy. Her feet faltered, weight shifting. Standing in place didn't mix with spike heels and afternoon cocktails.

Brock's frown deepened. "No, your daughter isn't safe at that house. She stays with us."

Mom shot daggers at him. What she was really upset over wasn't that I had gotten into a fight, but that I might have told Brock about what went on behind closed doors at the Pattersons'. "I don't know who you think you are—"

He bulldozed over her, cutting Angie off. "Isn't it your daughter's safety all that's really important here?"

She recoiled like Brock had slapped her. "Leave my daughter alone. She doesn't need *your* help."

They didn't care that we were on school property. This was their turf. "Too bad. She already has it," Fynn said as he took a step so I was slightly shielded by him.

"How dare you," she protested, her chin lifting.

Brock glowered. "It's time you understand how things operate in this part of town. Nothing happens without us knowing, including behind closed doors."

Oh shit. He just hit Angie's sore spot.

Grayson eyed her up and down, scorn dripping from his glare. "Go back to your rich husband. We'll take care of your daughter."

Her shoulders dropped an inch, and yet she spoke my name firmly. "Josephine."

Refusing to meet her gaze at her, I said nothing. Truth was, I didn't want to go home, and if the Elite had the power to make that happen, so be it. I moved closer to Brock, making my intention clear. "I'm not coming home."

A soft bitter laugh escaped as he turned her shrewd gaze to Brock. "Do you know it is illegal to harbor a runaway. You'll be hearing from my lawyers."

Brock grinned mockingly. "I sincerely hope so."

Angie's grip tightened on the side of her purse. "This isn't over," she promised.

"That's what I'm counting on," Brock replied tartly.

She spun on her heels before he finished delivering the parting statement.

Great. Now Angie and my stepbrother had declared themselves Elite enemies. My eighteenth birthday never seemed so far away.

What had I done? And why didn't I feel bad about it? No regret. No sadness. Just peace.

* * *

Brock gave me one of his spare football shirts he kept in his locker to change into. And somehow, strolling down the halls with his football number plastered to my back was sweet revenge. For once, I didn't care about the attention or the whispers. It was exactly what I wanted, for the gossip mill to do its thing. By the end of the day, Ava would know whose shirt I wore thanks to her childish tactics.

Take that, bitches.

"You're loving this," Grayson said as he walked me to the football field. His helmet hung in his hand.

I grinned at him. "So what if I am? I think it's time someone showed Ava she isn't as important as she'd like to believe." I doubled my steps to keep up with his long strides. It still seemed unreal that he was my brother.

His cleats sank into the grass, kicking up little divots. "I'm so glad you're taking the initiative. Just be careful. Don't underestimate her. To girls like Ava, high school status is everything. And being the girl on Brock's arm is the highest position for a chick at this school."

He didn't have to tell me. "I won't let her intimidate me. I'm fucking sick of girls like her."

"Good. So am I," he muttered right before he jogged onto the field, joining Brock, Micah, and Fynn, who were already huddled up with their teammates, including Carter fucking Patterson.

Having to hang around after school to watch the Elite practice was the last thing I wanted to be doing. Yet here I was. The only positive outcome was seeing Brock's ass in his tight football uniform. God, what a glorious tush. But sitting in the bleachers also meant I had to watch Carter and his loser friends.

It was a double-edged sword. The Elite wouldn't let me out of their sight and yet, the person they were shielding me from was always around.

Whack. The sounds of bodies hitting bodies echoed throughout the outdoor stadium as the first scrimmage got underway. Things got heated on the field as Micah slammed Carter to the ground for the fourth time during their practice.

I sat in the first row of bleachers, not far from where Micah and Carter crashed into the turf. Micah rolled off Carter, but not before giving him an extra shove as he got up. He readjusted the strap on his helmet, sporting his wicked grin. Catching my eye, Micah winked at me. A second later, Carter was on his feet, pushing Micah in the chest.

"What the hell is going on?" Coach yelled from the sidelines, tossing his ball cap onto the ground in frustration. Poor Coach Q. He had no idea what was really going on during his practice. It had become a battleground between the Elite and Carter.

A definite division had been declared in the team, which would only hurt the Academy's chance at the playoffs this year. Not that I gave a shit about football, but the school prided itself on winning, and many of the players needed the games to be scouted for college ball.

Carter included.

Yet, since Friday night, they'd been at each other since practice started. None of them needed to play football, not with the amount of wealth the Elite and Carter would inherit, but for Carter, it wasn't about the money. It was expected of him.

Ava and her cheer whores glared over at me from the sidelines like this was my fault.

In truth, I was partially responsible, and since that seemed to bother Elmwood's queen mean girl, a petty beam of satisfaction swirled inside me. Unable to help myself, I smirked and flipped her off. She returned the gesture before flashing her ass in my direction, the ruffled skirt hardly covering half her butt. Just the way she liked it.

"We have a game on Friday. You guys better get it together," Coach demanded. "Leave your shit off the field. I don't care about your drama or your girl problems. Not when we are here. Hell, I don't even want to know when we're not in uniform."

A few of the players snickered, including Micah. "Got that, Patterson?" he sneered.

"Fuck off, Bradford," Carter snarled back.

"Enough!" Coach Q warned. "Get back into the game."

Despite the coach's warning, the jabs continued. Coach called practice early after Grayson took a hit that sent his helmet spiraling across the ground and earned him a split lip. That was how players ended up with concussions.

Jumping up from the bleachers, I hustled toward Grayson,

only to stop short at the sight of Carter. He noticed me and sneered.

Grayson shoulder-checked Carter as he brushed past him. "I catch your eyes on her again, I'll crack more than your ribs," Grayson's dark voice threatened.

"I was just admiring my handiwork. It looks like it hurts," Carter replied, a man who had a death wish.

"Bastard," I cursed under my breath, and then Carter was flat on his back, Grayson looming over him.

The whistle blew long and hard over the field.

I winced.

"What the hell was in the lunch today? The two of you just earned yourself Saturdays," Coach Q barked, his face turning ten different shades of red.

Well, damn. Saturday detention should be all kinds of fucking interesting. Might as well make it a party.

CHAPTER SEVEN

"What the fuck was that?" I asked as Brock steered the Range Rover out of the school parking lot.

Brock shrugged. His damp hair smelled like shampoo from a quick shower in the locker room. "Just some friendly competition."

I made a disbelieving sound. "Uh-huh. I call bullshit."

"He needed to be reminded who owns this school. If he steps out of line, there are consequences," he said, his voice rough.

Shifting slightly in the seat, I angled toward him. "Don't you ever get tired of keeping everyone in line? Being the guy who calls the shots?"

His gaze flicked off the road for a second to glance at me. "Honestly, this is my life. Has been for a long time. I wouldn't know how to be any different."

I could understand that to a degree. When you don't know

anything else, it doesn't seem unusual. "These last few months have just been so surreal to me. Some days I wake up and can't believe this is my life."

"It won't always be like this," he assured.

"Is that what you tell yourself?"

He grinned.

The SUV ran over a bump in the road, jostling me in my seat. "Grayson told me what's on the thumb drive."

Brock liked to drive fast. And now was no exception. His foot hit the gas and the engine roared. "I know."

My fingers tightened on the seat belt strap, yet I wasn't worried Brock would crash. Despite everything, I trusted him with my life. "You can't let Carter get his hands on it. God knows what he would do with that magnitude of information. The lives he would destroy."

His expression went grim. "Carter only cares about saving his own ass."

"He will use me to get it. I don't know what he planned, but it's not good, Brock." Traces of the nervousness I felt leaked into my voice.

"We're expecting him to do just that. And we'll be ready for him."

I wished I felt a tenth of Brock's confidence. "It's because of Grayson that you took an interest in me. All this time, I thought it was because of that night at the wedding." It was completely out of character for the Elite to take notice of a new girl, yet from day one, I'd been on their radar.

Holding the steering wheel with one hand, he turned down the radio with the other. "I already told you I didn't go to the wedding to sleep with you. It's the truth. That was not my intention. You took me by surprise."

"And you just couldn't say no."

He shot me a sideline glance. "Would you have? Besides, you looked like you needed the distraction. I didn't know that night that you were his sister. It wasn't until a few days after we found out."

Boy, had I ever needed a distraction. "How long after did it take you to tell Grayson about what happened between us?"

Frowning, Brock turned onto Rosewood Lane. "I actually didn't. Carter saw us that night and couldn't wait to give me shit at school. Word got around."

"What a prick," I hissed, shaking my head as I glared out the front window at the cars in front of us.

The muscle along his jaw clenched. "Grayson was livid with me. You weren't supposed to be part of this, not until we figured you out. But Carter..."

"He changed everything," I finished.

"Something like that." I heard the underlying anger in his voice, regardless that his expression never changed.

Talking about Carter only pissed both of us off. There were so many unknown obstacles in my path. I didn't want Brock to be one of them. I didn't know where we stood, and I needed at least one answer I could count on. "So what the fuck *is* going on between us? Are we friends?" The question felt like sandpaper in my throat. Friends with benefits? Friends who couldn't seem to keep their hands off each other? That wasn't the kind of friend I was looking for.

But on the flip side, I definitely wasn't interested in a relationship.

Right?

I tried to envision what a serious romantic relationship with Brock would look like. Holding hands in public. Sharing his fries on dinner dates. But it was what happened behind closed doors that got me hot and bothered.

Then he said, "I have all the friends I need,."

Talk about a dagger to the heart. "Oh." I did a shitty job of hiding my disappointment as my expression fell. It wasn't like I was expecting him to declare his undying love, and I didn't think I could just be friends with him, despite that I was the one who put it out there. But...

Brock's lips twitched as he swung his car into his driveway and slipped the car into park. He shifted in his seat, leaning an elbow on the center console. "I've said it before. You and I, we can never be just friends, Firefly." His eyes darted to my lips and stayed there.

My body grew warm despite the heat in the car fading. "And why is that?" I asked, conscious of his eyes devouring my mouth as it moved.

"You know why," he murmured, moving closer.

Maybe, but I wanted to hear him say it. I lifted a brow.

His thumb grazed over my lower lip, leaving behind a trail of tingles. "We have too much chemistry."

Like a magnet drawn to metal, I leaned closer to him, aligning our lips. "Is that what this is? Chemistry?" The temperature inside the Land Rover went up a thousand degrees. Molecules. Elements. Atoms. Ions. Whatever it was, I was helpless when it came to Brock. Powerless.

Tiny flecks of annoyance fluttered inside me at the idea of Brock having that kind of influence over me. It was overrun by swift desire.

My brain clicked off the moment Brock's lips touched mine. Only with him did the world fall away, all my problems with it. He offered me sweet oblivion, a place where only he and I existed. Where no fear, no pain, no hurt lived.

Because I wanted to hold on to that feeling for as long as possible, I slid my hand into his damp hair and deepened the kiss. My mouth became more urgent, my fingers greedy, curling. It took some maneuvering as Brock drew me across the seat into his lap, giving his hands access to my body.

God, yes.

His lips almost made up for the incredible shitty Monday, but his hands, they made forget what day of the week it was. He cupped my breast through the borrowed shirt, and I groaned into his mouth. My hips rotated, pressing against the front of his pants. He was hard. So hard.

Brock wanted me. *Me.* Headiness rushed into my head at the thought.

His lips fell to my throat, and my head dropped back. I gripped his shoulders, relishing each sensation that rocked through my body. How could someone make me feel so free?

I shifted to get closer. I had to feel him. My fingers went to the button on his pants and—

Beeeeep!

The car horn blared, and I jumped, knocking my elbow into the door. *Son of a bit—*

It continued to blast as Brock and I stared at each other for a disorientated moment and then broke out into laughter. "Your ass is on the horn," he said, his hands moving to my backside and pulling it away from the steering wheel.

The fact that it was my ass only made me laugh harder. I dropped my head on his shoulder, letting the laughter roll through me. God, when was the last time I laughed? It was amazing how a bit of amusement could lighten the pressure on my chest. I'd lived with it for so long, I'd forgotten it was even there.

Until Brock.

Don't you dare get dependent on him. You don't need anyone, Josie James.

Desire still glittered in his aqua eyes as I lifted my head. "I don't think this is better than the couch," he said with a lopsided grin.

Humor tugged at my lips. The first two times that I'd had sex with Brock had been on a couch. "Are we sleeping in separate bedrooms tonight?" I asked breathily. That had been the deal, but after this kiss, I kind of hoped we could do more than sleep in his bed. I couldn't go another night sleeping beside him and not touch. There was no sleep happening. Not when my mind and body couldn't stop thinking about the guy beside me.

"I don't see the point in starting tonight, Firefly," he responded roughly.

All bets were off.

* * *

"So rumor has it you're living with Brock Taylor," Ainsley said two seconds after I picked up her video call. We hadn't had much time to catch up over the weekend, and I had a lot to fill her in on, but it appeared she was well informed.

I picked at a piece of thread on Brock's bed, staring at her face on the screen. Brock and I never made it to his bed after the hot kiss in the car. His phone had gone off. "It's my dad. I've got to take this." His whole demeanor changed at the mention of his father. Taking the call, Brock locked himself in his dad's office and had been there ever since.

"I'm not living with him...exactly," I corrected.

"Uh-huh." She grinned, flipping a rainbow curl over her shoulder. She sat on her vanity, doing her makeup.

My sigh was genuine, born from several feelings, including frustration from the sexual tension that always lingered between Brock and me. I didn't know how much longer I could stay here without losing my heart or getting pregnant. Not that we'd actually had sex, but once we did... game over. "I don't have much of a choice. Things are so fucked-up."

"Angie is probably going apeshit," Ainsley theorized, knowing my mother well.

"That's an understatement," I mumbled, not wanting to think about her. I propped my phone on a pillow as I lay flat on the stomach, feet dangling in the air behind me.

"Jesus Christ, Josie. You had me worried sick. What that asshole did..." Ainsley's nose wrinkled in disgust, rightly so. "He needs to be in jail."

"If it were only that simple," I replied with bitterness.

"You know I will always have your back."

"And I appreciate it." She was a good friend—the best. It didn't matter how serious or how illegal, if I asked, Ainsley would show up, no questions asked. I'd do the same for her. She was my best friend.

She brought a mascara wand to her eye, darkening her lashes. "Are you sure nothing else is bothering you? Not that being kidnapped and assaulted isn't enough, but are you okay, you know, staying with *him*?"

Ainsley knew me better than anyone, so it shouldn't have been a surprise that she sensed something else ate away at me. I promised Grayson though not to tell anyone. It was so hard keeping something this fucking huge from her. The words were right there on my lips just waiting to tumble out of me. Instead, I said, "I'm fine."

"You're not fine, but that's okay. Who really is okay? We're all a little fucked-up inside, some more than others." She pulled out a tube of lip gloss and unscrewed the top. "So what are you going to do? You can't go home. Do you want me to try and talk to Angie?"

"No, don't bother. It will only make things worse if she finds out I've been talking to you." I didn't want her involved or near the house as long as Carter lived there.

Putting away the tube, she turned and faced the phone. "I know you, Josie, and something else is bothering you, so spill."

I frowned, seeing no point in denying the truth. "I can't talk about it. Not yet."

Her lips were deep berry and shiny now. "Fair enough.

How about we talk about you and Brock?" Those bold lips curved wickedly. "Are you two doing more than just banging and living together?"

My eyes glanced to the closed door before turning back to Ainsley. "You mean dating? No. I don't know what we're doing."

"Holy shit, Jos, you want to, though. Date him. You're totally falling for him."

"I am not," I rushed to object, glancing at the closed door. "With everything going on, dating is the last thing I'm thinking about. That much I can tell you."

She pressed her glossy lips together, suppressing a grin. "Hmm-hmm." Leaning her chin on her hand, she looked at me through the phone, a concerned expression dropping over her features. "I just want you to be happy."

"Thanks. I wouldn't be able to get through any of this without you, Ains." The bedroom door opened, and Brock leaned against the frame. His eyes found mine, a shadow that hadn't been there earlier darkened them. It made me wonder what his father had said. "I've got to go. Call you later," I said to Ainsley. We disconnected, and I sat up on the bed, facing Brock.

He remained in the doorway staring at me. Something was wrong. The tension vibrating off him charged the room.

"Do you want to talk about it?" I asked, already knowing the answer.

He took a purposeful step toward me. Then another. "I don't want to talk at all."

I understood what he was implying, and I could do that—

give him what he needed. He had done the same for me. Was it fucked-up that we used each other in this way, to forget our problems and just feel?

Fuck yes.

Did I care?

Not at the moment.

But down the line, if we kept doing this to each other, someone would catch feelings. That someone would be me. Already I was afraid I felt more for him than I should.

He reached the edge of the bed, and I shifted so I was on my knees in front of him. My hands traced up from the flat of his belly to the hard planes of his upper chest.

His eyes blazed. "You and I...we'll never work. This is wrong. I shouldn't want you like this," he declared in that seductive, dangerous voice.

That was supposed to be my line. I was curious why he thought this was wrong. Was it because of his stupid rules on dating or did it have to do with Grayson? Or something else entirely? I looped my fingers around his neck, closing the space between us so our faces were just inches apart. "No talking, remember."

His hands came around me, grabbing my ass, and he lifted me off the bed. My legs wrapped around him as a muscle ticked along his jaw, underlying anger residing within him. Not at me. But someone had pissed him off. "Are you sure?" he whispered with a darkness that hinted of things to come.

I must have gone temporarily insane, lost all control. Messing around with Brock was bad. He said so himself. "I can handle you, Brock Taylor." I closed the distance between us, fusing that glorious mouth to mine in a kiss that demanded a response.

He didn't disappoint.

Our tongues tangled in a frenzy of desire, anger, and desperation. My fingers pressed into the base of his neck, weaving into a mess of wavy hair as I gripped him tightly.

Brock and I had issues. God, did we ever, and drowning those problems with sex only made them magically disappear for a brief moment. But it didn't matter, because all I wanted was to lose myself in him. This was the only time I felt normal.

With his lips still fastened on mine, he dropped us to the bed, covering my body with his. He trapped my hands behind my head and pressed a collection of hot kisses down the column of my neck. Every inch of him sank into me.

His name fell from my lips.

A smile curved on his lips. "Say it again," he demanded, his breath sending warm tingles over my skin.

My nose wrinkled. "No, I can't do it when you ask me."

Staring down at me, his eyes glinted as if I'd challenged him, and I realized what a mistake that had been. He kissed the spot just behind my ear, and my back arched. "Say it, Firefly," he murmured.

Powerless to do anything else, I breathed, "Brock."

He reclaimed my lips with a satisfied purr, in a kiss that set me on fire. My legs wrapped around his, keeping his body pinned to mine. His fingers slipped under my shirt, unhooking my bra, and my nails dug into his back. This was what I craved —his touch.

I pushed at his shoulders, and he pulled back, giving me

just enough space to take off my shirt. I tugged at the hem of his and bit my lip at the sight of his bare chest. He was a magnificent specimen of male, hard and firm in all the right places.

Speaking of hard...

He ground that part of him into the V between my legs. There were too many clothes between us. My lips parted as my fingers fumbled with the button on his jeans, and I slipped my hand inside.

"Fuck, Josie." He groaned at the touch of my fingers gliding over the velvety tip of his hardness.

Not Firefly. Josie.

He wasn't the only one who loved hearing their name. "Say it again," I whispered, wrapping my fingers around the length of him.

He glanced down at me from under a fan of black lashes, eyes heavy with need. "What?"

A small smile curved over my lips. The way he looked at me, the confusion in his voice, made me feel like a seductress. I loved every second of it. "Say my name," I demanded as I moved my hand, stroking over him.

He hissed, threading his fingers into my hair. "You play dirty... Josie," he breathed, tilting my head back.

And he liked it.

Urgency slammed into us as we rid ourselves of the rest of our clothes. Brock had no sooner tossed my panties to the ground than he sunk a finger inside me. The pad of his thumb rubbed over that spot, and I shivered, fingers digging into the sheets.

"Condom?" I asked. I took the pill, but I knew he liked to be extra cautious.

"Shit," he swore, withdrawing his finger and nearly making me cry in protest.

He was kidding. Right? No way the Elite god didn't have a condom. Was it because he had a strict rule of not bringing girls into his room?

"You should see the look on your face." He reached over into the nightstand drawer and pulled out a purple wrapper. "We're good."

I snatched the condom from his hand and unwrapped it. "I should leave you naked in this bed alone for that shit." We both knew it was nothing but an empty threat. I unrolled the rubber over him with deliberate slowness.

"You wouldn't dare, Firefly." His murmur was preceded by a moan as I positioned the tip of his dick just at the opening between my legs. Then with one quick thrust, he was fully inside me. I'd been so ready for him that he went in with ease.

My insides clenched around him, and we both just took a moment to bask in that intense desire. When he started to move, gliding in and out of me, my head spun, my heart thundered, and whispered curses escaped from my lips.

It didn't take long for my orgasm to tear through me, rocking my body from the inside out. Brock kissed me, absorbing those little noises of pleasure as he continued to pump in and out of me, chasing his own climax.

He came seconds later, the pleasure of his release pulsing inside me.

Brock dropped a damp forehead to mine, still buried inside

me. We just lay there, wrapped up in each other, still riding the wave of really fucking good sex. I was a sweaty mess, my skin glistening.

Did we just have sex in a bed? In his bed? Brock had broken one of his cardinal rules.

CHAPTER EIGHT

The rest of the week went by without incident, and I started to relax, which was the worst thing to do. When you put your guard down, that's when shit hit, when you least expected it. Carter kept his distance. Ava ignored me. And Angie eventually stopped calling and texting me a dozen times a day. The earlier messages spanned from, *Josie, I miss you. I love you so much. Come home.* To, *how can you do this to our family, to me? Wait until your father hears about this. I've called my lawyers.* And other threatening random bullshit.

If she did tell my father, he didn't call, and he would have, which made me believe everything out of her mouth was a form of manipulation.

Tomorrow was Halloween. It was also my first Saturday detention, something I wasn't looking forward to despite it just being for two hours. But two hours in the same room with Carter equaled utter torture.

One of us might just kill the other before detention ended.

Neither Carter nor Grayson was playing in tonight's game against the Thornlake Tornados thanks to their escapades during practice. Grayson antagonized Carter every chance he got, and getting my stepbrother riled up proved not a difficult task. By Thursday's practice, Coach Q had enough and tossed them both out of practice, suspending them from the game.

The Elite were up to something. I sensed it.

I dragged Mads with me to the game. Somehow over the last week, football had become a part of my life. I didn't like sports, except for swimming, but I couldn't deny something magical happened when the Elite took the field.

And I wasn't the only one who felt it. The entire stadium fell silent in anticipation of the announcements and went up in a deafening roar as their names blared throughout the stands.

Seeing all the Halloween makeup, masks, and costumes at the game gave me PTSD. Not to mention, the last time I attended a football game Carter had been waiting for me in the parking lot. His scare tactics went too far, and he ended up in the hospital that night.

Douchebag.

Knots formed in my belly, and my chest tightened. I thought I might be on the verge of a panic attack. My fingers pressed into my jeans; the hoodie suddenly felt like it was choking me.

Brock Taylor. His name boomed over the speaker.

My gaze connected with Brock's as he jogged onto the field, his black helmet swinging from his fingers, and all the beads of unease and prickles of fear dissolved. That had to be unhealthy. A single shared look with Brock, and the gray-and-white world was suddenly filled with color.

Sandwiched between Grayson and Mads, I waited for all the players to make their way out of the locker room. Two names were missing from the Elmwood Gargoyle lineup. "Is it weird not being down there with them?" I asked Grayson.

"Nah. It's kind of nice just watching," he admitted. He wore a baseball hat backward, strands of his dark hair peeking out the back.

I rubbed my hands together, chasing away the chill that fogged the evening air. "I can't believe you started all that shit with Carter in practice just so you could babysit me."

Grayson shrugged in his Academy hoodie. "Sacrifices must be made. Besides, it was a win-win."

My brow lifted as I tugged the ends of my sweater over my fingers. "How do you figure?"

A sinister, almost calculating grin passed over his lips. "It got Carter out of the game," he remarked.

"Okay." I failed to see how that was important.

Grayson pointed down at few rows in the bleachers. "You see that guy? He's with Penn State. And that guy over there? He's from Clemson University."

Understanding dawned. "They're scouting."

He nodded. "Two of the best football colleges in the country."

"I get the idea behind your plan. Carter is missing out on a huge opportunity." And Steven Patterson would be livid. Although I was sure he'd make a few calls on his son's behalf. "But what about you? Aren't you missing out as well?"

His expression took on a sort of sad look. "Football isn't my dream. It's something the guys and I did together. But I don't want to play pro."

"So, what is your dream?" I asked, genuinely curious. This was information as his sister I should know. The realization that Grayson and I were still virtually strangers hit me with a pang in the chest.

Mads leaned in, invading my personal space, but I didn't mind. "He wants to be a fireman, or was it a sharpshooter?"

Grayson rolled his eyes at his cousin. "When I was like ten. Honestly, I don't know yet."

"You better figure it out soon. Graduation will be here before you know it," Mads informed.

Not soon enough for me.

The two of them stayed plastered to my side throughout the game. There was no sign of Carter or Ava for that matter, but that didn't mean the bastard wasn't lurking about. We stuffed our faces with hotdogs. Grayson ate three, and all I could think was how the hell did he stay so fit?

Elmwood Academy pulled off a win in the last two minutes of the fourth quarter, keeping the fans on the edge of their seats the entire game. For someone who didn't like football, I managed to have fun. I'd almost forgotten what fun felt like. This was what senior year should be, not running from home, being harassed by my dickless stepbrother, or sucked into a teenage war far beyond my years.

In Elmwood fashion, a victory after-party was being held at

someone's house, but honestly, it was no different than any other Friday or Saturday night. Someone was always having a party. Usually one of the Elite. But not tonight.

Mads left as soon as the game was over. I hung out with Grayson, waiting for Fynn, Brock, and Micah to change and get cleaned up after the game. Grayson, Fynn, and Micah hopped into Grayson's Jeep, while Brock and I followed in his Rover. We pulled out of the school parking lot. "Are you sure you don't want to skip the party?" Brock asked, his gaze focused on the dark road in front of us.

I pulled the visor down and checked my face out in the mirror in an attempt to distract myself from jumping across the seat and attacking him with my mouth. There was something damn irresistible about Brock after he showered. The scent of his freshly shampooed hair and earthy soap filled the car, driving me wild. "Is that even allowed? Brock Taylor not showing up to a victory party? Seems criminal."

The corners of his mouth lifted in a small smug grin. "It is if I say it is."

I made a sound of indignation and rolled my eyes. "Nice."

Brock turned into the gas station, Grayson's Jeep trailing behind. As Brock stopped the car beside the pump, a girl in the next lane caught my eye. She sat on the hood of her car, cell phone in hand. "Is that Mads?" I asked, looking closer. The girl angled her head toward us, a cigarette pressed against her lips, and she was wearing the same sweatshirt and jeans.

His amusement slipped, eyes narrowing. "Looks like it."

I got out of the car with Brock, leaving him to fill the gas tank, and walked over to Mads. "Hey. I thought you were going home."

A smile pulled at the corner of her lips around the cigarette. "I am," she retorted, releasing a puff of smoke with the word. I doubted a lecture on smoking at a gas station was what she was after. "I stopped to fill up and my car won't start."

I glanced over the fairly new white BMW. "No shit."

Jumping off the hood, she bent down and snuffed out the smoke. "I just had the damn thing in for maintenance too. Makes no sense."

"Little does to me when it comes to cars. I just drive them, and even that's questionable. Did you call someone? We can give you a ride home, if you want," I offered.

"If Brock doesn't mind the detour. My dad called AAA or some shit." She spotted Grayson's Jeep beside Brock's SUV. "I can always get Gray to drive me."

"I'm sure it will be cool," I assured as a gust of wind blew through my hair. It was getting colder by the minute.

A familiar Escalade came zipping into the gas station, coming to a screeching halt. My stepbrother even drove like an ass. He and two of his football buddies jumped out of the car. Carter's eyes zoned in on me, followed by an arrogant smirk.

Mads's eyes narrowed. "What is he doing here?"

I folded my arms, prickles of unease running down my skin. "Starting trouble."

Leave it to my fucking stepbrother to ruin a perfectly good night.

"Oh, shit," Micah said, catching sight of Carter.

Brock stiffened, jamming the gas nozzle back into the pump,

and came to stand beside me. His lips turned down into a frown. "Get in the car. Both of you." Brock's tone turned cold. The ice dripping from his command wasn't directed at me, I knew that, but I hated being ordered about.

But this was one time I might actually listen.

A knot formed in my gut, and I told my legs to move.

"Shit," Mads cursed under breath, reaching for my hand. "I've got her," she assured Brock.

I would have gone willingly with her if Carter hadn't opened the back door. If a girl hadn't stumbled out. If the girl didn't have familiar rainbow hair woven into two braids.

Son of a bitch!

It couldn't be.

She would never.

Would she?

But the facts were: Ainsley Fisher liked to party. Carter Patterson liked to slip drugs into girls' drinks. And Carter was on a desperate mission to ruin the Elite and using my best friend wasn't beneath him.

I froze. My heart jerked in my chest, ice freezing in my veins. I got the message. If I didn't comply, didn't help him get what he wanted, Carter would hurt those I loved.

Dammit, Ainsley.

The sleaze put his arm around Ainsley, helping her stay on her feet. "Whoa, there."

His hands were on my best friend! I stopped thinking, my legs carrying me away from Brock's car, but I didn't get very far. Firm arms wrapped twined around my waist.

"No fucking way, Firefly," a voice hissed close to my ear.

"Let me go," I gritted. "That's my best friend."

"We'll handle this." He jerked his head at Grayson, Fynn, and Micah. In a few seconds, I had a human wall of Elite in front of me. Frustration bubbled up. My friend needed me. She was in trouble. If anything happened to her because of me, I'd never forgive myself. I had to do something before Carter hurt her, like really hurt her.

Then it happened.

Brock stepped forward. Murder gleamed in his eyes as he glared at Carter. "I thought I told you to stay away from Josie."

Carter had an excuse for everything. Now was no different. "It's a gas station. How the hell was I supposed to know she'd be here?"

Micah let out a swift curse. "You see our cars. First clue."

"I don't know how much clearer we can make this. Stay. The. Fuck. Away from her," Grayson rumbled, the veins in his neck throbbing.

"That includes her friends, you asshole," Fynn added lethally, his voice deep and dark.

"You want her. Here," Carter shoved Ainsley across the gas station parking lot. "She's all yours. I'm done with her now." My stepbrother's blue eyes flashed to mine with the satisfaction of a serial killer who just got away with another murder.

Shawn and Porter chuckled as Ainsley stumbled and fell to the ground.

"How pathetic." Porter spat on the blacktop at Ainsley's feet.

Fynn scooped her up, his scowl flat and cruel. "Funny, I was thinking the same thing about the three of you. I can't believe I ever considered you teammates. That's what really gets me. You're nothing to us, on or off the field."

"Look at the lights," Ainsley said as her head fell back, gazing at the floodlights surrounding the gas station. She was drugged out of her mind.

I pushed forward, somehow managing to wedge myself between Brock and Micah. I shot Carter a look of pure venom as I rushed to Ainsley in Fynn's arms. No one stopped me this time. "What the fuck did you do to her?" I hurled at Carter.

The bastard grinned. "Nothing she didn't want to do."

Carter Patterson's famous last words. "Bullshit! If you touched her, I'll kill you." Ainsley might like to party, but she had a strict policy against drugs.

Carter jiggled the phone in his hand. "Better watch what you say, sis. You're on camera."

I didn't give two shits.

Grayson cracked his knuckles. "She's not your sister."

Carter must be glutton for punishment. "What? It's okay for you guys to pass her around as your whore? But I can't have a little fun with her best friend?"

"Your kind of fun ends with you behind bars. I'd be careful not to drop the soap though. I heard things get a bit slippery in the showers," Micah sneered.

"Don't fuck with me. When I'm done with you, Carter, you're going to wish my mom never married your dad." The threats just flew out of my mouth. I had no real ammunition to back it up, and yet, somehow having the Elite stand alongside me gave me too much courage.

It was dangerous.

I was relying on them, using them as a safeguard. I had to stop before I got hurt. Not by Carter. But by one of them.

Brock, Fynn, Micah, and Grayson all had the power to hurt me now. They had become important to me. I didn't even know how or when it happened. They didn't deserve it after lying to me, but I also understood why they had. In this world, the four of them could only trust each other.

Now they had me.

And I had them.

The Elite stared Carter down, silently begging him for a fight. They might just get their wish.

"Get her in the car," Brock ordered Mads with full authority, his tone so low.

Mads didn't hesitate. She took my arm by the elbow, leading me away from whatever would happen next. Fynn followed behind with Ainsley, loading her safely into the back seat of Brock's car. I climbed in beside her.

I didn't care what happened to Carter, Porter, or Shawn. My only concern was for Ainsley.

"Josie?" she moaned. "I don't feel so good." Her head landed on my lap as Mads opened the front passenger door and got in.

"I know. It's okay now," I assured Ainsley, stroking her hair, praying it would be. I rolled down the window slightly for two purposes. One, to let in some fresh air for Ainsley, and the other, so I could hear what was going outside.

Micah disappeared from my sight as Brock, Fynn, and Grayson moved toward Carter, Shawn, and Porter. The gas station had cleared out, leaving just four cars in the lot. Carter's,

Mads's, Brock's, and Grayson's. "We've warned you what happens when you step out of line," Brock snapped.

Carter snorted. "What are you going to do?" My step-brother puffed out his chest, feeling pretty freaking cocky. Idiot. It made me wonder what he was up to. He wouldn't confront Brock like this, not unless he had a reason the Elite wouldn't hurt him. Perhaps it was because we were in a public place with cameras. Something told me the Elite didn't care. They had Carter on camera, dumping my best friend who was clearly out of her mind, despite it not being enough to prove that he gave her the drugs. And they had power to erase footage, to make it look like nothing happened after this point.

That kind of pull frightened me.

In the distance, the first sound of police sirens went off.

Shit.

"You love this car, don't you?" Brock said, running a finger along the hood of Carter's SUV.

"Love" was an understatement. Carter worshiped his Escalade.

"You like to have fun, right?" I heard Micah say. I still couldn't see him, but the look on Carter's face... it was priceless.

Smash.

The windshield on the Escalade shattered. *Smash. Smash.* Out went the passenger side front and back windows. Micah grinned, a baseball bat in his hand. He didn't stop, putting dents in the side panels of Carter's car.

I didn't even want to know why Grayson drove around with a bat. I assumed it was for situations such as this.

"What the fuck, man!" Carter shrieked.

Porter and Shawn both backed away a step or two, eyeing Micah uneasily. "Calm down. We're not looking for a fight," Porter said, no longer grinning like a shithead.

"Really?" Micah's lopsided grin turned lethal as he thumped the end of the bat against his palm. "Because it kind of feels like that's exactly what you were hoping for."

"We're always down for a good fight," Grayson said.

Brock gave a jerk of his head toward Fynn. "I warned you."

Fynn took off toward the gas station building, I assumed to get the camera footage.

Micah came around the front of Carter's SUV, bat propped up on one shoulder. It was three against three. Fynn was inside talking to the attendant. "Get in your car and get the fuck out of here," Micah ordered.

Enraged, Carter's face turned red. There was shattered glass littered on the ground around the Escalade. And for a moment, I thought Carter would charge Brock. "This isn't over, Taylor. We're just getting started."

"Doesn't matter. I will always end it," Brock replied.

Carter, Shawn, and Porter climbed into the SUV, sweeping fragments off the seats. The engine roared, Carter giving it gas before he put it into drive and squealed out of the gas station. A long moment of silence stretched where I did nothing but stare out the window at Brock. Stunned.

"Holy shit," Mads gasped. "I can't believe that just happened."

The world came rushing back around me, all the sounds with it.

I sank into the seat, glancing down at Ainsley. She had

fallen asleep. I didn't know if that was a good thing or not, but I was still taking her to the hospital to be safe. Hopefully, it was nothing serious and she could sleep off whatever cocktail Carter had slipped her. "I'm going to kill him," I hissed through my teeth as the car door opened.

"Get in line," Brock mumbled, sliding into the front seat. His eyes met mine in the rearview mirror. "Are you okay?" A brief glimmer of concern crossed his expression, so quick, I wondered if I imagined it.

I nodded. "Yeah. This is only going to get worse, isn't it?"

"Probably." No denial or lies came from his response. Just flat acceptance.

It was late when Brock finally dropped Mads off at her house. I hugged her quickly and promised to text her.

He and Mads had both stayed with me at the hospital while the doctor checked out Ainsley and tested her for drugs. It was important for the police to know what type of drugs were in her system. The doctor assured the affects would wear off in a few hours. I stayed in the room with Ainsley. It would be a week or more before the results from the rape kit test were concluded.

The extent of the Elite's influence reached to the hospital and to the police. All I could do was stare at him as he informed the officer and hospital staff that Ainsley would be coming home with us and there was no need to notify her parents. He also advised that bills be sent to him and he would take care of it. Again, no questions asked.

A few blocks after he dropped off my cousin, Brock pulled the Land Rover up to his house and helped me get Ainsley inside. As I covered her with a blanket, I thought back to that day in the bathroom when Mads came up with the idea for me to be one of the Elite. The idea seemed preposterous then.

I was not exactly an Elite, but I had their protection, which was supposed to make me untouchable.

So far, that had not been the case. If anything, the closer I got to the Elite, the more dangerous my life became.

I brushed a strand of hair off the side of Ainsley's cheek as she slept on the couch. Tingles radiated at my neck, signaling Brock was near. I turned around, finding him darkening the doorway. Only a small lamp provided light in the spacious room.

"Thanks for letting her crash here. I know this isn't how you thought to spend your night."

Brock crossed one ankle over the other as he leaned against the frame. "It's not the first time someone sobered up on that couch."

"Still, I appreciate it. She's family." I knew he would understand the importance. Sometimes people with no blood relation could be more family than those with whom you shared DNA with. Brock and I both had that. Me with Ainsley. And him with the Elite.

He forked a hand through his hair. "I get it."

"Are you sure this is fine?" I couldn't help but pick up a ribbon of unease or agitation from him, like he was living a bad memory.

His mouth tightened. "It's not your friend I'm worried about. You're in danger, Firefly," he stated.

My shoulders relaxed as I exhaled. "You don't have to tell me."

The look on his face was born from years of pent-up anger toward my stepbrother. "Don't discard Carter's threats. He is desperate, which makes him unpredictable. I don't know when he will strike next."

I scowled inwardly, understanding seeping into my already overtired brain. "I'm the easy target."

His features grew more serious if even possible. "Yeah, but we put that target there."

Walking around the coffee table, I closed some of the distance between us, not wanting to disturb Ainsley. That's what I told myself. It had nothing to do with this irrational need to be near him. Not. At. All. Chewing on the inside of my lip, I hesitated over telling Brock about Carter blackmailing me. If I was going to trust him and I wanted him to trust me, then I needed to tell him.

Fuck it. No more secrets.

"I think Carter knows why you're protecting me." My voice came out just over a whisper.

In the dimly lit room, his brows drew together. "What are you saying? That he knows who you really are?"

I tugged the sleeve of my hoodie over my hand. "He's implied that he knows."

He made a low growl. "Firefly."

"Look, I was going to tell you," I snapped back. "Don't get your boxers in a wad."

"Tell me what exactly?" he prompted, his patience growing thin.

I huffed, wishing I had chosen to sit in one of the chairs rather than stand. It had been a long-ass night, and my legs weren't thrilled about supporting my weight. "When I went home last weekend, he commented that if I didn't help him get the thumb drive, he would tell my little secret."

Brock swore. "You should have told me."

"I was working on it."

The light from the table lamp reflected off the center of his eyes. "Trust doesn't come easy for either of us." Brock shoved off the wall, his gaze flickering to Ainsley. "We aren't the only ones with secrets to protect. I bet Carter's father wouldn't be too thrilled with his son's after-school occupation."

It was known around the Academy that if you were looking from some extracurricular activities, Carter Patterson had the hookup. I just assumed he knew someone. But was it more than that. Did Carter sell *the stuff,* mostly pills, more than just frequently? "That's assuming Steven doesn't already know," I replied. "He is very well versed in covering his son's tracks. I get the feeling he's been doing it all of Carter's life. Without his father's protection, Carter would be up shit creek."

Tension lines his body. "Then we need to find a way to shatter that shield of fatherly protection."

I shook my head, unable to believe the turn of events. This was not how my evening was supposed to turn out. "I don't know what she was thinking. She knows better than to mess with Carter. She knows what he is capable of."

A frown marred his lips. "She most likely didn't even know

he was there. Remember, he's been at this a lot longer than you have."

That didn't make me feel better. "Will she be okay?" I cast a worried glance at Ainsley. What had Carter done to her? Physically the doctor assured Ainsley would be fine. It was her mental state that concerned me—the trauma. She hadn't said much in the hospital, still too high, but I was scared of what she might remember or might not remember.

"I don't know," he admitted after a long moment of silence. "She'll sleep it off. We'll see tomorrow."

Tomorrow. *Shit.* I had detention in the morning.

With Carter.

CHAPTER NINE

I gave new meaning to dragging your feet. Only part of it was due to me not being a morning person. Seventy percent of my procrastination came from not wanting to go to the Academy on a Saturday.

Who the fuck enjoyed going to school on their weekend?

I guessed that was the punishment of a Saturday detention.

This early in the morning, all I could think was Principal Wallis could suck my ass.

I had Ava to blame for this early morning torture. Why in God's name did they demand we be there at seven in the morning?

Still half asleep, I slipped into my favorite pair of leggings and added a knitted black sweater that was frayed in random spots over the lacy bralette. I found Brock downstairs in the kitchen sipping coffee when I appeared barely functioning. He held out a cup for me. I didn't say it out loud, but I thought it: *Brock is a godsend.*

Savoring the first bold sip, I leaned into the counter, thinking it was the damn best coffee I ever had.

Or maybe it was Brock in the morning that made it taste so good.

He stared at me from the other side of the kitchen island, eyes smoldering. "I've never seen anyone consume coffee the way you do."

I took another long sip. "Then you need new friends. Coffee is the nectar of the gods."

His lips twitched. "Most people would say that about booze, not coffee."

"And that is what is wrong with this world," I replied, smiling at him. "You sure you don't want me to wake her up?" I asked for the third time. "I can call her an Uber." Ainsley was still fast asleep on his couch, but who could blame her. I wouldn't be up if it weren't ordered by the principal.

I cursed Ava.

"It's fine. I'll pump her full of electrolytes while you're doing time."

I gave him a sarcastic short laugh. "Hilarious. Be nice," I said over the rim of my cup.

Without an ounce of humility, he grinned. "When am I not nice?"

That damn smile. It was like a spider's trap, waiting to ensnare me in his web of sexiness. I snorted, practically shooting coffee out of my nose. "If I had the time, I'd make you a list."

"Good thing Grayson's on his way."

I took another drink of my coffee. "Anyone ever tell you that you guys are extreme?"

"Try and stay out of trouble, Firefly," he retorted. "Detention isn't good for our school transcripts."

I rolled my eyes. As if any of them cared about their files. "What's the big deal? You'll just have them altered anyway."

He lifted his mug in salute. "True."

I hated that I wouldn't be there when Ainsley woke up. Hopefully, she wouldn't freak out, waking up in a strange place and then realizing it was Brock's house. She was so going to freak out.

What mattered though was she was safe. And alive.

I didn't know how I would be able to sit in detention with Carter and not put my hands on him. Thinking about last night, what he could have done to her, what he might have done to her... it made me sick. My coffee rolled and sloshed in my stomach.

She had been alone with him in his car with Porter and Shawn, three of the biggest assholes at the Academy.

Was an expulsion in my future? If I got expelled, so would Grayson.

He wouldn't let me go down alone.

It was bad enough that Carter had drugged her, but if he had done something to her while she'd been out of it. If he had taken advantage of her... I'd lose it.

I understood the Elite's deeply rooted desire for retribution for Kenna. I was more invested than ever.

As much as I wanted to know what happened last night, I also hoped Ainsley didn't remember a thing. Sometimes it was the memories that were detrimental. They lingered. They popped up when you least expected it, bringing you back to that horrible event over and over again.

Grayson honked twice when he pulled up to Brock's house, letting me know he'd arrived. We drove a block or two in uncomfortable silence. Things were still weird between us. How could they not be? Neither of us knew how to act around the other. At some point, we would have to figure it out.

"So, are you angry you have to spend your Saturday morning in detention...with me?" I added, taking a sip from the to-go mug of coffee Brock had supplied me with.

Fynn wasn't joking about Grayson and his cars. Today he drove a silver Bugatti that was too damn fast to be driving to school. It was like a bullet shooting down the road, and Grayson handled it expertly. "I'm not thrilled about the detention but... Ava had it coming. The way I look at it, it's for a good cause."

"I thought you and her were *close*." It had seemed that way the night I ended up playing strip poker at Brock's. Oh, God. It made sense now why Grayson had been so quick to leave the room. Strip poker with your sister? Bad idea.

The thought had my cheeks warming, and I promptly drank more coffee.

"By close, you mean am I fucking her?" he remarked flatly. "No. Not currently. She's way too clingy for me. Brock only keeps her around so he can watch her."

"He doesn't have feelings for her?" I wanted to thump myself on the forehead. That sounded way too much like I cared who Brock had sex with.

"Are you fishing?" he asked, lifting a brow. "Look, I'm not

going to get in the middle of whatever is going on with you and my best friend. It's weird enough without me thinking about you sleeping with him."

Seeing Grayson squirm was sort of funny. The scrunched expression on his face made me want to keep making him uncomfortable. "Is that a problem for you?"

His head jerked toward me for a split second. "You having sex? Or you having sex with Brock."

A ghost of a smile played at my lips. "Both."

He nodded. "Yeah."

I wasn't letting him off the hook easily. "Which one?"

"Both," he replied, his lips curving.

I smiled back at him. "You'll have to explain this whole standby girl thing to me and how it works."

He shook his head at me like I was a pestering little sister, which I guess in a way, I was. "I can't give away Elite secrets."

We pulled into the almost empty school parking lot; only ten cars versus hundreds sat parked. I reached for my coffee only to find that it was empty. It would be a long two hours. Sighing, I unfolded myself out of the car and faced the school. An arm slung over my shoulder, pulling me against a firm chest.

"Is it true you screwed the quarterback last night?" a playful voice that could only belong to one person asked.

I rolled my eyes, angling my head toward Micah, and shoved lightly at his shoulder. "Ha. Ha. Brock couldn't be so lucky."

His light blue eyes twinkled down at me. "Anytime you get bored of sleeping at Brock's, my bed is always available."

He smelled nice. Not as intoxicating as Brock, but still really good. "I'll keep that in mind," I retorted.

Grayson came around to my other side, frowning at Micah, who still had his arm around me. "You do, and Brock will kill you. And then Micah," he told me.

I winked at the playboy, unable to miss the opportunity to ruffle Grayson's feathers. He made it too easy to rile him up. "I promise it will be worth it."

Micah tossed his head back and laughed.

"Can we stop talking about my friends screwing my sister?" Grayson groused.

Micah and I shared another smile as the three of us walked toward the front entrance. I didn't know if they did this on purpose, lighting the air right before things got tense. Regardless, it was just what I needed. "What are you doing here?" I asked Micah. As far as I knew, he hadn't done anything to earn detention. I would have heard about it.

"I couldn't let the two of you have all the fun."

The sun beamed over the Academy as the gust of autumn air blew through the open lot. I buried myself closer to Micah and his warm hoodie. "This can't be your idea of fun."

He didn't seem to mind that I was soaking up his body heat. Micah was the type of guy who loved to have a girl in his arms. Any girl would do. "I've given up plenty of Saturdays through high school. It's what family does. We stick together through all the good and bad shit," he said.

My heart jumped in my chest at the word "family." It was a simple word for some—a word that brought on feelings of security, comfort, joy, and love. For me, it was a mixture of both good and bad. The idea of the Elite considering me as part of their close-knit family opened an ache of longing inside me. "Am I family?" The question popped out of my mouth, and the second it did, I wished I could take it back. I didn't want to appear as desperate as I was to belong.

Grayson surprised both Micah and me when he said, "You're getting there, Lil' J."

Nothing like having a pair of escorts usher me into detention. We arrived at the designated classroom with two minutes to spare. My eyes panned the room, looking for a particular face. He wasn't there. Not yet.

Had Steven managed to get Carter out of detention? That would have been just like my stepfather, and in this situation, fine by me.

I didn't want to see Carter's vile mug this early in the morning.

The classroom tables were nearly filled as Micah, Grayson, and I took a seat in the back of the room. It was as if they had been intentionally left open just for us. I had a sneaky suspicion that they probably had been.

These boys.

They were unbelievable.

But the treatment they got from this school...

Over-the-fucking-top.

"Mr. Bradshaw, why are you here?" Mr. Schultz asked, glancing up from behind his desk. He was the teacher assigned to monitor this week's detention. Mr. Schultz taught in the science department, and he looked the part. Scrawny, nerdy, glasses that fell down the bridge of his sharp nose, and a voice just a pitch too high. "Not that I don't like seeing your face in detention, but I don't have you on the list."

Micah folded his hands behind his head like he was preparing for a nap. "It was last minute. Coach probably didn't have time to turn it in."

"If you say so. It's your Saturday, Mr. Bradshaw." Mr. Schultz was one of those teachers that called everyone by their last name. He returned to his list, crossing off students as they arrived.

I angled my head toward Micah. "You don't have detention, do you?" I kept my tone quiet.

Micah shrugged, grinning. "We decided two of us were better than one just in case someone decided to deliver a little payback."

My mouth opened to tell him how ridiculous they were, but that someone in question walked in. I snapped my jaw closed, clenching my teeth.

Tension descended like a dark ominous cloud over the room as Carter walked in, Ava beside him. They were laughing.

And I saw red.

My hands clenched along the edge of the table, knuckles turning white. It took all my restraint to stay seated. I wanted to hurdle over the table and banshee-attack Carter, rake my nails down that face he was so proud of. Then I'd pounce on Ava. Her smug, glossy grin made my blood boil.

Micah leaned closer and whispered, "Put the claws away, tiger."

I didn't know how they managed to stay so cool beside me. Anyone looking at Grayson and Micah would believe they were bored and uninterested. Their expressions were masks, because I knew that under the yawns and blasé attitude, they were simmering with anger. "How do I make it through the next two hours without strangling him or Ava?" I murmured for their ears only.

"Just think about waffles," Grayson suggested.

"Or sex," Micah added from the other side of me.

I guess I knew what they were thinking about. But neither of those would work for me.

Carter sauntered into the room like he just got laid. I wouldn't be surprised if Ava hadn't sucked him off in the parking lot before coming inside. A little morning pick-me-up.

Disgusting.

The two of them together equaled a really bad trip.

"Take a seat, Mr. Patterson. You too, Miss Whitmore. You're both late." The look Mr. Schultz gave them said he'd rather be anywhere but here as well.

Carter and Ava slid into the two empty seats at the table to our right. "Did you walk here or get Daddy's driver to drop you off?" Micah's eyes seemed to dance as he posed the question. He enjoyed tormenting Carter. He also enjoyed being the center of attention. Carter wanted to command a room with his presence when he walked in, but it was Micah who managed to do so effortlessly.

Snickers sounded through the room.

The incident from last night had already spread like a disease through school.

Mr. Schultz folded his hand over the paper with our names on it, pointing his gaze toward my table. "Mr. Bradshaw, you know the rules. This isn't a social hour. No talking or I'll move you to a different seat."

"I'd be happy to switch," Carter volunteered.

Grayson scowled.

Everyone in the room was aware of the sudden ice coating the air. Even Mr. Schultz felt it. My two personal guards stiffened beside me, all teasing gone. They became cold, with a vow of violence swimming in their eyes.

"That wouldn't be wise, Mr. Schultz," Micah warned, leaning back in his chair.

Silence fell.

Mr. Schultz pushed up his glasses as he shifted in his chair, clearly uncomfortable with the implication in Micah's warning.

Halfway into our detention, which was basically a long-ass study hall, a balled-up piece of paper sailed onto our table, landing on my notebook. Grayson's scowl deepened as he snatched up the wadded note before I could. Unraveling the ball, his eyes scanned the scribble, and the set of his jaw hardened.

Rolling my eyes, I took a glance at Mr. Schultz, and plucked the note out of Grayson's hands. Micah leaned over, reading the message over my shoulder.

They can't always protect you. I'll be waiting.

"This guy just doesn't know when to call it quits. I knew he was hard-headed, but shit…" Grayson snapped the pencil between his fingers in half.

Shadows crossed Micah's normally twinkling eyes. "Should we take him behind the school?" he whispered, deadly serious.

My gaze darted over to Carter and Ava's table. The two of

them kept their heads forward, but I caught the hint of a smirk on their lips. They enjoyed this. "I don't think beating the shit out of him will stop him. It didn't work before."

"No," Micah admitted. "But it will feel good."

Grayson cracked his knuckles. "I agree."

An hour later I dragged the two of them out of the school by the hoods of their sweatshirts before either of them made good on their claim to beat the ever-loving snot out of Carter. Again. They'd already broken his ribs. Shattered his car. Threatened him. What next? I didn't want to find out today, not when Ainsley was waiting for me.

Ainsley sat on the couch nursing what looked like one hell of a hangover when I walked into Brock's house. Her eyes were bloodshot and half-lidded as she sipped on a bottle of grape Gatorade. But at least she was awake.

Brock sat in one of the big, cushiony chairs, Grayson taking the other. I went to Ainsley, joining her on the couch. Strands of her rainbow hair fell out of the messy bun atop her head as I hugged her. "God, Ains. I was so worried. Are you okay?"

"Yeah, I think so." Her mossy green eyes were clearer than they had been last night and filled me with relief. "Fuck, Josie. I don't know what the hell happened," she admitted, her voice trembling.

Micah perched on the end of the couch arm, closest to me. "You were flying higher than a kite."

I shot him a dry look. "Are you sure you're okay?" That was

the most important detail to me. All the other questions could wait until I was satisfied my best friend was fine.

"I'd be lying if I said I wasn't freaking out inside, because I am. I've never blacked out before. Ever. Gotten so drunk I pissed the bed? For sure."

"Been there," Micah muttered, a grin of approval tugging at his lips.

I rolled my eyes.

"What do you remember?" Brock prompted.

She glanced at Brock for a moment before casting her gaze floor. "Not much. I went to Trenton's party with Rory and Trevor." Trenton McGuire was Public's center on the soccer team. He was the Brock of Public, but not, because no one was really like Brock. But I guess Trenton was as close as you could get. "It was just a typical party. Everyone was drinking. The next thing I knew, I was waking up in the hospital." The color in her cheeks heightened, shame sparkling her eyes as she lifted them.

"You didn't see Carter at the party?" Micah asked.

She shook her head, clutching the bottle of Gatorade. "That's what is so strange. I didn't. I still can't believe I left with him. You know I would never do anything that stupid, Josie."

"I know," I assured, squeezing her hand.

"What was Carter doing at a Public party?" Micah questioned. "Definitely not his scene."

"I think we know why he was there," Brock mused. All eyes looked to Ainsley.

Fresh guilt stabbed into me. "He went intentionally to look for me."

Grayson leaned forward in his chair, pressing his elbows into his knees. "Did you notice anyone from the Academy there?"

She nodded. "Yeah. But that's normal. Academy crashes Public parties all the time, same with Public."

That was true. "He could have had someone else slip her the drugs," I suggested.

Brock agreed. "Likely. Carter needs to be extra careful. Getting someone else to do his dirty work would keep him out of the spotlight. If no one saw him at the party, then we couldn't prove he was there."

"The coward was probably waiting in the car," Micah seethed, his voice dropping.

Ainsley unscrewed the top on her drink, taking a quick sip. "I don't understand. Why would he drug me? What was the point?"

I wrung my fingers. "Me. He is sending me a message, letting me know there are other ways to hurt me if I don't give him what he wants."

Confusion descended over her features as she ran a hand through her sleep-tousled hair. "What the hell does he want from you, Josie?"

My eyes met Brock's and held for a long moment before I turned back to Ainsley. "This is my fault. I'm sorry, Ainsley. I'm so sorry." I didn't want to involve her further in this mess. She'd been hurt enough.

"You can't blame yourself. These are Carter's choices, not yours," she argued, getting fired up. I preferred to see her angry than sad.

"She's right, Firefly." Brock's aqua eyes lingered on me.

"I won't let him hurt the few people I care about to get to me," I replied with determination, a fire spreading in my belly.

"If you remember anything, call Josie," Brock instructed Ainsley.

She nodded. "Of course. I should call my mom before she sends out an APB" Setting down the plastic bottle, she reached around to check her pockets, still dressed in the clothes she wore last night. Her brows bunched together. "Shit, my phone. I can't find it."

Ainsley was notorious for losing things, especially when she was drinking. Alcohol made her forgetful and careless. Not that I was any better. "Are you sure?" I asked, a horrible feeling pitching into my gut.

"Yeah. I had it in my pocket. You know I never bring a purse to a party." It was something we both had gotten accustomed to doing, leaving the handbags at home and keeping all our personal stuff on us. Less shit to lose at a party. "It's probably sitting under a pile of pizza boxes at Trenton's. Or it's stuffed in between the couch cushions," she speculated.

Those were all likely possibilities, but my gut feeling said her phone had been taken.

What the fuck would Carter want with Ainsley's phone?

"Here..." I dug out my phone. "If you need to call or text your mom. I'm sure she is worried. I texted her last night to let her know you were staying at my house."

"Thanks, Jos. For everything," she rasped.

"Don't thank me. None of this would have happened if it weren't for me."

Her lips formed into a scowl. "Stop blaming yourself. I won't have it. You're my best friend. What happens to one of us happens to both of us."

Her support was unyielding even after what she'd been through, but I still couldn't help feel somewhat responsible. No, I couldn't control Carter or what the asshole did. But it was because of my relation to him that the bastard sought out to hurt my best friend. "Maybe Rory knows where your phone is. Or can help fill in some of the blanks," I offered.

"I'll give her a call after I talk to my mom."

I hugged her again. "I'm so glad you're okay. I was so scared. I don't know what I'd do without you." It was true. Ainsley was family to me—the only real thing I had from my past.

CHAPTER TEN

B rock and I dropped Ainsley off at her house after seven o'clock. She wanted to sober up some before she went home and faced her parents. Although her coloring was better, less pale green and more rosy pink, she still didn't feel well. Nothing a bowl of her mom's homemade chicken noodle soup and some hot tea couldn't cure. The stuff was magic. Mrs. Fischer had made me a batch more than a time or two when I'd fallen ill. She knew Angie wasn't the cooking type; nor was she the mothering type.

She wasn't my mother at all.

A fact that still shook me and felt unreal.

How long did something like finding out your mother is not your biological mother really take to sink in? I didn't think there were any textbook answers for situations like that.

Brock took a left turn at the stoplight instead of a right,

taking us deeper into the old section of Elmwood, not far from where I grew up.

"Where are we going?" I asked, pulling my gaze from the passenger window to look at him.

"Grayson is racing tonight. I thought you'd might like to watch, take a moment to get your mind off all the crap."

"Oh." Grayson was racing.

His older brother Sawyer had also raced cars, and it had killed him.

"Unless you want to go back to my place, and I could entertain you in other ways," he offered seductively. His tone might not have changed, but all my ears heard was the smooth and silky timbre of his voice.

Brock's suggestion was appealing, especially since his and my idea of entertainment went along the same lines. Sex.

My body tingled at the prospect of having him inside me.

This unhealthy obsession with his dick had to stop. I was getting too attached.

I had to stop thinking about his dick.

Like now.

"No, street racing is great. Can't wait," I replied. This was something Grayson was into—something that I imagined made him feel closer to his brother, our brother. Holy shit. I just realized that Sawyer had been my brother too. I never got to meet him. Just another thing Angie took from me.

Sadness filled me for the brother I would never know —never see.

"Hey, Firefly, you okay?"

Brock's unusually soft voice pulled me out of space where

I'd gotten lost in my thoughts about Sawyer. Forcing a smile on my lips, I replied, "Yeah, I'm good. I think everything is just catching up with me."

Headlights from the upcoming traffic illuminated the shadows on his face. Despite how incredibly beautiful Brock's features were, he had an edge about him that roughed up some of that beauty. "I'm surprised it hasn't sooner."

"I've had years of practice suppressing shit," I admitted, returning my gaze to stare at the blur of dark trees streaking by. As usual, Brock drove fast, but tonight seemed like a night that called for speed.

He eased the car to a speed lower than fast as fuck. "You don't have to with me."

When he said shit like that, my heart fluttered in my chest. I wanted to reach across the seat and run my fingers through his hair. I bit my lip instead. "I'll keep that in mind."

"I told Grayson we'd swing by and pick up Mads from her mother's shop," he explained as we headed into the shopping district of old downtown Elmwood.

Mrs. Clarke owned a clothing boutique. Actually, she owned several in the surrounding area, all named after her daughter. Mads was sitting on the curb when we pulled up, a cigarette in between her fingers. Her leather-clad legs stretched out in the street, ankles crossed, and the forest-green sweater she wore hung off one shoulder. She was by far the coolest person I knew.

Brock stopped the car next to the curb in front of her, since Mads made no gesture to move. I rolled down my window and leaned out. "You looking for a good time?" I said, channeling my inner Micah. I'd been hanging around the Elite too long. They were starting to rub off on me.

Her smoky eyes glittered as she finally stood and walked to the car. "I'm not into kinky threesomes." Her gaze shifted to Brock's.

A memory of him flashed through my mind from the first night I'd met Ava and the bitch cornered me in the bathroom. I had stumbled upon Brock with a chick, and he had asked if I wanted to join.

"You're missing out." Brock smirked like he knew what I was thinking about.

Mads's gaze swept over me. She angled her head to the side, exhaling. A ring of smoke puffed from her lips. "She can't go to a race like that. We need five minutes." The car door opened, and Mads stepped back.

"What's wrong with how I look?" I asked, pouting a little as I glanced down at my usual jeans and T-shirt. Sure, I wouldn't win any beauty pageants, but I didn't see what the big deal was. It was a race. At night. Who would see me? I'd been to plenty before.

"Maddy," Brock rumbled, as if Mads was trying his patience.

She took one last drag on her cigarette, not giving a shit, and flicked it over the roof of Brock's car. "Five minutes, Taylor. She needs it." Mads grabbed my hand, pulling me into the shop. "Come on, girl, let's get you fixed up."

"You don't have to do this. I'm not sure going to this race is even a good idea," I protested.

Mads's firm grip remained unwavering. She wasn't going to

let me back out. "If the Elite are involved, it is never a good idea, which is precisely why we are going."

"That doesn't make any sense."

"Neither do french fries and chocolate shakes, yet they are fucking great together."

I rolled my eyes.

"Trish, I forgot something in the back. We'll be just a few minutes," Mads said the girl behind the counter inserting tags into a pile of folded pants.

The college-aged girl smiled as we walked by. "Sure thing. Your mom is still taking inventory."

I followed Mads into the back room of the shop. Racks and racks of new clothes freshly pressed lined the walls. Mads fingered through the pieces, pulling out a few items. Five minutes turned into ten. I walked out of Madison Clarke Boutique in pair of tight jeans, which I'd already been wearing, a red crop top that somehow made the amber flecks in my eyes brighter, a black leather jacket, and a seriously kickass pair of heels. Mads teased my hair, adding volume and texture to it. She made quick work applying a little bit of makeup, mostly mascara and eyeliner to darken my eyes. The bruise on my cheek was mostly gone and completely invisible with a tad of concealer.

I turned in the mirror.

Hot damn, I felt badass. "God, I needed this."

Mads admired her handiwork, taking the full view of me in from head to toe. "Yes, you did."

The heels on my black booties clicked with confidence as I strutted over the sidewalk toward Brock's SUV. His gaze devoured me, and my lips twitched when I watched them darken in appreciation. "What did you do to her?" he snapped to Mads.

She slid into the back seat. "I made her fucking hot."

The scowl on his lips increased. "No."

"No, what?" I grinned, loving the way his eyes flared at me. His lips and tone were disapproving, but his eyes betrayed him.

"Don't toy with me, Firefly," he deadpanned. "You can't go like that."

"Yes, she can," Mads insisted as she fastened her seat belt. "Now put the car in gear before we miss the take-off."

Brock held up a finger. "Maddy, I'll get to you in a minute."

She ignored him and replied snottily. "Okay, *Dad*."

I angled my head toward Brock. "Since when do you dictate how I dress?"

"You're not her keeper," Mads added, the two of us ganging up on him.

With a shake of his head, he rebuffed. "She doesn't need the attention."

"You mean you don't need the competition." Mads reached for a cigarette. "Admit it, Taylor, you have a thing for my girl Josie."

Before she could light her smoke, Brock snatched the slim white stick from her fingers and snapped it in half, tossing it out the window. "You know the rules. Next time you need a ride, call Grayson."

Mads scowled. "Fuck off, Taylor. Don't get pissed at me because you have commitment issues. The guys at the race are going to be all over her."

"This is for me. Not them," I defended. I wasn't looking for attention, but now that Mads mentioned it, I wouldn't mind making Brock jealous. In fact, it sounded downright fun.

His scowl remained etched on his lips as he hit the gas.

Fynn whistled when he caught sight of me getting out of Brock's car. "Sweet Jesus, you look hot."

I tossed my hair over my shoulder, shooting Brock a sidelong gaze. "Tell that to Brock."

His flat look annoyed me. "I never said you didn't look good, Firefly. I said you didn't need the attention."

I returned his look with one of my own. "No one will be looking at me."

Two seconds later Micah had me off the ground and in his arms. He twirled me once. "Damn, James. Leather suits you."

It did. It really did.

"Tell me that you're coming home with me tonight," Micah purred, his arms still locked around me.

I pushed at his shoulders, but it did no good. "Only if you promise to put me down," I muttered.

"Now that's a promise I'm not sure I can make." He flipped me over his shoulder, causing my ass to point up into the air, straining against my pants, and then proceeded to smack it.

"Micah!" I shrieked.

"Put her down," Brock demanded, his voice harsh.

Micah chuckled. "You know she isn't just yours."

"She is in the way that counts," Brock replied, a twinkle in his eye like he had the right to be protective, which he didn't.

We might have slept together, but he had no claim over me. We were not dating.

Mads snorted. "Sex doesn't mean shit to you."

My feet hit the ground as three guys strolled up, ending the conversation. I recognized them from Public. Two of them had graduated last year, Todd and Weston. The other was known around school as Stitch. I had no idea where the nickname came from.

"Look who's slumming tonight in the lower E," Stitch greeted, clasping Brock's hand first before moving to greet the others in the same manner.

"The fucking Elite," Todd, of the older guys, said with a wry smirk.

"Should I take my money elsewhere?" Grayson flashed a stack of bills alongside a grin.

Stitch eyed the cash, dollar signs beaming in them. "You're lucky you're Sawyer's little brother, man."

Grayson left eye twitched at the mention of Sawyer, but that was the only tell he gave.

"Your brother was a goddamn legend on the streets," Weston said with apparent admiration.

"He was," Grayson agreed, a forced emotionless expression on his face. "Which is why I'm definitely winning this race. It's in my blood."

Stitch's gaze landed on me. He took his sweet time looking me over. Tension radiated in the air suddenly, and Brock's jaw tightened. It took me a second to realize the four of them circled me. I hadn't even seen it happen. They were just there, surrounding me, but Stitch and his buddies noticed.

I was theirs. And no one was to mess with me unless they wanted a problem with the Elite.

"I told you the guys would be all over her," Mads murmured to Brock. "What are you going to do about it, Taylor? Let them hit on your girl?"

I poked her in the side as I hissed through my teeth, "Stop trying to stir up trouble."

Her lips curved at the corners. "I can't help myself. He makes it so easy."

Stitch smiled at me in slow appreciation. "Josie James. Heard you moved up in the world. Don't tell me you're running with these four."

"Hey, Stitch. When did you start racing?" I said, quickly changing the subject.

"I don't. I just organize them."

How did I not know about this? I'd lived in these parts of Elmwood my entire life. I went to school with most of these guys. I'd been to races on the track with my dad, but never any on the streets. Ainsley would eat this shit up. It seemed like one of those exclusive pop-up events you needed to know someone to get an invite to.

Ainsley and I were never that cool.

But the Elite were.

I glanced around the abandoned parking lot stuffed with cars of every make and model. Neon lights lit up from underneath many of the cars as music bumped. "Interesting little side hustle you have."

He shrugged. "It beats working a part-time job. Harvey's here."

"Harvey," I choked. Like my ex-boyfriend Harvey? Fuck. I hadn't seen him in months. After the asshole cheated on me, I'd be good with never seeing his face again.

"Who's Harvey?" Mads crooned beside me.

"You look good, James," Stitch purred before I could answer Mads, thank God, not that his comment was any better.

Stitch had balls to eye me like he was in front of the Elite. Brock's expression looked as if he was two seconds away from giving Stitch a bloody nose, race or not.

My cheeks warmed, and I tucked a piece of hair behind my ear. "Thanks."

Stitch didn't seem to be intimidated by the four guys surrounding me. Did that make him brave or just stupid? "Please tell me one of these assholes is not your boyfriend."

"She's dating them all," Mads spoke up, a fast grin on her lips.

The hell I was. "That is so not true."

"Well, except for that one," she added, her gaze shifting to Grayson as she bulldozed right over my denial.

Stitched lifted his brows.

Mads pulled out a cigarette. "It's complicated."

Brock rolled his eyes as Micah slung an arm around my shoulder. "Sorry, she's taken, dude."

Grayson shot Micah a WTF look but didn't say anything as he leaned against the most beautiful piece of machinery I'd ever laid eyes on. His ride tonight was sleek, shiny, and looked fast as fuck. That was enough for me. I was in love.

I wiggled out of Micah's arms and strolled over to the car. "This is yours?" I said in awe, running a finger over the smooth midnight blue paint. "My dad would go apeshit over this." I liked to pretend I knew shit about cars. Thanks to my gearhead dad, I knew more about cars than I cared to.

"'67 Dodge Challenger. My dad helped me build it," Grayson said, coming to stand beside me as I petted the hood.

His dad. My biological father. I knew nothing about him... except that he liked to build cars. How strange that both my fathers had something common.

Weirdness hung in the air. Would things ever be normal between us?

Luckily the race was about to start. More cars started to line up on a long stretch of road. Grayson paid the entrance fee. Brock and Mads were preoccupied talking with the guys while Grayson and I admired his car.

The corners of his lips pulled into a wicked grin. "Want to ride shotgun?"

Only a moment passed before I responded. "Thought you would never ask."

He nodded to the other side. "Get in then, Lil' J. Better hurry before Brock has something to say about it."

I didn't give it a second thought and scrambled around to the passenger door, slipping inside before anyone noticed. The Charger's engine hummed to life underneath me, a gentle rumble like a lion purring, but once Grayson pressed on the pedal, giving the car a little gas, it roared like a furious beast.

Grayson's smile was that of pure joy, one he rarely displayed, and I found it impossible not to smile in return. I glanced out the tinted window. Brock scowled back at me, shaking his head as he folded his arms. There would be hell to pay, but that didn't matter right now.

Grayson and I were having a brother-sister moment, something I'd missed out on for seventeen years.

We moved into position in the lineup. Grayson revved the engine as we waited for the signal to begin. My heart beat against my ribs in anticipation, equal parts excitement and fear. The white flag lifted, and Grayson shifted the car into gear. He stole a glance at me. "Brace yourself, Lil' J."

The flag went down and Grayson slammed his foot on the gas. I was tossed back against the seat. A rush of adrenaline tore through me. And I laughed.

Grayson handled the car like a pro—like he was born to drive. His fingers fit snugly over the vibrating steering wheel, his other hand shifting the car from one gear to the next. We weaved in and out of traffic, passing racer after racer. I didn't think I exhaled until we cleared the busy street, heading into a rural part of town where the road opened up.

And that was when Grayson let the Charger free.

I was never so damn thankful for a seat belt in my life. It kept me strapped securely against the seat. The guy beside us kept neck to neck with Grayson's car, not giving an inch.

"This asshole wants to play."

Grayson didn't flinch as he shot through a red light, foot pressed to the floor. "Holy shit," I whispered, bracing my feet against the floorboards, while my hand clutched the ceiling. I nearly shit myself and decided if I was about to die, I didn't want to see it coming. My eyes squeezed shut. This was intense. I didn't know if I was cut out to race.

"Did we win?" I asked moments later, noticing the car was losing acceleration.

Grayson laughed. "You can open your eyes."

He sounded happy. Like truly happy, so I took that as a good sign.

I slowly opened my eyes, ready to congratulate him for crossing the finish line, but the second I blinked, a pair of blinding headlights beamed through my window, barreling straight for us. I was about to be smashed like a pancake.

"Hang on!" Grayson ordered.

Is that panic I hear in his voice?

I was panicking enough for both of us. My scream got caught in my throat as his foot hit the brakes hard and he cranked the wheel to one side. The car drifted, throwing me against the door.

It felt like the car would never stop coasting over the road, the Charger turning parallel with the oncoming car. The world blurred, the night's sky nothing but a streak of darkness. Then it all went still except for the thumping of my heart.

"Oh, my God, how did you do that?" I would have frozen, let the oncoming car hit me. Not Grayson. He managed to avoid a collision like he was a damn stunt driver.

His frown turned into a grimace as his gaze swept over me. "Are you okay?" Concern glittered in his features.

"I'm fine because of you," I replied, residual tremors of fear still shaking through my body.

"The fucking car came out of nowhere." Anger vibrated in his voice, the lines around his lips hardening.

I recognized the car, and no amount of wishing otherwise would make it less true. "That's one of Steven's cars," I said, staring at the taillights that lit up the vanity plates. IGROWL. It was pretty difficult to mistake a car with plates like that.

"Carter," Grayson snarled right before he punched the gas, causing the Charger to go from a dead stop to full speed as he gave chase. "That asshole is dead."

"Do we want to take a moment to think about what you're doing?" I just barely lived through my first race and managed to escape a car crash. I wasn't super eager to engage in another.

His foot didn't let up, conviction flaring in his eyes. "He could have killed you."

"He is trying to scare me. He is upping the stakes until I agree to help him."

"This has gone too far."

My fingers gripped the edges of the seat as I pressed myself further into the seat. "You think?" The Charger lurched over a dip in the road, gaining ground on Carter. "What do you plan to do if you catch up to him? Run him off the road? It's not worth it. And this car doesn't deserve to be wrecked over him, no matter how satisfying."

He released a grim exhale. "I'm sick of his shit, of waiting for him to be accountable for the shit he's done."

"No one more than me wants to see him pay."

"Dammit." Grayson slammed his hands against the steering wheel. For the second time, I saw my life flash before my eyes as

Grayson spun the car around in a one-eighty, taking us back to where the race ended, letting Carter get away.

Quite a crowd had gathered by the time we pulled in and parked. I glanced around, searching for Mads, but it was Brock who found us.

He got in Grayson's face as soon as he stepped out of the car. "What the hell was that?" I'd never seen them fight before, not like this. And I didn't want them to start.

Not over me.

I never wanted to be that girl, the one that breaks up a friendship.

Grayson didn't back down under Brock's burning glare. He stayed nose-to-nose with him. "She's fine. So am I, thanks for asking."

"That's not the point," Brock growled. The crowd that had gathered for the race now turned their attention to Grayson and Brock.

"What is the fucking point?" Grayson shot back at Brock. "If you think I'd let anything happen to her, then you don't know me as well as you think."

"Stop!" I yelled, shoving my way in between them, a dangerous maneuver, but I didn't think. I just reacted and hated seeing two people I cared about arguing. This was Carter's doing, and I refused to let that little shit get in between the friendship these guys had. Their bond was supposed to be fucking unbreakable.

I needed it to be.

Micah stepped to defuse the tension as he normally did.

"Well, that was an interesting race. The winner doesn't usually take off."

A scowl locked onto Grayson's lips. "Carter made a surprise appearance."

All amusement fled from Micah's handsome face. "That was him in the car at the finish line?"

I nodded.

"Why don't we let the asshole think you're helping him?" Mads said to me. "Just hear me out, before the four of you get all 'me man, hear me roar.'"

The sudden intensity dripping off the Elite thickened the air.

"What if we make him think that Josie is willing to snoop around and find the thumb drive? It would get him to let up on the scare tactics for awhile at least." Leave it to Mads to hatch a crazy plan.

Grayson blinked, regarding his cousin with a blank expression. "The way your mind works sometimes scares me."

"You're not the only one it scares," she mumbled.

"There are so many things that could go wrong," Fynn said, being the voice of reason.

We had formed a circle as we talked, closing off the crowd around us, our voices lowering. "So you just want to sit around and see what crazy thing he is going to do to her next?" Mads argued. "At the very least, it might buy us some time, make him believe she has succumbed to his blackmail."

"She has a point," Micah agreed, meeting each of the other three guys dark stares. "A person can only handle so much. We need him to think this was Josie breaking point."

"Absolutely not." No one was surprised by Brock's refusal.

"Shocker, the king disagrees," Mads retorted sarcastically, pulling out a cigarette. Her lighter flared in the dimly lit area.

Brock gritted his teeth. "We're not using Josie as bait. Not again."

"And if I volunteer? You're not using me then. We don't have any other options that I can see."

Every muscle in his body went rigid. There was a bit of wariness too. "If we do this, we do it my way, on my terms," he finally said after a long moment of consideration.

We shared a look, and my brows lifted. "Is there any other way?"

With Brock, there wasn't.

My ears still rang as I laid my head on the pillow and closed my eyes. I swore the bed rumbled like an engine underneath me.

Eventually, my mind and body must have quieted enough for me to fall asleep, somewhere between reliving the thrill of the race and Brock's angry face. The next thing I knew, I was locked back inside Carter's car, blindfolded and bound. *Fear hit the back of my mouth, coating my tongue with the sharp tang of panic. My hands trembled against the twine tying them together.*

A door squeaked open, and a spear of terror lanced through me. Seconds later, Carter's voice pierced the roaring of fear in my head. "I warned you what would happen if you chose the wrong side."

"No," I screamed, my head shaking back and forth wildly. "Carter, stop."

The blindfold ripped away from my eyes, and I stared into the twisted face of a madman.

Carter showed no remorse, no emotion as his fingers wrapped around my neck like a thick noose, tightening until air was impossible to get into my lungs. My eyes went wide as I bucked, struggling to dislodge his body. But Carter had the weight to keep me pinned to the back seat.

I thrashed, but it was useless.

I couldn't breathe.

He was going to kill me.

No one was coming to save me.

"Firefly."

The gentle voice nudged me out of that place of horror that trapped me, urging me out of the nightmare and into wakefulness.

Through the well of hot tears, it was Brock's face hovering close to mine. Not Carter's.

I swallowed a cry of genuine fear and blinked just to make sure.

"Firefly, hey. It's me. You're okay. Do you hear me? You're safe. I won't let him hurt you. Not in my house."

"Brock?" I whispered, my voice raspy like I'd been screaming.

Had I?

Thump. Thump. Thump.

My heart still hammered in my chest, despite the realization that it was only a dream. Carter wasn't here. And I wasn't trapped in his car. I was in Brock's bed. It was his body warm against mine, chasing away the chill of fright and helplessness.

Brock brushed his knuckle along my cheek, and I stared into his eyes. It was those eyes, the color of the ocean at night, that calmed the racing panic. His touch banished any lingering traces of Carter's fingers wrapped around my neck.

I lifted my arms and touched his face, needing to feel that he was real. His skin was warm and comforting. I slide my hands into his hair, pulling him down against me. "Hold me," I murmured.

His body became flush with mine. If there was one thing Brock was exceptional at, it was making me forget. I needed that now.

I needed him.

Brock didn't protest when I guided my lips to his, not that I thought he would. In this area, Brock never denied me. I didn't let myself think that meant anything. Brock wasn't the kind of guy to get tangled with a girl—physically, yes but not emotionally.

CHAPTER ELEVEN

We put the beginnings of Mads's harebrained scheme into motion Monday at school. The Elite would make it known over the next few weeks that I was one of them, I was in the inner circle of trust. All the while Carter would think I was using this newly gained trust to stab them in the back.

Thinking it caused a pang in my gut.

But first, I had to convince Carter I was willing to help him *if* he stopped harassing my friends. He was never to touch Mads or Ainsley again or the deal was off. That part needed to be very clear.

If he had a problem, then he came directly to me.

It was a dangerous game but the only way I could see to pacify Carter long enough to come up with a way to take him down. Nothing so far had worked. Like the Elite, Carter had money and a powerful father in his corner. But I had the Elite.

Nothing about this would be easy. And I realized the Elite were putting a lot of trust in me.

I had to do this not just for them, or myself, but for the sister I'd never met. Kenna deserved justice and closure.

I thought about Kenna often, particularly when I was alone with my thoughts. It had only been a little over a week since I found out my life was nothing but a lie. That rage at being deceived and taken from my family still burned bright inside me, and I knew my silence on the matter wouldn't last much longer.

There were answers I needed from Angie, answers only she could give me.

To say I hadn't yet dealt with being kidnapped as a baby was an accurate statement. How the fuck did someone cope with that? On one hand, my parents were all I knew. They raised me; however good or bad that had been was debatable. But to me, they were Mom and Dad.

Then there were the Edwardses. It was stupid but a part of me was afraid of how they would react when they found out their dead daughter wasn't dead after all. Logically they would be happy. Shocked, for sure, but happy. Right?

The whole thing was so fucked-up.

There was too much shit in my life to dissect it, compartmentalize my feelings, and know what the right way to handle Angie, Dad, Grayson, Kenna, and my birth parents.

One problem at a time, and right now, Carter took precedence.

My stepbrother was smart. I refused to do anything that might jeopardize his faith in me. I had to convince Carter that while I was living with the enemy, I wouldn't double-cross. He would expect that of me because it was no secret how much I hated him.

I couldn't fake that shit.

The hatred was real.

But it was a mutual animosity he would trust.

It took two hours of arguing on Sunday during my first Elite takedown, which Mads demanded she be a part of, before I finally got Brock to agree to let me meet Carter alone. The fact he wanted to hook me up to a wire shouldn't have been a surprise. Nor should my refusal.

We came to an agreement. The Elite would give me space to talk to Carter, but it had to be in a public place. The Academy was our best bet. In between classes. The lunchroom. Anywhere but the parking lot. Carter and I had history with parking lots and I wasn't keen on having those memories in my head when we talked.

Third period had just ended when the announcement of a mandatory assembly echoed through the school. A unanimous groan went through the halls. "Any idea what's going on?" I asked Fynn, who had been waiting at the corner for me.

Fynn shrugged, seeming unconcerned. "Probably some lecture on safe sex or bullying. They usually do them once or twice a year."

Sometimes when I walked down the halls of Elmwood Academy, I was still struck by the unusual and gothic design. Huge cathedral ceilings hung overhead as I passed into the auditorium. The doorway was arched, black carved wood framing the entrance.

I spotted Carter walking in from the other side. "I'll catch up with you. There's something I need to take care of," I told Fynn, catching his eye.

Fynn's gaze narrowed but only briefly when he noticed Carter. Fynn gave me a short nod and took off down the aisle to find the Elite.

When opportunity strikes, you take it. This was the safest place to talk to Carter, in a crowded room with lots of noise and witnesses, including the Elite.

"Carter," I called out as I rushed to the other side, catching him before he turned down the aisle leading to rows of black seats. "Carter!" I said again, this time louder to be heard over all the voices talking.

I finally caught his attention. My skin immediately crawled as his eyes ran over me. It was the first time I'd been at school without a guard dog since my stepbrother decided to get gangster and take me hostage. Despite all the crowds, my veins tingled with unease. "Hey, you got a minute?"

Carter kept his eyes trained on mine. His lips slanted into a spiteful grin. "For you, sis, always."

Gag me.

I kept my face neutral even though my stomach felt like I'd eaten an entire bag of pop rocks and washed them down with a case of pop. It was all fizzy and crackly inside. "Look, you've made your point. I don't want to see any of my friends get hurt, okay?"

"So you've finally come to your senses. Good. Thanks to you, the police came knocking on our door. Dad wasn't too happy when he found out you were involved."

Bastard. He would try to make me somehow responsible. Since he was so smug, I assumed nothing came out of the police speaking with him. Typical. I swallowed against the gloating in his eyes, forcing myself to keep going. "What is it you want me to do?"

He shifted closer to me. It was a struggle to not back away. "Are you still crashing at Brock's?" he asked.

Nodding, I replied, "For the time being."

His grin turned into a triumphant smirk. "Why are you exactly? Don't tell me it is because of me?"

I snorted. "You aren't that important." But he was in all the ways that were bad about this world.

A crowd of kids weaved around us, but Carter ignored them. "Not like your fuck buddy, huh, but that's where you're wrong."

My heart plummeted, but I refused to let it show. "Can we cut the shit? I don't have a lot of time. They're watching."

"In that case, we better make this look convincing." He shifted his stance so he was in front of me, using his body as a blockade, a maneuver that screamed Carter. He had a way of isolating someone even in an auditorium filled with hundreds of students.

The flutters of restlessness that entered my belly increased tenfold. "Do you want the fucking thumb drive you're so obsessed with or not?"

Cater's mouth flattened. "I'm not sure I can trust you."

I expelled a ragged breath. "I know I can't trust you. But you're not giving me much of a choice here, are you?"

The last few stragglers made their way into the auditorium.

Carter and I were running out of time. "The rules are simple. Get me the thumb drive. I want everything the Elite have on me," he stated, like it was as easy as stealing candy from a baby.

I saw it then, for just a fracture of a second. Fear. "You're scared. You're afraid of them." Of course, I knew Carter had every reason to fear them. With what they had, it could ruin a lot of people's lives, including the reputation of the Academy.

That kind of information didn't belong in the hands of someone like Carter. The safest place was right where it was.

"Get me the thumb drive," he restated, his voice firmer this time. "And the passcode to his phone."

"What do you plan to do with it?"

"Not your business, sis."

I had a sickening thought. What if Carter didn't just want to destroy any evidence that could hurt him? What if he wanted to do some destroying of his own? Grayson said there was information on the Elite that could hurt the four of them. There was also information on Kenna, Grayson, and me, proving Angie had kidnapped me from the hospital.

I didn't want him to see just how much fear the idea of him having that information caused inside me. I lifted a single shoulder, feigning indifference. "Whatever. Keep your end of the deal, and I'll find out where the thumb drive is."

"And Brock's passcode."

I gritted my teeth. "What good is the passcode if you don't have the phone?"

His smile turns smug. "I don't need his phone, just access to his cloud."

"Fine," I barked out as needles tiptoed down my spine.

He reached out and grabbed my elbow as I turned to leave. "You've got two weeks."

I jerked out of his hold, my brows slamming together as I suppressed a shudder of revulsion. "Are you kidding?"

That stupid smirk was back plastered on his face. "It shouldn't be too hard. You are fucking him."

"After this, you never speak to me again," I spat.

Carter tugged on his black-and-blue tie. "We're family. We're stuck together."

Fuck. I was going to be sick—all over the Academy's plush carpet in front of the entire school. I was due for a round of gossip. What better way to get the school talking about me again than spewing right before an Academy announcement?

"You're nothing to me." I shoved my way past him and scanned the seats for Brock. It took me a minute of searching before I spotted them near the back of the auditorium.

I sunk into my seat next to Mads. "Girl, you look hung the fuck over."

My hands shook. I shoved them under my legs. "Carter has the kind of effect on me."

She shuddered. "Shit, he has that effect on most girls. Except for maybe Ava."

I followed her line of sight, seeing Carter take a seat next to the Queen B herself. Porter and Shawn were in the same row. Carter leaned close to Ava, whispering something in her ear. Ava said something back, a satisfied smirk on her painted lips.

Mads crossed her legs, a look of disgust on her face. "Nothing good can come out of that pairing. Please tell me they're not fucking."

I scrunched my nose. "How would I know?"

"Rumor is, she and her groupies are no longer standby girls."

The whole concept of having girls to hook up with was disgusting. "Good," I said.

Mads's eyes jerked back to mine. "Things are changing around here, and it is all because of you."

"Wonderful," I muttered as Principal Wallis took the stage.

* * *

Brock pulled me into his lap, his fingers lingering over my hips. I turned my head toward him, my eyes resting on that too gorgeous face. "What are you doing?" I asked shortly, despite the ache his touch started inside me.

"Setting a precedent," he said with a deliberate sneer to his lips.

His familiar heat pulled at me, and I could feel myself leaning into him. "And that is lap dances in the lunchroom? Which I am most definitely not doing, by the way."

He chuckled as one of his fingers hooked into one of the belt loops on my skirt. "That's not a bad idea, Firefly."

Mads scrunched her nose as she sat across from us at the table. "Gross. Can we not do this while I'm eating?"

I had to agree with Mads. This wasn't a lunch-worthy conversation. But my body was like *let's get it on*.

"I think you might be onto something," Micah added, grinning like a fool. "Imagine all the stress it could relieve in between classes."

Relaxing against Brock's chest, I rolled my eyes. "If you

have stress to deal with, hit the weight room," I suggested, lacing my fingers with Brock's for two reasons. First, because I wanted to touch him. Second, to keep his hand from going other places.

Grayson shook his head. "Why is it the moment Josie is around, the conversation somehow always turns to sex?"

"Because your sister is fucking hot."

Brock's eyes blazed at Micah as he kicked him under the table. Micah only laughed.

My lips twitched as I caught Micah's sparkling light blue gaze. "You guys realize this is not normal."

Micah shoved a handful of fries into his mouth. "Talking about sex?"

Someone shoot me.

Mads snorted a laugh. I had a feeling my friend wasn't as over Micah as she liked to believe. No one laughed at Micah's jokes but Micah.

"At Public, you'd never get away with having a girl on your lap. The teachers shut down the first signs of PDA. No kissing. No touching. No lap sitting," I said, shifting purposely in Brock's lap. He made a small groan that caused my lips to twitch at the corners. If he planned to make me sit on top of him the entire lunch period, then he would suffer for it.

"Public sounds like a drag," Micah groaned.

Fynn shrugged, a hint of a smile on his lips. "Your normal is not everyone's."

Very true.

"What happened with Carter?" Mads asked, changing the course of the conversation, thank God. Not that talking about Carter was any less stomach-turning.

"He took the bait," I said with a touch of bitterness. This was what we agreed on, but now that it was happening, I was having second thoughts. *This is the only way to keep your friends safe.* That's what I kept telling myself. But it wasn't just for Mads, Kenna, and Ainsley that I was willing to risk my safety. I had to do this for myself as well.

Fynn shook his head, picking at the pepperoni on his pizza. "So predictable."

Brock slid our joined hands in between my legs, the warmth of his touch seeping into my thigh. I told myself not to shiver under his touch. "His eagerness will be his downfall," he said, his voice remaining even whereas I was afraid to speak.

"Let's hope. He lacks the discipline to see this through," Fynn said, pointing out Carter's fatal flaw.

"Then we better make it convincing." I should have noticed the sudden change in Brock's tone, the husky texture that came into it. I might have been prepared when his fingers slipped into my hair and he fastened his lips to mine.

A voice told me I shouldn't be kissing him during school, not like this with his tongue tangled with mine. I didn't abhor public affection. It was the principle behind Brock's kiss. It would be one thing if he were my boyfriend.

That was not the case.

This kiss claimed me as not just a standby girl, but also Brock's current favorite, a position Ava prided herself on holding.

Not anymore, bitch.

Of course, the entire thing was a sham.

I definitely was not a standby girl.

As for Brock's favorite... that might have had a bead of truth to it. As far as I knew, he wasn't sleeping with anyone else but me.

I told myself not to let it go to my head.

A difficult task when my toes were curling under the table. I melted into him, sinking deeper into the kiss.

Someone cleared his throat.

"Enough," Grayson grumbled. "I can't sit here and watch the two of you make out."

Micah reclined in his chair, looking rather relaxed, a crooked grin on his lips. "I disagree. I'm rather enjoying myself. It's kind of like watching porn at school."

My cheeks flamed.

Brock's gaze cut across the table at Grayson. "This is part of the plan. We need Carter to believe Josie is—"

Grayson dropped a hand on the table with startling force. "My ass. Let's not pretend you aren't enjoying every second your lips are attached to hers. This isn't a game. When are you going to admit that something is going on between you?"

Mads's jaw dropped. She was thoroughly enjoying this, despite my discomfort. Micah too. He had his chair leaned back, balancing on two legs.

Brock scowled at my brother. "Josie and I have an under-standing."

"Oh, do you?" Grayson snapped, his expression calling Brock a liar.

I sat forward, putting a small amount of space between Brock and me. Not that it mattered. The lazy circles he drew on my inner thigh were driving me crazy. *Focus, Josie.* "I'm confused. Is this part of the plan?" Brock and Grayson bickering with each other was not a good thing.

"Who fucking knows," Fynn groused, staring at Brock and Grayson with disapproval.

I never did get an answer. The bell rang.

* * *

On my way to ninth period, I got a text from Ainsley. She must have finally found her phone.

I need to talk to you. Can you meet me after school? I don't want to be alone right now.

I read Ainsley's text twice as I sat down at my desk. Did she remember something from the other night?

My best friend needed me, the same friend who had always been there for me, and here I was thinking only about myself, that all the problems in the world revolved around me. Selfish. That's what I was being. And after what happened to her on Friday night, I'd be a shitty friend not to help her with whatever she was going through.

Of course. Are you okay? Should I be worried?

While I waited for her to respond, I leaned into the aisle toward the desk next to mine. "Hey, Mads. I need a favor."

She lifted a brow, popping a piece of gum into her mouth. "Anything."

I lowered my voice. "Can I borrow your car after school? I wouldn't ask if it wasn't important."

She raised a slim brow. "Everything all right?"

"I don't know. Ainsley texted me. She needs me."

"Enough said, girl. Here...." She dug out her keys and handed them to me. "I'll cover for you for as long as I can."

The second the bell sounded, announcing the end of class, I shot out of my seat before the teacher could excuse the class. I had only a small window of opportunity to sneak out of school without the guys knowing. Word traveled like a bad STD around here. They had practice and expected me to be there.

Brock would be livid but this was Ainsley. And now that I had a moment to dwell over her text, I was concerned.

Just meet me at Tommy's.

CHAPTER TWELVE

Tommy's was a local food joint on the other side of town not far from where I used to live. Lots of kids from Public hung out there after school. They had the best hotdogs on the planet. It was also where Ainsley worked part-time after school, so meeting her here wasn't a surprise.

From the Academy, it would take me twenty minutes to get to downtown Elmwood. By the time I sped out of the Academy parking lot, the Elite would realize I was gone.

I drove carefully across town, afraid to put so much as a fingerprint on Mads's car. At this time of the day, the roads were light until I got closer to downtown Elmwood, close to where Tommy's was. I found a parking spot with little difficulty and made sure to lock up as I got out. A car like this stuck out like an orange in a basket of bananas on this side of town.

Scanning the one-way parking slots, I didn't see Ainsley's

car. My fingers flew over the keys, sending her a text. **I'm here, where are you?**

Her reply came a moment later. **Around back.**

I left my stuff in the car, grabbing just my phone and Mads's keys. A gust of wind tainted with the scent of fried food brushed over me, tossing my hair off my shoulders. Dry leaves blew over the sidewalk, crunching and swirling at my feet as I made my way toward the employee entrance.

There was something so familiar and comforting being back in my old stomping ground. I knew every inch of old downtown. If you could look past some of the run-down buildings and debris littered on the ground, it had a charm about it that I found quaint and comforting.

Hooking a left at the corner of Tommy's, I waved at the shopkeeper from the next building who was outside straightening her sale rack of vintage clothes. I wasn't too far from Mads's mom's shop, just a few blocks.

The sun still provided plenty of sunlight, but shadows darkened the back of the alley. For a split second, a tingle of unease tapped over the nape of my neck but I brushed it off. It was the middle of the day, only a handful of steps from the main road, with people popping in and out of shops and restaurants.

How unsafe could it be?

This was my town.

And from what I'd learned living in the upper part of Elmwood, it was more dangerous there than it was here. My shoulders relaxed as I glanced past the dumpsters and folding chairs used for smoke breaks, looking for my friend.

"Ainsley?" I called, my voice echoing off the brick alley walls.

Footsteps clattered over the blacktop behind me, where I had entered the alley. I turned around expecting to see my friend's rainbow hair shining in the sun.

Not Ainsley.

Ava.

And she wasn't alone.

A string of F-bombs went off in my head.

She stepped into the alley, Izzy and Emily following. The three of them made a wall across the exit. The only exit. They were dressed in all black, the hoods on their sweatshirts pulled up. Even in the nefarious attire, they still looked like rich bitches, but I wasn't stupid enough to mistake what this was. Or underestimate them.

My stomach dropped.

Despite the unease worming itself within me, I glared openly at the three of them, my gaze eventually settling on Izzy. She and I had unfinished business from when she had lured me into Carter's trap. I still didn't know why she had done it or what she gained from helping my stepbrother.

Or did she just hate me that much?

It didn't matter, the reasons why.

Not now.

I shook my head, forcing my lips to curve in my best I-don't-give-a-shit smirk. It wasn't as snarky as I'd like. "How original. Mean girls gang up on the competition to deliver a painful warning. If pushing me down the stairs didn't work, you think this will?" I had no intention of making this easy for them; nor did I understand how my voice remained steady, but I was damn proud of myself.

"This is just the beginning," Emily sneered.

"The beginning of what?" They had me cornered, and unless I could make a run for it and get past the three of them, this wouldn't end well.

Could I scream for help?

It was doubtful with all the noise from the kitchen equipment running and music filtering through a cracked back door that anyone would hear me.

Did I have time to call 911 or Brock? Someone?

Ava took a step closer, Izzy and Emily shadowing her every move. "You shouldn't have come to the Academy," Ava said, her warning clear.

"Things will only get worse from here," Izzy added.

How much worse could it get? "All this because I slept with Brock. You guys have some serious territorial issues. You do realize you don't own them. Any of them. I'd say that they own you. Do you have any idea how pathetic this makes you look?" I was literally rambling, anything to keep them from putting their hands on me. Maybe I could keep them talking long enough for me to use my phone before they beat the shit out of me.

My thumb swiped up on my phone as I gripped the side of it.

Ava shrugged as if my insults bounced right off her. "The Elite have their rules, and we have ours."

"Let me guess, I broke your rules by fucking Brock." I hit

the number nine button on the phone. At least, I was pretty sure it was the right one. The stupid keyboard made a clicking noise, drawing Ava's glare to my phone.

Fuck.

A sneer touched her lips as her hand shot out, smacking into the hand that clutched my phone. "This is your punishment."

I groaned as my phone went tumbling to the ground, clattering over the blacktop.

Shit.

"I'm not a fucking child," I hissed, adjusting the key in my hand. Thank god Mads's house key dangled on the little ring, because the car fob was absolutely useless in a fight. But a key...

It wasn't great. But it also wasn't nothing.

"I warned you." Ava held up a familiar-looking phone. It was Ainsley's. I recognized the custom case splattered with photo booth pictures of Ainsley and me from last year at the Elmwood Festival.

I glanced from the phone to Ava's smug face. "How did yo—?" My heart started to race as I put together pieces of the last few days. "You were at the party last weekend," I concluded, remembering she hadn't cheered that night. I hadn't thought much of it.

A wicked grin graced her shiny lips. "She was too easy of a target. It was so pitiful. I'd never seen anyone so desperate to be noticed."

"Bitch," I hissed, my fists bunching at my sides.

"You think you can replace me?" Ava snarled, her eyes turning wild like a feral beast.

"Not think, I already have." So not smart to antagonize the

skank and her evil minions, seeing as I was outnumbered and it was clear I'd been set up, but when it came to Ava, I lacked caution.

I despised the girl.

She had done nothing but make my life hell since I'd come to the Academy.

Fuck it.

I shoved forward and braced myself for the torment that was about to follow, but I'd at least have the satisfaction of delivering the first hit. And I was going for the queen bitch herself. My fist thrust forward, Mads's key tight in my grip as it slashed along the side of Ava's cheek. Not quite the spot I'd aimed for but as long as it left a mark, I didn't care.

Someone grabbed my hair, another my shirt, the material ripping. I was yanked backward while Ava cursed, a clutching the side of her face. "You bitch. This is going to hurt twice as much for that." With an open palm, she slapped me across the face.

As someone who's been slapped more than once, the sting that flared over my cheek was familiar, but damn, it still hurt every fucking time.

I blindly punched and smacked at the hands holding me, nails scratching. I kept fighting them. It didn't do much good once the first kick blasted me in the gut, knocking the air out of my lungs. I hit the ground, gasping wildly. Before I could catch a breath, a shoe landed into my side.

Sweet Jesus.

Pain burst through me from the force of the hit. I clamped

my mouth closed, swallowing the cry of agony. I kicked out at them, over and over again.

"She's insane."

"Ouch. Dammit."

"Hold her down."

A hand latched onto my leg, another stepped on my ankle. Instinctually, I turned onto my side and lifted my arms to cover my head as I tried to curl myself into a tiny ball. I grunted as I took another hit in my lower abdomen, then one to the hip. The torture seemed to go on infinitely. Logically it had probably only been a minute or two, but they were the longest minutes of my life.

No tears. No pleas. No cries. I refused to make a sound.

Blood dripped along the side of my head, and one of my eyes was swollen shut. I tried to fight them off. I definitely didn't make it easy for them.

"Hey!" someone yelled. "Get off her!"

Had I imagined a male voice? *Please, God.* The beating stopped, and a shudder of relief went through me.

"The fun's over," Ava hissed. "For now."

"We're not done with you yet, James."

"Let's fucking go."

Footsteps scrambled, pounding away. "Stop!" someone yelled. Seconds later, a shadow moved above me.

"Oh, dear God," someone else choked out, an elderly woman.

"Call 911," the deep voice ordered.

Whoever this person was, they just became my hero.

If this guy hadn't stumbled upon me, how much further would Ava have gone?

He crouched down, careful not to touch me. "Don't move."

I don't think I could even if I tried. Through my good eye, I stared up at his face, but his features were blurry, my vision hampered from the swelling that was only getting worse. I wanted to thank him, but making my lips form words proved to be too damn painful.

"Just hang on," the guy reassured over and over. His voice was deep and solid, which I found soothing. Strong but gentle fingers wrapped around my hand. "I've got you."

Closing my eyes, I gritted my teeth against the throbbing pain and turned my thoughts to the long, long list of ways I'd make Ava regret what she'd done. I didn't even want to think what the Elite would do when they found out.

Lose their shit.

Kill Ava and her bandit of whores.

Not that they didn't deserve it, because right now, I was feeling all sorts of vengeance.

He stayed with me and I was so grateful. "I'm sorry I didn't get here sooner," the guy said, regret heavy in his tone.

I drew in a quivering breath, the air like shards of glass and fire in my lungs. Sirens blared in the distance. It grew harder to breathe, but I forced myself to take it slow and steady. I didn't attempt to move but just lay on the ground, bleeding and clutching this stranger's hand.

Getting the ever-loving crap beat out of you was an experience words failed to describe. I could taste blood.

The next few minutes after the first responders arrived and

then the ambulance were a whirlwind of questions, needles, and finally meds. I was most eager for them to kick in and take the edge off the agonizing suffering of my body.

"Thank you," I managed to whisper to the guy who helped me, finally letting go of his hand as I was wheeled into the ambulance.

He smiled. "No more alleys, okay?"

CHAPTER THIRTEEN

I woke up disorientated and sore as fuck. Someone knocked on my hospital room door, and I realized that woke me up. I must have fallen asleep after the doctors patched me up and administered more pain medication. My eyes cracked open slowly as the door squeaked and my dad walked in. His eyes went through a range of emotions as he got his first look at me, and it was enough to tell me I was a fucking mess. I didn't need a mirror to tell me that. It was written all over his face.

"Dad?" I rasped.

"Hi, honey." He forced a smile, adding extra doses of happiness into the deep timbre of his voice. It didn't help, but I knew he meant well. What else could a parent do when their child was hurting and there was nothing they could do to take away the pain? You faked it.

I was so damn relieved it was him and not Angie. Someone

upstairs must have taken pity on me after the shit day this was turning out to be.

"How did you know I was here?" I rasped.

His face paled after stepping into the room. The old band T-shirt he wore had a grease stain on it, so I knew he had rushed over from the shop. "The hospital called me."

Why him and not Angie?

"They weren't able to reach your mother, and I'm still listed as your secondary contact," he explained, seeing the unspoken question crossing my expression.

Oh, thank God. "I'm glad," I said, making the mistake of attempting a smile. The cut on my lip protested, and I thought it might have started bleeding again.

"How are you feeling?" he asked, pulling the chair in the corner close to the bed. He sat down as he waited for me to respond.

"Like I got the crap beat out of me," I admitted.

"You don't look so hot. I've had my fair share of split lips and black eyes. Who did you get into a fight with, a troll?"

A hollow chuckled escaped which turned into a wince. "No jokes. I can't laugh. It hurts too much."

"I can do that, considering you always thought my jokes were lame."

"Dad," I groaned.

"You want to tell me what happened?" he asked, all humor aside. His expression sobered, those blue eyes brimming with concern.

I averted my gaze, staring at the foot of the hospital bed where my feet were. "I got jumped. It was stupid."

His rigid shoulders dropped a fraction. "What were you doing at Tommy's? Shouldn't you have been in class?"

Ugh. Busted. "It's complicated." I didn't want to go into the details.

He wasn't going to let me get off that easily. "How about you uncomplicate it for me, Josie? The police want to speak with you."

I frowned, or rather I attempted to frown. "Now?"

"It's best to do this while the details are still fresh in your head but if you're not up to it..."

As much as I didn't want to deal with the police, I'd just as soon get it out of the way. "Okay," I agreed.

"You're sure this has nothing to do with school or at home?" he pressed.

Why would he ask that? I tried to remember our conversations and if I'd mention anything about the mean girls at the Academy. He knew how I felt about Angie and Carter.

Tears finally sprang to my eyes, hot and biting. It all came crashing down on me, and I felt so out of my depth.

Dad reached over and grabbed my hand, giving it a gentle squeeze as he placed his other hand on top of our joined ones. "You don't have to tell me. Not now, if you don't want to. I didn't mean to..."

It was difficult to see him for so many reasons. He was clearly upset and struggling to control his emotions while also maintain that solid father figure persona I'd always depended on. But it was also difficult because seeing him reminded me he wasn't my biological father, a surreal concept I still struggled to grasp. "Dad." My lips trembled.

"It's okay. Everything will be okay. The doctor said there is no internal bleeding. A few bruised ribs, but most of the injuries are superficial."

Well, pop the confetti and break out the champagne. Nothing about my body felt superficial.

Despite the sarcastic thoughts, it was a relief knowing no real permanent damage had been done. The cuts and bruises would heal. I did sort of remember the doctor explaining the same thing, but the pain had been too severe to retain the information.

But everything wouldn't be okay. Not a chance in hell.

I couldn't tell that to him, so I just nodded, tears pooling in my eyes.

He patted the top of my hand. "The doctor said I could take you home soon. They just need to wrap up the paperwork. All your X-rays came back satisfactory. Once you finish giving the police your report, we'll go home. Okay, kiddo?"

Home?

Did he mean to the Pattersons'? My head shook too hard and too fast, but I didn't care. "I can't go home. Dad, I—"

"I know that you haven't been staying with your mother," he interrupted before I went on a panicky tangent. "She called me last week after your detention."

My racing heart slowed. "Oh."

Unfolding his hand cautiously from mine, he fussed with the blankets. "I think it's best you stay with me while you recover. I'll handle your mother. That's if it's okay with you."

This time I nodded slowly. "Yes," I exhaled.

A nurse came in then, asking for some signatures on the

release papers. She went over some instructions with my father, prescriptions that needed to be filled for stronger pain medication and how to care for the wounds.

Buzz. Buzz. Buzz.

My phone vibrated on the bedside table. Two seconds later, it went off again and again. I was afraid to look at the notifications coming through. Word had probably gotten around. Ava would see to that. I didn't want to talk to anyone. Not yet. I just wanted to get out of the hospital and go home. I wanted to be surrounded by my things, the few I had left behind, sleep in my old bed, and forget for a few hours that Elmwood Academy existed.

I also really, really wanted Brock, but I refused to let myself admit that I needed him, that I wanted to see him because that rang too close to girlfriend vibes.

My phone went off again. Both the nurse and my dad snuck a glance at it. "It might be your mom," Dad said, offering what would be a responsible excuse for most teenagers. Not me. He probably couldn't tell with my face all messed up, but I shot him an are-you-kidding-me look.

Dad reached over and handed me my phone. "You should check it just in case."

The screen had a crack in the corner and the protective case had a few scratches on it from being knocked to the ground. Now I really needed a new phone. Unlocking the passcode, a slew of notifications ran down the screen.

But only one stood out.

Firefly, where the hell are you?

That had been sent over an hour ago. He had texted six

more times after that. Stalker much? But in truth, he had every right to be worried. I was known to take off, disregard Brock's rules. Along with over a dozen messages from the other guys and Mads, there were also numerous missed calls, including three from Ainsley's house phone.

Had she heard?

I sent a quick text to Brock, assuming he would let Mads and the others know. I'd call Ainsley later tonight when I got home.

Home.

I was going home.

The thought filled me a contentment I hadn't felt in a long time.

I'm at the hospital with my dad.

I should have known that a quick simple text wouldn't be enough for Brock. My phone vibrated seconds after I sent the message. **What hospital?** I could almost feel the sudden uptick in emotion through the phone. Concerned? Maybe. But also pissed off.

I was guessing more pissed off.

Uh, no way would I tell him what hospital. He'd be here in two seconds, most likely followed by the rest of the Elite. The hospital didn't need the distraction, because the four of them sauntering down the halls would incite a riot. **I'm leaving after I give my statement to the police. They are discharging me.**

We need to talk.

A part of me wanted to see him...but for all dangerous reasons. I wanted to fall against him and have his strong arms hold me. I wanted him to tell me that he'd take care of Ava. That she would cut out the insane, jealous girlfriend act and leave me alone. I wanted him to make impossible promises that for a short time, I'd believe.

Those all screamed boyfriend. *Brock is not my boyfriend*, I reminded myself. Before I told him to get his fine ass to the hospital, I sent back a one-word reply. Short and to the point. **Later.**

Brock would not be satisfied until he got answers. **Tell me you're okay.**

I'll live. Much to Ava's disappointment.

Firefly.

Damn him. Reading that stupid nickname caused a knot of emotions to rise into my throat, where it got clogged. I could hear him growl my name in my head. It was almost like he was in the room with me. That one word spoke volumes.

I sighed and put the phone down, lacking the energy to keep texting. Whether he liked it or not, Brock would have to wait.

* * *

My body screamed at every bump and curve in the road during the car ride home. I didn't say much, just closed my eyes and listened to the low rock music coming out of the speakers. After speaking with the police and recounting what I could remember and who was involved, I was exhausted.

Dad helped me get from the car to inside the house. It sucked having to rely on someone for the simplest of tasks, but my injuries could have been much worse.

Looking at my bloodstained shirt, you would have thought I died. It was amazing how much blood a few cuts, even deep ones, could produce.

"Bedroom or couch?" Dad asked as he paused in the entryway, waiting for me to give him a direction.

I took a long second to soak in the familiarity of being home, the scent more manly than before but still somehow the same. The small ranch had only two bedrooms, but for the three of us, it had been enough.

At least, it had been enough for Dad and me.

Nothing was ever enough for Angie.

I shook off the thought, not wanting to think about her. "Actually, I want to take a shower." I had blood crusted in places that blood shouldn't be.

He dropped his car keys into the little basket on the table by the door. "Good idea."

"Then couch," I added. "Do you have to go back to work?" I didn't want to be alone, and I was afraid that feeling might linger with me for a while.

Damn Ava.

He walked in front of me, clearing a few discarded cups and things lying around. "No, I'm not leaving. I'm taking a few days off. How about you take that shower, and I'll make us some soup. You pick the movie."

"Thanks, Dad. For everything."

He paused, his eyes meeting mine. "You don't have to thank me, Josie. I'm just sorry I wasn't there." His voice grew rough.

"There is no way you could have possibly known." I berated myself for not being more careful and guessing something was wrong. I'd just been off-balance since Carter messed with Ainsley.

"Well, when you're ready to talk about it, I'm here. In the meantime, I think you might still have some old clothes in your room." He gestured down the hall.

Was there anything better than old, comfy clothes? Not in my world, particularly when I didn't want anything pressing or rubbing against the raw parts of my skin. The wrappings and bandages kept some of them protected. Dad helped me cover them with plastic wrap and keep them from getting wet.

Alone in the shower, my mind went to all those dark places I didn't want to relive. Yet, I couldn't stop the memories. Ava's, Izzy's, and Emily's faces flashed behind my eyes. Their laughs echoed in my ears. The thud and whack of the shoes hitting my flesh, inciting quick bursts of pain that brought fresh tears to my eyes.

I was fucking angry. And angry tears were the worst.

I didn't like to cry. And crying because of Ava only fed that force of hot rage. The tears made me angry. The anger made me cry. It spun in a vicious cycle until I had no more tears left to fall.

Shivering despite the water turned up to hot and the steam billowing around my face, I turned off the water before my skin could wrinkle any more.

When I emerged from the bathroom in a pair of pink sweats and a baggy T-shirt out of my old closet, Dad was waiting with a glass of water and two pain pills. My hero.

He got me all settled on the couch, propping me up on a pillow from my bed and draping a plush throw over me. It reminded me of when I was little and sick. He always made a bed out of the couch for me to lounge in so I wouldn't be alone in my room. I was one of those people who didn't like to be isolated when they felt like shit.

"I called your mother while you were in the shower." He set a bowl of steaming cream of chicken rice soup in front of me. My favorite. "She isn't thrilled that you are here, but we both agreed it was for the best. At least for a few days." He took a seat on the love seat. "She's worried about you, Josie."

A ridiculous snort escaped me. That was the joke of the century. If she were truly worried about me, she would take my claims about Carter seriously instead of brushing me off and caring more about the Patterson reputation.

My sarcastic skepticism wasn't lost on Dad. "And so am I," he added. "Your mom might not be affectionate or motherly, but she does care about you, Josie."

"I'm sorry. I just have a hard time believing that right now." This might have been the opportune moment to tell my dad about me not being his biological daughter, that Angie had taken me from the hospital. But staring into his rugged face, I couldn't bring myself to do it. Not yet. His reaction scared me. Right now, I needed to be here. I needed him.

My time with my father was limited. I didn't want to ruin what little we had or hurt him, because if he didn't know what Angie had done, I couldn't imagine what kind of blow it would be to learn your daughter wasn't biologically yours and that in fact, your daughter died at birth.

If he did know, he wasn't the man I thought he was.

But between my two parents, I chose him.

"You don't have to be worried," I said, lying through my teeth. "I'll be okay."

"Worrying about you is my job," Dad replied, ripping a hunk of bread off for me before dipping his own into his soup.

I managed to spoon down a small bowl, nothing impressive, and sipped on hot tea during the movie. Somewhere between "Yer a wizard, Harry" and "Five points to Gryffindor," I dozed. The movie was more than half over when the doorbell rang.

Yawning, I went to stretch, forgetting for a split second that my body felt like it got hit by a wrecking ball. It was quick to remind me. I winced and swore under my breath as my dad stood up to get the door.

"Expecting company?" he asked with a raised brow.

"Uh, I don't think so." But as soon as the words left my mouth, I had a sneaking suspicion who was at the door.

That inkling was confirmed when I heard a familiar voice ask, "Is Josie here?"

Brock. If I'd been able, my head would have whipped around over the back of the couch. This house was a fraction of the size of the one Brock lived in. With slow movements, I could glance in the direction of the front door and catch a glimpse of my dad.

He stood so he blocked the opening. "Now isn't a good time."

"Dad, it's okay," I said from the couch. "He's a friend." Why did that sound so strange coming off my tongue? Friend? Brock wasn't just a friend, but I couldn't define what he was to me. Whatever was going on between us couldn't be defined.

It was better to get this over with before Brock did something stupid and reckless.

Dad gave Brock another long stare, assessing this guy he didn't know and deciding whether or not he would let him into his house. "Five minutes. That's all," he finally conceded, stepping to the side to let Brock in.

Brock walked in, and instantly the room seemed smaller. My eyes devoured him, or what they could with the swelling. Once my gaze landed on him, I couldn't look away.

Dad must have picked up on the vibe that something was going on between us. "I'll give you guys a few minutes. I'll just be in the other room." He gave Brock one last glance, an unspoken warning passing to him—*you hurt my daughter, I will hurt you.*

Brock rounded the couch and flinched. The master of control and feelings struggled now to remain unaffected by my injuries. I'd seen myself in the mirror. I knew it looked bad. Really fucking bad. And over the next few days, it would get worse.

His jaw tightened, the muscles along his neck pulsing. He sat down on the old wood coffee table close to me, looking me up and down with a frown, which turned into a nasty scowl. Something like murder flashed in his eyes and then was gone in the next instant. "Wow, Firefly. You look like you walked into a wall. Repeatedly."

"Fucking funny. What are you doing here?"

"You didn't honestly believe I wouldn't find you. When I heard what happened..." His voice went gruff.

"Everyone knows?" I asked, trying to decide how I felt about the entire Academy knowing Ava beat me to a bloody pulp. It was a tad damaging to my pride.

His next words were said with dark venom that caused a shiver to tiptoe along my spine. "I'm not just going to kill her. I'm going to torture her first. Izzy and Emily too." When Brock made a threat like that, it was believable. Did I really think the Elite were capable of murder?

Yes.

The admission should have frightened me, and yet, it had the opposite effect. Having Brock close only filled me with security. No one would mess with me. It was those times I found myself alone that I got into trouble.

But also, screw that.

I refused to spend my life suction-cupped to a guy. I was not the girl who depended on a guy to keep her safe. I was fucking capable of doing it myself. Had done it my entire life. Brock was a magnificent lay, but I'd be damned if I stopped taking care of myself and leaned on him wholly. There had to be a balance. I had to be able to hold on to who I was. My identity could easily get swept up in the Elite if I weren't careful.

"Not if I get to her first," I replied, meaning every punch behind the threat. I hoped Ava, Izzy, and Emily had a few bruises of their own.

Leaning forward, he lifted his hand toward my face but then halted. "I'm so fucking sorry, Firefly. I should have seen this coming. I knew the bitch was crazy, but..."

You never know what a person is capable of. Ava showed Brock her true colors. I reached out and took his hand. "This isn't your fault. I'm the one who ditched out on class. It was so stupid." I could say that now, looking back.

"I wish I could've—"

"Wish you could've what?" I folded my arms and looked him up and down. "Wish you could've stopped it?"

He drew back, frowning. "Something like that."

Tears filled my eyes and I hated them. I hated all the emotion welling up in me, burning me from the inside out.

I hated most of all the way I wanted him to make it better. Dangerous thoughts, leaning on someone else to make you happy, to take the pain away.

It wasn't healthy. Nothing about *us* was normal.

And I needed to stop using Brock as a crutch. At some point, he wouldn't be there for me to lean on. I didn't need another toxic relationship in my life.

And yet, Brock didn't feel destructive.

He felt... right.

He made me feel alive and safe. All the things I longed for.

"What happened?" he asked, his tone gentle despite the storm in his eyes. "The security guard detailing you got there too late."

So that was who saved me. Any other time I would have ripped into Brock for having someone follow me. Today was the only exception. I explained about the phone and how Ava used it to trick me into meeting who I thought was Ainsley.

Brock made a sound of aversion in the back of his throat. "This smacks of Carter. I can't help shake the feeling he is behind this, and Ava is his pawn."

Besides being a cold bitch, I had to wonder... "What do you

think he has on Ava?"

He scratched at the stubble under his chin. "A whole slew of shit. She is no angel. But I mean to find out." He broke off with a curse. "It seems the harder I try to protect you, the more hurt you get. I promised Grayson you'd be safe and if there is one thing I'm not, it is a liar. She won't touch you again. I'll take care of everything."

"That's what scares me," I admitted, picking at the tape securing the bandage around my wrist.

"You're okay here?" he asked, his gaze intense.

"With my dad?" I nodded slowly. "Yeah, I think so."

"After what happened, 'I think so' won't cut it. Not anymore, Firefly. I won't leave you unprotected."

"I appreciate the gesture, I really do, and for letting me stay with you, but I need to be here."

His gaze turned thoughtful. "Yeah, I get that, which is why I'm staying."

I blinked and shook my head. He had not just said he was staying at my dad's house. I had been kicked in the head too many times. "Excuse me?"

Brock cracked a grin for the first time since showing up. "You heard me."

I lowered my voice as I replied, "I hate to be the one to tell you this, but there is no way my dad is going to let a guy stay in my room or his couch for that matter."

He leaned in close to my ear. "Make it happen."

For the love of God, this guy... he was fucking impossible. "Fine," I conceded. "But you have to come back tonight. I'll sneak you in, if you're that concerned."

"I like how your mind works, Firefly." A butterfly kiss brushed over my ear and he pulled back with a satisfied expression.

"Like you gave me a choice," I grumbled, telling myself those were not fireflies zooming around in my belly.

"Now that is settled..." He reached into the pocket of his pants and pulled out a set of car keys. My car keys. "I had your car dropped off just in case you need it once you feel better. I didn't want you stranded without an escape."

"Thank you." And then I remembered. "Oh, I have Mads's keys."

"I'll have someone get the car." A few moments of silence passed between us. "Am I really just a friend, Firefly?"

His gaze ensnared mine, holding me captive. The heat in them flared up, or maybe it was just the temperature of my body. Either way, Brock had to stop staring at me like he wanted to join me on the couch and make me forget how much pain I was in.

How fitting.

Our relationship seemed based on us covering up our pain in each other.

"A-hem." From behind me, Dad cleared his throat. Brock and I both jumped like we'd just been caught doing some heavy making out on the couch instead of just gazing at each other. Don't get me wrong. It was some heavy-ass gazing.

"Josie," Dad called from where he hovered in the hallway, his tone disapproving. "You need to rest."

I carefully shifted on the couch so I could see my dad, moving with slow deliberate movements. "I have the whole week to rest," I countered, not quite ready to see Brock leave, regardless of how tired I was. The doctor wrote me a pass to stay home from school for the remainder of the week.

Brock stood, and my heart sank. "He's right, Josie. I should probably get going before the other guys decide to come see you themselves."

"Other guys?" Dad echoed, his brows raised, arms crossed over his grunge band T-shirt.

"Friends, Dad. Chill," I explained, groaning.

Brock glanced down at me. "You have a right to be cautious, but I don't want to see your daughter hurt any more than she already is." His gaze slid to where my dad still stood in the door-way, seriousness firmly rooted in his features.

My dad's resolve didn't waver. "Then you and I want the same thing. You might not have been involved, but I think it is best you stay away from my daughter."

My mouth dropped. "Dad!" I protested. "You don't know what you're doing. It's not Brock you should be worried about. Believe it or not, he is protecting me. I need him."

Did those words actually come out of my mouth? Could this get any more embarrassing?

Fuckkk.

Color stained my cheeks but I kept my chin up, letting my father know how important this was to me. I guess also, how important Brock was to me.

Shit. Shit. Shit.

I was so falling in love with him.

Without an ounce of contrition, Brock replied, "I can't do that."

A hush fell over the house, my dad's jaw set. I could see he was about to say something, but his attention and Brock's were distracted as they both glanced in the same direction. Red and blue lights flashed through the drawn curtain hung over a large picture window that faced the front of the house, saving me from further awkwardness. Dad's narrowed eyes went from the window to Brock and back to the window with accusations in his eyes.

Despite what my dad might be thinking, I knew there was no way in hell Brock would have called the police. "Did you call the cops?" I hurled at my father. Hurt and betrayal laced my voice.

"No, of course not," he retorted, still staring at the window and the lights rotating through it.

I didn't bother to ask Brock. Brock strutted to the window and peeked through a small crack in the curtain. "There is a squad car parked out front. Two officers are on their way up to the door."

"I'll handle this," Dad said, striding toward the entryway.

The doorbell rang a moment later. Brock gave me a look, conveying a message. *Don't say anything. I'll take care of this.*

I rolled my one good eye, peeking over the back of the couch to the door.

Dad greeted the two policemen, the cuffs hooked to their belts clanging together. "Mr. James?" one of the officers prompted.

My fingers clutched onto the blanket as Dad answered, "Yes. Is there a problem?"

"That's what we're here to find out. Is that your Lexus in

the driveway, sir?" the officer asked.

Dad angled his head slightly out the door, taking in the sight of the red Lexus parked in his driveway for the first time. "No."

"Uh, Dad. It's mine," I said softly from the couch. "Brock dropped it off." I deliberately left off confessing that the car had been parked at Brock's house. He had driven me to school today, as he did most days.

"It was reported stolen by the owner an hour ago," the shorter police officer informed.

My mouth dropped as the reason for their visit registered. An hour, huh? Not long after Dad had gotten off the phone with Angie.

That fucking bitch.

I couldn't believe she'd stoop so low, especially after what happened to me.

Wait. Yes, I could.

And that was sad. So very sad.

Dread pitted in my stomach, disbelief twanging in my chest.

"You're telling me my ex-wife reported our daughter's car stolen?" Dad reiterated as if he too was shocked.

"We can't release that information," the other office stated.

Brock snorted, earning a scowl from everyone in the room, including the two cops.

One of them handed my dad the paperwork. "We'll be taking the car into possession," he informed as his walkie-talkie started sputtering information.

There went my chance at escape. Not that I wanted the car. Angie and Steven could have it.

Fuck them both.

CHAPTER FOURTEEN

"What happened to your car, Josie?" Dad asked as the Lexus was being loaded onto the tow truck. Brock took his leave after the news of my car being impounded with the whispered promise of seeing me later. The look he gave before he left was one full of wickedness, threads of sympathy, and underlying tendrils of anger.

I pouted, still on the couch, facing my father. "Mom sold it," I told him. "She wanted me to fit in." The bitterness was evident in my tone. I still held a grudge for her selling my old car right under my nose.

Dad swore under his breath, losing his usually neutral position in this divorce. Rarely did he ever badmouth Angie, despite her deserving the bulk of the blame in their failed marriage. Dad deserved so much better than her.

And I hoped one day he found a woman who appreciated

him and was worthy of his kind heart. For that to happen, he had to start dating.

He rubbed at his temple. "Why didn't you tell me?"

"I didn't want to hurt you. And I was angry at Angie."

He flinched just a fraction at me calling her by her first name. "I'll talk to her tomorrow. I'm sure this is just a misunderstanding."

"You're kidding, right? When are you going to wake up and see her for who she really is?" The words "she's not my mother" nearly tumbled off my lips.

He loosed a tired breath. "I know you and your mother have been going through a difficult time."

"Do not make excuses for her. You don't know what she is capable of. The unforgivable things she has done." I'd said too much, but I couldn't seem to stop myself. Venom brewed within me.

"What things, Josie?" he asked suspiciously, his hand dropping away from his face.

He couldn't possibly not have any inkling. "It doesn't matter now. She has Steven and Steven's money. I don't want anything from them."

I could see that he wanted to press me, but when I snuggled deeper into the couch and closed my eyes, he just sighed and let me be.

* * *

By nine o'clock I was ready for bed, partially because I was tired, but mostly because I wanted to see Brock. Living with him these last weeks, I'd grown more accustomed to his presence than I'd realized. Not to mention sleeping in his bed. My ten-year-old twin mattress didn't cut it. And I missed the warmth of this body, the gentle breathing of another person next to me, the sense of knowing I wasn't alone. The sex was an added bonus when it happened, which hadn't been often.

I kept staring at the clock, willing it to move faster, wondering when Brock would show. I waited for the text that never came. Ten o'clock rolled around and my dad came to check on me in my room and say goodnight.

Things were different, I realized.

And it just wasn't our disagreement about Angie.

Dad had changed.

But so had I.

And knowing the truth about my birth... rocked my world.

I'd thought coming here had been what I wanted. I'd thought putting miles between the Academy and me would clear my head. I'd thought space from the Elite would give me a new perspective.

I was wrong.

Their world had stained me, bled into my soul, and there was no scrubbing it clean.

I lay in the dark, trying to trick my mind into thinking my body didn't hurt or that my pride wasn't bruised. My thoughts turned to the cops. A sense of foreboding entered into my chest like a little seed. As the minutes went by, it sprouted roots, growing and tangling around my organs.

It had nothing to do with the Lexus being impounded. I didn't give a shit about the car.

Yet, I couldn't pinpoint what troubled me, only that it was bad.

A small knock tapped on my window, pulling me out of those dark thoughts. My heart spun, overwhelming the shroud of darkness within me. That's what Brock did. He chased away the evil. I eased out of bed to unlock the window. *What if it is not Brock?* A ribbon of doubt crossed my now paranoid mind.

My bedroom was on the side of the house with a window that faced my neighbor and another the backyard. Being a ranch, there were no heights to contend with.

Believe it or not, this was the first time I'd snuck a boy into my room. My parents had loved Harvey, but we hadn't spent a lot of time in my bedroom.

I peeled back a corner of the floor-length black curtain and held my breath. It came out in a relieved whoosh at the sight of Brock's gorgeous frowning face.

God, even upset he was ridiculously attractive. It was like the devil and an angel had a baby, producing the most heavenly-looking male who had a naughty streak that went deep into his core. Fearless. Calculating. Ruthless. Powerful.

Brock leaned against the window frame as I slid the glass pane up. Moonlight splintered across his face as he lifted his eyes, and my heart thrust against my chest. Hands shoved into his pockets, the starlight made his eyes glitter.

I was so falling in love with him, even as I told myself not to. My pulse raced faster. "You climbing in or just going to lurk like a creeper?"

He snorted. "As if I have a creepy bone in my body."

True. But his ego didn't need me to confirm it. He eased

himself through the opening and closed the window behind him as I hobbled back to the bed, waiting for him to join me. When he just stood near the window, I angled my head to the side, regarding him. "You can't just stand there. It's making me nervous."

A single brow arched. "Since when do I make you nervous, Firefly?"

"Just sit down," I groaned, patting the bed.

Seconds later, the mattress dipped under his weight, but there was still too much space between us. From the moment he showed up at my house earlier tonight, I wanted to be in his arms, engulfed by his scent and strength. I didn't know why it was so hard for me to ask.

He brushed a stray piece of hair behind my ear with the greatest care, a gentleness I didn't know he was capable of possessing. "Is this okay?"

"Yes," I whispered. "I'm not going to break... any more," I added with a lopsided grin.

He shook his head. "I don't know how you can have a sense of humor about any of this."

"If I don't, I'll lose my fucking mind." A flash of something like respect or admiration passed over his features. I put a hand to his chest, just over his heart, giving in the urge to touch him without asking him for what I wanted. "Why are you here?" I asked. I was done with the games. If I took away anything from what happened today, it was that the lies stop; the secrets too.

No more.

No more excuses.

And that included my own secrets.

He cleared his throat. "I promised Grayson I wouldn't leave you alone."

Propped on a pile of pillows behind me, I retorted, "Bull-shit. Why are you really here? What is this we are doing? You and me?" I came right out and asked what I couldn't get off my mind.

His fingers forked into his dark, windblown hair. "I don't know, Firefly. I just know that I can't stay away from you. Even though I should." The confession didn't seem to make him happy. If anything, it had the opposite effect, his lips turning down.

It was a start. Not a very good one. He literally told me nothing, other than he too was struggling to figure out what was between us.

Brock shook his head. "I never should have involved you. I didn't expect this. I don't like surprises, and you definitely took me by surprise."

I placed a hand on his arm, drawing his eyes to me. There were shadows there, hidden in his face. "You're not the only one who was surprised. I had plans, you know."

His lips twitched, and the shadows faded just a sliver. "Oh, really. Like what?"

"Well, for starters, I was going to get the hell out of this town, go to college."

"Has that changed?"

"No." But at this rate, I might not make it out of high school. "I just feel as if I've fallen off track. I thought I'd be applying to colleges, visiting campuses. Instead, college has been the last thing on my mind."

He nudged gently near my hip. "Make room, Firefly. You need to lie down and I don't plan on sleeping sitting up."

When he reached out, I shifted into his arms and let myself rest fully against him. I guess that was my answer, and for the first time since the alley, I could breathe. The pressure on my chest lifted, the weight on my shoulders eased. I didn't have to handle everything on my own.

Not that the warmth and support of his arms changed anything.

I don't know how, but he managed to fit onto my bed and tuck me into his arms. I was more or less lying on top of him. Not that I was complaining. Not in the slightest.

"Are you comfortable? Are you in pain?" he murmured softly, his woodsy scent hitting my senses.

"No," I whispered. "Not in the slightest." Thank you, painkillers. They gave me the chance to spend the night smashed into my twin-sized bed with Brock Taylor.

"Don't worry, Firefly. You'll get back on track," he assured softly with such conviction anyone would have believed him. "The guys and I will make sure of it."

Snuggling deeper into him, I finally let my heavy eyes drift closed, the steady beat of his heart pulsing under my cheek. I had just fallen asleep when something woke me back up. My gaze lifted to see Brock's eyes already open.

A tiny ping hit the glass pane. And then another. "Is someone throwing rocks at my window?" I groaned, annoyed that I'd been woken up. I was far too comfortable to fucking move.

Brock ran his knuckles along my underarm. "Don't tell me. Old boyfriend?"

I yawned and followed it up with a hissing wince, the cut on my mouth protesting against being stretched. "Not funny. What if it's Carter?" Ribbons of unease wove through me, banishing the last remnants of sleep.

"I hope it is. I'll kill him." Brock's temper flared to the surface as he untangled himself from the bedsheets and me. He did so carefully.

Was that anticipation I saw in his eyes? I put a hand on his arm, halting him from getting out of the bed. "Maybe you shouldn't look."

His dark brows bunched together. "I'm not scared of Carter."

"I never said you were." But maybe he should be. Besides, I was suddenly plenty worried for the both of us.

I chewed on the inside of my cheek as Brock went to the window, brushing aside the curtain. From where I lay on the bed, I could only see the darkness of night, but the visible relaxing of the muscles in his back told me it wasn't Carter.

I couldn't think of a single person who would use my window other than Ainsley, but she'd definitely call first or text. We had talked briefly. She had been worried and pissed, all the appropriate responses to your best friend getting jumped by a gang of mean girls. She'd gotten a new phone, so I didn't bother to tell her what happened to her old one. Knowing Ainsley, she'd harbor guilt that it was her phone that drew me to the alley.

Brock muttered a curse. "I should have guessed."

"Who is it?" I inquired from the bed, hardly able to stand the suspense.

A devilishly handsome blond stuck his head through the window, shooting me a dimpled grin. "Hey, Josie Jo."

I blinked from where I lay on the bed. "Micah?"

"They're all here," Brock said, looking anything but pleased. He tousled his dark hair, fluffing up any bedhead.

"All?" I echoed.

Brock's lips twitched.

"We had to see you for ourselves," Fynn's said from somewhere behind Micah.

The next thing I knew, Micah, Fynn, and Grayson had climbed through my window. My bedroom was not big enough for four guys, especially four high school football players. Not to mention, my dad was down the hall. It was one thing to sneak a guy into my room. It was a fucking other level to sneak in four.

But a part of me was touched they cared enough to show up. Their concern squeezed my heart. How the hell had the Elite manage to weasel so quickly not just into my life but my heart as well?

Grayson jerked his head in greeting to Brock. "Figured you'd be here." A look passed between them.

I maneuvered myself into a sitting position on the bed, eyes glancing warily at my locked bedroom door. Hopefully, Dad was fast asleep. He tended to be one of those people who not even a bomb going off would wake up.

Fynn whistled as he got a look at me. "Damn, JJ, you took a beating."

"She didn't hold back, did she," Micah added. "Stupid bitch. She should know better than to mess with ours."

Grayson's jaw hardened. "No one messes with family."

Tonight, for the first time, I felt like part of the Elite. I almost didn't care that it took getting my ass beat to get here. Feeling like I belonged like I was family, and it made me want to tear up and cry.

So not very Elite like.

I shoved back the tears threatening to spill out of my eyes.

"Fuck this," Grayson bit out. "I'm done dicking around, being patient. This asshole is going down. Ava too."

"What do you have in mind?" Micah asked, the corner of his mouth curving.

Plotting seemed to be an Elite pastime.

They guys got comfortable in my room, finding wherever they could to sit or lean against the wall. "I appreciate you guys stopping by, I really do," I interrupted before any nefarious plans could be made. "But I can't have you all in here."

Grayson rolled his eyes. "You and Brock can take one night off from bonking. Jesus. You just got out of the fucking hospital."

I pinned my brother with a hard look. "For your information, my sex life is not open for discussion or any of your business, but this has nothing to do with sex. My dad is down the hall," I explained. They were doing a decent job at keeping their voices low. I had to give them credit for that, but at some point, someone was going to knock something over. Not that my dad would hear it. There was just something in the anticipation of being caught I couldn't handle right now.

A mischievous smile touched Micah's lips. "This isn't the first time we've snuck into a girl's bedroom. We got this under control."

"Individually or together? Like all four of you in one girl's room?" I questioned, and then I shook my head. "Never mind. I don't want to know."

Micah's stupid grin widened. "I have to admit, I always wondered what your room would look like." His eyes spanned the cramped space, taking in what he could see in the small amount of moonlight streaming through the window. "It's pretty much how I imagined."

"They aren't all spending the night, are they?" I asked, turning to Brock.

"No," he stated firmly from where he perched on the edge of the bed closest to me.

"Hell, yes," Micah said at the same time. "Slumber party. When was the last time we had one of those?"

"Last weekend," Grayson stated flatly. "Every weekend. What do you think all those parties that you end up crashing all night are?"

"Good point. Josie Jo, you got anything to drink? Something strong. I needed a damn bottle after what you put us through."

I snorted. Not to mention what *I* went through. "No one is raiding my dad's beer stash."

Micah wasn't the only one to groan, but even I had to admit, I could use a drink.

"Ava and Carter think they've gotten the upper hand," Brock stated, steering the conversation away from booze before things derailed, because, with Micah, the nonsense could go on for hours.

Fynn sat on the floor under the window, his knees bent, elbows resting on them. If he had stretched out his long legs, they would have taken up over half the room, I swear. "We need to destroy that alliance," he said.

"And how do we plan to do that?" Grayson asked, tone somber. His baseball cap was pulled down low, shielding most of his eyes and making him look damn right criminal.

Brock tapped his thumb against his knee. "We give her what she wants."

"Does anyone know what that crazy lunatic wants?" Micah questioned.

One by one, the Elite turned to Brock, and my heart plummeted. They couldn't possibly be thinking...

"Me," Brock said without any infliction in his voice or change in his dark expression.

I, on the other hand, had an array of emotions. Mainly horror and disgust.

He wasn't serious.

Oh, but he was.

The idea of Ava and him together made me want to hurl.

"She wants to be at the top. I can do that just as quickly as I tossed her aside," he added grimly.

"More importantly, she wants to be the It girl. The one who snags Brock wholly, no sharing." Fynn's gaze shifted to me, and my cheeks warmed. Was he suggesting that I was the girl who snagged Brock?

No way.

Not possible.

He just didn't understand the strange and unhealthy arrangement Brock and I had.

"No," I hissed, making sure to keep my voice from rising like it wanted to do. My chest tightened. I'd been around these guys just long enough to start to understand how their minds worked. What they were suggesting, implying... "No," I said again when not a single one of them refuted me or tried to pacify me.

Just the opposite.

"I'm going to crush her," Brock said coldly. "Since murder really isn't an option."

"There has to be another way," I rebutted, absolutely hating the idea of Brock and Ava. Why was I getting so defensive? I was acting like a jealous girlfriend, and everyone in the room was thinking the same thing. I wasn't Brock's girlfriend. I had no claim on him.

But... Brock and Ava...?

Fuck no.

Fury flooded me, making my head throb and dulling the effects of the painkillers. The web of lies and deception these guys wove just went deeper and deeper. I felt as if I was stuck in a dark tunnel with no end in sight, no light to guide me out; I was just steeped in darkness.

My lips pressed tight together as my heart thundered.

"It will probably work," Fynn said in agreement. "Ava doesn't know who she is if she isn't the most popular and desired girl in school."

"You can't be serious," I gasped to Brock.

"Ava's motives were purely selfish. I won't let what she did to you go. It's been decided," he said with an air of finality, like a judge slamming down his gavel. His words hung in the air.

As I glanced around the room and saw the resolve in each of their faces, I knew I was outnumbered. Nothing I said or did would change their minds. I let out a sigh of defeat. "I don't know how much longer I can keep lying," I said, my eyes drifting eventually to Grayson. It got harder and harder by the day, and after what happened today, I wanted the lies to stop and the truth to come out. Selfish, a little, because I was only thinking about myself, not all the other lives that would be impacted by this monstrous secret. Including the man sleeping down the hall.

Grayson's identical shade of brown eyes as mine studied me. As his sister, I wondered what he saw. Then he nodded. "I know."

It was more than an hour before Brock ushered the guys back through the window. By then, my body was beyond drained. I fell asleep within minutes of my head hitting the pillow, and I slept through the night uninterrupted without nightmares. When I woke up in the morning, Brock was gone but his scent clung to my sheets.

There was also another scent wafting through the air, seeping in from under the doorway.

Coffee.

As foretold by the doctor, my body hurt twice as much as it did yesterday. Specks of purple started to paint under the skin, the bruises becoming visible. Not even with the draw of coffee was I ready to get out of bed. It required moving, and I wasn't certain that was such a good idea.

Hugging a pillow to my chest, I contemplated rolling over and going back to bed but ultimately, the aroma of coffee drew me out of bed. My poor body ached everywhere and besides coffee, I really needed a pain reliever.

As I rounded the corner to the kitchen, Dad had a fresh cup of coffee in hand and a gruff smile. "Morning. I thought you could use this." He extended the mug to me. Dad to the rescue.

"You have no idea," I mumbled, memories of last night inundating me.

"Did you sleep okay?" he asked, setting my bottle of medicine on the kitchen table.

I sighed and slide into a chair. "Better than I thought." Thanks to Brock. No amount of pleading had changed his mind. Eventually, I had given up.

As the coffee began to filter into my system, I had a devastating thought. Would Brock ignore me now that he planned to destroy Ava? What about the other guys? This was a stupid fucking plan, and I wasn't sure I could idly sit by while Brock pretended to be into another girl—particularly Ava Whitmore.

CHAPTER FIFTEEN

The next few days sucked.

But they also were like the old times, like the last six months were nothing but twisted nightmares.

Except it took only one phone call from Angie to shatter the illusion. I'd been ignoring her since before I got beaten up and still was, which meant she'd taken to calling my father. I sort of felt bad putting him in the middle.

She called to complain, of course, about my staying with him. I could tell by my dad's face. He pinched the bridge of his nose, dropping his head like he was fighting off a headache. I knew and felt a similar headache induced by Angie.

He tried to keep his voice low as he sat at the kitchen table, but I got the gist of a familiar argument. They were nine out of ten times about me. I sneakily turned down the TV so I could listen, which turned into a toxic idea. Knowing Angie was

forcing my dad's hand enraged me. She could be such a manip-
ulative, control freak.

I wanted to storm into the kitchen and hang up on the
phone.

Instead, I sat on the couch, clenching my fists until the call
ended. Dad sat at the table for a full minute in silence, presum-
ably taking a moment to compose himself. I'd be cussing her out
and throwing shit.

I don't know how he remained so chill.

"You want some pancakes?" he asked, emerging out of the
kitchen and leaning up against the doorframe.

"Was that Angie?" I asked from where I curled up on the
couch.

"Your mother was checking up on you," he declared.

I didn't correct him. "You don't have to lie to me or pretend
everything is okay. I'm not five anymore."

His expression registered surprise before settling back
into something like resignation. "Protecting you is habit.
And it doesn't matter if you're forty, I'll still want to shelter
you."

My spine straightened. "Does she want me to go home?"

"She misses you, Josie," he said like he actually believed
that.

Biggest crock of shit.

I pursed my lips.

"She told me you've been living with that boy," he added
coolly.

I rolled my eyes. She would try to pit my dad against me.
How funny that I couldn't stomach calling Angie "Mom," but I

couldn't stop referring to Easton as my father. "It's complicated. He's a friend."

"Your mom told me he is bad news. That you got a detention because of him."

"She would say that. I'm not comfortable at home. Carter is the one you should be concerned with. Not Brock." It wasn't much of an explanation for why such a rift had been created between Angie and me or why I refused to stay in that house.

Dad studied me carefully. "If you're in some kind of trouble, Josie, let me help you."

It was too late. There was nothing he could do.

My body slowly started to heal, dampening the pain to manageable aches. All good things, but it also meant that I'd have to go back to school come Monday. A task I loathed as much as going to the dentist.

I hadn't seen Brock since the first night, since the Elite concocted one of their takedown schemes. My fear was confirmed over the last few days. No calls. No texts. No middle of the night surprise visits. I hated to admit it, but dammit. I missed him. That stupid, cocky crooked smirk. The depth those ocean blue eyes that always saw too much. How his arm always wrapped around me in the middle of the night.

Brock might not know it, but in sleep, he was a cuddler.

Fynn, Micah, and even Grayson stopped by to see me after school, dropping off lecture notes so I could keep up with my schoolwork. The Academy was known for moving at an accelerated pace. The last thing I needed was to fall behind... well, more than I already had. The Elite had been an unexpected distraction.

If Dad thought it odd that my friends were four hot guys, he didn't say anything.

I peppered them each day with questions, hungry for information about Ava, Carter, and Brock. They weren't always forthcoming, and I could tell talking about Brock and Ava made them super uncomfortable, which gave me cramps. Not the period kind.

But the real information came from Mads. She became my eyes and ears at school while I was out. I heard all about how Ava and her band of bitches were back sitting at the Elite table, Ava assuming her position on Brock's lap. She couldn't be that dumb in thinking he wanted her back.

From what Mads said, she was.

I guessed the Elite were right. She was disgustingly desperate to be on top. For someone who had never been popular nor cared to be, it was unfathomable to me how someone could go to such extremes to be the most envied girl at the Academy.

Fuck that.

Micah showed up at my house after school on Friday, sporting a devilish grin, two dimples winking at me. "Who did you hit on today?" I asked, because he had that look of someone who was about to score.

He lounged on the porch swing beside me, throwing an arm along the back as his lips twisted. "How much time do you have?"

I rolled my eyes, tucking my legs up on the cushion underneath me. "You're unscrupulous."

He threw me an arrogant smile. "Thank you. Mads said something about meeting up with me later." The way he said her name and the goofy glittering of his eyes sent a warning bell chiming in my head.

I narrowed my eyes. "You leave my friend alone."

"She still has a thing for me, doesn't she?" He sounded so damn pleased with himself, like God's gift to women.

I shook my head, narrowing my eyes. "I swear to God, Micah. I'm not joking. Don't mess with her. Go play with the million other girls falling at your feet."

He put his hands up in surrender like he was calling a truce before I ripped him a new one. "For you, Josie Jo, I'll do my best. Any chance you're included in all those millions of girls?"

"You mean now that Brock and Ava are a thing?"

He winced. "Ouch. You know it's not like that."

"Maybe not, but I am still salty as fuck about it." An autumn breeze kissed my cheeks as I turned my gaze to the house across the street. It was so nice to be outside. Today was one of those rare Indian summer days. The sun still shone brightly in the sky, warming the earth. Bold, crimson leaves stuffed the large tree in the front of our yard, and a robin hopped from branch to branch, occasionally chirping.

Micah shoved his foot against the ground, sending the swing moving. "It's not permanent. And if it helps, Brock is miserable. I think he actually misses you."

I snorted. "I find that hard to believe."

"No one knows Brock better than the three of us. He hasn't

come out and said it, but we all see it. Brock's different with you."

"Is that supposed to make me feel better?"

He scratched his nose. "Who knows? I can't figure girls out."

"But you're the playboy," I countered, enjoying the sun and the banter. "I thought girls were your specialty."

"Only the ones that don't matter," he replied, surprising me.

Was he saying that Mads mattered?

As I contemplated, Micah tugged on the end of my hair. "You're looking better, James. Less like a punching bag and more like a stubborn girl."

I gave him a mildly amused, mildly annoyed look. "You kind of suck at giving compliments."

His cockiness knew no bounds. "That's not what most girls say."

"I might have to question your taste in women. Mads excluded. You really fucked up there, buddy." I poked him in the chest.

He chuckled, but the husky sound was cut off by a cop car rolling up in front of my house and parking alongside the curb. Micah's Hummer sat behind my dad's car, taking up the small driveway.

Micah's expression hardened, his light blue eyes sharpening to ice chips. "You expecting company?" The Elite knew about my car getting impounded.

"No." They already took the Lexus. What could they possibly seize now?

Micah's arm dropped around my shoulder, pulling me

closer to him. "I don't like this, Josie. Twice in the same week... Something is up."

I thought the same, but hearing Micah say it sent a chill down my neck, despite the heat seeping from his body into mine.

Micah and I watched as two officers got out of the patrol car together. "You should probably get your dad," Micah muttered.

With a sense of dread, I hopped off the bench and stuck my head inside the door. "Dad!" I hollered through the house. "There is someone here to see you."

He made a grunting noise, followed by, "I'm coming."

"Afternoon," one of the officers greeted as I let the screen door swing closed and turn back to face the policemen.

Micah grinned, flashing teeth. "Well, if it isn't Elmwood's finest. What brings you by?"

The other officer cleared his throat. "We're looking for Easton James. Is he home?"

Micah remained lounged in on the swing like he didn't have a care in the world. "Depends."

"Micah," I hissed, giving the cops an apologetic smile.

"Are you Josie James?" the other officer asked.

"She isn't at liberty to say," Micah answered before I could.

"Ignore my friend. Yes, I'm Josie," I told the cops, ignoring the frown Micah sent at me.

"If your father isn't home—?"

"He is," Dad said, stepping out onto the porch. "What's this about now?" He sounded exhausted, and I realized the past few days had taken a toll on him. Taking care of me. Dealing with

Angie. The cops. Disrupting his routine. The Elite. Trying to keep the peace.

"We're here to serve you this." The officer handed over some official-looking documents.

Dad's eyes skimmed over the first sheet of paper. His brows furrowed, features pinching into something akin to anger. "This has to be a mistake."

"Dad, what is it?"

At the sound of my voice, his head jerked up like he'd forgotten I was there. I saw something in his face that sent alarm through me. I didn't want to believe there was anything that could frighten my father, but whatever was typed on that report had him clearly upset.

"Josie, go inside," he ordered.

"Dad?"

"Just go," he clipped out. "I'll handle this." Dad rarely used that tone of voice with me. It threw me off guard, and I flinched. I turned to leave, Micah straightening to his full height beside me. He had a good four inches over both officers.

They eyed him warily before turning back to my father. "Sorry, sir. Your daughter needs to come with us. She's been reported as a runaway and we've been asked to return into her mother's care."

Wait. What? Did they say they were taking me into custody? My heart began to race, pumping hard in my chest.

"Josie is not going anywhere," Micah stated, adamantly, positioning himself just in front of me.

I clutched the back of Micah's arm as if it was the only way to keep me grounded, to keep them from taking me. "You don't understand. I can't go back there. It's not safe." My voice wavered, giving away the panic quickly rising to hysteria.

"Is that who did that to you?" he asked, indicating to the bruises and acknowledging them for the first time.

Lie! Lie! Lie! A voice screamed inside my head. *Tell them it was Angie or Carter.* "No," I exhaled. *Idiot. You should have lied. Now you have to go back to that house.*

The officer gave me a sympathetic look. "We don't want to make this more difficult than it has to be, but if you don't come with us, your father could be charged with harboring a runaway."

"This is insane. She is my daughter," Dad argued.

"But unfortunately, her mother has full custody."

But she's not my fucking mother, I wanted to scream. How had I not seen this coming? Of course Angie would pull some kind of bitch-ass move like this. It was the only way she could get me under her control. For as much trouble as I caused her these last months, I didn't know why she just didn't wash her hands of me. I was like a possession she couldn't let go of. It didn't matter how many times or different ways she forced me to return to that house. I'd just leave again and again.

"She is seventeen," my father pointed out.

True. But we were dealing with assholes who used money to manipulate and bend the laws in their favor. Having a runaway daughter wasn't good for Angie's image. I was a trophy for her, something to show off. If I didn't return home with her, she would continue to find ways to make my father's life hell. I couldn't let that happen.

"True. And there is nothing we can do to prevent her from running away again," the officer informed.

"Fuck," Micah growled, a low rumble that of displeasure.

"Micah?" my voice came out in a soft plea. I don't know what I was asking him to do, but I wanted him to make this nightmare go away.

"Don't worry. We'll get you out of this. I promise, Josie," he said vehemently. "I'll call Brock We'll make some calls."

"Are you sure there isn't a mistake?" Dad asked, looking dumbfounded and helpless. "I talked to my ex-wife this morning. She never mentioned anything about calling the police or wanting Josie home."

"I wish I could help you, but unfortunately, we're just doing our job. I suggest getting in touch with your lawyer to straighten this out," the officer advised.

"You better believe she will," Micah retorted.

Dad ran a hand through his hair roughly, his features solemn. "I'm sorry, kiddo. I'll get to the bottom of this as soon as I can."

I almost told him not to bother. What was the point? Steven Patterson's team of lawyers battling it out with my dad's small-town guy. My only hope was Brock, but I didn't want to tell that to my father.

I had only wanted one week with my dad before my entire life blew up. Angie stole it from me. This was probably the last time we'd be together like this, as father and daughter. The next time I saw him, he'd be looking at the stolen girl who wasn't biologically his.

My gaze lingered over the only dad I had known for just a

bit longer. A part of me wanted to fight or make a mad dash. Instead, my shoulders slumped, and I gave my dad a long hug before following the officers down the driveway.

Micah trailed after us. "Can I ride with her?" he asked.

The officer's boots clattered over the driveway as we made our way toward the squad car. "Sorry, we can't allow anyone else to accompany her."

"But you can't stop me from following you," Micah speculated.

"No, we can't," an officer responded on a huff like he was having a long, shitty day. Couldn't be worse than mine.

I took one last glance out the back of the cop car at the house I grew up in. Dad stood on the front porch watching me with a forlorn expression. He might not be my biological father, but he was the only dad I knew. He loved me, and this was breaking his heart.

Angie couldn't be more of a bitch in my eyes.

* * *

I said not a single word as I rode in the back of the police car. My first ride in a cop car. A metal gate separated me from the officers, making me feel criminal. They didn't handcuff me, but they might as well have.

Micah's Hummer rolled behind us, offering a thin ribbon of comfort. It wasn't enough to overpower the anxiety that crashed inside me like a raging storm.

The Patterson mansion came into view. I rested my forehead against the window, my stomach tied in one giant knot. It had been almost a month since I lived under the Pattersons' roof or with Angie. Just the thought of seeing my insufferable mother made my skin crawl.

I refused to call that place home. It was sure as hell wasn't mine.

The officers announced themselves at the gate, waiting for it to swing open. How could I live here and pretend everything was normal? I didn't know how long I could do it, stay under the same roof as Angie and Carter. If I left, how many times would Angie threaten those who helped with harboring a runaway?

Micah parked his Hummer at the end of the driveway behind the iron fence, keeping an eye on me as I was let out of the police car. It was his way of letting me know I wasn't alone. They hadn't abandoned me. He had no idea what his presence meant to me. It gave me the strength to walk up to the front door, flanked by both officers as if they were afraid I might try something stupid. Good call, because that was exactly what rolled through my head. Each step closer I took, the louder the panic grew to bolt, to save myself.

Angie opened the door before we got to the porch landing. Her hand flew to her chest in a gesture of relief. There were fake tears in her glittering eyes. "Oh, thank God," she proclaimed.

She reached out for me, taking me into her arms for a hug. I stood limply frozen in place, not returning her embrace. It took everything inside me not to shove her away, and I bit my tongue. I thought about creating a scene but coming here had sucked all the energy out of me.

"Look at you," she said like a concerned parent, surveying

my face. Her tongue tsked. "What did you do to your face?" The keyword in that sentence was *you*. Somehow getting the crap beat out of me became my fault, as if I'd somehow caused it or initiated the fight.

My nostrils flared.

"Nothing a little cover-up won't fix right up," she said, tweaking the end of my chin with a smile. She then turned those deep red lips to the policeman standing behind me.

"Thank you for bringing my daughter home," she gushed, batting her eyes. If there was one thing Angie excelled at, it was using her looks to make men forget their names. It was her game and how she moved up in the world. I'd always known she used her body and face like a weapon, but I was just realizing how far she might go.

This woman was unpredictable and every bit as dangerous as Carter.

She exchanged a few more pleasantries with the drooling officers before ushering me toward the front door. I threw a glance over my shoulder, desperately searching for the white Hummer. My chest squeezed when I saw Micah still parked on the street.

How long did he mean to stay there?

Would he try to break me out once the cops were gone?

A brief spark of hope flared inside me.

Then the door closed.

Poetic. And symbolic. It felt as if Angie had just slammed the door shut on my life, imprisoning me inside this massive tomb.

I faced her, my expression resigned. "Well, you got what you wanted. I'm here."

Angie crossed her arms, some of the sweetness leaving her voice. "Now, honey. Let's not fight. You're home where you belong. This is a day for celebration. Not pouty faces and complaining."

I blinked. "Are you bipolar? Or just insane?"

"Josephine," she scolded, losing her smile altogether. "This is where you belong."

My hands dropped to my sides, nails curled against my palms. "You're wrong. What you did today, to Dad, to me, I'll never forgive you," I ground out.

"Of course you will. I'm your mother," she said dismissively.

Heat flared inside me. "You're not my mother." The denial was punctuated. She had no idea the truth behind those words, no clue that I knew her deep, dark secret.

Shoulders straightening, she drew up to her full height as if it gave her power over me. "Josephine!" she snapped. "Enough!"

My body jerked from the fierceness in her voice.

She pressed a hand to her temple. "I know you've had a difficult time, but living with that boy is not the answer to your problems. Look what happened. And your father—"

"This was not his fault. Both of them are only trying to help me. You might want to point the finger closer to home."

Exasperation edged into her eyes. "You have got to let go of this vendetta against Carter. Without him, I wouldn't know how you've been faring these last weeks. He's been a godsend."

"I just fucking bet. Where is the little angel?"

She smoothed at invisible wrinkles over her white cotton

pants. "Out, but he will be home for dinner," she said, composing herself. It was like watching an actress prepare for a role of a lifetime.

"I'm not hungry. I think I'll just go to my room," I said through gritted teeth.

"Good idea, get settled," she said, remaining a pillar of calm. "Your bedroom has been prepared for your return. You should find clean clothes to change into."

There was nothing wrong with the cropped sweats and hoodie I wore, but if I told her so, it would open up another battle. Yet, my mouth moved before I could stop. "I didn't know I'd be leaving the house today," I snapped back.

Taking a deep breath, I spun around and marched off toward the stairs. If I stayed in her presence any longer, I wouldn't be able to hold my tongue. Accusations would fly, none of them good.

I rushed up the stairs to my room and went to flip the lock, except... There was no fucking lock. *That bitch.* She took the lock off my door. I let a shrilling scream of frustration, slamming the heel of my palm into the wood.

Turning around, my back hit the door as I forced myself to take slow, steadying breaths. *Breathe, Josie. In. And out. In. And out.*

After a minute or two, I came to the conclusion that breathing exercises were a crock of shit. They never worked for me, not for long at least. It could also be that I just didn't give myself enough time or fully complete the process. Not that it mattered, because no amount of inner chi would help under this roof.

I had to get rid of the tightness in my chest and the dull ache behind my eyes. A swim was out of the question. That would require me to leave this room, which I most certainly would not do that and risk running into either Carter or Angie.

Not tonight.

I dug out my phone, my back sliding down the door until I sat on the floor.

What I wanted was Brock.

But Brock was pretending to date Ava.

Chewing on my nails, I wrestled with the idea to call him, beg him to break me out of this jail. He would come. Once he found out I was no longer at my dad's, he might very well show up guns blazing, screaming my name. He'd probably burn this place to the ground, which was precisely why I couldn't call him.

He would do something stupid, irrational, and damaging to his future. That would not be on me. Giving the ideal time to settle couldn't be a bad thing.

I huffed, dropping my head back against the door. My phone vibrated in my hand a moment later and I glanced at the message.

Grayson: **We're coming to get you.**

Me: **Don't bother. She won't stop.**

Grayson: **You can't stay there.**

Me: **I know.**

Grayson: **You okay?**

Me: **Define okay.**

Grayson: **Brock isn't going to let you stay there.**

Me: **It's my choice.**

Grayson: **Just don't do anything stupid. Avoid Carter.**

Me: **I can't make any promises.**

Grayson: **I mean it, Josie.**

On a huff, I closed my phone.

Now what?

My gaze panned over the room. It stood exactly the same. Cleaner than I'd left it. Bed neatly made. Not a stitch of clothing thrown on the floor. The bedroom appeared more like a guest room. Nothing of me lived inside, not like my other room.

My chest seized.

Angry tears clouded my eyes.

Before I made a blubbering mess of myself and climbed into the big bed to wallow all day, which I still had plans to do, I made use of the bathroom, one of the very few things about this house worthy of missing. It was spacious and luxurious, with a large white soaking tub that screamed my name.

I drew a bath, and as the water rumbled in rhythm with the ceiling fan, I released the tears. It was stupid, but in a way, it felt as if everything had been taken away from me. Dad. My old life. Brock. My self-respect. Even my mother. How much more could I lose? How much more could they take from me?

Utterly alone.

Utterly hopeless.

Devastatingly broken.

Dipping my toes in the steaming water, I sank into the tub, not bothering to dry my running nose or the tears that streaked down my cheeks. I let the sobs overtake me—let the emotion rip through my body and pouring out from deep in my soul. I stared out the big window overlooking the pool, a beautiful view, but I found no beauty in the world today.

An hour or more went by, and all the bubbles were gone, the water cold. I toweled off, cautious of the bruises covering my body. I stared at my reflection once I got out of the tub, wiping the mirror clear of steam. The girl staring back at me was a stranger.

She looked... afraid. Scared. Alone. Terrified. Damaged. And I didn't know how long I could stand feeling that way before something cracked within me.

It wasn't just the bruises that looked worse than they felt.

For a split second, I wished I had snuck a bottle from the liquor cabinet, anything to numb the emotions. I hated that my first thought was to reach for a drink just like Angie. That would not be me. I would find some other way to deal with my shit. Might not be less toxic, but alcohol would not be my vice, I refused to be anything like the woman who stole me—who pretended to be my mother—who lied to me my entire life.

At least I understood where some of her ridicule and emotionlessness toward me stemmed from. The unconditional love I should have felt from Angie had never been there.

I steered clear of the walk-in closet and all those expensive clothes waiting to be worn. Instead, I went straight for the dresser full of comfortable pieces that according to Angie never should be worn outside the house.

After slipping on some clothes, I plopped onto the bed, checking my phone. I don't know why I expected to hear from someone. I told myself it didn't matter that Brock hadn't texted me, but it was a lie.

It did matter.

I did care.

I shot a text off to Micah; I needed information, needed outside contact from the house of horrors. It was stupid to think Micah would sit outside my house all day, but since he was taking too long to text me back, I ventured out into the balcony. Just a quick peek. I also wanted to test how far I could get, test the boundaries. Could I just walk out of here anytime I wanted? Would someone stop me? Would she call the cops again if I took off?

The grounds echoed in emptiness as I walked down the wooden stairs. I welcomed the silence.

I paused at the bottom landing, my fingers gripping onto the banister. Glancing over the lawn, I headed to the patio on the right side of the house.

No Angie in sight.

No staff.

"Going somewhere, Ms. James?" a deep voice asked, stopping me dead in my tracks.

Spoke too soon. I whirled around, staring up at Edmund in his wrinkle-free black suit. His dark hair was slicked back, giving him mafia vibes. "At ease, Sergeant. I just need some air." I faked a mock salute.

Did his lips just twitch? Certainly not. Edmund was incapable of facial expressions. "I've been advised to keep you safe."

"Is that so?" I choked out. "Or do you mean you're being paid to keep me inside this house?" My eyes darted to the open patio. Freedom. So close I could smell it. Would he stop me if I made a mad dash to the door? How much force would he use? I had a split-second vision of Edmund tackling me to the ground. It wasn't a pleasant sight.

From his stony expression, I predicted a big yes to detaining me by any means necessary. "It would be best if you stayed inside."

"This is utter bullshit, Edmund," I spat, letting him see my outrage.

Edmund lowered his voice, his eyes bearing directing into mine. "A word of advice. Keep your head low until you turn eighteen."

"That might be some solid advice, Sergeant. That's assuming I make it to eighteen. Have you seen my face?" I made a circle around my head.

His expression remained neutral. "All the more reason to stay inside."

Fists clenched, I made a shrieking noise in my throat before spinning on my heels. I returned to my room, intent on staying there for the rest of the weekend. To pass the time, I texted Mads and Ainsley, the two people who never blew me off. We had a lot to catch up on.

Deep in my bitch-fest texting to my besties, I didn't hear the door to my room open. Angie announced, "Dinner's ready."

I jumped, dropping my phone quickly on the bed, screen down. "I'm not hungry," I retorted, despite not having eaten anything since this morning. My traitorous stomach growled at the mention of food, and I scowled.

She stepped into the center of the room, her long dark hair gathered into a sleek bun low on her head. In a cream cashmere sweater and tailored black pants, she almost looked sophisticated, but there was something off, something in her face, a sexiness that denied her from achieving the look of polish she craved. "Josephine, it's your first night home. I had all your favorites prepared; a little welcome home gathering."

Was she fucking with me?

How many ways did I have to express or say I didn't want to be here before it sank into her thick-ass skull?

The last thing I wanted to do was sit down to a fancy fake-ass dinner where we all pretended to be a family. Yeah. Not happening.

Couldn't she see how tired I was?

But no, she kept rambling on, her trilling floating across the room as she came to sit on the edge of the bed. "Carter's bringing a friend."

I stopped breathing. "Who?"

She fumbled with the massive rock on her ring finger. "I'm not sure. They should be here in a few minutes."

"I can't do this." I sighed.

She patted my leg, and I forced myself not to flinch or knock her hand away. "Josie, you have to eat. I know you are not happy with the situation, but you belong at home, with me."

"And you belong in a mental hospital." The words hurled out of me, like a sword cutting through the air, intending to hurt.

She lifted her chin, eyes hardening. "We're not doing this. You will not provoke me. Not tonight. Steven just got home. He is looking forward to seeing you. He missed you. Now get up and get downstairs before I drag you out of your room."

Ooooh, I wanted to argue. It was exactly what I wanted. To rage and scream at each other. I itched for a fight, like a storm brimming on the surface crackling with lightning before the thunder struck.

"Fine," I reluctantly agreed. "If it will get you off my back. One dinner, then you leave me alone."

She rolled her eyes as she stood up. "You don't have to be so dramatic, Josephine. You act as if I'm the one who hurt you."

Hadn't she though? I'd spent my entire life being hurt by her. Living with Angie was like watching a yo-yo tournament. It was also like watching a train wreck.

Candlelight filtered into the hallway from the dining room. As I entered the room, the large table was set with polished silverware and gleaming white plates. Flowers graced a white vase at the center of the table.

"I had the chef prepare Chicken Vesuvio for the main course," Angie informed, babbling as she weaved her way around the table. "Remember how much you loved it at that little Italian restaurant we used to go to?"

I did remember. "You mean with Dad?" The snappy retort rolled off my tongue.

Her lips pinched and she reached for the glass of wine on the table. "Let's try to have a nice meal, for my sake." She pulled her chair out and sat down.

I froze not five paces from the table at the sound of the front door slamming shut. The moment I'd been dredging was here. Carter was home. And he wasn't alone.

A husky female laugh danced from down the hallway from which I'd just come.

That voice. I knew that fucking voice. Only it was usually sneering, full of sarcasm and nastiness. Still, I wasn't imagining it.

A combination of sickness and rage came over me in one staggering wave.

That bastard. That goddamn bastard.

My first night home, and he pulled shit like this to get under my skin.

What made it worse was, it worked.

The sound of the two of them laughing sent me into a tailspin.

"Welcome home, sis," Carter said, his eyes practically glowing with sick amusement. The grin on his lips caused my stomach to pitch.

My gaze shifted to the girl standing at his side. Ava fucking Whitmore. She was the *friend* he brought to dinner.

"Are you fucking kidding me?" I spat.

CHAPTER SIXTEEN

Dinner was about to get interesting, especially when I leap across the table and tackle a bitch. No one's life could be this cruel.

Fury licked through my veins as the room fell into a dark void. Mouths were moving, but I heard nothing but the ringing in my ears as I stared at the viper who just slithered into the house.

Bold red curls hung to frame Ava's pretty face made up to perfection, except for the scratch she tried to cover up on her cheek. A small amount of satisfaction went through me. Other than the barely visible mark, not an eyelash was out of place. No bruises to hide like mine. The black flared skirt was short enough without being slutty and the forest green sweater accentuated the hue of green in her hazel eyes. Angie would love her. This was her idea daughter. Polished. Put together. Worldly.

Anybody who didn't know the witch in front of me would

think she was the cutest, sweetest thing in the world. The bitch was full-on pretending to be somebody else.

At parties, Ava wore a crop top and shorts cut high enough to leave her butt cheeks showing, or she'd wear a tight top with no bra. And always, always enough makeup to practically hide her actual face. The girl was going all-in to impress the parents.

What the fuck for?

To discredit me?

I didn't have the brain energy to figure it out, not when I had to use all my wits to keep up with their game.

Ava hung on Carter's arm, her laugh cutting through my ears like glass, and when those unstable eyes met mine, I stiffened. "Hey, Josie. I'm so sorry about what happened."

I could take that statement two ways. One, she was actually apologizing for what she had done to me. Or two, she was pretending as if she had nothing to do with it.

I honestly didn't give a flying fuck which one it was.

Don't let them see what this is doing to you. Don't give them the satisfaction of seeing you rattled.

That was the entire point of this. To fuck with me. To show me that she'd won. I was beginning to support Brock's plan to destroy her wholeheartedly. It was so much simpler to give myself a pep talk in my head than it was to carry through with the charade.

No matter what Ava did, no matter what Carter said, I couldn't let either of them know how their presence affected me.

"What a surprise." I offered as natural a smile as I could and forced my legs to move, taking my seat across from Ava and Carter.

She had such nerve showing up here. In the hospital, all I thought about was how I'd exact my revenge. That fire kept me going, and here she was, rubbing her fake-ass tits in my face. Had the police talked to her after the attack?

Steven walked into the room and smiled when his eyes landed on me. "Josie, we are so happy to have you home. Your mother has been beside herself with worry." He gave my shoulder a light squeeze before moving to kiss my mother on the cheek and sit at the head of the table. Still dressed in his shirt and tie, he unbuttoned his cuffs and rolled up his sleeves. "Carter." He nodded to his douchebag son. "Hello, Ava. It's so nice for you to join us. It's been too long since we've seen your pretty face around."

"Thank you for having me, Mr. Patterson." Ava smiled wide, flashing pearly white teeth. "Everyone's been so worried about Josie."

I flipped her off under the table. Someone should have warned me to take an anti-nausea pill before coming downstairs. If this was how the rest of the night would go, I wouldn't last two minutes. I wondered what would happen if I blurted out that this was the bitch who jumped in the alley. Would everyone just keep on eating?

"I always thought you and Carter made such a power couple." His choice of words had me scowling. Did he know what the two of them had schemed? That they were behind the attack?

"She has a boyfriend, Dad." Carter groaned. "Let's not make this embarrassing."

I choked on my glass of water.

"We're better friends," Ava added, grinning at me.

"I just bet," I mumbled, earning a round of frowns from the adults. "You're a pretty *friendly* girl."

"Josephine." Angie said my name with warning as the first course came out.

"Ava is Elmwood's head cheerleader," I explained with a grin so wide my cheeks ached while twirling a piece of hair.

"You are?" Angie squealed, as I knew she would. Angie had been a cheerleader in her day before getting knocked up. How weird to look back at the story I'd heard a million times and realize it was not about me. I was not the little girl who derailed her entire life. Now that I thought about it, why hadn't the loss of her baby been the answer to all her problems? She hadn't wanted to be a teenage mom.

While Angie gushed cheer with Ava, I dug out my phone to send out a quick text to Brock. **Your girlfriend is here.**

Just as I hit send, Angie scolded, "Honey, you know the rules. No cellphones at the table."

I blinked, slipping the phone back into my pocket just as it buzzed with a new message. "Since when?" I replied.

Carter snorted, forking a bed of lettuce drenched in ranch dressing.

I made a face at him. "How's the football scouting going, Carter? I heard you missed a big opportunity during detention. Penn State, was it?"

My stepbrother no longer found me funny. "And whose fault was that?"

Blinking innocently, I replied, "You can't possibly think I had anything to do with it."

"Maybe not directly, but your boys did," he snapped.

Angie jumped in before things got ugly, steering the conversation back to a more pleasant topic. "We're so proud of how Carter is playing this season." Funny, since she had never been to a game, probably because Carter didn't want her there. "He will be scouted in no time." She lifted her glass in salute and helped herself to half its contents.

"We're proud of him too." Ava turned her shark smile on to me, and it seemed to broaden just a little. "Everybody at school is rooting for Carter to go pro. Right, Josie?"

I wondered if I could throw my knife hard enough that it would lodge between her eyes. Or maybe in her chest, that might be easier. Though the thought of Ava with a beautifully carved knife handle protruding out from between her eyes made me smile back at her, at least. "Oh, sure. He's Mr. Popularity."

Steven topped up Angie's and his glasses with white wine. "Carter has nothing to worry about. He's already received several promising offers from schools."

This was the first I'd heard about them. Then again, I'd been absent for the last few weeks. A lot happened while I was away, except... I didn't give two shits about any of it—any of them.

"Congratulations." Ava beamed.

"Have you decided where you will be attending college?" Angie asked Ava.

The two of them launched into a discussion about her top two favorite schools and how she'd already applied. I played with my salad, pushing the cherry tomatoes off to the side.

"What about you, Josie? Have you thought about where you will be applying?" Ava asked smugly.

My head snapped up at the sound of my name. I more or less had checked out of the conversation, but Angie was all too eager to respond for me. "Josephine is going to Hamilton University, isn't that right, honey? She's been talking about Hamilton since she was five."

"That's the plan," I said, slapping a forced grin on my face.

Salad plates were cleared away as the staff brought in the main course. "Didn't you and Ava get into a fight a few weeks ago?" Steven asked. "The same week Carter got detention, wasn't it?" He looked to Angie for confirmation, as if it just occurred to him. Why would he bring that up?

Ava opened her mouth, but I answered before she had the time to say a word. "It was a misunderstanding. Girl stuff." I speared a stalk of asparagus and bit off the tip while looking at my stepbrother, who rolled his eyes.

Rage flashed behind her eyes, and she lifted a hand to touch her injured cheek, but she recovered quickly. It made me wonder what she had said to the police. If she denied being a part of the attack.

Angie delicately cut into a piece of chicken. "It's no secret Josie is having a hard time making friends, which is why I'm so glad to have you over for dinner."

"Mom!" I gasped, reverting to old habits. I couldn't keep up the farce. Not with Ava. Not with Angie. Not with Carter.

Fuck this. Why was I pretending to like this girl? We were enemies, and I no longer would play her games. "Ava and I are not friends. We'll never be friends."

Silence fell upon the table, silverware suspended midway to a mouth or a plate, but I didn't give two shits. Screw decorum.

I didn't have any.

Ava dabbed at the corner of her mouth with a cloth napkin. "Do you have something you'd like to say to me?"

I stabbed a potato aggressively with my fork. "I don't even know where to begin. Let's start with fuck off."

"Josephine," Angie hissed. "I will not allow you to speak to our guest so."

Carter threw his head back and laughed.

I ignored my mother and the deep scowls from Steven, who seemed to be struggling to keep up with my sudden change in attitude. "You have a lot of nerve showing up here." I pointed my fork at her, spattering sauce all over the pristine white tablecloth.

Ava's eyes brightened. "I don't know what you mean."

"Don't play coy with me," I retorted shortly. "You're not a dumb blonde, Ava. You're a cunning redhead."

She angled her head to the side, regarding me with a tight smile. "What does that make you? A dark-haired witch?"

Finally. The bitch emerged. "Yes. You're going to wish you never met me," I said bluntly, meaning every word of the threat.

Angie stood from the table, tossing her napkin onto her barely touched plate. "Josephine, I think it is time you went to your room."

Fury simmered in my blood. "Gladly." I shoved out of my seat.

Angry tears shined in Angie's eyes as she shook her head at me. "We couldn't have one nice dinner as a family. You just had to ruin this, didn't you?"

"As you're so keen on reminding me, it's what I'm good at." With that parting statement, I stormed from the room. I'd never been so glad to walk away from a meal.

What a shit show. We never made it to dessert; not that I cared. Was anyone surprised about the outburst? Not at all.

As I climbed the stairs, I remembered the text I had received but never checked. Turned out I had a handful of messages and two missed calls, all from the elusive Brock. Quickening my pace, I slammed my door shut, and since it didn't lock, I bolted myself inside the bathroom to call him back. He answered on the first ring as if he'd had his phone in his hand, waiting for me. "Why is she there?" his deep voice immediately demanded.

It had only been four days since I last heard his voice, but to my ears, it felt like months. My heart flipped in my chest as I leaned against the bathroom sink. "To gloat. To rub it in that she won."

"Are you okay?" he growled, and when I didn't answer immediately, he repeated the question.

I sat on the edge of the tub and bit out, "Like you care."

"Firefly," he said, a tad tensely.

I sucked in a deep breath, realizing I didn't want to fight with him. "I'm fine for now. But I can't stay here much longer."

"You don't have to," he vowed, saying the exact thing I wanted to hear. "I'll come get you."

A chasm of pain, hurt, and longing opened up in my chest. "Don't bother. Besides, your girlfriend is here. Wouldn't want her to see you sneaking into my room." I wanted to ask how his fake relationship with Ava was going, but at the same time, I didn't want to know. Just thinking about her in his lap, running her nails through his hair, or kissing those soft, skillful lips sent me into a dark place. In my head, I knew Brock wasn't mine. He was free to date or fake date whomever he wanted. But in my heart, Brock was mine. And only mine. Even after I told myself not to fall for the jerk.

My first night back in the Pattersons' house of horrors was nightmarish. I slept like shit. The bed had nothing to do with my restless sleep, as it was literally one of the most comfortable things I'd ever lain in. How could I close my eyes with Carter down the hall able to creep into my room at any time?

The winds howled outside, ramming against the house with enough force to rattle the windows. I jumped up out of bed for the twentieth time, staring into the shadowy room, searching for signs of movement or eyes glowing in the corners. Storms didn't bother me. I rather liked them. It was the shadows that lurked inside that concerned me.

The floor outside my bedroom door creaked, and my head whirled in that direction, intently watching the door handle to see if it moved. It was difficult to tell, given I was sleep deprived, and the shadows were dancing and laughing at me.

On a frustrated groan, I flung back onto the mattress, head

hitting the pillow with a soft thump. I gave up on sleep after that. What was the point in trying to force my body to do something it refused to do?

I watched the sunrise from the floor where I sat by the doors that led out to the balcony. Such a beautiful sight; the sky glowed a watercolor of deep reds, pinks, and purples. I skipped breakfast. Shelly, one of the staff, brought me a carafe of hot coffee, and I thanked her profusely. I did my best to ignore the looks I got from the staff, the glimmers of pity or expressions of worry. They never came out and asked about my injuries, but I could see they were curious. How could I blame them? They worked in *this* household. God fucking knew the shit they saw.

I was sipping my third cup of coffee when the house phone on my desk rang. I stared at it, debating whether to ignore whoever was on the other end. Since mainly only the house staff used this line, I hit the speaker button. "Hello."

"Ms. James, you have a friend to see you," Shelly said from the other end of the line, her kind voice echoing through my room.

My brows drew together. "A friend?" I echoed doubtfully.

"Yes, a Ms. Clarke is here to see you," she explained, a hint of excitement brimming in her tone, like she knew how much I needed a friend right now.

OMG. Mads! "I'll be right there," I said, quickly disconnecting and rushing out of the room. Too much time had gone by since I'd seen her. We talked and texted, but it wasn't the same as hanging out in person.

As I approached the first floor, tendrils of excitement burst inside me. I missed her so much, her no-bullshit attitude. Her ability to make me feel like I belonged. Her friendship, and keeping me sane.

My lips grew into a broad grin as I caught sight of her hovering near the door. Her jaw worked tiredly over a piece of gum as she turned in my direction at my approach, lips splitting into a smile.

"You're really here," I shrieked, giving her a tight hug.

She squeezed me back, smelling faintly of smoke and mint that mixed with her shampoo. Her long hair was straight and sleek, honey highlights gleaming from the sun streaming through the glass windows that framed the door. "They kept me away long enough."

"They don't know you're here, do they?" I guessed, knowing Grayson wouldn't want her anywhere near this house.

She shrugged, her mouth still curved upward. "What they don't know what hurt them."

"God, I love you, bish." I grabbed her by the hand and pulled her upstairs to my room before she disappeared on me. I was hungry for company, to not be alone in this hellhole, even if it was just for an hour. "I can't believe you're here."

Her eyes scanned over my face, taking note of the bruises, the split lip, and the cut at my temple. "Oh girl, shit. Look what they did to you."

"You should have seen me a few days ago. This is nothing. An improvement." It was a sad attempt to make light of my injuries, but I didn't want Mads's pity.

Heat flared in silver eyes. "That fucking bitch. I'm gonna cut out her black heart."

"That seems to be the consensus going around." My gaze

dropped to the floor as I thought about dinner last night and how good it had felt to come unhinged.

She dropped a pile of papers on my desk. "The gall of that bitch. She just made an enemy out of the Elite. Biggest mistake of her miserable life."

"You shouldn't be here. It's not safe."

She touched my shoulder, drawing my eyes back up. "Probably not, but I had to see you. Besides, with your mom and Carter's dad here, I doubt he will try anything."

"I'm sorry about the car." I had already apologized for her car being stranded at Tommy's but I felt the need to say it again.

Like before, she replied, "I don't give a shit about the car. Besides, Grayson and Brock brought it back before my parents even knew it was missing." Mads sank onto my bed, legs dangling over the edge as she kicked off her shoes. "How are you doing? Really. Don't bullshit a bullshitter."

I plopped down on the other side. "Like a caged tiger, clawing, hissing, and scratching to get out of here. She took the lock off my bedroom door. Who the fuck does that?"

She grimaced. "Harsh. And really frightening."

"Tell me about it."

"Does Brock know about the lock?" she asked.

"Brock is too busy shoving his tongue down Ava's throat and fingering her," I grumbled, salty as fuck.

"That is not true," she retorted, her delivery half-assed. Even she didn't believe it.

My brows inched up. "Which part?"

"Well, all of it... mostly."

I heaved a long sigh and dropped down onto the bed. "I

don't know whether to thank him for distracting Ava with his dick or fucking scream my lungs off."

Pulling both her legs up and weaving them like a pretzel, a glint came into her eyes. "Why choose? I'd go with both. I find screaming to be a huge stress reliever."

The corner of my lips twitched. Leave it to Mads to make a joke of this messed up situation.

"He misses you," she added.

A sarcastic snort blew from my nose.

"I mean it," Mads emphasized.

"Does it matter?" My words came out flat.

"Maybe not, but it's clear you're ridiculously jealous. You care about him, even after I warned you."

She had warned me. The first day we met. God, that seemed like a lifetime ago rather than just merely months. "What about you and Micah?" I countered, turning the tables around on her. I was done being in the spotlight.

Our gazes met, and I swore I saw something like amusement flicker through them. "There is no Micah and me."

I pressed my lips together, the smile I tried to hide peeking through. "I see the way you've been dancing around each other. The way you look at him."

She rolled her eyes, fidgeting on the bed. "You need glasses. And I need a cigarette."

"What are those?" I asked, indicating to the stack of pamphlets she had set on my desk.

Her gaze followed mine, landing on the papers. "College applications. I thought they'd be a good excuse to see you if I needed one and they might help get your mind off, you know..."

"Getting the living shit beat out of me," I supplied.

"Does it hurt? Because it looks like it hurts like hell."

My mind flashed back to that alley. "Not so much anymore, but yeah, it fucking hurt."

She shimmed off the bed and went to the desk, gathering the pamphlets. "If it makes you feel better, the whorish trio skipped school the day after. Heard the cops had a nice chat with the three of them. You got a few good swings in. Izzy had a black eye that no amount of makeup could disguise."

I lifted my hand in the air, pinching my thumb and index finger close so only an inch of space separated between them. "Yeah, it makes me feel a little better."

"So, college?" she prompted, dropping the stack on top of the bed in front of me, resuming her spot on the other side.

I grabbed one of the flyers. "I missed a few days of school, and everyone seems so college focused suddenly."

"They had a college fair on Thursday," Mads explained. "More or less kicked our asses into gear, realizing how close our deadlines are."

"Oh, great. I missed it. Just another thing I can blame Ava for. That skank is damn determined to ruin my life."

"Only if you let her. And besides, you have me. I brought you a packet from like every school there." Her jaw worked tirelessly over a piece of gum.

I thumbed through the information on the University of Westly. "Thanks, Mads. You really are the best. I don't know what I would have done this year without you."

She picked up the next pamphlet and held it up. "Where should we start? Dupage College?"

"You don't have to do this."

She shrugged. "I've got nothing better to do, and I miss my best friend."

"It's been like five days."

"Exactly. So, which school first?"

"None," I muttered, dropping the flyer back onto the pile. "I'm still hoping to get a scholarship, otherwise I'm not sure college is an option. I won't take a dime from Angie, for obvious reasons. My dad doesn't have the money, and then there is the little tidbit that neither of them are my biological parents."

Mads eyes softened. "Perhaps it is time the truth came out."

There was nothing I wanted more, but it was the after that worried me—the unknown. "Where would I go then? Back to Brock's? I can't stay there forever. Besides, his parents came home this week. I doubt they are looking for an orphan to put up."

"You could stay with me," she offered graciously. "My mom would love to have you, cuz."

A pure grin crossed my lips, not even the tightness from the cut could stop it. "Holy shit. I keep forgetting. We're fucking related."

Mads smiled. "Hell yes, we are. Seriously, come stay with me. Get out of here."

The offer was damn tempting. I'd met her parents, who I absolutely loved, even before I realized they were my aunt and uncle. Mads also had another brother, Jason, who I hadn't met yet. I had fucking cousins—a family that I could bring into my mess. "And have the cops show up at your house? I can't do that or put you in danger. Shit, Carter might try to burn down your house next."

Her gaze shifted to the closed door, twinkles of unease and specks of silver flames mixed in her eyes. "Has he said anything to you?"

I twisted the ends of my hair. "Not, yet. But he is going to want his information on the USB drive."

She set down the paper in her hand, her eyes turning serious. "If he wanted it bad enough, he should have put a leash on his pet. She fucked up when she took you out of Brock's house."

I blew out a breath. "I can't figure out if that was something they planned together or if Ava went rogue."

"Jealousy is a powerful tool," Mads mused.

"Ugh, I don't want to talk about the losers anymore. It's giving me PTSD." The next thing I knew, we were laughing, and God, did it feel good to let loose, release all the tension built up over the last twenty-four hours in my muscles. There was nothing funny in what I said. It was sad but true. Maybe Mads just knew how much I needed a friend and all the benefits that came with it, like laughing for no reason.

"What about you? Did you send in any applications yet?" I asked. Dwelling on my pathetic situation would not make me feel better. I didn't want to spend my time with Mads depressed and feeling sorry for myself. I could do that when I was alone.

All this talk of college had my thoughts turning to Ainsley. Our plan to go to school together seemed like a dream. A million years ago instead of just months. How sad. My future was sinking before my eyes. I had no choice but to sink or swim, and I was quickly drowning.

Mads picked at her black nail polish. "Yeah, I sent out a lot of applications, actually, to a bunch of schools. I don't know where I want to go and figured I'd pick one from whoever offers an acceptance."

"Solid plan. You don't sound excited. Aren't you looking forward to college?"

"It just so much has changed over the last year. I know you can relate to that. Nothing is how I thought it would be."

"It's like you read my mind." I'd fallen so far behind without even realizing it. Sometimes, it felt like I was forgetting myself, forgetting who I was.

I was really winning at life.

CHAPTER SEVENTEEN

There was nothing fucking scarier than seeing a man's face in your window at night. A scream rose in my throat, seconds away from shrilling throughout the dark room. My first thought was someone was trying to break in or Carter was snooping around. Tucked inside my bed, I swallowed the cry for help, the guy's face coming into focus.

My speeding heart went from racing in fear to skipping with excitement. "Brock?" I mumbled, squinting through the dark. Unfolding myself from the tangle of sheets and downy comforter, I padded over to the balcony doors. "Are you insane? How did you get past security?" I asked through the glass.

He glowered from the other side. "Firefly, open the door."

I quickly fumbled with the lock, sliding the door open. Startling aqua eyes ensnared mine, and before he finished walking over the threshold, I was on him. I don't know what came over me. Perhaps it was the sudden surge of fright to realizing there was no danger at all. Well, not the kind that would stab me a million times and then toss my body into the pool. Maybe it was the separation from Brock. Or knowing he was with Ava during the day and probably nights too. The uncontrollable urge to possess him rushed over me.

Lifting on my toes, I drove my fingers into his hair as my lips sought his in the dark. I wasn't thinking, because if I had been in my right mind, I wouldn't have kissed someone who was possibly kissing my enemy, no matter the reasons behind those kisses.

But the only thing on my mind was how much I needed to remind him that I was real. That this thing between us that took control over us both couldn't be denied or shoved aside. I wanted him to forget Ava existed. I wanted him to claim *me*, to possess *me*, to scream *my* name, to...

I couldn't dare think l-o-v-e.

So I kissed him like my life depended on it, and in a way, it felt like it did. Kissing Brock was one of the things in my life that felt real. Despite all the drama surrounding us, when we were alone, just him and me, nothing else mattered. The games, the lies, the disorder all stripped away, leaving just the two of us.

He couldn't fake this, not with me.

And whether he was ready to admit it or not, there was something between us. I could no longer lie to myself. He was like a drug I had no intention of kicking my addiction to.

Brock nipped at my lower lip until I parted for him. He slid his tongue between my lips, caressing my tongue, tasting, teasing me. My mouth opened wider as I angled my head to the side, kissing him deeper and longer. His tongue stroked over mine, inch by inch, and he moaned into my mouth.

I slowly ended the kiss but stayed wrapped up in him. "You liked living with me," I murmured, our faces still so close, we shared breath.

He tilted his head to the side, his gaze roaming over my face and lingering over my lips. "What gives you that idea?"

"This," I said, kissing him again. Heat flared through me, warming every corner of my body.

His hands moved to my hips, guiding me deeper into the room, toward the bed. "Are you sure we should be doing this?"

"Yes," I breathed, attacking the button on his jeans.

"But your—"

I gave him a feline smile and tugged his ass to the edge of the bed. I sat down on the mattress, slipping my fingers into boxers. "Is asleep."

"Josie—"

"I need you." My fingers closed around him, freeing him the confines of his open jeans and boxers.

God, he was big, so hard. And I wanted him. Now.

I dipped my head, but right before I wrapped my mouth around the tip of him, I glanced up. His eyes burned like glowing stars as he glanced down at me. "I want to taste you," I whispered, letting my warm breath brushing over his erection. My fingers stroked down the length of him as my mouth finally closed over him.

His head fell back, fingers twisting into my hair. "Fuck," he hissed, coming out in a partial groan.

I squeezed him, my hand tightening while sucking him into

my mouth. He was so silky and smooth, yet hard as steel. The muscles in his legs tightened, and a shudder rolled through him, sending need burning into me.

His breathing became ragged, and I smiled, stroking him again as my tongue rubbed over the tip of him. "I need to be inside you," he growled, pulling my head back. He hooked a finger into the side strap on my panties, wiggling them down over my hips.

I wiped at my mouth with the back of my hand, staring at him from under heavy-lidded eyes. Brock picked me up by my hips, dropping onto the middle of the bed. And then he was on top of me, his weight sinking into me. The muscles on his back trembling as pulled out a condom and wrestled with the wrapper open with his teeth. Once it was securely in place, he pressed himself in between my legs. "Fuck, I missed you, Firefly," he moaned.

The broad tip nudged at my opening, finding me wet and ready for him. I pushed my hips down slightly, pleading with him to bury himself into me.

He entered in slowly and just an inch. It wasn't enough. Nowhere near enough. I clamped around him, my body arching into his.

His mouth fastened over mine, devouring me. I melted like ice on a hot summer day as he filled me completely.

He made lazy circles over the small of my back as I lay naked in his arms, gazing at the intricate ink tattooed on his body. "This isn't why I came, you know."

My lips twitched. "I know. But I'm glad you came. Literally."

He chuckled, the sound rumbling against my chest. "Funny." He adjusted his head on the pillow, a comfortable silence falling between us. My body still buzzed from the pleasure Brock gave me. "I'm not sleeping with her. I want you to know," he said, killing that lingering tingle.

I lifted my head, staring down into his face, my palm lying flat on his chest. "Are you really thinking about her after we just..."

He brushed his thumb over my bottom lip. "No, the point is, I'm only thinking about you. Even though it might not seem like it or my methods conventional, in the end, Firefly, it's you."

My heart pounded. This was my chance to tell him how I felt. "I know we said this between us was casual."

"About that... I've never been in a relationship, not the kind you want or deserve. I'm going to fuck this up."

I searched his face, my hand coming to cup his cheek. "I don't care. I come from the most fucked-up family. I'm willing to bet my heart on you."

He shook his head, and I could see the doubts that lived in his eyes, but he only brought my head down for a kiss.

I fell asleep on his chest, listening to the steady beat of his heart. I never imagined I'd be able to find a shred of happiness in such a gloomy time in my life. Brock became the person who grounded me, who sheltered me and completed me. Never in a million years would I have believed someone like him would choose someone like me. It didn't make sense. And yet, everything about us fit perfectly. We both had our fucked-up lives that somehow interconnected, locking us together.

I'm falling in love with you. The words whispered in my head. At least, I thought they were in my head. I was too tired to care.

* * *

I had this plan that involved me waking up and smothering Brock with kisses, thanking him for last night, for staying with me. I had needed him. The only time I ever slept anymore was when he was near. Last night had been no different—except for the part in the middle of the night when he had roused me out of sleep with his fingers. I had woken up on the verge of an orgasm, disorientated and horny as hell. A whimper of pleasure had escaped before I even opened my eyes, my center contracting around his index and middle finger as he stroked the orgasm from me.

I had groaned when he pulled out, the waves still rocking through me, but seconds later, he replaced his fingers with his cock, filling me completely. And the pleasure started over again, more deeply, more intense.

Afterward, I had fallen instantly back into a deep, satisfying slumber, a smirk on my lips, tucked tight in his arms.

I should have known... my plans never work out. The idea of waking him similarly this morning seemed like sweet revenge. Instead, I barely had time to register that I was coming out of a glorious dream involving Brock in an interesting position when I was jostled and tossed on the mattress. Grumbling, I shoved the hair out of my face, my mind trying to figure out what the fuck was going on.

I opened my eyes, a flash of Brock's bare ass streaking past the bed as he bent down, collecting his clothes and dashing out the balcony doors without so much as a kiss goodbye.

WTF.

I blinked, a new thought entering my brain.

OMG. Brock is running around my backyard buck-ass naked. I imagined my neighbors were getting more than they bargained for with their morning coffee.

If my bedroom door hadn't flown open a second later, I would have broken out into hysterics. Angie stood in the doorway, her eyes finding me in bed. She then panned the room, searching for something or someone. Holy shit. That had been close. If she had found Brock in my bed...

I shuddered to think what kind of psycho would have emerged from her. "Knock, much?" I snapped, tugging the blanket close to my neck, seeing as I was utterly naked.

She schooled her expression, disregarding my tone. "I thought I heard something."

"I was on the phone with Ainsley," I lied, doing my best to avoid the slightly parted glass door, not wanting to draw her attention to the balcony.

With her chin high, she leaned a shoulder on the doorframe, crossing a foot over the other ankle. "How long are you going to be angry with me?"

I glared. "Forever. What you did... it's unforgivable." I

wasn't just talking about ripping me from Easton or having the Lexus impounded. The majority of my disgust was born from the knowledge that she had stolen me.

"Since when is loving and caring for my daughter a crime?" she countered.

Anyone who looked at Angie would see a put-together woman, but I could see that she was lonely and unhappy. The difference was, I didn't give a fuck. The woman had what she always wanted—the money, the cars, the house, the staff, the husband. Everything Easton could never give her, everything she dreamed about. And yet, she was still miserable.

It didn't take a shrink to tell me that Angie would be chasing happiness her entire life. She couldn't love and accept herself, let alone the people that should be important in her life.

My fingers curled around the comforter. "You don't love me. You love the idea of a daughter," I hurled at her.

She flinched and took a visible step back like I'd hurt her. "How can you say such a cruel thing?"

I ran a hand through my disheveled pink hair. "Because you forced me to come home when you know I don't want to be here. You threatened to have Dad charged with harboring a fugitive. I'm his daughter! I'm tired of pretending."

"Pretend?" she echoed, her voice pitching. "Is that what you're doing? Pretending to be my daughter?"

"I thought that's what we were both doing in this house. You pretending to be an important, rich housewife, and me... Actually, I no longer give a shit. The pretending stops. I'm done. You don't believe me when I tell you what's happening right under your nose. You don't seem to care about my safety. You let Ava into this house, the same girl that beat the crap out of me. This feels like a joke. A dream. That's it. I'm still dreaming and this is some warped alternate reality like I'm stuck in a funhouse, the one with all the mirrors." I was staring at a million reflections of my life, all of them wrong.

Her eyes darkened. "You're being dramatic as usual."

"And you're being a bitch as usual." If Angie was my actual mother and not a liar and a kidnapper, I might have felt bad about calling her a bitch.

Her pretty features contorted into something ugly. "At some time, you're going to have to accept this family." She whirled to leave back the way she came.

"Not likely," I muttered to her back.

Boom. The door slammed closed, the sound echoing through the house. I swore the frame splintered from the force of the impact.

But at least I was alone, no longer in her presence, and I sat in bed, wondering if the rage I felt would ever subside. Would I ever be able to forgive the woman who had raised me? Look at her again without being filled with contempt? I had loved her. Loved her still...?

Perhaps that was part of where all the anger stemmed from. A part of me still loved the woman who raised me, no matter how shitty of an effort she put into it.

The mood for the day had been set and only continued to grow gloomier. I missed my friends. I missed the Elite. I missed Brock.

Lightning cracked, flashing the room in a bright glow of yellow before it submerged into gloominess again. The storm reflected my mood. Turbulent. Unpredictable. Angry. Volatile.

In my sweats, I watched the rain pelt against the window, running down the glass in big fat drops. Mist gathered over the panels, and I drew mindless circles in the dew, letting my mind wander. Tomorrow was Monday—my first day back at the Academy—and I was starting to feel the nerves.

It wasn't Ava or her band of bitches that had me worried, nor all the gossip that would undoubtedly swirl around my return. It was having to see Brock with Ava. Together. I couldn't stomach the thought. Not after last night. Not after he still refused to end this charade.

Carter's voice suddenly filled the room. "Contemplating running away again?"

My head whipped in his direction. He wore a smug smirk. Damp, slightly curly sandy hair fell over his forehead, like he'd just come from the shower or had gotten caught in the rain. I never heard my door open, the storm covering up the turning of the knob. I pulled my knees up to my chest, wrapping my arms around them. "What do you want?"

He shoved his hands into the pockets of his jeans. "Just checking in."

"Like you actually give a fuck about me. If you're looking for information, you're shit out of luck. Thanks to your *girlfriend*, I never got the chance to find it or figure out his passcode." Thunder struck, rumbling the house. I had only a small lamp on in the corner of the room. It flickered as the power cut out and back on.

Half of Carter's face was shrouded in darkness, the storm snuffing out the sun, but I still caught the gleam of his grin. "She's Brock's girlfriend now or haven't you heard?"

If he was looking for a reaction, he got his wish. I couldn't control my emotions, not when I had just been thinking about the two of them and how much it would hurt seeing Brock with her. "Get the fuck out. I'm not in the mood for your shit." I returned my gaze to the window, not caring if Carter still stood inside my room. Turning my back to my stepbrother was never a good idea, but I was all out of fucks to give.

"You owe me. One way or the other, I'm going to get what's coming to me." He stepped further into my room, a slash of lightning cut across the sky, lighting up the side of Carter's face. The look on his face...

I shivered. I didn't think about my actions, only reacted. Grabbing the nearest thing I could reach, I hurled the Bath and Bodyworks candle across the room at Carter. "Get out!" I screamed.

He ducked, narrowly missing being clobbered in the head. Too bad it hadn't been lit. The glass tumbler hit the wall with a thud, shattering into chunks of glass that clattered to the floor. "You're as crazy as your mother." His hand went to the side of his neck where a sliver of glass had nicked him.

I lost it then. Jumping up to my feet, I faced my asshole stepbrother, flames igniting in my veins. "Don't you dare compare me to her. She is *not* my mother." The pressure behind my eyes warned me I was about to cry. Nothing I hated more than angry tears. I don't know why I let my emotions get so bottled up that they came out in a gush.

Carter's lips twitched.

"What is going on up here?" Angie demanded, hovering just outside the doorway behind Carter. He turned to the side so Angie could see us both.

I stood facing them, fuming. "Where do you want me to start? I don't know, how about the fact that your stepson is trying to blackmail me? Or that this family is so disturbed? Do you have any idea what he has done to me? To Ainsley?"

Confused crinkled at the corners of her eyes. "Ainsley? What does she have to do with any of this?"

"How can you stand there and pretend you don't know why what is going on? This is your fault. If you would just listen to me..." I shook my head, my body physically shaking with rage. "You have no idea how much shit he has put me through."

Carter touched the small scratch on his neck, smearing a bead of blood. "She's off her rocker. She needs help."

"You would love that, wouldn't you?" I snapped, temper simmering in my blood. "Have me sent away, committed to a psych ward. It wouldn't fix your problems. If anyone needs to seek treatment, it's you."

"It might be good for you," he pressed on like he hadn't heard a word I said. "You've been under a lot of stress."

I straightened my spine and raised my chin. "Hell no. This is not happening. You're sick in the head. I'm not the one who needs help."

Defeat slumped in Angie's shoulders, the fire in her eyes extinguishing. "Josephine, stop. Just stop. Carter has a point. Steven and I have discussed you talking to someone. We think it might be a good idea."

This wasn't happening. Just when I thought my life couldn't get any more mucked up. "I don't need a shrink. Besides, do you really want me to air our dirty laundry to stranger?"

Angie tilted her head slightly to the side. "Carter, would you mind giving Josephine and me a moment alone?"

"Don't bother. I'm leaving." I went to grab a hoodie from the end of my bed.

Both Angie and Carter stood like a barricade at my door, neither of them budging. Since when had then become a unit working against me? My supposed own mother. Fuck this. I whirled toward the balcony doors.

Angie rushed to get in front of me, putting herself between the exit and me. A tinge of sadness worked its way into her pretty yet tired features. "You are not going anywhere. Not until we discuss what is going on with you. I told you that boy was no good. Look where hanging out with him has gotten you."

"This is not Brock's fault," I ground out, my voice dropping an octave.

Carter made a snort of disbelief that did not help the situation. "The Elite do nothing but cause problems. They ruin lives. They've been trying to ruin mine for years."

Okay, I'd heard enough. Brock, Grayson, Fynn, and Micah weren't here to defend themselves, so I took it upon myself to do so on their behalf. "You don't have a leg to stand on. You raped my sister. And god knows how many others are out there too afraid to come forward."

Carter's face went beet red. I first thought it might have been shame, but then quickly realized it was undiluted rage that trembled through him. He wanted to hurt me.

"Do you hear yourself? You don't have a sister, honey," Angie said in a voice that was full of pity and meant to pacify an uncontrollable toddler.

This time it was my turn to grin nefariously. "That's where you're wrong, Angie. Turns out, I have a sister and brother. Triplets. Imagine that."

Her face drained utterly of color, all the confirmation I needed, not that I required more proof. I'd seen enough. "This is nonsense. I'm making you an appointment with a doctor."

The surprise in Carter's face only lasted a brief moment before he quickly put together the pieces. Perhaps he hadn't known my secret after all; not that it mattered now. I was just glad I was the one who unveiled the truth. Not him.

"Oh really, so you didn't have a baby girl who was born premature and died in the NICU at Elmwood Hospital?" And just like that, I unraveled Angie's deepest, darkest secret. I blew the lid off it.

Shock turned to a calculating gleam so quick, I couldn't believe it. She was already looking for a way to spin a web of lies. It was impressive and scary as hell. This woman was more than a drunk—she was a con artist. Nothing about her life was genuine or true.

Angie schooled her features, morphing her face into one of shock and disbelief. "Why would you say such hateful things to me? Do you really hate me that much, Josephine?"

So she was going for the woe-is-me innocent mom act. I was not buying it. And surprisingly, neither was Carter. Perhaps it wasn't that surprising at all that he believed me. Carter was, after all, his father's son and a conman in his own right. It looks like Angie finally found a family who fit her perfectly.

I was the odd man out.

And I finally understood why.

None of us were cut from the same cloth. I had morals and a fucking conscience. I believed in shit like right and wrong.

Carter's eyes narrowed, bouncing from me to Angie and back to me. "No shit," Carter muttered, staring at me in a different light. "That's why you look just like her. I had a hunch."

I rolled my eyes. "Please, don't pretend you hadn't figured it out."

"I hadn't," he said mildly. "But I'm guessing the Elite did. It's on their little thumb drive, isn't it? All the gritty details. Imagine what that would do to this family—to your mother if it got out."

"She is not my mother." The statement was laced with venom, all the anger built up since I found out burning in my words.

"Josephine." Angie took a seat at my desk, sinking into the chair like a fragile porcelain doll about to shatter into a million pieces. Was this part of her act, a ploy for sympathy? Her breathing grew rapid, a delicate hand resting over her heart. The realization that the truth couldn't be buried seeped into her bones.

I steeled myself, refusing to find compassion or empathy for her. She didn't deserve it. And yet my heart still twinged inside. "Is that even my name? Or was that the name of the baby you lost? Do you even know my real name?"

"Mikayla," she whispered.

I hadn't expected her to answer me, let alone give me the truth. *Mikayla*. The name boomeranged inside my head and a weight I'd been bearing for weeks—for my entire life finally lifted off me. Hearing my name, an admission of the truth from Angie, set me free.

I'd been kidnapped as a baby.

"Holy. Fucking. Shit. Wait until my dad hears this."

"Carter!" Angie snapped, her head whipping up, defeat no longer glimmering sadly in her eyes. Hardness. Desperation. Panic reflected in them now, a woman who would do anything —*anything*—to save the life she'd fought so hard to obtain by any means necessary. She would not go down without one hell of a fight. "Your father should hear this from me," she said, leveling out her voice and schooling her features.

I snorted. "So you can weave more lies? Does it never end?"

She looked at me now. "This isn't simple, Josephine. Not for me."

"What about me? Do you have any idea what it is like to find out that your entire life is a lie? That I have an entire family I know nothing about?" I let all the anguish and hurt seep into my voice.

"Stop," Angie whispered. "That is just not true. I loved you. I love you still. You are my daughter. It doesn't matter that we don't share blood. You will always be mine."

"I am not a possession. You don't own me. Were you ever going to tell me the truth?"

"No," she stated flatly.

Another truth. The blows kept going. This was what I wanted, but still hearing it wasn't easy. "This is some serious shit. You actually stole a baby." I wanted her to understand the deep impact that decision had on not just my life, but hers as well. She was damn lucky she'd gotten away with it and wasn't behind bars.

A heavy sigh left her chest. "It was all a long time ago. I was only thirty-four weeks pregnant. She came too early." The story poured out of her as if she had waited almost eighteen years to unload this secret she had kept to herself. Her gaze was focused just past my shoulder like she was reliving those moments that happened nearly eighteen years ago. "But she was a little fighter and she seemed to be doing okay, which was why her sudden death was such a shock to me." She took a deep breath, Carter and I remaining quiet as we waited. "The hospital had been in a buzz the day I'd given birth. Another mother came in pregnant with triplets. The three of them were born just a few hours after my little girl. But less than twenty-four hours later, I lost her. I just kept thinking, why does she deserve three? Why had my little girl's life been taken, yet all three of them lived? It wasn't fair."

"So you decided to take one of them?" My sharp voice cracked through the room.

"It wasn't planned. It just happened," she defended, her gaze finally connecting back to mine. "An emergency broke out that sent the staff in the nursery out in a rush. Moments after they left, my little girl just suddenly stopped breathing in my arms. I hit the help button, called out for someone to help. I even tried to revive her myself. But it was too late. She was gone. Before I knew what I was doing, I switched out the ID bracelets and swapped you with my baby, laying her little body in the incubator. Letting go of her, saying goodbye was the hardest thing I'd ever done. But then you looked up at me with those dark eyes. You became mine. I loved you instantly."

"Is that supposed to make it okay?" How this woman had ever raised me I'd never understand. Did she not have a remorseful bone in her body? No conscience?

Lightning zapped across the dark sky outside the windows. "You don't understand. You don't know what it's like to lose a daughter." Her eyes pleaded with me.

But my resolve didn't waver. "No, I don't. But I do know what it's like to never have something. I have a brother and a sister. You took them from me."

"I can't lose you too. I can't." Her voice trembled.

"You already have." I didn't care how many times the cops brought me back. I couldn't stay here. Not any longer.

I had to leave.

"You don't mean that," she said, the words breaking over a sob. Tears glossed her eyes.

"I'm not your daughter. I never was." Shoving past Carter, I rushed from the room, unable to stay another second in this house. I couldn't breathe. I was suffocating, drowning in a sea of lies and truths.

"Josephine, wait," Angie called out, shoving to her feet. "Where are you going? You can't leave."

Like hell, I can't.

I reached the stairs and from behind me, I heard footsteps

chasing after me. "Josephine!" she screamed, panic causing her voice to shriek. "Josephine!"

I didn't stop. I didn't look over my shoulder. I just ran out the front door and into the stormy night with only my phone and the clothes on my back.

CHAPTER EIGHTEEN

The wind howled like a wounded animal alone in the woods. Plumes of rain poured down over my head, but I barely noticed. It was difficult to focus on anything else when my life was such a mess. I don't know what I thought would happen when I confronted Angie. Had a part of me actually believed she could discredit the proof I'd seen? That she would have a rational explanation?

And yet, I was also relieved she wasn't my mother.

Mikayla. My name was Mikayla Edwards.

What a strange thought. I'd only ever been Josie James.

Grayson. Kenna. And Mikayla.

What would the three of us become if we'd been together?

I continued to walk mindlessly in the rain, my hair being tossed around my face by the wind. Why the fuck couldn't it have been sunny and cheery on the day my world imploded? It was as if the universe felt my deep-rooted sadness and mourned with me.

Time to say goodbye to this life. Metaphorically and literally.

And I did just that, never once looking back.

I didn't know what my future held, but the storm would not last forever. At some point, the sun would come out, a new day would be born, and hope would rise on the horizon.

It just really sucked at the moment.

Flipping up the hood on my sweatshirt, I ducked under a tree and pulled out my phone. I stared at the screen as it lit up, gnawing on my lower lip. *What do I do now? Who do I call?*

I was essentially homeless. Again.

I couldn't go back to the Pattersons'. Not now. Not ever.

Brock was the first name that popped in my head, not surprising and my finger hovered over his name, but then I remembered. His parents were home.

There were several other friends I could call, including Ainsley or Mads. I also could always call Easton. Now might be a good time to tell him the truth, but I didn't have the energy to have that conversation. I was fucking exhausted after dealing with Angie and Carter.

I knew where I wanted to go. I didn't want my friends. Or even Brock. Not today.

Today, I needed someone who would understand. I needed my brother.

With my mind made up, I sat on the curb and dialed his number. It rang and rang, before going to voicemail. *Shit.* I had nowhere to go and couldn't stay out in here in the rain, so I requested an Uber through the app on my phone.

Twenty minutes later, I stood outside the Edwardses' home. Even the somber storm couldn't dim the beauty of this house. The windows warm glow reflected like a lighthouse in the dark, guiding me home.

Except... this wasn't my home, no matter how much I might want it to be.

A crash of thunder vibrated at my back as I pulled the white hood from my sweatshirt closer around my face, not that it helped all that much. Soaked to the bone, I stood on the porch, wondering if I'd made a mistake in coming here. Before I could change my mind, I pressed the doorbell, my fingers shaking from both the cold and from the residual effects of my fight with Angie.

I wrapped my arms around myself as I waited, my hood shielding most of my face. It wasn't long until I heard shuffling from the other side of the door. The lock flipped, and a woman's laugh filtered over the rolling storm.

Did Grayson have a girl over?

I wouldn't doubt it.

Shit. I should have called first.

The door swung open, and my heart dropped at the sight of the tall woman with sleek dark hair. Sparkling deep gray eyes fell upon me, and the smile on her lips slipped just a notch. Her familiar face glowed in the light of the foyer.

I couldn't help but gape. I had thought about this moment for weeks. What I would say. What she would look like. I could see myself in her features. The same skin coloring. The same dark, glossy hair. And the same slim nose.

Whereas Angie had a natural sex appeal, Mrs. Edwards was stylish in a classic way born from wealth and an upbringing you couldn't fake.

She was beautiful.

And I wanted to hug her.

The air in my lungs halted. I hadn't expected his parents to be home, let alone to come face-to-face with my birth mother.

Suddenly tongue-tied, I stood in the rain looking homeless, like a stray kitten that had wandered up to the front porch.

"Can I help you?" she asked, her tone gentle and a bit confused. When I didn't answer right away, the smile faded completely from her lips, and her eyes grew concerned. "Are you alright? Do you need help?"

My throat clogged with emotion, and feelings surged out of nowhere, catching me off guard. *Shit. I am going to cry.* Quickly, before I made a fool of myself, I blurted out, "Is Grayson here?" My voice trembling. The rain blended with my tears, hiding them, but then again, perhaps I wasn't fooling anyone.

Mrs. Edwards's grey eyes softened. I must have looked pathetic. "Grayson!" she hollered, angling her body slightly to the side so her voice projected through the house. "Come in, please. You must be freezing." She ushered me inside with a wave of her hand.

Some of my brain returned. "I'm a mess. I wouldn't want to ruin your floors."

"Nonsense. Come in," she insisted.

Crap. Perhaps I should turn and run? This wasn't how I pictured meeting my birth mom for the first time.

But my feet had a different idea as they stepped over the threshold into the warm and cozy foyer. Something about her presence changed the vibe of the house. It was cheerier and homier.

Flipping down my hood, I attempted to fix my wet hair and knew the second Mrs. Edwards got her first real look at me. An audible gasp rang over the room, and I watched a flare of recognition washed over her. A manicured hand flew to her heart, eyes brimming in confusion. "Kenna?" She blinked and realized that she must have made a mistake. "Sorry, you just look so much like my—"

"Josie?" a deep voice interrupted.

My gaze went to Grayson as he descended the stairs.

His eyes swept over me, his mouth turning down into a serious frown. "Josie, are you okay? What happened?" He came to stand beside his shocked mother, whose gaze still raked over every inch of my face.

My shoulders heaved, a sob bubbling out of my lips. I was a fucking mess. This was all too much. I didn't know what to do. Without saying a word, I walked right into his arms, which came instinctually around me. I buried my face into the familiar scent of his shirt.

"Did he hurt you?" Grayson demanded, the muscles in his arms tightening.

I shook my head, still unable to form words. I wanted to hide in Grayson's arms, never lift my head again, not until I felt strong.

But then I remembered we weren't alone.

"Grayson, what is going on?" Mrs. Edwards asked.

He kept an arm around me, probably because he thought I would crumble to the ground if he left me go. He wasn't far off. "Mom, this is Josie."

I sniffled, lifting my tear-streaked face. Was he going to tell her who I was? I didn't know if my heart could take it. I'd dreamed of this moment, but as it stared me in the face, I wasn't prepared.

"She's a friend from school," he explained.

My chest exhaled, even as a ribbon of disappointment curled within me. I wanted to be done with the lies, but I needed a day to collect myself and Grayson somehow sensed that. He gave my arm a gentle squeeze.

She shook her head as if to clear the confusion. "Forgive me. I don't meant to stare. It's just you look so much like my daughter. The resemblance is uncanny. You took me by surprise."

I am your daughter, a voice inside me said, but I kept that voice quiet for the time being.

"We're going to go upstairs," Grayson told his mom, a look passing between them.

"That might be a good idea. I'll get you a towel." She offered me a comforting smile as she went down the hall. She glanced over her shoulder, and our eyes met again.

Grayson rubbed a hand over my back, bringing my attention back to him. "What is going on?" he asked.

"I'm sorry. I didn't know where else to go. I didn't know they were home," I rushed out quickly when we were alone, wiping off my face with the end of my sleeves.

"It's okay. Really," he assured. "Do you want to talk about what happened?"

"No," I answered honestly. "But you deserve to know."

His brows drew together. "Is that why you came here?" The front of his shirt was imprinted with wet spots.

"You mean instead of running to Brock?" I concluded.

His lips twitched. "That's not what I said."

"No, but you were thinking it."

"Yeah, I was. It's just I know how close you've become."

I snorted. "Except he's with Ava now."

"This has more to do with you just being jealous over a bitch like Ava," he said seriously. When had Grayson begun to understand me so well? "Especially when you know it is all bullshit."

Mrs. Edwards came back with a fresh white towel in her hand. "Here you go. Grayson, why don't you see if there is anything dry she can borrow from your sister," she offered.

Chilled, I replied, "Thank you. I'm sorry to just show up like this," I apologized, finally able to find my voice in front of her.

"Nonsense. Don't you worry about that." It was obvious she could see the hurt and bruises on my face, that I'd been through an ordeal and needed a friend.

Not just a friend—my brother.

I was embarrassed to have her see me like this, but the damage was already done.

Slipping off my drenched shoes and hoodie, I wrapped the towel around my shoulders as Grayson said, "Come on, let's get you into something dry. Then we can talk."

Mrs. Edwards's gaze followed me as I trailed Grayson up the stairs as if she couldn't take her eyes off me. But I understood the feeling well. I also wanted to just stare at her, soak up every detail of the woman who should have been my mom.

Inside Grayson's bedroom, I toweled off my face and hair, waiting for him to return with some dry clothes for me to wear. What had I done? Was it right to come here, to bring my problems with me? The last thing I wanted to do was implode their lives.

Grayson came back holding a pile of clothes. He kicked the door shut behind him. "I didn't know what you wanted."

I could care less about making a fashion statement. I just wanted out of these heavy, wet clothes. "Are you mad?" I asked, unable to read Grayson's face. Or perhaps it was his lack of attitude that threw me off.

Grayson rubbed at his jaw. "At you? No, why would I be mad?"

I could think of a dozen reasons. "For showing up here."

"It's not like you planned it. Besides, it's time the truth comes out, don't you think?"

Once again, he surprised me. "I'm not sure of anything," I mumbled.

"How about we get you dry first," he suggested, nodding his head toward the door behind me. "The bathroom is in there. Take your time; I need to make a call."

"Brock?" I assumed.

His phone was already in his hand as he nodded. "Yeah, he needs to know where you are."

"Because he said so, or because he gives a damn?" I couldn't stop the snappy retort. I would have thought after last night, things between Brock and me would be clearer to me, but everything was so fucking muddled in my head.

Grayson grinned. "Both."

I took the clothes from him and walked my soggy ass into the bathroom. Alone, I gave myself a moment to just breathe, to allow myself to feel safe. I didn't know how long I'd be able to stay here or where I'd go for the night, but for now, I wouldn't think about it. I'd deal with it when the time came.

Peeling off the wet clothes plastered to my body, I picked through the few pieces of clothes. They smelled of laundry soap with a hint of vanilla. I held up a pair of purple jogging pants and a white knitted top with a floral print in the logo. These were Kenna's. Her style was different than mine, cute and super girly. I didn't mind purple, but floral... not my thing.

Slipping into the cozy joggers, I opted for a plain V-neck T-shirt in cream instead of the white floral. They fit perfectly. But as my triplet, it shouldn't have come as a surprise that we were similar in stature. It was a weird feeling, wearing something that belonged to a sister I'd never met. In a way, it made me feel close to her.

Grayson just ended his call to Brock as I came out of the bathroom. He sat on the edge of his bed and glanced up at my approach. "Let me guess, he demanded to come get me," I said.

The look on his face told me I was right before he even spoke. "More or less. I convinced him it wasn't a good idea. You'll stay here for the night."

I sat on the bed beside him, leaving plenty of space between us. I would have thought being alone in Grayson's room would be awkward. It wasn't. Just the opposite. Being at his house felt right. For the first time since I'd left my old house on the other side of town, I felt as if I belonged. "What about your parents?"

He shrugged. "They'll be cool with it."

I let him see my gratitude. "Thank you."

Setting his phone aside on the nightstand, he replied, "I figured you came here for a reason."

I tugged on the end of a damp strand of my hair. "I got into a fight with Angie. Carter was there."

"Did they hurt you?" His brandy-colored eyes darkened as he scanned over my face looking for new marks.

Here went nothing. "No, but I told her I knew what she had done. I couldn't pretend anymore. I couldn't let her or Carter control me further."

Grayson ran his fingers through his hair. "You didn't have a choice, Josie. It's okay."

"Mikayla."

Grayson's dark eyes flickered. "What?"

I frowned slightly. "She told me my name was Mikayla."

Grayson's voice dropped. "Yeah." Silence followed for a moment, as we were both absorbed in the past and the deception that brought us here. "We need to tell my parents before Angie tries to pull the harboring a runaway bullshit. It's the only way to keep you safe."

I agreed, but the idea of telling them filled me with trepidation. It was stupid to think they would reject me, but the fear was there, like a little thorn stuck in my heart. They didn't know me, and I didn't know them, but that bead of doubt wondered if they would even want to know me. Nearly eighteen years later. Perhaps they were happy with the two children they had.

I picked at my nails, needing something to do with my hands. "Carter was there when it all came out."

"All the more reason that you and I take control of the situation. We don't need your... hell, I don't know what to call her, your kidnapper?" he tested, and then shook his head. "Whatever, what is important is that we have a legal leg to stand on if she tries to pull the cops into this again. She tried that shit with your, uh, dad because she knows he doesn't have the financial means to fight. That isn't true here. My parents will fight her."

I chewed on the inside of my cheek. "How can you be so sure?"

"I don't think my mom ever really let you go. Call it motherly instinct or whatever, but she's never forgotten you. Then of course there is the fact that you look so much like Kenna. It won't be hard for them to believe you're their daughter."

"Is your dad here?"

"Our dad," he corrected, a concept my mind still was learning to accept. "And he won't be back until late tonight. We'll tell them tomorrow. Together. Tonight just try and get some sleep."

I flung back on the bed, staring up at his ceiling. "I can't believe this is happening. I'm not sure I'm ready now."

He nudged one of my legs hanging over the bed with his foot. "Everything will work out. You're back where you belong, with us."

I wasn't sure if he was talking about his family or the Elite. It didn't matter. I wanted both. Turning on my side, I propped my head upon my hand, looking up at Grayson. "How did you feel when you found out about me?"

The question hung there. Then he exhaled. "Like I'd been kicked in the gut. It was difficult to believe what I saw, reading over the files the PI sent. Even though the truth stared me in the face, I didn't want to believe it. My first thought was how this would affect my family. My parents had been through so much, Kenna too. And believe it or not, I thought about you."

My nose wrinkled. "Me?"

"You'd been taken. I wondered what kind of life you had. If you were happy. But it didn't take long after reading the rest of the information to draw conclusions. Then I saw you—saw the woman who took you." His voice turned cold.

"It wasn't always bad, you know," I told him softly. "There were happy times. I had Ainsley and my dad."

"I'm sure there were. But I also think you don't know anything different than the life you've had. God, I was such a prick to you."

I snorted. "That's putting it mildly."

A half-smile played at his lips. "I'd like the chance to show you what a family can be like."

My heart stuttered. "A part of me thinks this is a dream or a game."

"No games. Not anymore," he assured.

I rested my hands over my stomach. "I don't want to put any of you in danger. Angie won't give up. And Carter...he hasn't forgotten about the flash drive. If he can't use me, he will find another means to obtain it. And now that he knows the truth about Angie...there is no telling what he will do with the information."

"We'll deal with Carter. Together. The five of us. And as for Angie, she won't dare come here or send the cops. You're safe."

For now. But I couldn't shake the feeling something bad was about to go down. Lies and deception had a way of untangling themselves when you least expected it. I had to be prepared for whatever happened next.

I had to stay strong.

I had to survive the disorder that was my life.

"I'm sure it's been a long night. Come on," Grayson hopped off the bed. "I'll show you where you can stay." He waited for me at the doorway and led me down the hall to the room next door. Reaching his hand just inside, he flipped on the wall switch, flooding the bedroom in light.

My eyes took a quick pan of the very girly space. "Is this...?"

He nodded. "It's Kenna's room. I hope that is okay for tonight. I'll have one of the guest rooms made up tomorrow."

Wearing her clothes, sleeping in her bed... I was almost starting to feel like the sister who left, but looking into Grayson's face, I could see that was not his intention. "Thank you, Grayson." I smiled.

His hands shoved into his back pockets. "Stop thanking me. Seriously. It makes me feel all saint-like, and I'm definitely not."

I chuckled. "That you are not."

He lingered, an awkward silence falling between us. Grayson and I didn't spend loads of time alone. It was obvious we still had to work on being at ease with each other. "If you need anything, I'm in the next room."

I opened my mouth.

"Don't you dare thank me," he warned before I could form the words, knowing exactly what I'd been about to say.

I playfully shoved at his shoulder. "I wouldn't dream of it, asshole."

"Better." He leaned against the wall. "You ready for tomorrow?"

Fuck. I'd all but forgotten about school on Monday. "There are some things you just can't prepare for."

"Like finding out your sister's not dead."

"Or that you were kidnapped."

His lips morphed into a smirk. "Precisely. You got this, Josie. Or should I start calling you Mikayla?"

I made a face. "I'm not sure I can handle a name change. I'm still in the middle of an identity crisis."

"You know who you are. You're still you. You're one of us." His words were sincere and washed over me like a warm blanket. Secure and soft. He had no idea what that meant to me.

Because my throat clogged with emotion and the urge to thank him yet again rose, I said nothing and only nodded.

"Get some sleep," he said, before he left, shutting the door quietly behind him.

Alone, I stood near the door, uncertain about everything, including what to do next. My arms folded around myself in a hug as I waited for the surge of panic to grip me, but it never came. After a moment of just breathing, I realized it was because I felt secure here, just as I did with Brock.

Curious, I wandered through my sister's room, trying to get a sense of the virtual stranger who was a part of me. Fairy lights framed the white headboard of the queen-sized bed. In the corner near a window hung an egg-shaped chair, a fuzzy lavender blanket draped over the cushioned seat, the same color as the walls. I ran a finger along the dresser, reading the labels on the perfume bottles. Unable to help myself, I picked up one and sniffed the cap. Pictures of Kenna and her friends framed the vanity mirror. Mads was in almost every one. I recognized a few of the girls from school, including one with Ava. Apparently, Kenna had been on the cheerleading squad.

So much personality lived in this room.

It allowed me to learn a little more about Kenna.

Hesitantly, I padded over to the bed and sank down. I should probably text Mads and Ainsley, let them know where I was, but as I stared at my phone, I didn't have the energy to make those calls or send the texts.

Tomorrow. I'd tell them tomorrow.

I had just settled into bed when a soft knock came at the door. "Come in," I called.

Mrs. Edwards's reassuring smile greeted me as the door gently opened. She carried a tray with a small plate and a white cup. "I thought you might like some tea before bed. It might help warm you up after being out in the rain."

I tried to recall if Angie had ever brought me tea in bed. "Thank you, that sounds wonderful, but you didn't have to go to the trouble."

"No trouble at all. It helps me, reminds me of times when my children needed me." She set the tray on the nightstand, and I saw the plate had cookies on it.

"You miss that," I said.

Her gaze swept over the room before landing back on me. "Very much. The only time they allow me to dote on them now is if they're sick, and even then it's not the same."

"Well, you've done a remarkable job raising them. I wouldn't have gotten through the last few weeks without Grayson."

"You have no idea how nice it is to hear. It hasn't always been easy for him. I hope you don't think it too forward, but I want you to know that you are safe here. If there is one thing we don't tolerate in this house, it's bullying." She'd already had one daughter subjected to something traumatic and lost a son.

My heart ached for both of us. Tears misted in my eyes. I hadn't been or felt safe in a long time, not like I did right then.

"Well, I'll let you get to bed. It's very nice to meet you, Josie."

CHAPTER NINETEEN

I wouldn't call what zoomed inside my belly butterflies. It was more like a swarm of bees buzzing around inside me, stinging me, poisoning me with their venom.

Today I went back to the Academy.

My nightmare hadn't ended the moment I stepped foot inside the Edwards' home, despite how sheltered I felt within the walls of this large house. Sure, last night I slept soundly and without any horrible dreams, but it didn't matter.

Awake or asleep, my demons waited.

Grayson drove me to school after a quick breakfast. Both his parents were already deep in work when we trotted downstairs. His dad was in the middle of negotiations for a new film, which meant long days and nights while he was home. I had yet to see him, but it was probably for the best. My stomach couldn't handle any more anxiety. I was already seconds away from hurling the toast I managed to wash down with a cup of coffee.

Grayson steered the Viper onto Crest Boulevard, heading to school. "Are you nervous?"

I pulled my gaze from the window to regard him. "No, why?"

"Because you can't sit still," he commented, eyes drifting to my bouncing knee.

"Shit," I mumbled, placing my hands over my legs to stop the jumbled nerves. "Honestly, I just want this day to be over. Fuck, I want this year to be over."

"Look, I won't lie to you. Things will be different when we get to school," he warned.

"You don't have to explain," I insisted. I tugged at the hem of my plaid skirt. Another borrowed item from Kenna.

"We're not abandoning you. But we have to keep our distance," he explained, looking uncomfortable doing so. "At least, we're supposed to make it look that way." He flipped his blinker on as he switched lanes. "Brock needs to keep up appearances."

I didn't bother to suppress the eye roll. "For your information, I could care less what Brock fucking Taylor does."

His lips mustered up into a smile. "Keep telling yourself that, Josie. Keep telling yourself that."

I would.

And did the entire way I walked up to the school with Grayson by my side. The looks were expected. I had gotten the shit beat out of me, enough that I'd missed nearly a week of school. Of course people were curious. Not all the bruises had faded, but they were easier to conceal with makeup. This morning I looked almost normal, most of the evident traces of the fight hidden, unless you got up close and personal.

Grayson stiffened as we reached the pathway that led to the front entrance, and I lifted my head to see what tangled his boxers. I assumed it would be Carter, enemy number one, and prepared myself.

Nope.

A pair of glacial aqua eyes snagged my gaze, and I swore the world froze. For a long moment, I could only see Brock.

But the bastard wasn't alone.

Ava had her arms looped around his neck as she pressed her slim body into his. He lounged against the side of the building, and I couldn't shake the feeling that he did so deliberately—as if he waited for me.

Ava's lips curled like those of a possessive feline who had trapped the mouse. So damn proud of herself. She got rid of me and won the prize.

I wanted to slam her face into the concrete and paint the ground with her blood.

She had another thing coming if she thought there wouldn't be payback. I'd never thought of myself as vindictive. I could probably let the beatdown go, but seeing her clinging to *my* guy...

Fuck no.

I doubted he would appreciate it if I walked up and slapped Ava, although Grayson and I might find it amusing. Brock would be annoyed his plan had been foiled. It was all about the deception for him—seeking revenge.

Grayson bent down and whispered in my ear, "He is going to ruin her. Just remember that."

Brock's lips curved arrogantly, but what no one noticed was the firming of his jaw. He fought to keep the sneer in place. This guy... he wasn't my Brock.

Grayson guided me to the entrance under the sharp archway of the Academy, and as he went to pull the door open for me, a group of girls giggled. Grayson rolled his eyes. "Ignore them."

Micah appeared on the other side of me just as I walked inside, looping an arm around my neck and pulling me against him for a sort of half hug. "Finally, you're back. This place is so fucking boring without you." His light blue eyes twinkled like he was up to no good, which he usually was.

"Hey to you too," I greeted, leaning into him.

"You've been here for like two seconds and already got the school buzzing." His platinum hair was messily styled so it stood up on one side. Two dimples kissed either side of his cheeks.

"I live to entertain," I grumbled, eyeing the halls that stretched out on either side of us. Chatter echoed off the stone walls as everyone prepared for class and caught up on their weekend. It died down just slightly as the three of us passed by, but that was fairly normal when the Elite were around. "Aren't you supposed to ignore me or something?"

Micah kept his arm around me as I headed to my locker, but I didn't mind. There was something nice and comforting about being snuggled by him.

Grayson scowled as we turned the corner. "If your hands go

any lower, bro, I'm going to have to kick your ass," he warned Micah. I hadn't even noticed Micah's wandering hand on the small of my back. He had slipped a finger into the belt loop on my plaid skirt.

Micah's grin widened. "I'd like to see you try."

"Besides, Brock just walked in, and he looks like he wants to kill you," Grayson added, glancing to the side.

The smile on Micah's lips remained in place. "Good. He should have to suffer too, don't you think, Josie Jo?"

I grinned up at Micah, avoiding Brock. "I knew you were my favorite." I grabbed my notebook out of my locker and shoved it inside my bag alongside my laptop before facing the guys.

Grayson frowned.

Micah winked at me. "I'm everyone's favorite."

Shaking my head, I started walking to my class. "I can't believe I thought I missed you guys."

Grayson snorted.

"Where's Fynn?" I asked. I'd seen them all but him this morning.

"With Mads," Micah replied, striding alongside me and sharing a look with Grayson.

"She's got security detail?" I guessed, doing my best to ignore all the glances we were getting.

Micah nodded. "Brock's orders."

I imagined Mads was cursing Brock to seven different kinds of Hell. "Oh, I'm sure Mads loves that."

Micah snickered. "She's lucky it's him and not me."

The material of my plaid skirt rubbed against the side of my legs as we strutted down the hall. "When are you going to admit that you have a thing for her?"

His retort was quick. "As soon as she admits she can't live without my dick."

Grayson made a noise in the back of his throat. "That's my cousin, dude."

I was with Grayson on this one. "Oh, my God, you're impossible. I should punch you in your dick for saying that," I said to Micah.

"Go ahead. I dare you," the bastard challenged, grinning the entire time like there was nothing he would love more.

"Dude! Stop fucking flirting with my sister. I can't take it," Grayson blurted. "It's bad enough she's banging one of my friends."

Hearing Grayson call me his sister brought a smile to my lips, so I overlooked the fact that he'd brought up Brock.

Micah shrugged, looking anything but remorseful. "It's not my fault she's hot."

"But it is your fault that you're a horny douchebag," Grayson pointed out.

"God, I really need to get laid," Micah muttered, his gaze shifting to me.

I lifted my hands in the air and took a step away from the wickedly charming smile on Micah's face. "Don't look at me. I'm not a damn standby girl. I'm only screwing one of you. Period. Not one of you at a time. Just one. Ever. And stop looking at me like that."

Grayson shoved him halfheartedly on the shoulder. "Go to class."

As Micah turned to go down the opposite hall, he slapped my ass. Not hard, but enough to cause me to squeal and Grayson's frown to deepen. "I swear to God, some girl needs to break his heart," my triplet grumbled, his glare burning into Micah's retreating back.

My morning in general went by pretty uneventfully. I didn't have any classes with either Ava or Brock, which allowed me to just concentrate on making sure I was all caught up. But of course, my mind wandered frequently. I couldn't seem to get the picture of him and Ava together this morning out of my head.

I never thought I would admit it, but I actually missed having the guys walk me to class. I found myself looking for them after each bell and the disappointment as the day dragged on never lessened.

Mads waited by my locker at lunch. Fynn was with her. It was the first time I'd seen him all day.

He offered me a grin. Fynn had a smile that literally melted hearts. He was the sweetheart of the bunch—a big guy with an even bigger heart.

I didn't know why the fuck he hung around with the others.

Shoving my shit into my locker, I steeled myself, taking a deep breath. *You can do this. No big deal. It's pretend. Fake. Just like the bitch herself.*

But when I walked into the cafeteria and saw Ava and Brock sitting at the Elite table, there was nothing fake about what I felt. Jealousy slammed into me—hot and fierce, lancing through the anxiety I'd been feeling.

"Josie."

It was only then that I realized Mads had called my name more than once. "Sorry. I can't help it. I just want to kick her in her kitty."

Fynn chuckled.

Mads glared in Ava's direction. "I'll hold her down. You do the kicking."

Forcing my gaze away, I glanced at Mads. "You're such a good friend."

Fynn towered over me as we moved into the lunch line. "Girls are crazy. This is exactly why I don't date. You totally strike me as the kind of girl who would slash my tires and key my car."

I was pretty sure he didn't mean that as a compliment, but I took it as one. "Fuck yes, I would."

"Don't forget to take a crowbar to the windows," Mads added.

Fynn grabbed a food tray and two milk containers. "Should I be worried about Brock or his car?"

"Both," Mads and I said at the same time.

"I hope you know I'm not sitting anywhere near that bitch." I grabbed a water bottle and a salad off the buffet, not really hungry. I lost my appetite the second I laid eyes on my guy with another girl.

"Same. I'm with Josie," Mads agreed as she reached for hummus wrap. "The whole situation is fucked-up enough as it is."

My back was to them and yet, I felt their eyes on me, particularly Ava's. "I can't even be in the same room with them."

"I know you don't want to hear this, but no part of this is easy for him either."

Something in Fynn's voice, the way he said the statement felt true, but I ignored that intuition. "Well, he does a shitty job of showing it."

Fynn had a tray full of food. If I didn't know him and his never-ending appetite, I would wonder where he put it all. "You know Brock. He isn't going to let it show. He'll ice everyone out until it's done."

"Don't try and pull on my heartstrings, Fynn. Not cool. Right now, I just need to hate him."

Mads looped her arm through mine, steering me to the opposite side of the lunchroom. "And hate him we will."

When Fynn, Micah, and Grayson joined the table Mads and I sat at in the far corner of the room, I was taken aback. Even Mads seemed surprised. She lifted a brow at Micah as he spun the chair next to her around and straddled it, dropping the tray of food. "What are you doing?" she demanded, eyeing the playboy who'd broken her heart. "You're supposed to be avoiding her."

Micah flashed her a grin, and I swore the girls at the next table sighed. "Making your day."

Mads was immune to those dimples. "Try ruining it more likely," she griped.

Micah wasn't deterred. He rarely was. "Come on, Mads, you know deep down you harbor a lady boner for me."

She peeled open her sandwich, showing more interest in it

than in the gorgeous platinum-haired guy beaming at her. "I honestly don't know what anyone sees in you."

His smile brightened. "It's the dimples. Kills them every time."

I wasn't sure I could sit here and watch them weirdly flirt. I wanted no reminders of love. And once the two of them got started...

"So, what lie did Brock tell Ava to explain why the three of you are still talking to me?" I quickly interjected before the sexual banter continued.

Grayson and Fynn both looked relieved. "That you're a standby girl," Micah explained, looking all too happy with the lie.

I choked. "He did what?" That prick. I did what I'd told myself not to do. I snuck a glance over at Ava and Brock. Pain lanced through my chest. He couldn't have come up with a better excuse? I swear he did it on purpose, just because he knew it would rile me up. "How much longer is this going to last?"

Fynn cast a glance at the table duo in question. "Until Brock destroys her."

Grayson's gaze followed Fynn's, his lips pulled into a straight line. "What she did was unforgivable in his book. She never should have touched you. That was just as good as issuing her own death sentence. He is ruthless when he needs to be."

"What happens next? What will he do to her?" I asked, not that I was the least bit concerned about her. It was Brock who I worried about. These kinds of actions left scars.

Micah dug into his burger. "Who knows. But it will definitely create fireworks," he said as he munched. "Shit, it will be memorable as fuck."

I found it impossible not to sneak glances at Ava and Brock's table, despite how hard I tried to resist. My willpower when it came to him was pathetic. The other Elite might have chosen to sit with Mads and me, but that didn't mean Brock and Ava were alone. A few other football players and Ava's squad gathered around.

I didn't know if Ava noticed, but Brock seemed to be looking at me each time my gaze roamed in his direction. So many questions relayed through those quick glances, and I ached for five minutes alone with him, except I knew we wouldn't get much talking done. Those few moments would be spent doing sinful things to his mouth.

Relief poured through me when it was nearly time for my next class. Mads and I took our ritual pit stop to the bathroom, Micah trailing behind us.

Outside the girls' bathroom, no Ava in sight, Mads spun around and put a finger into Micah's chest, halting him. "We're going to the bathroom. Alone," she emphasized at the playboy who would have happily trailed us inside.

"You got five minutes before I come in there," he warned, which didn't really hit the mark when he grinned as he did.

"There is such a thing as smothering." Mads quickly put her hand over his mouth as it opened and narrowed her eyes. "Don't think about giving me some snappy retort about smothering me in some perverted position."

Micah lifted a brow, his eyes dancing with humor and hints of desire.

My best friend ripped her hand away from his mouth. "Did you just lick me?"

"Just a little taste. As good as I remember."

I rolled my eyes and shoved past them into the bathroom before things got kinky. Mads followed a second later, shaking her head. "He is unbelievable."

I glanced at her reflection in the mirror. "Are you going to admit that you still have a thing for him?"

She sighed, leaning her butt against the sink. "Depends, are you going to admit you're in love with Brock?"

I grimaced as she pulled out her routine after lunch cigarette. "Is it that obvious?"

She put the smoke in between her lips and flicked the lighter. Flames jumped to life. "Only because I know you and I've known Brock most my life," she mumbled with the cigarette still clenched in her mouth and then lit it.

I groaned and locked myself into one of the stalls to pee.

"Grayson told me what happened with Carter and your mom. Are you okay?"

Flushing, I waited until I was at the sink to reply. "I think it might be a while before I'm truly okay. But for now, I'm just happy to not be alone. I don't know what I would do without you or them."

She held the cigarette between her fingers, a trail of smoke floating into the bathroom. "There was a reason we came up with that stupid plan. It's like the universe knew how much you would need the Elite."

I turned on the water and washed my hands. "I'm not sure I

believe in fate, but if I did, I'd say destiny or whatever is a twisted son of a bitch."

"I'm just happy you're here."

That made one of us. Being back at the academy was harder than I envisioned. Seeing Brock... made me want to run for the hills.

Mads boosted herself up on the sink, taking a long drag on her cigarette. "What did Aunt Liana do when she saw you?"

"She was a little confused," I admitted, drying off my hands.

Her eyes grew wide as if to say, *oh shit.* "I imagine you gave her quite the shock, seeing you standing there."

"God, she is so nice."

"She is. She is going to freak out when she learns the truth. And I mean that in a good way. To get a child back after all that she's lost..."

"I thought this was what I wanted, but now I'm not so sure I'm ready," I stated.

"You don't have anything to be nervous about. I get this is some life-altering shit and probably scary as hell, but if you don't take this step, can you honestly say you won't regret it?" she posed.

I met her reflection in the mirror as a defeated breath left me. "No."

Mads crossed her legs. "That's your answer. Now, tell me what's it like sleeping in her room?"

Leave it to Mads to make something sound simple. "Weird. Super weird. But also...kind of nice. I get the chance to see Kenna, if that makes sense."

She nodded, a speck of sadness moving into her eyes. "It does. I get it."

I turned around and glanced sidelong at her. "No one here seems to like to talk about her."

Mads blew out a cloud of smoke. "It's been two years. People forget what they don't see every day. But you remind them, those who knew her at least."

The five-minute warning bell shrilled through the bathroom. "We should probably get to class." Mads took one long inhale from her cigarette before putting it out in the sink and washing it down the drain. She hopped off the sink, fluffed her hair, and offered me a piece of gum as we walked to the door.

Micah's head turned in our direction from where he leaned on the wall waiting. His brows were drawn together and his eyes lacked their usual twinkle. It didn't take me long to figure out why.

Ava and Brock headed toward us, splitting off to go to class like everyone else. Ava's eyes locked with mine, and her entire demeanor changed. She grinned like a demon swinging its pitchfork.

She slid her fingers into Brock's hair, possessively.

Everything clenched inside me. Anger rose within me, swift and violent. My hands trembled as I curled them into fists and his eyes lifted to mine. For a split second, they pleaded with me to understand.

They looked like the perfect couple. The quarterback and the cheerleader. So very clichéd.

Brock was everything I wasn't. Popular. Gorgeous. The idol of Elmwood Academy. How did we make sense?

Maybe he was better off with someone like Ava?

Those old doubts and insecurities of not being good enough crept inside me. I hated them, hated the way they made me feel less.

The flame built and built inside me until I felt as if I would explode. I was a light fuse, waiting to detonate.

Fuck this.

I stormed off to class.

I thought when the day ended my nerves would be gone.

So not the case.

Going home with Grayson meant the bomb I'd been waiting to drop was about to explode, which gave me anxiety like a motherfucker. It was difficult to explain what I felt. On one hand, it felt as if the truth would never come out. On the other hand, I was so scared of what would happen when it did. This was what they called a double-edged sword.

First I had to sit through Grayson's grueling football practice, which I'd forgotten about or blocked from my memory. It was anyone's guess.

Carter hadn't shown up for school today. That added another layer to my uneasiness.

What had happened after I left on Sunday?

Had he told his father?

I'd expected Angie to blow up my phone, and her radio silence was cause for concern. It wasn't like her to give up, to let go. She was a relentless bitch—a trait I thought I had inherited from her. Or perhaps it was learned behavior.

I sat in the back of the stands, my face hidden behind my laptop as I attempted to get my homework done. It was next to impossible when all I wanted to do was watch Brock.

How could I ignore him in ass-tight pants?

My self-control was at an all-time low or MIA altogether. If only I could make Ava disappear for good. Practice was almost fun since Ava and the cheer squad were practicing their annoying routines in the gym.

I leaned my chin on my hand, glancing over the rim of my laptop as Brock tossed a perfect spiral down the field. His gaze flipped to me the second it went into the receiver's hands. These stolen glances between us were killing me. Did he not understand how difficult this separation between us was for me? Especially, since I pretty much had gone and done the one thing I told myself not to. I'd fallen for him.

Sweaty and stinky, Grayson drove us home after practice. Being confined in a car with a seventeen-year-old guy who just rolled around on the grass for an hour was not something I recommended to anyone.

I chewed on my chipped painted nail, a bundle of nerves. "Grayson, are you sure this is a good idea?"

He opened up the sunroof, allowing more air to move through the car. "Are you having second thoughts?"

At this rate, I'd have no nails left by the time we got to the Edwardscs' house. Clasping my hands together, I sighed. "I don't know. Maybe."

Grayson eased the Viper to a stop at a red light and looked

at me. "It's better if we tell them than finding out on the evening news. We have no idea what Carter will do with the truth. Hell, as far as we know, your mom could be in jail already."

With everything that happened, I'd been consumed with my own emotions. "Do you really think he would turn her in?" A thread of something like fear raced through my blood.

Grayson lifted a brow.

I thumped myself on the forehead with the palm of my hand. "I can't believe I just asked that. Of course he would." But I would know about it first. The police would open an investigation.

The light changed to green, and Grayson eased his foot onto the gas. "When the truth comes out, will you be okay with the fallout?"

"Honestly, I haven't let myself consider it. She wasn't a wonderful mom or an easy person to love."

The wind whipped through his damp dark hair, drying the sweat. "But you do love her."

I took a moment to consider, to try and put aside all the hurt and betrayal I felt. "Despite everything... I do. How fucked-up does that make me?"

"You can't just erase seventeen years of history."

Those emotions I suppressed for just a minute came gushing back. "I'm angry. I'm hurt. I'm sad and confused. A part of me will always care about her, but I can't forgive her. Not yet."

"And you don't have to. I think it might be best if we told our mom first. Alone," he said.

Our mom.

My heart gave one giant yank in my chest. I turned my gaze out the window before Grayson caught the sudden water that sprang to my eyes. *Don't cry. Don't cry.*

But I hadn't been quick enough.

"Are you crying?" he asked softly.

God, you would think I was on my period, as unstable as my emotions were. "No," I replied, my voice sounding funny, giving me away. I snuck a glance at him, trying to hold back the tears.

His eyes returned to the road, mouth flattening. "Well, my triplet telepathy is calling bullshit."

I rubbed at my eyes angrily. "That's not a thing."

He shrugged. "It could be. Kenna and I occasionally have had weird premonitions before."

"I'll keep that in mind the next time I get a strange feeling."

Grayson turned the steering wheel with one hand, the other hand downshifting. "It's okay, you know. You don't have to be this brave badass chick all the time."

My stomach fluttered. "You think I'm badass?"

He shook his head, one side of his mouth lifting. "Don't let it go to your head. I'm trying to be serious here."

Tears one minute and a grin the next. What a fucking car ride this was turning out to be. "Fine, continue having your big brother moment."

He rolled his eyes. "You ruined it. But what I was trying to say is I can be brave for both of us, if you let me."

I blinked, staring at him like Grayson was a virtual stranger. "Were you abducted by aliens recently? Where the hell is Grayson the prick? Since when are you a nice guy?"

The car ride wasn't long enough. Grayson pulled into the

long driveway, the Viper's engine purring. He put the car into park and faced me, a dark smile twitching on his lips. "I'm not."

That was better. Nice Grayson made me nervous, and I didn't need any more help in that department. My eyes shifted to the enormous house looming in front of me. Shit was about to get real.

This was my do-or-die moment. I swallowed a knot that suddenly formed in my throat.

CHAPTER TWENTY

I don't think my heart ever hammered so hard before as it did walking through the front door of the Edwardses' home. Grayson's dad was still at the office. My brother grabbed my wrist, tugging me down the hallway. Such an odd phrase—my brother. Would I get used to this? Would I always feel like the odd one out?

My legs seemed to weigh a hundred pounds each. Walking became difficult, like I was trudging through a swamp of mud.

We found Liana in her office, eyes scanning the computer screen. Grayson knocked softly before he said, "Mom?"

She lifted her gaze, a soft smile forming on her lips, eyes lighting up at the sight of her son in the doorway.

Shit. I can't do this.

Grayson's hands tightened on my shoulders, keeping me in place. "There something we need to tell you."

Her eyes noticed the seriousness on her son's face, heard it in his voice. Sensing that what he had to say was important, she closed her laptop. "Okay, what's up?"

There was a worn leather couch on the opposite wall of her desk that looked like it got plenty of use. Grayson navigated me to the couch, sitting down beside me. I didn't know what to do, so I laced my hands together to keep from fidgeting. I couldn't bring myself to look at her and kept my eyes averted to the floor. My nails dug deep enough into my palms that I was afraid of finding blood on them once I unclenched my fists.

Grayson shifted as he searched for the right words. "I don't know how to say this, so I'm just going to come out and—"

Her gasp drew my gaze upward to see her hands flying to cheeks. "Ohmygod, your pregnant. She's having your baby."

Color stained my cheeks. I was mortified at Liana's conclusion, as was Grayson. His face scrunched. "Ew. That is literally the grossest conclusion you could have come up with. Seriously, Mom, I'm going to be sick. Josie and I are not... dating," he finally settled on, unable to mention sex in the same sentence as him and me. I didn't blame him.

After getting over the initial humiliation, I found the whole thing comical. It relieved some of the pressure clamping down on my chest.

Grayson raked a hand through his hair, shaking his head. "God, when you hear what I tell you, you're going to realize how disturbing the imagine of Josie and me together is."

Liana looked confused. "Why? Because she looks like your sister? I will admit the idea worried me that you'd bring home a girl who is the spitting image of Kenna."

"Mom, just stop," he interrupted before she could dig

herself into a further hole. "Josie is not my girlfriend. I repeat. We are not dating. She's sort of hook—uh, seeing Brock," he quickly amended.

My cheeks flamed again. This was not going at all as I had planned. It was way worse. The last thing I wanted was to be made out a slut. I thought about pinching Grayson under the arm, but I realized I wasn't the only one who was nervous.

A tension had moved into the room between the three of us. It was best if Grayson blurted it out like ripping off a Band-Aid.

He must have had the same idea. "She's your daughter," he finally spat out. "I should have told you when she showed up."

A pin could have dropped in the room, and it would have sounded like a shotgun going off.

No one said a thing. The three of us just stared awkwardly at each other as Liana digested the information.

Shock. Confusion. Fear. Uncertainty.

The range of emotions flooding the office bounced from one spectrum to the other and could be seen in her face. Her posture was so straight. She blinked. "What did you say?"

"Josie is your daughter. The one you thought you lost," Grayson explained, speaking just a little slower this time instead of rushing the truth.

Her eyes so much like mine dashed from her son to me. She looked at me with a different perspective, considering. The resemblance was undeniable, but not proof enough. "Why would you believe that?" she asked Grayson. "Don't get me wrong, her resemblance to your sister is uncanny, but Grayson, that doesn't mean she is your sister. She died."

"I have proof," Grayson disclosed. "The baby you thought died had been switched in the hospital. Josie is that baby."

Paling slightly, she scolded, "Grayson, this isn't funny. Don't play with my emotions. If this is one of your—"

"Mom, this isn't a game," he interrupted. "She is your daughter. She didn't die. She was taken."

"Taken?" Liana echoed, disbelief shining in her eyes. "You're implying she was kidnapped."

I could do nothing but remain silent as the two of them went back and forth.

"Not implying, Mom. I'm telling you she was," he said frankly.

Liana's gaze slid to me, doubt finally breaking into her features. I could see her mind turning, trying to decide if what Grayson said could be true and what she saw with her own eyes. "How can this be possible? I don't understand."

Grayson shifted forward so he sat on the edge of the couch. "Another woman in the hospital had also given birth to a baby the same day. That baby ended up in the NICU with us, but sadly, the little girl didn't survive."

"Oh, God," she proclaimed, anticipating where this was going.

"Seeing that you had three healthy babies, she switched her little girl with Josie. I have a DNA test that proves she is the baby you thought you lost."

"Grayson—" Her voice caught. Then she looked at me. "Y-You're really her?"

I nodded. I'd never felt so exposed before in my life, so damn vulnerable.

"Sweet Jesus. I think I might pass out or cry. Probably both. I'm definitely going to cry," she blubbered, tears already filling up her eyes. "I-I can't believe it. I've dreamed about you so many times over the years. I wondered what you'd look like. You're beautiful. Can I hug you?"

I nodded again, unable to get my mouth to function words.

We both stood up, and surprisingly my wobbly legs held me. At any second, I thought I might crash to the ground, but then her arms were around me. When she pulled back to frame my face with slim fingers, tears followed freely down her cheeks. "Let me look at you." Soft and gentle fingers brushed strands of my hair off my forehead. "I should have known to trust my gut. When you walked through that door, something told me you were special. I just didn't know how much."

"She looks so much like Kenna, doesn't she?" Grayson said.

Liana bit her bottom lip, her head bobbing up and down in agreement. "Yes, she does. I can't believe this is real." She hugged me again, her shoulders shaking as her overwhelming emotions got the best of her.

I hugged her back, my face and eyes wet. Once the tears started, I couldn't stop them. They fell and fell, tearing through me. She held on to me, letting me purge the onslaught of emotion we both needed.

"What time is it?" she gasped when we'd both regained a semblance of composure. "We have to tell your father. He is going to be beside himself. God, I have so many questions. Have you been living here this whole time?" She coaxed me back onto the couch.

I nodded, wiping at my eyes. "Well, on the other side of town up until this year."

"And your... mother? The woman who..." She swallowed, stopping herself from finishing. This had to be difficult. Someone had stolen her baby. I could only imagine how she felt about Angie Patterson. I'd had weeks to get used to the idea, but honestly, it wasn't enough time.

"Angie," I supplied. This was a sensitive subject, one both of us were uncomfortable discussing. I didn't know what was the wrong and right thing to say.

"I have so many questions for you. I... I can't believe this is real, that you're real." Her hand clutched mine as if she were afraid to let me go, that I might somehow disappear. "It's really you. When I saw you... for a split second I thought... but then I told myself it couldn't be true. It was impossible. But here you are."

"I was pretty much in denial for days when I found out," I admitted. "This is some heavy news to learn about yourself."

Understanding and compassion touched her features. "I'm sorry you had to go through that. I imagine it has been quite an adjustment, learning your parents aren't your parents. I'd like the chance to get to know you, if you let me."

"I'd like that," I whispered. More than I could express.

Her beaming bright eyes glanced at her son, and then back to me. "You and Grayson found each other? What are the chances?"

I met Grayson's gaze from where he lounged at the far side of the couch, Liana between us. "I guess we did. But it was mostly Grayson."

"I'm too overwhelmed to care how he found you. Knowing my son, there is definitely a story there."

Grayson cleared his throat. "It's best you don't know."

Liana rolled her eyes. "Try that excuse on your father." Her fingers brushed over my hair as a gracious smile spread on her lips. "You're beautiful. Absolutely beautiful. I want to know everything about you."

"Maybe not all in one night, Mom," Grayson suggested. "She's had a long day."

"Fine, but I'd like you to stay with us, at least for a little while. I'll have one of the rooms made up for you. I don't know what happened, but I got the impression you're in trouble. I'm not prying, just giving you an option."

An option I couldn't refuse. This was why I had come here, what I had hoped for, a chance to know them, know what it was like to be a part of their family, what life might have been. "Thank you. I think I'd like that very much."

She put her arm around my shoulders. "Good. It's settled. Let's go see what Elise is making for dinner, and I'll try not to stare at you too much. I'm half afraid if I blink, you'll disappear."

All the anxiety I felt before vanished as she led me out of the office, Grayson behind us. I had a feeling it would be an emotional night in the Edwards household, but a good kind. And long overdue. The secret was out, and I could finally start figuring out who I was, who I wanted to be.

* * *

As expected, Chandler Edwards had a similar reaction when his wife told him the news. It was a lot to spring on someone the first time meeting him. Grayson showed both his parents the tests and information the Elite had collected proving who I was.

Chandler was so different from Easton, and I didn't just mean in looks. It was neither a good nor bad way, just different. Chandler had an air of importance about him, a sophistication Easton lacked. My dad growing up had been hands-on, not afraid to dance in the rain, wear a pink tutu, or make mud cakes and pretend to eat them. I had a hard time picturing Chandler doing any of those things. I envisioned him throwing the football in the backyard with Grayson, having movie marathons on the weekends, and getting all technical about it. One didn't seem more fun than the other.

Grayson looked like his father... correction, our father. They shared the same serious dark eyebrows, chiseled jaw, and were nearly the same height, Grayson just an inch taller.

Once Chandler got over the shock, he engulfed me in a bear hug, squeezing me. The disbelief lingered for days, every time I walked into a room. I answered their many questions about my life and childhood, careful to skirt around details of my parents. They were a touchy subject, understandably. I had yet to break the news to Easton, a conversation I dreaded. But we all agreed to keep this quiet for a while, not looking for the attention a revelation like this would cause.

The Edwardses were a prominent family, and the return of their presumed dead baby would cause headlines and media attention. I didn't want it.

There were two problems with this. Carter and Angie.

And their silence made me nervous.

The next few days flew by, and I adjusted quickly to my new routine and staying with the Edwardses. I didn't know if I'd ever be comfortable in referring to them as my parents. For now, Chandler and Liana would do. It was difficult to think of two people who were still strangers to me as Dad and Mom.

I didn't hear from Angie, and despite being relieved, a piece of me was also hurt. Don't get me wrong. I was grateful for the space. It was exactly what I wanted—time to figure out who I was and how I felt about what she'd done.

One thing that remained steady was how I felt seeing Brock and Ava together. Each moment kindled my jealousy. By the end of the week, I was sure my rage would rupture from me. God help the Academy when that happened.

Carter had returned to school on Tuesday. I braced myself for the verbal attacks, the threats, for him to exploit my secret. Instead, he treated me as if I had an infectious disease. No eye contact. No sneers. No side comments. I didn't know this Carter.

It made me suspicious and uneasy. I'd lived with Carter long enough to know he never stayed quiet for long.

Nothing sucked more than waiting for the shoe to drop and not knowing when it would come.

Not true. I changed my mind. Brock being with Ava sucked way more.

The separation weighed on both of us, but it was the knowledge that this was his choice that kept me angry with him.

There were other ways to get back at the bitch.

The first time Brock's hand brushed mine as he passed me

in the hall, my heart lurched in my chest. I was so hungry for his touch. I almost believed I imagined it until it happened again and again, little stolen touches.

Soon, they weren't enough.

We both needed more.

Friday, during gym class, Coach Q ordered us to head outside for a mile run around the track. Groans erupted throughout the gymnasium. I was one of the last out the doors into the hallway as the class dragged their feet to the exit at the end of the corridor. I just made it into the hallway when someone grabbed me from the side, tugging me around the corner.

I whirled, fists ready to face my assailant, panic clawing at my chest. Then my eyes clashed into a sea of aqua. "Brock? What the hell? I almost punched you in the dick," I hissed, staring up at him. God, I missed his gorgeous face. My eyes devoured him. It had been too long since we'd been this close.

A finger pressed to my lips, silencing me. My brows furrowed in response. As the rest of my class filed outside, Brock pulled me into the boys' locker room.

"What are you doing? Shouldn't you be in class—?" The lock flipped, resounding over the tiled walls. He had a look in his eyes that sent my blood rushing to the surface. "What is wrong? Why are we—?"

His lips covered mine, cutting off the rest of my words. Both of his hands came to frame my face, the pad of his thumb running along my right cheekbone.

For a heartbeat, my mind went blank, and then there was only the warmth of his lips slanting over mine. Rising on my toes, I curled my fingers into his shirt and hauled him against me. The firmness of his body pressed into mine, and I groaned into his mouth.

Conflicting emotions swam within me. Should I be kissing Brock? I was pissed at him. Wasn't I? But for one minute, I wanted to forget all the crap, all the hurt and pain. I just wanted to bask in this intense high only Brock could induce.

Living with my bio family was wonderful. But being in Brock's arms, that felt like coming home.

The taste of him was goddamn cosmic..

I moaned again as his tongue slid over mine, enticing and teasing me.

Someone cleared his throat. A someone that wasn't Brock.

Brock tore his lips from mine with a growl, an icy scowl marring his lips. "Get out of here," he told Jason, one of his football teammates, his gaze never leaving my face. Heat flared in his eyes, his voice harsh, breathing uneven. "And you say nothing. You saw nothing. Understand?"

"Got it, man," Jason replied, holding up his hands. He quickly dashed to the door, flipped the lock, and rushed out.

Brock's gaze flicked to my lips. I could still taste him, and need throbbed between my legs. He leaned forward to reclaim my lips and finish what he'd started, but despite just how much I wanted him, I needed to know what the fuck was going on. I pressed my hands to Brock's chest, applying enough pressure to keep him a bay. "Don't. We're done here," I said in my best stern voice.

His hands encircled my wrists, not hard but firm enough to grab my attention. "No, we're not. We're just getting started."

As if to prove his point, he switched direction of his lips, grazing my jawline with them instead before moving to my ear.

Damn him!

"I can't keep doing this, Brock." He knew what I was referring to, this shit with Ava, avoiding me, and pretending he didn't give a shit about me.

I think the only person he fooled was the bitch herself, but maybe that was the point.

"Just a little longer," he murmured, taking the lobe of my ear into his mouth. His teeth pressed down, tugging. My back hit the wall, Brock lining up his body into mine.

We fit so fucking perfectly. It was like God had crafted him just for me.

My head dropped back onto the wall. "Then what?" I demanded, his assurance not pacifying the growing frustration within me, but it no longer was about this scheme he was carrying out, and quickly became about how much I wanted him.

He dropped his forehead to mine and whispered, "I need you, Firefly."

Well, shit. Why did he have to go and say that? Brock and I had this unspoken agreement when it came to sex, and I knew what he was asking. He had been there for me every time I had needed him in the same fashion. How could I refuse him?

Moreover, did I really want to?

Because the truth of it was, I missed him, more than I wanted to admit.

"Then what are you waiting for? Fuck me, Taylor."

"God, I missed you," he said as lips descended over mine in

a kiss that shattered any last bit of shield I had around my heart. His fingers dug into my hair, angling my head to the side for deeper access as he claimed me.

Desperate to show him what he made me feel, I ran my fingers under his shirt and over the plane of his stomach, reveling in the power I had over him as the muscles bunched and quivered under my greedy hands.

Then there was just his mouth and the unbelievable things he could do with his tongue and teeth. He kissed me thoroughly, and I wondered if he planned to spend the entire class period torturing me before giving us both the release we so wildly hungered for.

He cupped my breasts through my cotton Academy gym shirt, and tingles radiated from that part of my body. As his lips devoured mine, his fingers teased and kneaded.

Oh, God.

"Brock," I groaned. My breasts ached in his hands and I lifted them further into his touch, seeking more. He didn't disappoint. The pad of his thumb flicked over a budding nipple, and it instantly went rock-hard. I groaned, my head falling back, exposing the column of my neck.

He traced a line of kisses on my throat, dragging his tongue over my pulsing vein. I felt his teeth and shuddered.

It should have occurred to me that we were still in school, where anyone could walk in at any time, including a teacher.

I was past the point of caring about anything other than Brock's hands, his lips, and the pleasure his body could give me.

I didn't just need him.

I craved him.

His fingers slid around me, clasping my ass to lift me up. I clamped my legs around him, feeling the hardness of his desire pressed between my thighs. He ground his hips against mine, and I arched my back, begging for more. The center of my core burned for him. I burned for him. Every part of me.

I barely noticed or felt him walking us further into the locker room; my sole focus consisted of Brock. He placed me down on a hard surface, his fingers tugging at the hem of my shorts.

"Shorts off," Brock growled.

"If you want them off, you're going to have to do the work," I breathed.

His husky chuckle brushed over my lips. "With pleasure, Firefly." Hurried fingers hooked into the waistband as his half-lidded gaze found mine. His eyes never wavered. "Better hold on." He gave a yank, pulling the shorts down my hips.

I let out a small laugh, my hands finding his shoulders for stability. "I was thinking the same thing," I murmured, guiding my fingers into the front of his pants.

He hissed at the first touch of my hand wrapping around the velvety yet hard length of him. A smile curled my lips as I teased him with slow, deliberate strokes. "Josie," he breathed. "Jesus, I missed you."

"Then show me," I dared, my need for him reaching the point where I wanted him deep inside me.

I got what I asked for.

Shoving aside the black lace panties, he sank a finger inside me, and my muscles instantly clutched around him. One finger turned into two as he moved in and out. His thumb rubbed over that sensitive spot, driving me fucking insane. No matter how close I grew to a shattering climax, Brock eased back just enough to keep me from sailing into bliss.

A curse escaped me as my fingers tightened around him.

Digging a condom out of his pocket, he held the foil wrap for me between his fingers. I gladly obliged, ripping it open and sliding it down over each marvelous inch. I knew the reasoning behind using a condom even though I took the pill, but a part of me wanted to feel him inside me without any barriers.

He drew me to the edge of the counter, aligning himself between my legs so the tip of his erection pressed into me.

"What are you waiting for?" I panted, my eyes clouded with desire.

"Always so impatient."

In one quick thrust, he buried himself inside me, my wetness surrounding him. As I rode that first wave of pure pleasure, my lids fluttered shut and my head fell back. Nothing in the world came close to the feeling of Brock moving inside me.

I tightened my legs around his waist, keeping him pinned close to me as I angled my hips, seeking more of him. Brock brought me right to the cusp of pleasure with each stroke, but holding back and drawing it out instead of sending me over the edge. He knew it wouldn't take much to rip the orgasm from me.

"Please," I whimpered. "Brock, please."

"You're mine, Firefly. I want to hear you say it," he murmured, his breath a hot kiss against my skin.

Asshole.

But just as quickly I went from cursing him to worshiping his name. He thrust into me again, and I would have said anything, but I meant the words that tumbled from my lips with everything in me. "You're mine. Only mine."

"Say it again," he rasped, tendrils of his hair falling forward over his darkened eyes.

Brushing aside the strand, I returned the sentiment, never meaning anything more in my life. "You're mine, Brock Taylor." My fingers plunged into his hair, a soft cry and a moan following the burst of my orgasm. I swear I saw the twinkling of stars behind my eyes. Or maybe they were fireflies.

"Firefly," he whispered, nuzzling his face into the crock of my damp neck as his seed spilled into the condom.

For a long moment, we just stayed where we were, neither of us moving. Our breaths evened out, our hearts returning to a comforting rhythm that beat in time with each other. I was the first to shift, my hands dropping away from him. He sensed something changed between us and pulled out of me, but he didn't step away.

Brock hooked a finger under my chin and tipped my face up until my gaze met his. "What's going on in that head of yours?"

A million thoughts, but all I said was "We should probably get to class."

He shook his head, not letting me wiggle off the counter. "No, I'm not buying it. That was not what you were thinking. Since when do you hold back telling me how you feel?"

He had me there. Fine. He wanted to know how I was really feeling. I would lay it all on the table. What the fuck did I have to lose?

Everything, an evil voice inside my head whispered.

Not true. I'd already been done the road of losing everything.

"Depends, are you going to tell me what happened?" I asked. He'd needed me for a reason. I wanted him to open up and share that part of himself. The good. The bad. And the ugly.

"We fucked," he stated crassly because he knew it would rile me.

"Don't be stupid. That's not what I meant. You know it." I pushed a finger into his chest, giving it a hard shove. The bastard didn't move or flinch, just blinked at me like he was made of steel.

Brock pressed his lips together, his emotions a mask, tucked and hidden away. "I thought we had an agreement. Isn't that what *you* wanted, what you suggested?"

"Screw you for tossing it back into my face." My hands pressed on his chest as I jumped off the counter, adjusting my panties back into place. I bent down and reached for my shorts. "You're saying nothing has changed? You are still going forward with your idiotic plan?"

"Josie."

"Don't Josie me. And don't pretend you're doing this for me. You're the one who wants to punish her. I am more than capable of hurting Ava my own way, in my own time. I never asked you to do this."

He tucked himself back into his boxers, zipping up his pants. "No, but it's what we do."

"And if I asked you to stop?" I pressed, not letting let up for a heartbeat. I would challenge Brock every step of the way. He had become important to me—too fucking important. And that was where the problem lay. I had set the ground rules. Now I wanted to alter them, but not just alter, I wanted to knock them all down.

I wanted him to love me.

Silence. His straight lips didn't budge.

"That's what I thought." Straightening the rest of my clothes, I shook my head. "I'm done. This thing between us, whatever the fuck it is, it's over. Next time you need a fuck, go find Ava." I spun, intending to storm out. Brock didn't let me.

His hand flashed out, grabbing onto my wrists, twirling me back around to face him. "It's not over until I say it is, Firefly."

"Bullshit," I spat. "Those words we shared, they meant nothing. It was just a fuck, right. You might think you own me, but you don't. The sooner you get that through your thick skull, the easier this will be. You might run this school, but only I get to say who touches me. After today, you lost that privilege."

The fingers on my wrist tightened. "Are you saying what just happened was a mistake?"

"Fuck yes. Never again," I swore.

"Now who is bullshitting? You can deny it all you want, Firefly, but you want me as much as I want you. That is something you can't just flip off. We belong together."

Those words were so damn close to what I wanted to hear that I nearly caved. My heart soared in my chest, urging me to throw myself into his arms.

I didn't. I stayed firm and planted. "Maybe I can't just flip off my feelings, but I've decided I don't want to do casual. Turns out, I'm not as impervious to catching feelings as I thought."

He released my wrist, forking a hand through his hair, a deep scowl on his swollen lips. "You expect me to just let you walk out after you say something like that?"

I shot up a brow. "Do you really have a choice?"

"Don't do this." His face contoured into something that almost mirrored hurt.

My chin lifted just a fraction as I strengthened the last bit of shield around my heart. "I think we both know you won't give me what I need." This time when I turned to leave, he didn't stop me. That was all the answer I needed.

I walked out of the boys' locker room without a glance back, despite my heart splintering into a million little pieces.

CHAPTER TWENTY-ONE

I must have emitted bad day vibes. I'd never been through so many highs and lows in a single week. It had to be a record, and I couldn't help thinking the universe had to cut me a break. I was due one, right? Like gacha games, I had to be approaching pity; the odds had to be in my favor after all the shit I'd been through.

Being that it was Friday night in November, Elmwood Academy had a football game. One of the few left in the season. After my incident with Brock in the locker room, I was in no mood to don my pom-poms and cheer from the stands, not that I would ever do that. The point was, I just wanted to stay home and wallow in my heartache, because it turned out, walking away from Brock ripped my heart to pieces.

I fucking loved the jackass.

Couldn't he see that?

I had myself to blame. Why had I ever thought I could keep

things casual? And despite his reasons, I couldn't sit by and watch him with another girl, even it if was all a sham. My heart wasn't built to withstand that kind of pain, jealousy, and betrayal. I felt all in abundance.

A part of me knew Brock would never really let me go, but the big question was could I stay away from him? Did I want to?

Not really, a loud voice boomed in my head.

If I could admit that to myself, then I also realized something had to change. I needed to do something. Drastic measures and all that shit.

I skipped the Friday night football game for several reasons; my horrible track record with football games and avoiding Brock were the top two contenders. Instead, I stayed home with Liana and Chandler, who also missed the game at Grayson's suggestion. When they were home, his parents usually went to watch him play, but Grayson thought it might be nice if the three of us had some time alone.

Grayson knew precisely why I didn't want to go to the game, and he didn't push. I silently thanked him.

It was nice, spending a night with my bio parents. They succeeded in diverting my thoughts from Brock, if only for a few hours. Chandler grilled kabobs, like grilled them himself. Of course, the kitchen prepped the kabobs, but still, I was impressed. When he noticed my lifted brow, he told me grilling calmed him and made him feel manly.

Liana and I laughed. It felt so good to laugh—to be worry-free, if only for a few hours.

I often found them gazing at me like they couldn't believe I was real. That feeling also resided in me when I looked at them. Surreal.

The night ended too quickly, and before long, I was surrounded by darkness, tossing and turning in bed. No matter how many diversions I tempted my brain with, my thoughts always went back to Brock. Was I really giving up? I'd meant what I said. I was done waiting, done with the games.

If Ava weren't a factor, would Brock want us to be more than just fuck buddies?

Sometime after midnight, I heard Grayson come home. I contemplated rolling out of bed and talking to him, but it wasn't fair to him put in the middle of Brock's and my drama. I couldn't do that.

So I suffered with my obsessive thoughts alone in the dark, refusing to cry. Brock Taylor was not worth my tears... so I kept telling myself.

I slept very little, my emotions flip-flopping between gut-wrenching sadness and such flaming anger that when the sun rose over the hills, I hoped Brock had suffered as much as I had. More so.

I planned to do absolutely nothing all weekend and managed to do just that most of Saturday until the Elite showed up. Well, three out of four. Brock was absent, which should have been a good thing, considering I wasn't ready to see the asshole yet, but somehow that wasn't the case. The disappointment that settled within me was very fucking real. I assumed they were here for

Grayson, but when I noticed Mads was with them, it became clear that the group was up to something.

I should have headed upstairs and locked myself in Kenna's room. That would have been the smart option.

Grayson turned on the gas fireplace on the backyard patio. It was cool tonight. The air had a bite to it, and the warmth that emitted from the fire was nice. Grayson sat down on one of the beach-style chairs that circled the fire pit. He stretched out his legs and asked me, "What happened between you and Brock?"

Unease twisted in my chest. Had Brock said something to them? "Nothing, why?" I replied, trying to stick to the plan to keep Grayson out of the middle.

Orange and yellow flames licked over the lava rocks, casting shadows over Fynn's face. He sat directly across from me. "Because he is acting as mopey as you are. We almost lost the game last night. His head wasn't in it."

I'd heard about the close call at breakfast this morning. "What makes you think that has anything to do with me?"

The three guys gave me pointed looks that apparently spoke volumes.

I sighed. "Whatever. Tell him to stop being a stupid prick. This shit with Ava has gone on too long. I told him I was over it yesterday. That's what happened."

"You did what?" Surprise fluttered over Mads's face. For once she didn't light up.

Micah rocked his chair back on two legs. "You know, you are the first girl he has ever treated like this. That means something."

I shrugged. "Maybe, but he has a funny way of showing it."

Fynn tossed a stray lava rock into the fire. "That might be true, but for Brock, this is his way of showing you just how much he cares. He wouldn't go to such lengths for anyone. He's doing it for you."

"Stop being reasonable," I muttered, stretching my feet closer to the warmth. "I don't like it."

Fynn's lips twitched.

"What you need is to relax—cut loose—party," Micah exclaimed. Always needing physical contact of some sort, he scooted his chair an inch closer and put his arm around me.

Suddenly, the reason for this gathering began to make sense. "I'm not much in the mood for a party," I admitted honestly.

Micah's impish grin sent a warning through me. They weren't going to be easily brushed off. An internal groan went off in my head.

"Hey." A familiar voice came from the house. I didn't have to look up to know who it was. A trail of tingles danced up my spine, and as if they moved of their own accord, my gaze lifted. Brock strutted toward us, his eyes locking with mine.

Why did he have to look so fucking good? Drop-your-panties-instantly good. He had a way of making basic clothes like jeans and a T-shirt look phenomenal.

A few awkward seconds stretched over the group as Brock and I stared at each other. Someone finally cleared his throat, breaking through the silence.

Brock took the only empty seat. At least he hadn't brought the bitch with him. I didn't know what I would have done if he had brought Ava here of all places.

Definitely made a scene. And I wasn't quite ready to show the Edwardses just how crazy I really was.

"You guys ready?" he asked, the white shirt stretching across his chest. I told myself not to think about what was under that shirt, the hard planes of muscle and swirling ink of tattoos.

My thoughts betrayed me.

"We're working on it," Grayson replied.

Brock's eyes zeroed in on me once again, and he arched a brow. "She being difficult?" he asked.

Suspicion grew in my belly, and I frowned. "What the fuck? I am sitting right here, you know. You don't have to talk around me."

Brock eyed me closely. "I see what you mean."

My gaze swept around the circle, realizing this shit was planned. "What is this, some kind of party intervention?"

Micah crossed his arms over his chest. "Hell yes, Josie Jo."

"You can't hide out here forever," Mads said. Whose side was she on anyway?

"Yes, I can," I clipped out. "Besides, it's only been a week."

"Two weeks," Fynn clarified, as if I needed him to. "You were injured the week before."

I rolled my eyes. "You're all going to gang up on me, aren't you, until I give in?"

"Pretty much, Firefly. Save yourself the trouble and just say yes." It was the first time he'd spoken directly to me since strutting his fine ass into the Edwardses' house. Not that I noticed his ass or anything. I was on a Brock hiatus. Indefinitely. So I reminded myself.

If only he didn't smell so good, which I wouldn't have

noticed if he hadn't chosen to sit beside me, a deliberate maneuver on his part. Here, when it was just the group, he didn't have to pretend; not that I gave a shit.

But apparently, I did. Or at least, my body did. His nearness fucked with my ability to stay mad at him.

"You guys suck. Does anyone remember what happened the last time I went to a party?" I pointed out.

"Don't let the bastard keep you from doing things you love, from living, from experiencing life. We're seventeen. This is the time in our life when we are supposed to party." Mads's eyes glittered with strong intensity.

Everything she said was something I'd already thought myself. But thinking was entirely different than executing.

"Fuck yeah," Micah added at the end of Mads's speech.

I couldn't help but shake my head and try to cover the smile that tugged at my mouth. Leave it to Micah to make a joke out of everything.

"You, Josie James, should not be contained. We're not going to let that asshole keep you in a box," Mads declared.

Damn right, I shouldn't. My lips curled into a half smile. "Thanks, Mads. I fucking needed that."

She offered me a smile of her own, the glow of flickering flames highlighting her face. "Girl, it's what I'm here for. To lift you up and set you straight."

Grayson blinked at Mads. "Are you done yet?"

Mads rolled her eyes.

"Okay, fine," I surrendered. "Let's go out. Give me ten minutes. And I better not get abducted or beat up tonight, clear?"

"So that leaves room for shot or buried alive," Micah joked.

Mads whacked Micah on the back of the head. "You're a morbid asshole."

"Damn, Clarke. Lay off the weights." He rubbed at the back of his skull and then ruined any sympathy he might have received by winking at her.

Dumbass. He never learned.

Before I changed my mind, I made a quick trip upstairs into Kenna's room, only to realize I didn't have shit to wear. Brock had given Grayson the few items I left at his house, but it consisted mostly of stuff to wear to school and lounging items for the weekend. All of my actual clothes were still at the Pattersons'.

Chewing on my lips, I stared at the closet doors, mulling over the idea of borrowing something from Kenna.

"She won't mind, you know," a voice said from the doorway. Mads walked into the room, the black jeans she wore hugging her curves as threw open the closet door. The deep purple sweater hung off one of her shoulders, flashing a bit of ivory skin. Mads always looked good and ready to kick someone's ass. She had this rich girl rebel quality only she could pull off. All the other girls at the Academy were so prissy, like they grew up thinking the movie *Clueless* was the holy grail.

"It just feels like I'd be invading her privacy," I admitted.

"She's your sister. It's like a rite of passage or something to borrow her shit." Mads scanned through the racks of hanging clothes. "Now, let's see. There has to be something in there that would suit your tastes..." She continued to comb through the soft pink sweaters, the ivory shirts, and cute skirts until she came across something black. "Here we go. Put this on and grab a pair of jeans. She has like a hundred of them."

Padding into the adjoined bathroom, I quickly changed into the black sweater that was intentionally shredded in random spots and slid into a pair of dark, buttery jeans, feeling almost more like myself.

Mads eyed me with approval as I stepped out. "See. That shirt was made for you."

"I can't see Kenna wearing this." I touched the hem of the knitted material. All her other clothes were so preppy.

"She bought it for Halloween, I think. Never wore it. Didn't get the chance." Mads reached into the vanity, pulling out a tube of mascara and eyeliner. "Close your eyes," she stated with a grin, pulling off the cap on the eyeliner.

I obeyed. Having Mads help me get ready reminded me so much of Ainsley. I missed her like crazy. I couldn't look at eyeliner without thinking of my best friend. Since the whole Carter incident, things between us had grown distant. I knew it was safer for her this way, to not get mixed up in this mess, but she was that piece of my old life I refused to let go of.

"Open," Mads instructed, pulling me from my somber thoughts.

She applied a thick coat of mascara to my lashes. "It will be okay," she said. "You will find a new normal. I did, because of you."

"Mads," I said softly, blinking.

Screwing the cap back onto the tube, she said, "You have no idea how much I needed a friend, needed you, even if you look just like my other best friend."

A low laugh escaped me. "You're gonna make me cry."

"Not tonight. Tonight we dance our asses off."

* * *

The party turned out to be at Brock's. Go figure.

There was something calm and reassuring about coming back to his house, like a haven, despite the place being overrun with teenagers, most of whom I recognized, including a few I'd like to hit with a baseball bat. Like my archenemy—Ava Whitmore.

Now that I was here... what did I plan to do?

"Do you want to leave?" Mads asked like the good friend she was, noticing what caused the sudden deep scowl on my lips. "We could take this party elsewhere. Somewhere less... skankish."

I thought about it, and to be honest, my gut reaction urged me to do just that, but then another thought snuck in. Sometimes my brain scared the shit out of me. This was one of those times. "Nah. This gives me the opportunity I've been waiting for, but I'll need your help. I have a bitch to take down." Getting the shit beat out of me sucked, but what Mads said earlier struck a chord within me. I refused to shrink or run out of the room every time I laid eyes on Ava. I would not give her precisely what she wanted. Fuck no. I'd do what she'd least expect.

From across the room, the redheaded twat flipped her hair as her eyes clashed with mine. A venomous grin curved over her lips, like a cat playing with its prey before the kill.

Mads lifted her hand, shooting Ava the middle finger. "I

love devious plots of destruction. You had me at take down. What do you need me to do?"

"Be my decoy. Just long enough for me to slip past my guard." My gaze shifted sideways to Micah.

"Really? You couldn't give me something more challenging?" She nearly sulked at the idea of having to distract the playboy Elite.

I rolled my eyes. "I'll let you know when. For now, let's mingle."

Both her brows shot up. "We mingle? Since when?"

Looping my arms into hers, I said, "Tonight we do." I was going to teach both Brock and Ava a lesson, the whole "kill two birds with one stone" tactic.

So for the next hour, I flirted with every guy who crossed my path, touching, laughing, twirling my hair, whispering in their ear, all while making sure Brock had a front-row seat with Ava on his lap. The problem with this plan was that I had to also watch her flirt with *my* guy.

I had told Brock I was done. And I was. Done with the lies and the games. But I realized something tonight... I could never be done with him. I just had to show him what he would miss. Before the night was over, Ava wouldn't be my problem, and Brock... he'd claim me, just as I would claim him.

What was a party without fireworks?

Ava got up from her cozy spot draped around Brock and meandered through the crowd. The opening I'd been waiting for came, and I jumped on it. Keeping my gaze focused on the target, I nudged Mads lightly. "Ready to put the girls to use?"

From the corner of my gaze, I saw her adjust her boobs and pull down the front of her sweater. "Ready."

Poor Micah. I almost felt bad siccing Mads on him. Almost.

As Mads spun, blocking me from Micah's line of sight, I followed Ava. She approached the bathroom and slipped inside, but before she could shut the door, I thrust out my arm, slamming my palm on the door.

"What the—?" Ava whirled, her hazel eyes colliding with mine.

I grinned, bulldozed my way inside the bathroom, and shut the door, flipping the lock. How ironic that the Ava had delivered me my first warning in a bathroom at Grayson's house. And now here I was, about to deliver one of my own. "Hey, bitch."

She stood smugly, a hand going to her hip. "What the fuck do you want? Another beatdown?"

If she thought she could intimidate me, she was fucking wrong. "I'd like to see you try. It's just you and me. Think you can take me?"

Her lips pressed in a tight line.

I positioned myself in front of the door, blocking her chance at escape, just as she had done to me. Sweet revenge. "I'm guessing not. One-on-one, you're not shit. Remember where I came from. Brawls at Public are a daily occurrence."

Her mouth twitched. "What's your point? I'm growing bored and I have people waiting for me... like Brock."

Fucking whore.

That was just the wrong thing to say to me.

I let a short laugh. And then another longer one. Before I knew it, giggles burst out of me as I leaned against the door.

She stared at me, her nose bunching up and a bead of concern flickering in her eyes. "What is wrong with you? Are you having a nervous breakdown?"

"Sorry to disappoint, it's just fucking hilarious that you actually believe Brock is into you." Satisfaction glowed within me. God, that felt so damn good to say.

Her eyes became sharper as they narrowed. "What are you talking about?"

"It's all a hoax. A fucking lie. He doesn't give two shits about you. It's all a ploy to ruin you by pretending to be interested in you. I'm not sure what he has planned, but I can't wait to find out." Except, I was spoiling his scheme purposely, doing a bit of my own retaliation. I didn't need the whole school to see. This was between Ava and me.

"You lie," she hissed, despite her face bleaching a little of color.

"Am I?" I countered, angling my head. "Think about it, Ava. I know there has to be a brain inside that pretty head," I said, tapping the side of my skull. "Does that sound like something the Elite would do? You've been around a lot longer than I have."

Fury sprang into her cheeks, turning them pink. "You're just jealous. He finally realized what trash you are."

I snorted. "Pathetic. I'll be the one laughing my ass off when he makes you a fool in front of the entire school. Did you actually believe there would be no repercussions for what you and your friends did to me?"

"Brock would never choose someone like you," she hissed.

Challenge accepted.

A dark smile graced my lips. "That's where you're wrong. I might be trash, but he will always pick me." Pretty sure he would. Brock had never told me he loved me, but I was a gambling kind of girl. I was betting on him and me. "Are you so confident to think that if we went out there right now and I demanded he choose one of us, that he would pick you?"

Doubt crept into her hazel eyes. Just a flicker, but it was enough.

I pounced. "In fact, just the other day at school, he fucked me in the locker room."

"That's all you are, a fuck." She flung the accusation at me.

I grinned. "And a damn good one. He comes to me. Not you."

The bitch stepped forward, a hand open at her side.

I thought she might slap me, and I would have welcomed the pain. I wanted her to hit me first because then it was game on. "I'm guessing by the fury in your eyes that you and Brock haven't been intimate since his sudden return interest in you. Didn't you think the timing was odd? That he would start paying attention to you again after what you did to me? You're lucky he didn't have the living shit beaten out of you." I advanced on her, getting in her face. "I'm more of a tit for tat girl."

"Perhaps I went too easy on you the first time." She shook with fury, her voice trembling from it.

Lifted my chin, I baited her. "Go on. Hit me. I dare you. It will give me an excuse to kick your fucking ass. You don't stand a chance against me alone, and you know it. Without your friends, you're nothing. Just a rich girl who can't get the guy."

"Get the hell out of here!"

I wasn't done yet. I was just getting started. "How about we just end this right here, right now?"

"What are you doing?" she asked when I turned the lock and reached for the door.

"It's not what I'm doing. It's what we're doing. Come on," I ordered over my shoulder, holding the door open. "Don't make me drag you down the hall by your nappy red hair."

"My hair is not nappy, whore."

I grabbed her by the wrist and yanked her out of the bathroom. She ripped her hand out from my grasp as I started forward down the hall. A few nearby partygoers turned to stare, and as I stalked through the house, Ava on my heels, we drew more eyes. I didn't give a flying fuck.

Micah pushed his way through the crowd and sauntered up beside me, keeping pace with my footsteps. "Josie Jo, what is going on?" He muttered near my ear.

I weaved around furniture, moving into the next room. "Just wait and find out. The entertainment is about to begin."

"I'm not so sure a strip show is the best idea," he muttered, eyeing me warily.

I rolled my eyes. "I'm not getting naked, you perv."

"Don't think I don't know what you and Mads did back there," he said, busting us.

I shrugged, my purpose unwavering. "I needed a moment."

His gaze flicked to Ava, who was now flanked by Izzy and Emily. "I see that."

I whirled on Micah, my emotions heightened. "Where is he?" I demanded.

Grayson suddenly appeared at my other side. "What's going on? You have that look."

I glared at my brother, pivoting to search the room. "I don't have a look. Do you know where he is or not?"

Grayson's gaze darted over my shoulder before returning to me; a shrewdness that hadn't been there before flared.

"She's lost it," Ava shrieked, her eyes also scanning the crowd.

I shot her daggers, suppressing the urge to slam my palm into her nose. "I told her the truth. Now, where is he?"

Grayson blinked. "You did what?"

"Hot damn, Josie Jo. Way to blow shit up. You are literally my idol." Micah chuckled with approval, flashing me his adorable dimples.

"Brock's going to be pissed," Grayson stated, his expression impassive.

I shrugged. "What else is new? I'll handle him."

"You might just be the only girl who can," he mumbled, signalling over my head to someone. I thought it might be Brock and lifted up to see over the crowd. It was Fynn and Mads.

The two of them wandered over, my best friend shooting Ava a death glare.

Grayson assessed the situation. I had drawn a line between Ava and me without even knowing it. She had her side, and I had mine, which I could admit was a helluva a lot better than hers. "This is a bad idea, Josie," Grayson muttered.

"Probably," I agreed as I wondered how many rooms in this house I would have to check before I found Brock.

Grayson placed a hand on my shoulder. "Nothing I say will stop you."

I slide my glance to him. "No. If you stand in my way, bro, we are going to have our first fight."

Turned out, I didn't need to find Brock. He found me, which looking back, I realized what a sight I must have looked, surrounded by the three guys. We drew all sorts of attention.

Brock's brows were furrowed together, his aqua eyes narrowed as he glanced between us. "What is going on?"

I faced him. "Ava and I have a score to settle."

Ava shoved her way forward. "Brock, she is fucking out of control. I demand you kick her out."

Micah rubbed his hands together, grinning impishly. "Ah, shit! This is going to be good."

Ignoring them both, I closed the distance between Brock and me with determination shining in my eyes. His brows narrowed as I approached, and he saw the trouble that brewed in my face. He knew I was up to something, and it wouldn't be good.

"Firefly—" he said firmly, but that was all he got out before my lips attached to his. I laced my fingers into his hair as I touched my tongue to his lips, demanding he open for me. He did, without hesitation. Desire flared between us at the first brush of our tongues.

I was semi-aware of the room going quiet, of the few gasps, but only for a second. Every thought of revenge eddied out of my mind at the taste of Brock. Nothing but him mattered.

"I need you. Tell me you want me," I murmured against his mouth.

"Always, Firefly."

Our bodies were pressed so close together I felt his heart beat. "Only me."

"Only you," he affirmed, his mouth seizing mine in another explosive kiss.

And that was all I needed.

I kissed him for a few more seconds before I regrettably drew away, ending the kiss. My arms were locked around his neck, his hands securing me to him. I turned my head to the side, brows raised smugly as Brock's lips brushed against my ear, taking the lobe into his mouth. Victory curled on my lips as I stared at Ava.

So much hate glittered in her hazel eyes, her cheeks flaring bright pink with shame. By the end of the night, word would spread about what I'd done. This time, I didn't care that I'd be the hot topic on Monday. I owned it.

Mine, I mouthed.

Ava whirled around, her red hair flying in the air. I swore I caught a glimmer of fresh tears springing into her eyes. She stormed off, pushing her way through the crowd, Izzy and Emily hot on her heels, hopefully to lick her fucking wounded black heart.

Bitch got what she deserved.

Brock was watching me when I turned back toward him. His brows pinched together. "Dammit, Firefly."

I didn't want to argue, and I could see the storm brewing behind his eyes. "Say it." He knew what I was asking, and his eyes darkened, but this time I wasn't backing down. I knew what I wanted. It was clear to me. He might not see it this way, but I was fighting for what I wanted. Him.

"This isn't cute," he said through his teeth.

We still had a crowd around us, but with the show over, they were starting to go back to their drinks and muttering amongst themselves. I didn't give a shit about them. "There is nothing cute about us. I want to hear you say it." My eyes stayed on his as I wound our fingers together.

"You want to hear that I'm in love with you," he said tightly, causing my stomach to drop.

I lifted my chin, still searching his eyes from some kind of emotion, a tell that he was half as crazy about me as I was him. "Yes."

He stared at me for a full moment in silence—a deafening quiet that had my heart hammering in my chest. What if he didn't say it? What if I was wrong? What if he didn't—?

"Firefly, I love—"

I kissed him fervently before he could finish the words. "I love you, Brock fucking Taylor."

He grinned. "God, I never thought there would be a girl who would be my match. You were made for me, James."

"I think I was."

CHAPTER TWENTY-TWO

"A bout fucking time." Fynn grinned, clapping Brock on the back.

Micah scooped me up, twirling me around. The room spun and squealed. "Put me down," I ordered, pushing at his shoulders, but his grasp only grew tighter. He did finally stop spinning, thank God.

Those damn dimples winked on either side of his cheeks. "Not happening. You're one of us now, Josie Jo."

Grayson grinned. "The first girl Elite."

"The only girl Elite," Fynn added as my feet touched the ground.

"Do you hear that?!" Micah yelled throughout the house, his arm slung around my shoulder. "She is one of us now!"

I rolled my eyes. The gossip train on Monday would be barreling through the Academy at full steam. "And what if I don't want to be an Elite?" I teased the four of them. They had formed a circle around me, including Mads in the group. I tried to keep a straight face, but I couldn't stop the grin from appearing.

The corner of Brock's mouth twitched up. "The only way out is death."

"Hardcore," I replied. But it didn't matter. I didn't want out. I wanted this. The friendship. The protection. The Elite was my safety net—always there to catch me.

I welcomed their disorder.

Mads gave me a hard hug once Micah finally released me. "I'm so happy for you. Despite all his less than stellar qualities, Brock is one of the good ones."

I agreed wholeheartedly.

Still riding the high of hearing Brock tell me he loved me, we rejoined the party, heading to the kitchen for a drink. Celebratory shots.

Mads had been right about the party. I had needed this, more than I knew.

I turned down the hall, heading toward the kitchen, trailing behind Mads. Micah and Fynn were already raiding the liquor bottles, while Grayson and Brock did a sweep of the party to make sure shit was under control. These parties were notorious for crashers, which normally weren't a problem, but Carter made it a problem after his recent shenanigans with Ainsley. They were monitoring who came into their homes.

As I passed the section of the hallway that broke off into three directions, I caught a flicker of movement that had me turning my head and halting. A shadow moved down the opposite way, the section of the house that was closed off to the party, that lead upstairs.

I don't know what possessed me to follow, but my legs moved down the hallway just to make sure I wasn't seeing shit. When I reached the stair landing, I glanced up, searching the darkness.

Click.

Was that a door I heard shutting?

I shouldn't investigate. I should go back, follow Mads into the kitchen, do a round of shots, and pretend I heard nothing. But... I couldn't do it. A wicked sense of dread overrode all those glorious feelings of being in love.

Perhaps it was just Brock or Grayson checking out the house. That had to be it. I'd feel stupid when I spotted one of them. Climbing up the stairs, I tiptoed down the corridor away from the party until I was staring at Brock's bedroom door. It was closed.

My heart jumped in my chest as a soft glow of light flashed from under the doorway. Someone had flipped on a light inside the room. I reached for the door handle, my pulse hammering, and turned the knob. With a gentle push, the door swung open.

I peered inside, a healthy dose of trepidation dancing within me.

Nothing.

Just the warmth of the table lamp situated at the corner of the large rich, mahogany desk.

What the fuck?

How the hell had the light just turned on? I was so sure the room had been absolutely dark when I first approached. It didn't make sense.

Laughter and music flowed from down the hall as I took a step into the room. And then another step as my eyes panned the shadowy corners.

Squeak.

The hinges on the doorframe echoed through the room, and I whirled around, watching as the door closed, followed by the click of the lock. Carter stepped out from where he'd been hiding behind the door like a ghostly predator.

Horror and dread grew in my stomach, both competing for top position, but really, neither emotion would win.

He leaned against the door, part of his face shrouded in darkness, adding an eeriness to his features. His lips curled up in a sneer. "I knew you were still fucking him."

My heart jumped into my fucking throat, fear surging to the surface. "What are you doing here?"

Carter chuckled, and the sound sent chills down my arms. "You and I have unfinished business, sis. You didn't actually think I'd forgotten about our deal?"

I gritted my teeth. "You could have just called or texted. *And* I'm not your fucking sister."

He wore a black hoodie, and his fingers fumbled with something in the front pocket. "Oh, right. Your mom is a kidnapping psychopath."

"Takes one to know one," I snapped back, praying it wasn't another knife he was concealing.

He chuckled again, sounding like a desperate man coming

unhinged. "What? You think that being the Edwardses' lost daughter makes you all high and mighty? You're still worthless."

My nerves were stretched thin as I tried to come up with a plan to get the hell out of this room. "I don't give a shit what you think of me."

"You never did."

"Brock will be here any minute." Yeah, this was the best plan I could come up with on the spur of the moment. Eventually, when I didn't show up in the kitchen, they'd come looking for me. And if Brock found me with Carter, he would kill him. Actually kill the bastard. "It's pretty stupid of you to come here alone." Carter liked to hear himself talk, so I'd stall until then.

A fight was just what Carter would love; anything to put the heat on the Elite. "Who said I'm alone?"

I was going to call his bluff. Maybe there was a chance I could bulldoze my way to the door, shove him out of the way just long enough to flip the lock and open the door. "Get out of the way." I attempted to walk toward him in hopes the asshole would move. He only shifted, blocking me further and yet somehow bringing us close.

Too fucking close.

I retreated a step, my insides churning.

"Let's make this quick and painless. I want his passcode and the thumb drive, sis. Now. Since you've interrupted my plans to get in and out unseen, you're going to get it for me."

The fact that he mentioned pain had my panic going through the roof. "I don't know where it is."

"Well, I suggest you start looking, because your life depends on it." He pulled his right hand out of the hoodie pocket. A sliver of moonlight from the window glinted off steel.

Carter clasped a gun.

An audible gasp fled from my lips. "Are you fucking insane? Why do you have a gun?"

He held it up, pointing the barrel at the ceiling. "Incentive."

I didn't know much about guns, other than what I'd seen in the movies, but it looked like it had an attachment on the it. A silencer perhaps? "Do you plan to kill me if I can't find what you want?"

His smugness rose, the gun giving him power. "You or whoever gets in my way."

I no longer wished for Brock or the Elite to find me.

"But... I don't even know if it's in his room."

"I have it on good authority that it is. Now move." He swung the gun in the air, indicating for me to start my search.

Ava. If he trusted anything out of that bitch's mouth, then he wasn't as smart as I gave him credit for. I realized he probably hadn't heard about Brock's latest scheme, and I wasn't about to tell him either. Brock would never have trusted her with that information.

Keep him busy, my mind encouraged.

With that thought, I cautiously turned and walked toward the desk.

"Sit," he ordered.

Once again, I did as he instructed.

"Put this into the USB," he said, pulling out a compact portal drive and handing it to me.

"Why?" I asked, taking the device.

"Just fucking do it."

Fear made my movements clumsy but after a few tries, I managed to get the plug into the USB port.

"Now open the file on the hard drive."

"I don't have the password to get in."

"Useless. Let me guess, you don't have the passcode for his phone either." He shook his head and dropped a slip of paper onto the desk below the keyboard. "Enter this. And do it quickly. The clock is ticking."

I snuck a glance at Carter and stared at the end of the gun. "I can't concentrate with you pointing that thing at me."

Carter stood over me, using his *incentive* to keep me motivated. "Try harder."

My tongue wanted to unleash a verbal fury like Carter had never heard. I curbed the desire and typed in the password written on the piece of torn paper. I didn't want to know how or from where he had obtain the information to get into Brock's personal computer..

After the computer logged in, I covered my hand over the mouse and moved to the folder located on the desktop, clicking it open. There was just a single file inside. *Black Widow*. I snorted.

"Open the file," Carter demanded, jamming the into my back.

Every second I spent alone in the dark with Carter made me feel criminal. "What does it do?"

"It doesn't matter. Just open it. Now."

"And if I refuse?"

He rammed his fingers into my hair, grabbing a fistful and yanking my head back as he leered over me. "Don't test me."

"Do it yourself," I hissed between gritted teeth as sharp pain shot through my scalp.

"Worthless bitch," he swore sharping, covering his hand over mine and clicking the file open.

I shivered at the touch of his skin on mine, which only made Carter chuckle, his hot breath fluttering over my neck. My eyes stayed on the computer screen, watching as a black box came up, text scrolling too fast through it for me to understand what it was doing. Nothing fucking good, that was for sure. As soon as the black box disappeared, Carter leaned forward and withdrew the portal drive, shoving it back into his pocket.

He stood straight and waved the gun in my direction. "Now find me the thumb drive, and I'll be out of your life."

Like hell, I thought. Carter was like a disease with no cure. "I don't know. And that's the truth. They don't tell me shit." My fingers clutched the front of the desk and brushed up against something small. Something fastened under the center drawer.

Holy shit.

Doing my best to keep my facial expression schooled, I wiggled the little rectangular device out from its holding clip.

"I suggest you start looking," Carter ordered, glancing to the locked door.

I took the opening and slipped the USB into my back pocket as stood up and turned around to face him. By the time his cold eyes returned to me, I moved to start opening the desk drawers.

Carter stepped up close behind me, so close his chest

touched my back and his breath stirred my hair. The barrel of the gun pressed into my lower back. "Do you want to show me what you found?"

My blood froze in my veins. *Remain calm.* "I don't know what you're talking about." I was proud of how calm my voice came out.

"I love that you like to do things the hard way. It makes this so much more interesting." His nearness made it feel like a million spiders crawled over my skin.

A string of f-bombs went off in my head as I stared straight ahead, afraid to move, even breathe. Carter slid his hand into my back pocket, the gun firmly pressed into my back. His hand basically cupped my ass, lingering longer than necessary.

The asshole was enjoying himself.

Fucking creep.

My jaw clenched. "Get your hands off me."

Carter's fingers finally removed the thing he'd been so desperate to find for months now. He jabbed me with the gun and commanded, "Turn around." I did as asked, facing him with slow movements, terrified that if I moved too quickly, he'd shoot me. I took my time lifting my eyes, hating what I knew I'd see on his face. Triumph glittered in his deranged eyes. "Now, was that so hard?"

I opened my mouth to tell him to go to hell, but the door handle jiggled, shifting our attention.

"Josie, are you in there?" Brock called from the other side. "Why is the door locked?"

About fucking time. Christ.

At the sound of Brock's voice, Carter's eyes grew wild, and

his face drained of color. All I could think was, *good. I hope he pisses his pants.*

Something spurred inside me, some basic instinct to survive. "Brock! He's here!" I yelled, forgetting for a brief moment about the weapon aimed at my chest.

"You stupid bitch," Carter hissed, shoving the USB into his pocket. I didn't see his other hand move until it was too late to deflect the blow. He hit me on the side of my head with the butt of the gun.

It wasn't hard enough to knock me out, but damn if I didn't see stars as pain burst into the side of my skull as I stumbled, struggling to stay on my feet and keep conscious. Groaning, I dropped my head, pressing a hand to where the pain radiated. A warm, sticky substance oozed onto my fingertips. Blood.

Son of a bitch—

Crash. The bedroom door shook under what sounded like a shoulder ramming into the wood, vibrating through the room.

Carter scrambled around the desk toward the other side of the room where the sliding door led out to a small private patio. I froze, unsure if I should run to the door or tackle Carter and try to stop him from escaping.

After another smash against the door, I took off toward Brock, reaching the exit just as Carter shoved open the glass doors. *Fuck. Fuck. Fuck.*

This was bad. Like the entire Academy collapsing bad.

As I flung open the door, Brock stood on the other side like an avenging angel. His eyes were dark and darkened further when he caught sight of the blood dripping down the side of my face. Stepping over the threshold, he glared at Carter with such violence that I nearly trembled. Brock's hands were fisted at his sides, and they unclenched, then clenched again.

"Where the hell do you think you're going?" Brock demanded.

Carter had one foot outside and the other in the bedroom, halfway to freedom. He lifted the gun in his hand and aimed it at me. Brock's kryptonite—that was what Carter had called me. I was the Elite's weak spot. "Don't fucking move or I blow her head off," Carter threatened.

Brock's gaze sharpened as his eyes darted to the gun before shifting so he put himself between the weapon and me. "Put the gun down, Carter. You don't want to do this."

What was he thinking, putting himself in the line of fire? Fear like I never felt crashed into me. It was one thing for Carter to aim that thing at me, another thing entirely to point it at someone I loved.

"You have no idea what I want to do," Carter fumed.

"I know that you don't want to go to jail or you wouldn't be here," Brock chided.

"It doesn't matter now. I have no use for her. You can fucking have her." Then Carter twisted, bolting down the stairs, taking the gun, the danger, and the flash drive with him.

I expected Brock to rush to out after him and gave chase, but he turned, facing me. In my next breath, he was in front of me, worry shining in his aqua eyes. "Firefly, are you—?"

"Brock, he has the USB," I cut in, unconcerned about myself. A small cut was nothing compared to the kind of damage the information on that external drive could do.

"Good," he replied. With gentle fingers that shook just

slightly, he brushed at my hair near my temple, surveying the cut. "I can't believe that fucker hit you again. I'm seriously going to kill him."

Okay, not the reaction I'd expected. I blinked, confusion clouding my mind. "What the fuck do you mean, good? You aren't going to go after him? He did something to your computer. Put some kind of virus on it or something. I don't know." His lack of response got me worked up and the words rushed out in one long ramble.

Brock shrugged, a hand moving to my hip. "He took what we wanted him to find. And as for my computer, I'll have someone uncover whatever the bastard did."

"You knew," I whispered, my gaze searching his face as clarity began to break through. "You knew he would try to break into your house?" I didn't want it to be true. None of it. But sometimes you don't get what you want.

He tugged me closer, and for some reason I let him. Maybe because I wanted him to comfort me and tell me I was wrong. "I knew he would try something," he affirmed, my body flush against his. "What Carter stole only has information we gave him. It's not the real USB. We wouldn't keep something like that in here," Brock explained.

"You did good, James." Fynn stood in the doorway with Grayson and Micah. I hadn't heard them approach.

My eyes volleyed between the three of them and Brock beside me. What did he mean I did good? It didn't take me long to draw a conclusion. "Was this some kind of twisted test?" When no one denied it, I shook my head and shoved out of

Brock's arms. "Fuck you. Fuck you. Fuck you. And fuck you," I said to each of them, unable to believe they would pull a stunt like this. Just when I thought I knew them, understood them, the Elite went and proved that I knew nothing. "I could have been seriously hurt. He could have shot me. What the actual hell?"

"We didn't know the fool would bring a gun," Grayson defended.

"We swear, Josie Jo," Micah reaffirmed, like that made it better.

This couldn't be happening. I felt betrayed by them, used. I get that I wasn't supposed to walk in on their plan and find Carter sneaking around, but it happened. And there was no undoing the events of tonight. A myriad of conflicting emotions washed within me as I let the words fly, "I don't need this shit. I don't need the Elite."

"Too bad, Firefly," Brock bluntly said. "Membership can't be revoked. Once you're in, you're in for life. Remember?"

What was this, the fucking mafia? Unbelievable.

I huffed out a breath, attempting to find a thread of Zen, for I would need it dealing with the four of them. "Then next time, you better fill me in on the plan first. You either trust me or you don't."

"Promise," Fynn agreed, speaking for the group, but it wasn't enough for me.

I eyeballed each of them, my back straightening. "I need all four of you to say it."

Micah's lips twitched, but I got what I wanted. Four deep, male promises.

Taking a step back, I leaned against Brock, the adrenaline quickly leaving my body. "Someone get me a damn drink."

He put a firm arm around me, and only then did I notice that my body was shaking. "Grayson, take her home," he advised gruffly as he kept his gaze trained on me.

"I don't need to be handled," I proclaimed, though the statement came out a bit chattering and not super effective.

Brock smirked down at me, pressing a kiss to the tip of my nose. "I wouldn't dream of handling you, Firefly, except for in the bedroom."

I wrinkled my nose. "Really? You thought right now would be an appropriate time to make a sexual innuendo?"

"Micah does it all the time," he replied.

Fynn cleared his throat, shuffling his feet from the doorway, trying not to smile.

Grayson just shook his head.

And Micah... he grinned like he just won the fucking lottery.

"It's cute when Micah does it," I replied.

Micah laughed, and the playfulness there eased some of the tension tied in knots around my chest. "Hell, yeah it is. Hand her over, man. I'll get her a drink," he told Brock as he waved me forward with a crook of his finger.

"Get the hell out of here." Brock halfheartedly shoved Micah's shoulder as he led me out of the room, Micah's laughter following us into the hall.

These four guys. What the shit was I going to do with them?

"I thought we shared everything." I heard Micah chuckle behind me as the guys followed us out.

"Micah, I swear if Brock doesn't give you a black eye, then I will," Grayson threatened, but there was no real bite to his words.

"Josie isn't just his. She's ours too," he defended.

Their nonsense chatter filled the corridor, warming me from the inside a little at a time, almost as effective as a shot of bourbon. I rested my head on Brock's shoulder as he shook his head.

"I'm with Micah on this one," Fynn agreed, surprising me.

"Jesus, not you too," Grayson groused. "Is there anyone that doesn't want to sleep with my sister?"

A beat of silence passed, and I felt my cheeks flush.

What have I gotten myself into?

"Believe it or not, it is possible to be friends with a girl," Fynn argued.

"And want to bang," Micah added.

"For fuck's sake," Grayson swore.

We'd just reached the party at the end of the hall when I spotted Mads as she whirled around at our approach. Something about the bright excitement in her eyes conjured a thread of unease within me. "You're not going to believe who I ran into."

Grayson's brows worked up. "It can't be worse than who Josie—"

A slim figure stepped out from behind Mads. She smiled timidly at the Elite, her fingers twiddling with the ends of her dark-haired ponytail.

And to think I thought all the surprises were done for the night.

I stared at the girl who shared so many of my facial traits it was damn right scary.

Grayson paused. "Kenna?"

Oh. My. God. It was really her—my sister.

I'd say it was seventeen years overdue.

Thank you for reading!

Brock and Josie will be back in the conclusion,
REVENGE!

xoxo,

Jennifer

P.S. Join my VIP Readers email list and receive a bonus scene told from Zane's POV, as well as a free copy of Losing Emma and Breaking Emma, bonus books from my Divisa Series. You will also get notifications of what's new, giveaways, and new releases.

Visit here to sign up: www.jlweil.com

READ MORE BY J. L. WEIL

ELITE OF ELMWOOD ACADEMY
(New Adult Dark High School Romance)
Turmoil
Disorder
Revenge

DIVISA HUNTRESS
(New Adult Paranormal Romance)
Crown of Darkness
Inferno of Darkness

DRAGON DESCENDANTS SERIES
(Upper Teen Reverse Harem Fantasy)
Stealing Tranquility
Absorbing Poison

Taming Fire
Thawing Frost

THE DIVISA SERIES

(Full series completed – Teen Paranormal Romance)

Losing Emma: A Divisa novella
Saving Angel
Hunting Angel
Breaking Emma: A Divisa novella
Chasing Angel
Loving Angel
Redeeming Angel

LUMINESCENCE TRILOGY

(Full series completed – Teen Paranormal Romance)

Luminescence
Amethyst Tears
Moondust
Darkmist – A Luminescence novella

RAVEN SERIES

(Full series completed – Teen Paranormal Romance)

White Raven
Black Crow
Soul Symmetry

BEAUTY NEVER DIES CHRONICLES

(Teen Dystopian Romance)

Slumber

Entangled

Forsaken

NINE TAILS SERIES

(Teen Paranormal Romance)

First Shift

Storm Shift

Flame Shift

Time Shift

Void Shift

Spirit Shift

Tide Shift

Wind Shift

HAVENWOOD FALLS HIGH

(Teen Paranormal Romance)

Falling Deep

Ascending Darkness

SINGLE NOVELS

Starbound

(Teen Paranormal Romance)

Casting Dreams

(New Adult Paranormal Romance)

Ancient Tides

(New Adult Paranormal Romance)

For an updated list of my books, please visit my website:
www.jlweil.com

Join my VIP email list and I'll personally send you an email reminder as soon as my next book is out! Click here to sign up: www.jlweil.com

ABOUT THE AUTHOR

J.L. Weil is a USA TODAY Bestselling author of teen & new adult paranormal romance, fantasy, and urban fantasy books about spunky, smart mouth girls who always wind up in dire situations. For every sassy girl, there is an equally mouthwatering, overprotective guy.

You can visit her online at: www.jlweil.com or come hang out with her at JL Weil's Dark Divas on FB.

Stalk Me Online
www.jlweil.com
jenniferlweil@gmail.com

Printed in Great Britain
by Amazon

15256142R00217